Praise

"A poignant and beau[tiful ...] second chances. Mich[elle Lindo-Rice weaves] a heartfelt story of two women reconnecting after years apart, reminding us that the bonds of friendship can endure even the deepest wounds. This book is a must-read for anyone who believes in the power of healing and love."
—RaeAnne Thayne, *New York Times* bestselling author, on *A Summer for the Books*

"An elegantly told story of friendship, full of meaty issues and wonderful characters, this is a book that will make you sob and cheer."
—Kristan Higgins, *New York Times* bestselling author, on *The Bookshop Sisterhood*

"*The Bookshop Sisterhood* is everything—dramatic, heartwarming, heart-wrenching, funny, relatable, and, most of all, a truly enjoyable read!"
—Kimberla Lawson Roby, *New York Times* bestselling author

"This is an enjoyable read, filled with drama, conflict and friendship. You'll laugh, you'll cry and you'll ultimately rejoice in the bond of sisterhood."
—Brenda Novak, *New York Times* bestselling author of *The Seaside Library*, on *The Bookshop Sisterhood*

"The ups and downs, joys and pains, and unyielding power of friendship are on full display in this funny, heartwarming tale of sisterhood. The perfect book club read!" —Farrah Rochon, *New York Times* bestselling author of *The Hookup Plan*, on *The Bookshop Sisterhood*

"An inspiring read about the power of women's friendships and how learning to trust those one loves best can be risky but ultimately rewarding." —*Library Journal* on *The Bookshop Sisterhood*

"Best friends, book lovers, drama . . . this story has it all!"
—*Woman's World* on *The Bookshop Sisterhood*

"Satisfying . . . Readers who enjoy stories about women overcoming life obstacles will be drawn in."—*Booklist* on *The Bookshop Sisterhood*

Little Free Library
Donated by Bob
and Jean Badger

Also by Michelle Lindo-Rice

The Bookshop Sisterhood

For additional books by Michelle Lindo-Rice,
visit her website, www.michellelindorice.com.

All my best 🙂

A Summer for the Books

Michelle Lindo-Rice

Michelle Lindo-Rice ♡

MIRA

/||MIRA

Recycling programs for this product may not exist in your area.

ISBN-13: 978-0-7783-3439-2

A Summer for the Books

Copyright © 2025 by Michelle Lindo-Rice

All rights reserved. No part of this book may be used or reproduced in any manner whatsoever without written permission.

Without limiting the author's and publisher's exclusive rights, any unauthorized use of this publication to train generative artificial intelligence (AI) technologies is expressly prohibited.

This is a work of fiction. Names, characters, places and incidents are either the product of the author's imagination or are used fictitiously. Any resemblance to actual persons, living or dead, businesses, companies, events or locales is entirely coincidental.

For questions and comments about the quality of this book, please contact us at CustomerService@Harlequin.com.

TM is a trademark of Harlequin Enterprises ULC.

Emojis © vadymstock/stock.adobe.com

Mira
22 Adelaide St. West, 41st Floor
Toronto, Ontario M5H 4E3, Canada
MIRABooks.com

Printed in U.S.A.

*For John, my love, who inspires
the wonderful men I write.
And for Mark, Naomi and Matthew.
Your auntie loves you.*

CHARACTERS

Shelby Andrews ~ Sugar Bean
Jewel Stone ~ Honey Graham
Declan Welch ~ Chance Hudson
Beryl McRae ~ Opal Graham
Hazel McRae ~ Topaz Graham
Augustina Welch ~ Arlena Hudson
Katrina ~ Janie
Roman Stone ~ Winston
Kendrick ~ Theo

A Summer for the Books

CHAPTER 1

Excerpt from That Was Then *by Jewel Stone*

∼

The deleted prologue—April 7, 2006

Honey

The skyline was black tinged with purple as the waves lapped against the sands of Eagle Point Beach. All was peaceful, a stark contrast to the crowds of children and families frolicking during the day, but the calm waters were a shield for the fright wreaking havoc on her insides. Honey glanced toward the far end of the beach at a huge bonfire. The giggles and yells of college students living out their last hurrah before midterms began drifted to her.

With just the moonlight as a guide, Honey Graham and her best friend, Sugar Bean, crept up the steps of the landmark bookstore by the beach, hunched over, panicking at every groan of the wood. They had dressed in black sweat suits, jackets, boots, caps with their hair tucked underneath and, though it was pitch-dark, sunglasses.

"We're missing all the fun," Honey whined. "And I'm pretty sure I stepped on a crab." Her top was soaked from perspiration brought on by the fear of being discovered.

"Would you hush? It was fun that got us into this mess in the first place," Sugar whispered, holding a special package close to her chest. "You're going to blow our cover. Besides, this was all your idea."

"Yes, but anything seems doable in the daylight." Even the most nefarious of plans. Especially those born out of desperation. Honey stepped on a loose board and froze as it creaked.

"Oh, for crying out loud," Sugar said. "Might as well just sound out on the blowhorn that we're here." She held out the package to Honey.

"I—I can't," Honey said, lifting her hands. "If I take it, I might not have the courage to do this."

Sugar released a drawn-out sigh. "We agreed."

"I know." Her lips trembled. She folded her long legs and sat on the wood. "But I'm scared."

"Everything will be all right," Sugar said, her voice gentle. But Honey could tell she was trying to be brave. She was just as terrified as Honey was. She had just as much to lose. Sugar put the package on Honey's lap, a gesture of defiance, and squatted beside her.

Honey touched Sugar's shoulder. "Is there another way?"

"I—I don't . . ." Sugar grabbed Honey's hand and pulled it to her chest. "My heart is beating so fast, I feel like I'm about to pass out."

"Breathe. Breathe," Honey huffed out. "I can't have you falling apart, because I'm already a basket case."

"Too late," Sugar said, a hitch in her voice.

Carefully, the friends hugged and rocked, crying, consoling each other but making sure the box stayed upright. Head to head, they reassured each other. *Everything will be all right.* Honey swallowed the rising nausea. "If we're going to do this, we have to do it now." Resolute, she got to her feet and held out her free hand, ignoring her shaking legs.

"O-okay." Sugar stood. She snatched Honey's hand in hers, and they inched to the front door.

Honey covered her mouth and sobbed. "I didn't know it would feel like this."

"Me either."

"Should we leave it by the entrance?"

"No . . . How about on the bench?"

"What if it falls? Or it rains?"

"I—I don't know what to do," Sugar rasped, sounding like she had chewed the end of her last rope. "There was no forecast of rain and the skies are clear."

Honey wiped her brow. She wished they had planned out this part because the uncertainty made her want to heave. "Let's leave the box by the plants in the back." As soon as she suggested that, Honey knew it wasn't the right solution.

"What if no one sees it? Or an animal comes by and messes with it?" Sugar wrapped her arms around herself. "We can't chance that happening. It's better if we leave it by the door, knock and then hide and wait to make sure Ms. Brown sees it." Ms. Brown was the sweet caretaker and new owner of the bookstore after Sugar's parents had sold it to her last year. She'd been very kind to them, allowing them continued free rein of her property. She would know what to do.

"We didn't give this enough thought, did we?"

"We didn't know about it until mere hours ago. How else were we to prepare?" A light came on inside the bookstore. Panic shot through her system like a rabbit with a bobcat on its heels. Honey swallowed a shriek. Her heart rate went into overdrive. "Oh my goodness. Ms. Brown is coming. We've got to get out of here."

"Put it down by the front door, and ring the doorbell. It's the best place."

Honey did just that, and then they gripped each other's hands as they dashed toward the bush by the steps to hide crouched together. They could see a shadow approaching from the inside. Sugar trembled beside her. Honey couldn't chastise her for it because her own body rattled so much her teeth chattered. They grabbed on to each other.

The porch light came on.

Emitting a moan, Sugar broke free and ran across the sand.

"Wait," Honey whispered, furious. They were supposed to make sure the box was discovered. She bit her bottom lip, debating what to do. Sugar didn't look backward. A sharp crack of thunder propelled Honey into action. Squaring her shoulders, she took off after her friend and grabbed her shoulders. "We can't leave yet. We have to make sure."

"I don't want to get caught." They stopped a few feet away.

"Then go without me." Honey hunkered down behind the umbrellas and waited for Ms. Brown to discover the package. A few seconds later, Sugar dropped by her side. They gripped hands.

"Anybody there?" Ms. Brown called out. The girls' bodies shook, but they didn't dare take a breath. After calling out a few more times, Ms. Brown looked down at the package. "Oh my! What do we have here?"

Sugar gave Honey a tug. "Let's go."

Sugar

The next morning, huddled in the safety of Sugar's bedroom in their campus apartment at the University of Delaware, both girls had their eyes glued to the morning news. Sugar's heart pounded, and her eyes burned. She hadn't slept that night out of fear that the police were going to come knocking on their door. In the two-hour ride back from Eagle Point Beach, she kept glancing through her rearview mirror for those flashing red and blue lights. It had taken some cajoling on her part, but Honey had slept about an hour, her head on Sugar's lap.

Suddenly, the camera operator zoomed in, and the announcer's smile transformed into a frown. Sugar leaned forward. "It's on. It's on." Honey's chest heaved, and her eyes held fear. In her haste, Sugar almost dropped the remote before she turned up the volume.

As soon as the tagline filled the screen, Sugar's breakfast soured in her gut. "I can't watch this." With her hand over her mouth, she raced into the bathroom and upchucked the omelet she'd had delivered. She glanced in the mirror at her matted hair and reddened, sunken eyes and shook her head. She couldn't go to work today and pretend her world hadn't been shaken off its axis. After washing her hands, she brushed her teeth, while she considered an appropriate excuse that wouldn't get her fired. As it was, she had missed work yesterday. And quite a few other days. This wasn't like before. She needed a job.

A loud screech echoed from the other room.

"What's going on?" Sugar yelled, her heart rate at a crescendo.

"They have a video."

"No. No. No." Hands on her tummy, she scurried back and forced herself to look at the twenty-six-inch screen. All she could see were shadows. She squinted. With the outfits they'd worn, it was hard to tell their builds. "It's murky, grainy. They can't decipher anything."

Honey sniffled as the tears poured down her face. "What have we done? Oh Lord, what have we done?"

She shuffled over to her hug her friend, her body tremoring as deep fear spread through her. "W-we just h-have to s-stay calm."

"Someone will know it was us." Honey wrestled out of her arms. "Maybe . . . maybe we need to turn ourselves in. They might go easy on us if we act now."

"W-we can't. We agreed. We made a pact."

Honey's lip trembled. "Yes, but . . ." She touched her abdomen. "I didn't expect the guilt to tear through my stomach like acid." Every time she closed her eyes, she saw that innocent face peering back at her.

"I didn't either." Sugar cupped Honey's cheeks with her hands. "It was a cryptic pregnancy. No one could tell. All we have to do is keep quiet."

Grabbing her hands, Honey repeated, "All we have to do is keep quiet."

They recited those eight words until they believed them. Their secret bound them tighter as the days flew by, each praying the news would die down. But within hours, it made national news.

Everybody was talking about the *Baby Abandoned at the Bookstore on Eagle Point Beach.* The phrase danced across the screens, haunting them. Those words became a hollow drum constantly beating in their ears in the days to come.

Yet the friends didn't break because they had each other. They consoled each other and squeezed their lips shut, their pact a tightly woven cord bringing them closer and closer.

Until eventually, eventually, there was nothing but blessed silence . . .

Jewel
Summer 2024

Sitting up in bed with her laptop on her thighs and her husband asleep next to her, Jewel McRae, known to the world as Jewel Stone, closed out the deleted scene of her debut novel, *That Was Then*, and leaned back onto the headboard. She'd just received word her book was going to be made into a series on a major network, and they wanted her on set as a consultant when they went into production next summer, which was why she was rereading the book. It was a chore, but fortunately, years had passed since its release, and it was all new to her again.

The network planned to create at least two seasons, so she was reading through her very first draft that even her agent and editor had never seen. It included about 17,000 words that were later cut, including the baby storyline. Her editor had never read that juicy subplot, and if Jewel continued to have her way, nobody ever would.

Honestly, though it was tedious work, the book-to-series was quite an accomplishment and a cause for celebration. Her followers were on social media posting memes and making actor suggestions.

But her celebration was bittersweet. The one person she wanted to share this with, her best friend since childhood, was no longer a friend. And the contents of this book were a part of the reason. Especially the deleted contents. Jewel didn't have the courage to share her truth with anyone, especially the man asleep next to her.

Releasing a huge sigh, she placed the laptop on her nightstand and massaged the back of her neck. With a yawn, she settled under the covers, and her final thought before fading out was *I miss my friend.*

CHAPTER 2

Shelby
June 3, 2025

The moment she'd dreaded had finally come. Only Shelby Andrews hadn't envisioned that it would happen in her eight-year-old sedan sitting outside her daughter's best friend's condo.

Shelby and Lacey had shared a pleasant two-hour drive from Lacey's apartment building in Wilmington, Delaware, to Rehoboth Beach where she would spend the rest of the summer. They had eaten ice cream while singing along to Beyoncé's "Cowboy Carter" at the top of their lungs, celebrating another successful year at the University of Delaware. But right after she kissed her daughter goodbye, Lacey had cracked the door open then broached the subject Shelby feared most.

"Mom, please don't get mad, but I want to revisit the topic of finding my birth parents," she said, oblivious to the dry heat slithering into the cab, warring with the cool air. Shelby was glad she'd wrapped her waist-length hair in a bun because the heat was intense.

Terror curdled the dairy in her stomach. She brushed a piece of cone off her teal shirt that served as a nice contrast to her sand-toned skin. "I thought you were done with it after that DNA Ancestry kit only led to some distant cousins. None of them had any viable information that you could use."

"Yes, but I can't lose hope that my parents might decide to look for me."

Shelby squared her shoulders. "And what if your birth parents don't want to be found?"

Lacey sucked in a breath and slammed the door closed.

Exhaling, Shelby reached over to hold Lacey's hand. "Honey, I know I sound harsh, but I don't want you disappointed if things don't go the way you'd like. I think you should redirect your focus back to your studies. You're about to start your third year, and you don't need any distractions." As soon as she said that, Shelby regretted her choice of words, but in all fairness, Lacey had caught her off guard. Sure enough, Lacey took umbrage. As she should. She pulled her hand out of Shelby's grasp and tucked it close to her chest.

"*Distractions?* Really? That's what you're calling my need to find out who I am?" She banged the door shut and glared at Shelby. Their close relationship had been forged over their love of the beach and books, but over the past six months Lacey's desire to search out her bio family had become a serious source of contention between them.

Shelby didn't fully get it. She gave Lacey her heart and everything she could want. Her daughter had a great home, a great life, great friends. She tried to compensate as best as she could to fill that gap. Why couldn't Lacey just let this go and be happy?

"I can tell you who you are. You're my tenacious, driven daughter who is rocking college by being on the dean's honor list every semester." Her attempt at humor fell flat. "I'm sorry. *Distraction* was a poor choice of words. I didn't mean it that way."

Lacey placed a hand on Shelby's arm. "Thanks for apologizing. Mom, I get that you're scared, but it's not like you're going to lose me. I love you, so there's no chance of that happening."

Oh, there was a 99.9 percent chance that Lacey would turn her back on Shelby if she learned the truth, which was why Shelby had to make sure that never happened.

Shelby gripped the wheel. She had a valid reason, albeit a selfish one, why she didn't need her daughter digging into her past. Every time Lacey brought it up, Shelby's heart hammered with fear. That was something she could be honest about. "You're right. I'm just . . . afraid. You don't understand. You're all I've got."

She bit her lower lip, hating her blatant use of emotional blackmail, but since losing her parents and then falling out with her best friend, Lacey was the only person Shelby had opened her heart to. From the moment eight-year-old Lacey had come into Shelby's bookstore with her foster parents, Shelby had been drawn the child with skin the color of sepia, deep brown thoughtful eyes, thick lustrous curls that fell mid-back, faint dimples and a smile that brightened her entire face when they talked about books. Their bond had been instant, and that grew into love, and all Shelby wanted to do was to keep Lacey sheltered from the ugly truth surrounding her existence.

"See, that shouldn't be the case," Lacey admonished, her tone gentle. "You need to socialize and make friends. I can't be your whole world, Mom. You have to have your own life. Just as you've always encouraged me to have mine. Anything that I've wanted to do, you've been my biggest supporter, and I love you for that, which is why I'm stumped that you're so against me finding my family."

"You aren't my *whole* world per se. Just a big chunk of my focus right now." Shelby waved a hand. "And I do have a life outside of you. I have the bookstore, and I've joined the cycling club."

"You don't know how relieved I am that you did. How many times I picture you at home all alone like a hermit while I'm up here living it up with Bea and my friends."

Shelby smiled. She had been the one responsible for introducing a shy Lacey to the gregarious Bea Bennett. From then, the girls had been as close as conjoined twins, attending the same high school and then university together. Their friendship was parallel to Shelby's own relationship to her former best friend, Jewel Stone. They too had been inseparable—until the day Shelby made a choice Jewel couldn't live with. She glanced over at Lacey. A choice she would make again with no regrets. Though, she did miss her friend something fierce.

"I'm not a hermit. I'm just picky about my friends."

"Yeah, as in you don't have any." Lacey gave her hand a squeeze. "Close ones, I mean. You talk to a lot of people and you're friendly, but you don't let anyone get close."

Goose bumps spread across her arms at Lacey's perceptiveness. It reminded her of . . . She shook that memory away. "I'm close to you," she said instead, booping Lacey on the nose.

Lacey lifted her shoulders. "See? That's exactly what I'm talking about. I can't bear the brunt of your unhappiness." Her cell phone buzzed. "Bea's texting me." Lacey's fingers flew across the screen of her phone as she typed her response, giving Shelby a moment to mull on those words.

Whoa. Was that what she was doing to her child? Lacey was such a sensitive soul. She had to be mindful of that during their conversations.

Once Lacey had finished responding to Bea, Shelby used her best Mother tone. "Relax. Don't worry about me. I'm perfectly fine taking care of myself. I was doing that long before you came into my life, and believe me when I say you're not responsible for my happiness. I'm . . . content."

"I know. But at least start dating or something." Lacey chuckled, the relief in her tone evident. "You shouldn't have any trouble getting hooked up. All you have to do is accentuate those high cheekbones with a little blush and add eyeliner to highlight your light brown eyes." She narrowed her own.

"Your lips are already pink enough, so just a light gloss would do and voilà! You don't need much."

She chuckled at her daughter's description. Kendrick, one of the men from her cycling group, came to mind. He seemed kinda cute, and he was super friendly. He had even asked her out, or she thought he had, inviting her to try out a new cycling route with him and then maybe grab coffee after. That sounded datey, right? "I'll think about it."

"Which means *no*." Her daughter sighed and opened the door again. "I've got to go, but I do want to continue talking about looking for my bio fam. It's really important to me."

Folding her lips into her mouth, Shelby reached over to give Lacey a hug. "We'll have a long talk about it soon."

After a reluctant nod, Lacey exited the vehicle. Shelby pulled off the curb, calling herself all kinds of horrid for trying to hinder her daughter from pursuing something that was her natural right as an adult. As a human. But she had to. To fail would implode the life she had built for them both, and the repercussions would be unimaginable.

ADRENALINE AND MOTIVATION KEPT SHELBY'S FEET ON the pedals as she pushed toward the finish line where she would clock in at thirty miles. Sweat poured from her face and back, her legs and thighs throbbed, but she gripped the handlebars of her bicycle and propelled herself to move even faster. After her encounter with Lacey earlier that day, riding with her cycling club was the perfect outlet for her pent-up frustration. She had sent her daughter a text to reach out when she was ready to talk, but Shelby had no idea what she could say to bring peace between them. Because there was no way she could give Lacey her blessing to find her birth family.

To do that would put everything she held dear in jeopardy.

A quick backward glance showed she still maintained a

significant lead on the rest of the team. Not bad, considering it had been less than a year since she had taken up this hobby. The only sound was the whizz of her bike as she sped past a deer poking its head out from the bushes.

Whew: 28.3 miles. Almost there.

She hunched her shoulders, the sun beating on her back. All she had to do was get around the curve. From ahead came the hum and throttle of a motorbike moving significantly under the speed limit. She put her head down and swerved into the other lane. Just as she did, her chain clunked.

Shelby looked down to see the metal trailing on the ground, her helmet shifting on her head with the movement. Just as she climbed off her bike to shimmy off the road, she heard a loud honk. She jerked her head up and gasped. A truck was heading toward her at full speed. She lifted her bike and rushed to the curb. A gush of wind rocked her body as the truck whooshed by, sliding into another lane.

"That was a close one," Deena said, pulling up beside her, along with the rest of the crew. Shelby looked into the kind blue eyes of the woman before her and fought back frightened tears. When she'd first joined the club, Deena had tried to befriend her, inviting her to house parties. But Shelby always found a reason to refuse. Her daughter was right about her reticence: she was friendly, but she kept her distance. She had lost too much and wasn't about to risk that happening again. She didn't do friends. She didn't do anyone. Not anymore.

What she did do was books.

Books were the perfect companion. Reliable. Her romances always had a happy ending, and her thrillers always ended with the bad guy dead or in handcuffs.

Shelby sank onto the grass, her fingers digging into the earth. One of the men picked up her road bike and took out a quick repair kit to fix her chain. Tears leaked from her eyes.

"You'll be okay," Deena encouraged.

She nodded and whispered, "Thank you." Her voice was croaky.

Drawing deep breaths, she attempted to slow her racing heart. Before they'd left, the team had performed safety checks on their bikes, but there was no foreseeing the chain malfunctioning.

"Hey, you all right?" a deep male voice asked. One belonging to a man who gave her the shivers and who'd had her checking her hair, her breath and how her butt looked in her shorts before she left for a ride.

Her eyes popped open, and she peered into warm gold ones set against a rugged face. He had a five-o'clock shadow. Besides her, he was the only other Black person in her group. "Y-yes." She straightened, almost bumping heads with his and dusted off her hair.

"Your bike's ready if you're good cycling back," he said, holding out a hand. "The chain should hold."

She ignored his hand and got to her feet. "I don't have a choice."

"You could call an Uber." He sounded like that's what he hoped she would do.

By that time, the other cyclists were on their bikes, waiting for her to make a decision. Shelby hated being an inconvenience. Of course, that was the moment they heard a crack of thunder, so she flailed her hands. "I'll catch a ride back. Why don't you all head off? Beat the rain."

With a nod, the others took off except for her unwanted sidekick. Well, at least she told herself he was unwanted. Taking out her phone, she tapped on the rideshare app and chose the deluxe option.

"You don't have to stay." She looked down at the app tracker. "My ride will be here in less than five minutes."

He gave her a wide smile. "I'd feel better if I waited. If something happened . . ." He shrugged, then chuckled. "Chivalry isn't dead."

A plop of rain hit her nose, and she tried again to get him to leave. "Thank you, but for real, though, I'll feel bad if you get caught in a downpour because of me."

Kendrick splayed his hands and showed her those straight, pearly whites. The man had a drop-your-drawers smile on him. And his chocolate skin was smooth and unmarred. "After a career in the military, this is nothing."

She gave him the once-over, taking in those powerful legs, well-fitted shorts and the shirt clinging to that broad chest before she remembered she wasn't interested in meeting anyone. Her vehicle approached so she gestured for him to get on his bike. The stubborn man waited and helped her load the bike in the trunk. Once she was seated, he left.

When she passed him on the way, Shelby kept her eyes on her phone, planting a fascinated look on her face. She did the same with the other cyclists, hunkering down in her seat.

It was pouring by the time she arrived back at the parking lot. She grabbed her bike out of the trunk and propped it against her sedan, hanging her helmet on the handle. Then she opened the trunk. But all she could think about was the 1.7 miles she had failed to finish. That equated to a couple minutes. Three, max.

She looked at her watch and debated. What she needed to do was get home, get showered and prep the bookstore for her Baby Boomers Book Club. Those ten women were her best customers, guaranteed weekly sales, and since her business wasn't exactly thriving, Shelby didn't mind staying open later for them. Which also reminded her, she needed to stop and pick up the pastries and juice.

She eyed her bike and threw up her hands. She had to get to thirty miles. Ugh. Why was she like this? The rain impeded her visibility, but she didn't have to go far. Just to the stop sign she knew was down yonder, and she would be done.

Snatching the helmet, she strapped the buckle under her chin and got back on her bike. Then she pedaled as fast as she could, her eyes on the stop sign. Right as she approached the intersection, she pressed the brakes and gasped. Her brakes were out. She dropped her legs to the ground, her feet sliding on the slippery road. Reaching over, she grabbed on to the metal pole of the stop sign and tilted her body. She came to a rough halt and hit her knee. But she was good.

Releasing a breath, she looked at her tracker and pumped her fists. She had done it. She did a jig before she heard the sound of screeching. Shelby's mouth dropped open. A vehicle was skidding toward her at rapid speed. She shook her head. No. No. This couldn't be happening. Shelby tried to jump off the bike, but she knew it was already too late even as she raised her hands to use as shields, bracing for impact.

CHAPTER 3

Lacey
June 6, 2025

Lacey Andrews had lied to her mom. What shocked her was how good she was at it, considering she had never been dishonest with her mother before. Well, she had told a fib or two—she forgot she had homework or a paper due—small-scale stuff like that. But never ever about the big things.

And telling your mother that you were just hanging at the beach with your bestie when you intended to play amateur sleuth was most definitely a big thing. Epic. Just thinking about it made her toes curl into the sand. She adjusted her straw hat lower on her head and crouched under the beach umbrella. The guilt had been messing with her equilibrium and her appetite over the past seventy-two hours.

She hadn't posted on her YouTube channel in days. As a wannabe mukbanger, eating in abundance was a must. But though she was a foodie, Lacey didn't have the stomach to back up her intentions. Try as she might, she had ended up dumping huge quantities of her meals into the trash. Still, she had about ten thousand people interested in watching her fail at mukbanging.

Her bestie, Bea, hobbled over to grab a towel from the chair beside her. "You really aren't going into the water?"

"Eh." Lacey shrugged, tapping her fingers on the handles of her beach chair. "I will."

"Lacey, you are nineteen years old. *Grown* grown. Choosing not to divulge your activities to your parent is your prerogative. News flash. It's called *adulting*." This from the girl who called her own mother three times a day for everything. If she stubbed her toe, Bea was calling her mother. Bea and Mrs. Bennett often spoke until her phone ran out of juice. Lacey hadn't minded because she was close to her mother too. They were the best of friends. Up until a few months ago, there wasn't anything she couldn't confide to her mom.

She rolled her eyes at Bea. "What it is, is irresponsible. Childish, even."

"But what other choice did you have? Your mom won't help you find your birth parents, so you have to take matters into your own hands," Bea said, rigorously drying her long blond tresses. She had the height and build of Bella Hadid, but Bea didn't like being compared to the supermodel because she was her own woman.

"I know, but I don't like lying to her that we're having an easy-breezie summer when I'm not."

"That was a necessary excursion away from the truth so we can search for your family without interference or hurting your mother's feelings."

Lacey winced. "No matter how you sugarcoat it, it doesn't make it right."

"It's not exactly wrong either. Not everything is black-and-white. We're simply swerving into the gray." She swayed back and forth, mimicking a skier.

"Really? Skiing in the summertime?"

She shrugged. "It's snowing somewhere." Then she ran her fingers through her strands. "Ugh, I am going to have to wash my hair at least three times to get all this gunk out of it." She picked up her phone to call her mom and ask her opinion on what shampoo to get.

Lacey scooted off the chair while Bea yakked with her mother, partly because she had to use the restroom and partly because she was jealous. Bea gave a nod and a little wave, occupied with her convo. Lacey missed her mother, and no matter how Bea tried to justify her actions, her guilt grew by the minute. Maybe she should call to check on her mom.

Since it was late afternoon, her mom was probably out bike riding with her new cycling team or hosting the Baby Boomers Book Club at her store. So she would call her later.

When she returned, Bea was ready and waiting.

"How about we go see the concert on the beach tonight?" Bea asked, her green eyes earnest. There would be local bands playing and quite a spread from the nearby restaurants.

Lacey lifted her shoulders. "I kind of wanted to stay in and chill."

"And we can do that. After."

"All right . . ." She dragged the last syllable out, while Bea did a happy dance.

"Great. Let's go home and get dressed. We won't stay long. An hour or two tops," Bea said. "The music will be the perfect distraction, you'll see."

The air had cooled, and the sounds of the band and ocean made for a pleasant summer night by the time they arrived at the makeshift party on the beach. Crowds of families and vacationers milled about, and though no one was allowed in the water due to currents, the lifeguards were out. As the evening yawned, she sipped on a virgin daiquiri, observing as Bea danced with two guys near the band, her little yellow dress bright and fun.

Lacey sat dressed in black under one of the umbrellas by the tiki lights, her eyes fixed on her phone. She had avoided eye contact with anyone who dared to talk to her and had eaten some Jamaican jerk chicken but would be hard-pressed to tell if it was good or not.

Glancing over at Bea who was looking her way, Lacey held up her hand and tapped her wrist, mouthing *Thirty minutes*. Bea gave a nod before gyrating her hips at one of the dudes. She was leaving right at the two-hour mark, with or without Bea.

A shadow loomed next to her. "Anyone sitting here?" She shook her head, willing him to go away. But no, he dropped into the seat on her right.

Ugh, the last thing she wanted was conversation. She curved her body to the left, making a point to bring up a YouTube channel. Maybe he would get the hint and leave. But dude didn't know how to read body language or he was purposely being obtuse. Either of those reasons annoyed her. He tapped his fingers on the glass table and said, "The band is killing it."

"Uh-huh."

"That guy is playing that guitar like I've never seen it played before."

"Hmm." Closing her eyes, she prayed for patience.

"Um, I can see that I'm bothering you," he said.

"Good observation." The minute she uttered those words, she hated how rude she sounded, but she bit the inside of her cheek to keep from giving an apology.

"Never mind. Forget it." The chair scraped as he stood. "I'll catch up with you."

It was the hurt in his voice that made Lacey lift her gaze and meet his eyes. She gasped, feeling sucker-punched. The guy before her was *delicious*. There wasn't a better word to describe that bronzed smooth skin, the firm jaw and those large hazel eyes. Plus, judging by the red cross on his shorts and shirt, she would say he was a lifeguard. She scrambled to her feet and raked a hand through her curls. "Uh, I'm sorry, I . . ." She exhaled. "I have a lot on my mind, but that's no excuse for my rudeness." She held out her hand. "I'm Lacey."

He studied her outstretched palm before placing his hand in hers. "I'm Mekhi James." He smiled, revealing a deep dimple and beautiful set of straightened teeth. A faint electric shock buzzed where their palms met, and she smiled back. Her first smile in hours. Her mood lifted a bit.

"Are you okay?" he asked.

She wasn't about to unburden to a stranger about her desire to find her parents. Instead, she tossed her hair and gave a slight nod. Hang on. Was she low-key flirting right now? She had better not be. Lacey hadn't come to Rehoboth Beach to find a hookup. She couldn't afford to be distracted, so she needed to stop making goo-goo eyes at this stranger when she had her lies to her mother and her search to think about.

Still, as they held eye contact, something shifted between them. Something propulsive. The beating drums around them only added to the tension forming. What in the world was happening to her right now? This wasn't the first cute guy to approach her, but it was the first time she had felt an instant attraction. A connection.

"Do you want to dance?" he asked.

She took a step toward him then froze. With a smile, he drew her into his arms. Their bodies aligned perfectly. Closing her eyes, she rested her head on his shoulder. His arms circled her back. They swayed to the music. He rocked his hips, and she moved in rhythm with him.

"Do you want to go somewhere a little quieter?" he asked, his voice deepening. He twisted one of her curls around his finger.

Her heart raced, her chest heaved and her mouth went dry. All the warnings her mother had given her when she had begun dating came back to her, but it didn't feel like he was a stranger. Which was folly since she didn't know anything about him other than his name and that he was fine as all get-out.

But her body was firing off some signals she wasn't about to follow up on. She had had two bed partners, but those had been long-term boyfriends, and she was seriously tempted to make this guy her third. That knowledge jarred her.

It was off the charts scary.

Lacey pulled her hand out of his and wiped it on her shorts. "I'm sorry. I've got to go." This could be her fears transposing into lust and jumping into bed with this man would be an unwise choice.

He held up his hands. "I meant just to talk."

If he thought that was all that would happen if they went off somewhere on their own, then he was deluded. She wasn't. "See you around."

"Wait!" he called out, but she took off.

Lacey dashed across the sand and headed for the boardwalk, regret enunciating each step. *Don't turn back. Don't look around.* Just before she turned the corner, she did just that, surprised at the keen disappointment piercing her gut when she saw he was gone. She might never see him again. With a sigh, she began her short trek to the condo.

Meandering onto the end of the mile-long boardwalk with its eclectic shops, restaurants and family amusements, Lacey waved at Ms. Carlotta, the ice cream shop owner, before walking a block over to the row of condos behind the boardwalk. Prime real estate. Especially since the boardwalk hosted festivals and concerts and all sorts of activities year-round. There was never a bad time to come to the beach.

She made her way up the stairs and unlocked the door to the condo then went to use the restroom. After she had refreshed herself with a cool shower, Lacey stretched out on top of the bed under the ceiling fan. A blend of modern and antique, the condo had been designed to meet the needs of even the most demanding occupants.

According to Bea, her family had owned this place for decades. Kind of like Lacey's mother and the bookstore at Eagle Point Beach. Her mom's parents had acquired it years ago, but they'd had to sell it because of mismanagement of finances. As soon as she could, Shelby had purchased the bookstore back. Because of its location, it was probably worth a fortune. But her mother had no intentions of selling. In fact, she had put it in a trust for Lacey. Her only request was that Lacey never take a lien out on the store. Lacey had been touched by the gesture, especially since it was the bookstore that had brought them together.

She had been adopted as a baby, but the Brooks got in some trouble—Lacey wasn't sure what exactly happened—and she had been taken from their home. She then entered the foster care system in Rehoboth Beach at age seven. The Smiths had been her third home, as she hadn't thrived in the first two. Her social worker told her they would take care of her and they had, including introducing her to books.

And books had led her to Shelby.

The Smiths had fostered Lacey for two and a half years, and Miss Edna had taken her to the bookstore for many trips, which was where she met Shelby. Their love of books united them, and when her foster parents had to go out of town or needed a sitter, Shelby would volunteer to watch her. She was now the only family Lacey had.

Was she being ungrateful seeking out her blood relatives? Her mom didn't understand what it was like to question your origins the way Lacey had been for the past year.

So it was either live in a constant state of uncertainty or dig for the truth herself—with Bea's help, of course.

Once she was back inside and under her covers, she texted Bea.

> I'm back at the condo. No need to rush.
> Have a good time for the two of us.

Ciao. Don't wait up.

Ok. Stay safe.

Always.

Resting her head against the headboard, Lacey closed her eyes and saw Mekhi's face. Her body lamented her running off. Her eyes popped open. Gosh, why hadn't she gotten his number at least? And why, oh why, was she thinking of some random meet-cute when she had bigger things to focus on?

Lacey scooted off her bed and decided to help herself to the Rita's Island Fusion ice that they had purchased the night before. She had just finished the treat when the lock jangled and Bea walked in, leaving the door wide open.

"What are you still doing up?" Bea asked.

"I had a lot on my mind . . ."

Lacey clamped her jaw to keep from yelling at Bea for letting in the flies. She had already cautioned her friend a couple of times about it and didn't want to nag. Or sound like her mother.

Bea tossed her straw hat on the table and wiped her face. "It's hotter than a love scene in *Bridgerton* out there," she declared, grabbing a spoon and reaching over to get a scoop of ice from out of the carton. "You just don't know how much until you're back under the cool air."

Lacey smirked. "Then close that door before you let all the cool air out."

"Yes, yes, I know." Bea shut the door. "I forgot to get a flyswatter."

"I ordered a couple from online already this morning. They should get here tomorrow before eleven."

"Cool beans." Bea picked up the remote and turned on the television. Lacey knew from experience that Bea hated silence. She needed white noise, as she called it. It reminded Lacey of the beauty salons or sports bars that had the televisions on at low volume with music blasting in the background. That's why Lacey was so grateful this condo had more than one bedroom: she needed it dark and quiet to fall asleep.

What was funny was Bea would be on her cell phone the entire time the TV was on. Half the time she didn't care for anything happening on the screen. There was no way Lacey's mom would go for that. She'd would be squawking about the energy bill. But that was Bea.

"I'm going to take a shower," Bea declared, wandering off to her room.

Lacey walked over to the couch and settled in, phone in hand, knowing regardless of what Bea said, it would be a while before Bea returned. She took ridiculously long showers, completely unconcerned about water shortages. Something Lacey's mom had drilled into her to consider.

Her mother hated waste of any kind.

And Lacey had to agree on this one. It was a pet peeve but, again, this was Bea, which was why Lacey found it best to tune out the things she didn't like and focus on the things she loved. Like Bea's generosity and loyalty.

When Lacey told Bea about her quest to find her bio parents, Bea had been all-in. And Lacey was grateful because she couldn't do this by herself. She only wished her mother was on board.

Lacey picked up her phone and scrolled to her last text message from her mom three days prior. **I love you honey. Reach out when you're ready to talk.** Mom was waiting on her to respond. Waiting and hoping that Lacey had moved on from this distraction. Lacey raked a hand through her curls and groaned. A *distraction*. She wished she wasn't so bothered by that word when her mother had apologized.

And what if your birth parents don't want to be found?

The question was like a bear's claw gnawing at her confidence. Flipping onto her back, she fisted her palms and stared at the ceiling. This quest was something Lacey felt compelled to do. She had to try. If she didn't, she would regret it for the rest of her life.

CHAPTER 4

Jewel
June 9, 2025

She was already a has-been at only thirty-nine years old. That was how she felt, though she couldn't show it. Not when she needed money. Lots and lots of money. Jewel drew in a deep breath, crossed her legs and gave her agent her best poker face, ignoring the intoxicating display of New York City at night through the glass window.

She had chosen her cream Alexander McQueen dress that complemented her java skin tone, knowing it wouldn't wrinkle during the two-hour ride from her home in the Hamptons to the writers' conference she had attended that day. Since she was in the city, she decided to visit her agent in person. When she stepped through the prestigious offices of Bianchi Literary, she looked like a woman who had her life together.

Though, she didn't.

Francesca Bianchi, her agent of twelve years, ran her fingers through her dark tresses. "Let's talk about your book proposal or, rather, your pitch." Francesca drummed her fingers on the dark cherry table.

Her stomach muscles clenched. "Did Marina like my idea?" She hated the doubt squeezing at her confidence. Marina had already passed on two other book suggestions.

"She thought a story about a couple opening their marriage bedroom to save it was a good concept, but she said she would need to see the synopsis and actual chapters stipulated in the contract before making a decision."

"Ugh. I wish I had taken your advice and requested a synopsis only when we were negotiating the deal memo. Because that I could get to you in a week or so," she croaked out. "Any chance of them changing that?" After the success of her debut, Jewel had had to deliver on every book that followed for fear of being touted a *one-hit wonder*. And she had churned out three more novels that reviewers stated weren't as good as her first. Those words chipped at her creativity because she'd had help with the first one. Actually, way more than help. And that person wanted nothing to do with her. Ever.

Francesca leaned forward. "Listen, I believe in you. You know I'm your biggest fan. But I can't see the publisher amending the contract to give you another advance without the stipulated proposal. We agreed to synopsis and chapters. Something you insisted on because you said it gave you accountability to start writing. Plus, let's not forget that you received a significant amount on signing."

That was true. She had. And for many people, that amount would be enough to last a year, possibly two. But she was the sole breadwinner after her husband had had to close his architectural firm five months ago.

She shifted her body toward the vent, welcoming the blast of cool air, while she thought of what to say besides the truth. That her mother and disabled sister were about to be evicted from their assisted living facility in Ronkonkoma, New York, and her roof was about to cave in. Add to that a housekeeper whom she owed months of wages and who had threatened to report her to a trash mag. And they would grab on to that, though Jewel was at best a B-list celebrity.

Jewel's chest tightened. "Tell Marina I need the money for . . . research. I know this isn't the way it's outlined in the contract, but surely they can make an exception." She pointed to the picture of her book, *That Was Then*, on display along with the tagline *Best friends falling for the same married man makes for one hot summer*. Francesca had come up with that pitch, and it had landed her a six-figure deal at auction for her debut. "My current books have been on every bestseller list. I'm a good risk." She cleared her throat. "I'll come through."

"You realize the publisher is contemplating asking you to return the signing advance. You're six months late with the proposal."

"I'll deliver." She lifted her chin, keeping her eyes locked on Francesca's. Smoothing her sweaty palms on her dress, she refrained from breaking eye contact.

Francesca curved her shoulders. "I'll talk with them, but I can't make any promises." That meant Jewel could expect to see an amended contract and the funds deposited soon. Francesca was worth every bit and more of her fifteen percent.

"Thank you," she said, standing. She held out a hand, but Francesca came around to give her a hug.

"How's Roman?" she asked, patting Jewel on the back.

Jewel looked down at the diminutive woman and spoke the words Francesca wanted to hear. "He's great. Couldn't be better."

Francesca nodded, her hazel eyes compassionate. "If you need anything . . ." So, her agent had seen the headlines about Roman's architectural firm closing.

"I'm good." Jewel stepped back and folded her arms. Then, realizing she must have sounded harsh, she softened her tone. "I appreciate your thoughtfulness."

Minutes later, she paid the parking valet before slipping into her year-old Mercedes SUV and heading back to the Hamptons. She had just decided to put on some music when the shrill tune of her car phone filled the silence. Seeing the name of the caller, she almost slammed on her brakes before pressing the Answer button.

"H-hello?" Her chest heaved, and she cocked her ears to take in the voice of the caller she hadn't spoken to in years. Breathing filtered through before the line went dead.

That was odd.

Jewel debated whether to call back, but this could have been a misdial. And she wasn't in the right frame of mind to hear the sneer in her former best friend's voice. The only true friend she'd had ever had. The one she had betrayed. And the one who had betrayed her.

She dabbed at her eyes. Ugh. Of course Shelby would call. A silent taunt since she couldn't find the words to put on paper. Words that made readers stay up until their eyes burned. Words that made the reviewers poetic. No, she thought as she wiped her brow, if she was feeling some type of way, it was because she missed Shelby as fiercely as she had ten years prior when they had slashed the bonds of their friendship.

With a groan, she turned up the music and swerved into the fastest lane. She needed to blot out the memories of the past. Her current career was very much in jeopardy.

Turning her radio to the latest gossip, the perfect distraction, she lost herself in it until she arrived home. Pressing the Off button, she pulled into her driveway and turned off the ignition, welcoming the quiet. Jewel tapped the steering wheel, pensive. How she wished she could postpone seeing her husband stretched out on the sofa watching TV and sighing. Make that watching *Star Trek*, eating and sighing. He had better not have finished her last tub of black cherry ice cream.

Her mind wandered to Shelby's phone call. Jewel decided to pull up Shelby's socials to see if there were any updates on her page that might give a clue as to what was going on. All she saw was a cute picture of Shelby and her daughter posing together with the caption *Nothing like some rocky road to celebrate your daughter's successful second year of college. #UDEL.*

They were cheek to cheek, eyes shining and smiling. Jewel

eyed the younger woman, her eyes greedily checking for details. Sharp longing rose within her that she squelched. She closed the page out, upset with herself for even looking. Dropping her phone in her bag, she yanked open the door and got out of the vehicle.

The temperature was a glorious eighty-eight degrees, down from the nineties, and the light breeze whisked her tendrils this way and that. She closed her eyes, transported back to Eagle Point Beach. A time when she had been carefree and her biggest problem was overeating black cherry ice cream and not finishing the latest must-read book before bed. But then she heard the slam of the screen door.

Roman stood there in all his fineness, with his arms crossed, in tan slacks and a shirt that read *Live Long and Prosper*. Normally, her eyes would travel the length of his fit body and she would do something suggestive like arch a brow, lick her lips and put on her sexy walk while she headed his way. Not tonight, though. Tonight, she stared, his muscles and flat stomach a reminder that he spent hours in their personal gym while she hammered out toss-away pages on her laptop.

"How did it go?"

The hopelessness of his voice softened her resentment. "Francesca's going to see what she can do."

He curled a fist. "I've got two job interviews tomorrow."

"Humph." Yup. That's all she could say. To say any more would reveal her lack of faith in his securing employment. Too qualified. Outdated skills. Yada yada yada. Roman had heard it all. She made her way up the three steps and patted his stomach to demonstrate her encouragement.

Ever the gentleman, Roman held open the door. She choked out a thank-you and slipped inside.

"How was the trip back?" he asked from behind her.

Jewel clenched her jaw to keep from snapping that she didn't feel like making small talk. "Good." She spoke through her teeth and sped up the stairs heading for their bedroom. He followed her. Ugh. She just needed a few minutes to herself, to decompress. But here he was. She could feel his eyes on her butt and clenched her butt cheeks to keep the natural sway at bay. Cause she was so not in the mood. The last thing she wanted was to make love when all she could think about was their rising expenses and her fib. *Fib?* She had told a straight-up, bald-faced lie.

I'll deliver. Deliver what? Air? The pages she had weren't fit for her own eyes.

Sure enough, she felt his palms on her butt. Since he couldn't see her and she didn't want to hurt his feelings, she rolled her eyes. "I've got to get some words down on paper," she said, her tone, saying *I really wish I could but* . . .

"It's okay. I understand," he said, agreeable, supportive, which made Jewel regret her churlishness. She scampered up the rest of the steps and turned toward their bedroom on the right. The left led to her home office, but she wrote in bed most of the time.

Or, rather, scrolled through social media, reading odd posts about celebrity kids all grown-up or what celebrities looked like before plastic surgery.

After changing into a silk pajama set, she snuggled under the covers with her laptop and Roman settled beside her wearing only boxer briefs. Jewel scooched over so she could rest her head on his shoulder. Of course, that impeded her ability to type but she exhaled. This was one of her favorite places to be. Reaching over, she cupped her hand in his and just like that, all was right in her world.

Until she noticed the cobweb in the high ceiling of their master suite and the light film of dust on the ceiling fan.

She sat up. "I thought you said you cleaned today."

"I did," he said. "You yelled at me for making all that ruckus with the vacuum when you were trying to write."

She had, but he could've done something during the five hours she was gone. "Ugh." She scooted out of the bed. "I have to do everything myself."

"Come back to bed. I'll get it done tomorrow." If only tomorrow would come for him. She didn't dare think of the state of the kitchen. Jewel had washed up before she left but she was pretty sure Roman had eaten, leaving a bowl or something in the sink. It was as if he didn't like seeing the sink clear.

"Whatever. I won't be able to sleep knowing the place is a mess." She stomped on the shaggy carpet to retrieve the duster and the Dirt Devil. "Must I do everything myself?" she hurled.

Roman simply turned on the television.

Their housekeeper, Mao, had said the week before that she wouldn't return until she had been paid what she was owed. Roman promised he would take care of the upkeep in the meantime. Her honey was better with his brains and in the bedroom than with household tasks. She had known that when she married him, but back then, he had been able to afford housekeeping services. It had taken months for Jewel to find someone who cleaned to her standards.

When she was in her young teens, she used to clean for the residents of Eagle Point Beach before she landed the job at the bookstore, and Jewel had been one of the top workers. She had outearned her wages in tips.

She dragged the vacuum into the room, attached the extender and plugged it in. Then took satisfaction when the loud hum overpowered the volume of the television. Roman bunched his lips and swung his legs out of the bed.

"I've got it," he yelled, attempting to take the machine out of her hands.

She curved away from him and stood on her tiptoes in an effort to get to the ceiling. Jewel was five nine, but she needed her step stool to reach those high ceilings. Roman bent over and pressed the Off switch. Then he held out his hand.

With a sigh, she ended their standoff by handing over the attachment. She plopped on their bed while Roman completed the chore. Her eyes fell on her cell phone: another missed call from Shelby.

This was no accident.

Her former best friend was reaching out.

Jewel looked to see if there was a voicemail message, but Shelby hadn't left any. There was, however, one from Francesca. Roman was now yanking the Dirt Devil across the room. Covering her other ear, she played the message. A few seconds later, she smiled.

Her smile led into a low chuckle. Roman glanced her way and stopped to ask what was going on.

"My publisher agreed to amend the contract. Once I sign the amended agreement, they will initiate payment. The funds should be in our bank account soon after that." She rubbed her temples, the grin wide on her face.

He whooped. "That's great, babe. We did it."

She raised a brow. *"We?"*

"Poor choice of words. You did it, babe. You." He dipped his chin.

Hearing the defeat in his tone, Jewel chided herself for putting it there. She walked over to him and placed a hand on his shoulder. He tensed under her touch. "I'm sorry. I shouldn't have said that."

"You only spoke the truth." He wrapped the cord around the vacuum, his movements stiff. "I'm the one leeching here. The one who can't provide." His bitter words rang in the air between them.

Jewel had felt those emotions over the past five months, but having him utter her thoughts aloud didn't sit well. Her stomach soured, knowing she had added to his self-flagellation. She felt shallow. This was not the kind of wife she wanted to be.

"You have been a good husband and an even better friend to me over the years. My partner," she said. "It's not your fault you lost your business, and I need to stop verbally whipping you and making you feel even more guilty than you must already feel. Please forgive me."

He nodded, his eyes averted.

"We're both stressed," she continued. "But this money will give us a reprieve."

"I'll get a job," he said, bunching his fists. "I'm speaking that into being. I put in close to ten applications today. Something will happen soon."

Her heart moved. Her honey was trying. And here she was being mercurial. Time to make things right. Jewel slipped out of her top and her silk shorties. Roman didn't even hesitate. She heard the whoosh of his boxer briefs hitting the ground, and then he swept her into his arms and rested her on the bed. His mouth found her neck, feasting on her sensitive spots like he hadn't eaten all day.

She groaned and closed her eyes, ready to indulge in the best kind of pastime and reconnect with the love of her heart. But the distinct buzzing of her phone penetrated her senses. Disengaging from Roman, she picked up her cell.

It was Shelby again.

"Are you really going to get that?" Roman huffed out, frustration evident in his tone.

"I have to . . . It's Shelby." She slipped on a robe and got a scrunchie for her hair.

His eyes went wide. "That's a name I didn't expect to hear."

"I know, but it must be something important." Squaring her shoulders and taking a deep breath, she answered the call.

CHAPTER 5

Excerpt from That Was Then *by Jewel Stone*

May 26, 2005

Honey

Honey dashed outside, exhausted but thrilled to have ended her first full week at the bookstore on Eagle Point Beach, Delaware. Her final shift before payday after pulling doubles four days in a row. To say she was relieved would be an understatement. Every year, she returned to the beach to binge-read while she worked to fill her pockets from the overstuffed tip jar. Vacationers tipped well. She couldn't wait for her check. Her phone buzzed. And neither could her mother, it seemed.

"Hey, Ma," she said, propping her phone to her ear. Her earbuds were acting up and Honey had hoped to purchase new ones, but with her ma struggling financially and in dire straits, she would wait. Just as she would wait to get a new pair of sneakers, she thought as her sandals dipped deep into the sand.

Honey usually sent her ma most of her paycheck to help out with the bills. But her ma never seemed to have enough, which meant clocking more hours on the job. It was hard to be resentful, though, because Ma worked hard as well. They were both committed to doing all they could to take care of Honey's younger sister, Topaz, who had been diagnosed with cerebral palsy. Picturing that little face alight with joy gave Honey motivation.

"Hey, Honey. Just reaching out to see how you doing."

That was code for *Did you get paid yet?* but her mother liked to cover her request with small talk.

"I'm good. How's Topaz?"

Ugh, she couldn't take the sand spilling into her shoes anymore. Wriggling her toes, Honey bent over to take off her footwear then knocked them together to get rid of the sand.

"She's having a good day. I think she's grown two inches."

And there it was. Subtle. But Honey was used to Opal Graham's way of asking-without-asking for cash. "Well, when I get paid, I'll be sending you money to get her a new pair of shoes."

"Oh, thank you, baby. You're such a good big sister," Ma gushed. "Topaz has been asking for you. When do you think you'll come home?"

"Uh, I'm swamped at work," Honey said, swallowing her guilt. "But tell Topaz that I miss her and give her a kiss for me." It wasn't that she didn't want to go home, but if she did, she would spend the entire weekend caring and cooking and cleaning, and then she would be too exhausted to stand on her feet for hours on end at the bookstore. Plus, she didn't have a car so she would have to rely on public transportation, and Delaware's DART system was spotty on the weekends.

"All right, baby," her mother drawled out with a sigh. She sounded tired herself. "I'll do that. Tell Sugar hello for me. Talk soon."

The urge to call her mother back, cancel her plans with Sugar and drag herself to the bus stop was strong. But she was young. And fun was at the top of her agenda for tonight. Plus, she had promised Sugar that they would talk about this book she had finally finished reading in between customers today. Thank goodness Ms. Brown was cool about letting Honey hang out in her apartment upstairs during break. Honey loved stretching out on her couch to take a power nap or read. Today she had done both.

She fell in love with books from a young age because they were the best kind of friends: they didn't judge, and they didn't talk back. Then when she hit middle school, the love of reading shifted to a love of storytelling. Her ma said she was good at it too. Which was true. How else was she going to get out of trouble for eating the last doughnut when her ma had clearly said it was for her sister?

Dropping the phone in her bag, Honey rushed down the rest of the path to Eagle Point Beach. Curving through the throng of beachgoers, she made her way to where her best friend, Sugar, sat on one of two lounge chairs under an umbrella. Sugar had snagged a great location near the water among other people their age. Beyond them were preppy parents running after their laughing toddlers, looking haggard, their tans streaked with sweat.

"It's about time you got here," Sugar said, looking fabulous in a red one-piece swimsuit.

"The checkout line went on for days. I was afraid they would ask me to put in some overtime, but the new girl offered to stay." She had clocked out one minute before five and rushed out of the bookstore before she got waylaid by a customer.

"Yay." Sugar clapped. She tapped the paperback on her leg—*The Mermaid Chair*. "Now we get to talk about this book." After their professor had recommended Sue Monk Kidd's *The Secret Life of Bees*, Sugar and Honey had decided to read her second novel as well. Both admired how Sue Monk Kidd was able to delve deeply into the psyche of her characters and thought that this was a way to study the craft of writing while feeding their love of books. Both girls were enrolled at the University of Delaware for creative writing. A win-win that bridged education with entertainment.

But Honey quickly learned that telling stories wasn't writing stories. There was a distinct difference. She discovered this when she received her first graded paper in her very first creative writing course. To be frank, she stank at it. The main reason was that her characters needed interiority. Honey hated talking about her emotions, much less putting them on paper. That was Sugar's thing. Sugar always had her nose buried in her diary. Maybe that's why she excelled in their classes: she was always exercising that writing muscle.

If it wasn't for Sugar's help, Honey wouldn't have passed the required courses the first semester. Although she was grateful, there was an underlying jealousy in her belly she couldn't excise every time she saw that A+ and glowing remarks on Sugar's papers.

The comments gutted her the most. *You were born to do this! A natural! I look forward to reading!* All that when Sugar would work on her stuff last minute.

Meanwhile Honey, who had spent days on hers, would get *I'm not connecting! You have more to give!* And the ever popular *If you need assistance, please visit the Student Center.*

"I'm so glad I got to finish reading today. I heard they are talking movie deals for this one." Honey lifted her face toward the sky. "Imagine seeing your book come alive on the screen. I'd like to see what that's like one day."

"You will," Sugar said.

"We both will."

They held hands briefly and smiled. Honey loved that she and Sugar shared the same dreams and would accomplish them together. Sugar was the best friend a girl could have.

"I'll be back," Sugar said, sliding off the lounge chair. "I'm going to get us some ice cream." No book club meeting was complete without them gorging on scoops of black cherry ice cream.

"All right. You need money?" She dug through her purse for her wallet but Sugar stopped her.

"I've got it. You get it next time."

Honey nodded, grateful, though her cheeks were on fire. There was never a next time. She only had seven dollars to spend, and Sugar probably knew it but was too kind to point it out. Her bestie's parents moved from Wilmington to their summer home permanently a year and a half ago since they owned a few businesses on Eagle Point Beach. Their wealth allowed them to dote on Sugar, their only child. She had a generous allowance, which she shared with Honey as needed, starting all the way back in kindergarten when they both lived in Wilmington.

All because Honey had defended her from the bullies. Sugar had been a scrawny, shy thing while Honey had been bigger and taller than most of the kids her age. Her ma bragged that it was because her father was some big shot basketball player. *Whatever.*

He wasn't here, and she and her ma were constantly on the verge of broke. Honey didn't even know his name, so for her he didn't exist. And Opal had never dated anyone after Topaz's father—a married man who would come by on occasion to string her mother along with the hollow promise that he was going to leave his wife and two kids for her.

Honey shimmied out of her shorts and shirt, revealing her white bikini. She loved how the bottom curved around her wide hips and hung on her butt. Just then, a young man— tall, bronzed with a head full of curls and a wide smile—sat next to her. *Nice.* The eye candy had just gotten better than at Rehoboth Beach, and she was here for it.

She stole a glance at the guy next to her. He wore designer

shades and had the look of money. Not old money. But that crisp dollar bill so new that you had to wet your finger to separate it from the other money. This was the kind of guy her ma would tell her to pursue and try to snag for marriage. Marriage. Ma had seen too many heartbreaks and their consequences to recommend anything less to Honey.

Angling her hips just so, Honey gave the boy a sidelong glance. He smiled. "Hey, I'm Chance Hudson, and I'm new in town. Any good places to dine around here?"

Oh, he wasn't wasting time. This brother was smooth with it. She smiled back. "Yes, and I know all of them."

"If you direct me, I'll treat."

"We'll see," she said, pinching her lips together to keep her smile from escaping. She needed to be a little aloof, somewhat mysterious, to keep the fellas guessing and wanting. But her brain wouldn't cooperate. She was grinning like when her mother used to send her to her room to read as punishment. This was definitely a case of like-a-first-look. She engaged him in small talk. "So what brings you here to Eagle Point Beach?"

"Uh, my, um, aunt bought a beachfront property, and since I'm an artist, I came to get inspired while she's away."

Beachfront? Dang, if she didn't have such high self-esteem, she would think this guy was out of her league. "What kind of artist?"

"I paint. I dabble in watercolors as well as photography. I was an art major. My dream is to open my own art gallery one day."

"Hmm, that sounds interesting." Honey didn't know much about the art world beyond da Vinci and the *Mona Lisa*—that was Sugar's thing—so she fiddled with her book, striving to think of something else to say. First conversations were tough.

Luckily, Chance had his own question. "What are you reading?" he asked, swinging his legs off the lounge chair to face her. When he met her gaze with those piercing eyes, she felt as if he was peering into her very soul. She broke contact because the very idea of that was ludicrous.

"You wouldn't know it," she challenged, playing with a tendril of hair.

A wide brow went upward. "Try me."

"The Mermaid Chair."

"You mean the story of a married woman who falls in love with someone else, even though she has a wonderful husband? That one?" He flicked sand off his legs. "Believe me when I say I can relate to that morally gray character. I find Jessie and Whit intriguing."

She leaned forward, forgetting she was playing it cool. "See now, you've managed to thoroughly impress me." This dude seemed to check everything off her wish list—brains, brawn and big money. She liked him.

Those luscious lips widened. "Well, everyone keeps ragging on Jessie, but love is never black-and-white. I get how you can be in love with two people at once." Again, a deep stare. Serious eye flirtation. And here she was having to remind herself how to breathe.

"See now, I know you didn't start talking about this book without me," Sugar said, arriving by her side holding two scoops of ice cream.

"No, no, we fell into this discussion by accident," Honey explained. Since Sugar gave her the eye, she made the introductions and filled her in on their conversation. Honey sat back into the lounger so the three of them could talk while she ate her ice cream.

Which was delicious.

"So, the very thing you loved about the book, I hated," Honey said to Chance. "I mean, I loved the imagery and the emotions that Sue Monk Kidd evoked. But Jessie was married with a good man. I didn't understand her motivation at all to engage in an affair with a monk."

"That's because you don't get how love can be messy, complicated even," Sugar said, joining the convo, eyes on Chance. "The monk was questioning his faith and his existence."

"And she was bored?" Honey shot back, splaying her hands. "That's not enough of a reason to hurt the people you love the most."

"Some things aren't black-and-white. Some things are bigger than you. Like passion."

"I agree," Chance said, his voice low and sexy. Wait a minute—was he putting on that bedroom voice for her or Sugar? Her eyes darted between them before Honey decided to burst that potential lust bubble forming right before her eyes.

She gave Sugar the side-eye. "That's easy for you to say because you have money. I choose security and commitment any day. Passion burns and fades, and all you're left with is regret."

Chance nodded.

"And a really good time," Sugar said and chuckled, wiping her brow before dipping into her ice cream. Sugar was licking her spoon all seductivelike, and Chance didn't need ice cream because he was eating that all up.

Honey rolled her eyes. "Whatever." Then gave her friend a warning glance before mouthing *Stop*.

Sugar gave her a look that said *What?* As if she didn't know what she was doing. Sugar was into Chance and was reeling him in.

Kicking at Sugar's sandals, once she had gotten her friend's attention Honey shook her head then mouthed *I like him*.

"Oh," Sugar voiced aloud, shoveling the ice cream in her mouth.

"Oh, what?" Chance asked. His phone rang, so he didn't wait for an answer, excusing himself instead.

As soon as he was out of earshot, Honey said, "Listen, girl, I feel a connection with him." She finished up her ice cream.

"And I saw him first, so you need to stop making googly eyes at him."

"What are we—in grade school?" Sugar snickered then held up both hands, juggling the ice cream container on her leg. "We're besties for life and you're into him, so he's all yours. No need to get possessive. I'll admit I thought there was a mutual spark, but I'll back off. It's not that serious for me, and you know it." Sugar viewed herself as a dating butterfly, refusing to be with anyone past thirty days, much to her parents' chagrin. They wanted her to settle down, preferably with a *good Jamaican man*.

Honey released a long breath. "Sorry if I'm coming off strong, but this feels like kismet to me. Of all the places he could have sat, Chance came next to me. I know it's only been a few minutes, but he's a potential for me. And he's a reader. Like me."

"I'm a reader too," Sugar chimed in, gazing in his direction. "I get it." There was a slight yearning in her tone. Dang, it seemed like Sugar was into Chance despite her assurance of the opposite.

"Is there going to be a problem if I holla at him?" Honey asked, gently. Chance was now making his way back to them.

"Nope." Sugar waved a hand before meeting her eyes. "No man could ever come between us. We're good."

Honey took Sugar at her word and snagged Chance's contact info. But there was a small knot in her stomach. An unease she decided to chalk up to slight lactose intolerance and not to the fact that Chance had also requested Sugar's number.

CHAPTER 6

Shelby
June 9, 2025

Water. She needed water.

Lying in a hospital bed in Eagle Point Beach, Shelby swallowed, her mouth dry, her eyes fixed on the cup of ice-cold water a few feet away on the overbed table. The condensation on the side of the cup tortured her senses. Since she had awakened three hours ago, she had given up on asking why she was here. The nurses who came in clucking their tongues and fussing with her linens while prodding her head and abdomen hadn't offered more than that she had been in a car accident and the doctor would be by to explain. They did emphatically tell her not to get out of bed.

Well, she needed an explanation quickly, because she was due to meet up with Jewel to celebrate her bestie's book release. If she didn't show up, Jewel would think Shelby was carrying a grudge because of what had gone down with the book. But she was past all that.

Slowly, she raised a hand to touch her head. It was bandaged. Shelby gasped. They probably had to cut her hair! A heritage of her Jamaican parents, her chocolate tresses flowed down to her waist. She knew it was vain to be worried about that when, judging from the beeps of the machines and all the cords attached to her body, it seemed she was fortunate to be alive.

She repeated that when the doctor entered and informed her that she'd had a concussion, multiple rib and a minor left ankle fractures and an abdominal injury. They had given her a light cast for the fracture in her ankle and would schedule the abdominal surgery sometime the next day. It was originally scheduled for this morning but had gotten pushed back because the doctor was pulled into an emergency surgery. But then they dropped the news that her concussion had caused some amnesia.

"I know my name and my birth date, I can recite the alphabet . . . How can I have memory loss?" she asked the doctor.

He held the clipboard close to his chest. "You think it's January 8, 2013. You said that specific date because your best friend was releasing her book on that date. However, it's June 9, 2025."

"T-twenty-twenty-five?" she gasped, hyperventilating. The beeping escalated. "How did I lose twelve years? Wait . . ." She tried to sit up, but the nurses prevented her. "Have I been asleep this whole time?"

Dr. Hassan gave her a sympathetic look. "You didn't lose twelve years, Shelby. You just don't remember them. You were in a coma for about five days after your surgery. Really six, because you were too groggy for much conversation that first evening."

She lost her breath. "I—I don't get it."

The doctor walked closer to her bed. "We did emergency surgery to reduce the swelling in your brain, but you are suffering from post-traumatic amnesia. Overall, you were very fortunate. The damage from impact could have been worse."

"I'm grateful. But . . . amnesia?" She shook her head. "This sounds like the beginning of a romance novel." Then she looked at the doctor. "How long will it last?"

"It could be a few days, weeks, even months." He clasped

his hands. "Or it might be permanent. You might never recall what actually happened. But physically, you're expected to recover, and physical therapy will help with that."

"W-what?" She gasped. "How am I supposed to piece my life together if there's a chance I might never remember?"

"Is there someone we can call?" the doctor asked.

"I . . . yes. I don't know," she stumbled around. "What if I have a husband?" She swallowed. "Or children?"

Dr. Hassan patted her hand. "The cops ran your license, but you didn't have a spouse listed." With another pat on her hand, the doctor left, saying he would be back after his rounds. The nurse remained with her to take her blood pressure and temperature.

So she had no one . . . Panic rose, tightening her chest. The beeping went off with a fury. Her shoulders shook as the sobs broke loose.

The nurse stuffed some tissues in her hand and ordered her to take deep breaths. That helped, but she couldn't control the overflowing feeling of helplessness, and it scared her. Wait. She straightened. She remembered. She did have someone. Her best friend.

Gripping the nurse's arm, she asked, "Has Jewel been here yet?" As far as she knew, Jewel was listed as her next of kin on her license. The police would have notified her. But knowing her friend, Jewel would have been calling the town hospital if she hadn't heard from Shelby in days.

"Who?" The nurse tapped her chin. "You haven't had any visitors."

She waved a hand. "You must be mistaken. Jewel's my best friend, and I'm pretty certain if she knew I was here," she said and pointed to the armchair in the room, "Jewel would camp out right in that chair."

The nurse shook her head.

"Then that means . . ." She released short, staccato breaths.

"Was . . . was she . . . was she with me during the accident?" She stiffened. "Is . . . she . . . ?" Her voice rose. "Has she passed away and no one is telling me?"

"No, you were hit by a driver who plowed past the stop sign," the nurse supplied. "You were standing with your bicycle at an intersection when—"

"A bicycle?" Her forehead scrunched. "That makes no sense. I haven't gone bike riding in years. Literally."

"That's what the report said."

Shelby's shoulders curled, and she dipped her chin to her chest. "I don't know who I am." Those words pierced her to the core.

"Be patient with yourself."

She rubbed her eyes. "C-can I eat?"

"The doctor still has you on soft foods, so I'll see if I can get you some soup and Jell-O."

She was too hungry to complain. The nurse went to get her some sustenance, leaving her alone. Shelby looked outside at the evening sky, the hues of oranges and blues painting an exquisite picture. The opposite of her life. The nurse returned with broth, Jell-O and toast. Shelby thanked her and then pressed the remote by her bed to turn on the television and clicked through to a news channel. Sure enough, the date signified it was 2025. She had no idea who the president was . . .

Shelby massaged her forehead. "It's surreal that I can't remember that kind of history." She took a tentative sip of the broth.

"You made history yourself. You're a miracle." The nurse gave a bright smile and made notations on her laptop. "You're making great strides—eating on your own and talking coherently despite your trauma. That's a big deal and a great sign. If you keep this up, you'll be back to yourself in no time."

"I guess . . ." Shelby had more questions than answers. Foremost on her mind was *Where was Jewel?* She ate some more of her soup. The nurse stood watching over her, extolling her progress. The broth warmed her insides. It was saltier than she expected. "Hey, did I have my cell phone with me?"

"I don't know, but I'll check around. It might have been destroyed when . . ." The nurse trailed off.

"Ah." She straightened before hunching over, forgetting her ribs were bandaged. "Luckily, I remember Jewel's phone number."

The nurse clasped her hands. "Another really good sign." She brought the hospital-room phone closer to Shelby's bed. "Eat first, then call your friend." Shelby gave a nod. "I'll be back to check on you."

The minute the door swung closed, Shelby's appetite deserted her. She pushed the meal aside. Everyone was so upbeat and praising her, but her insides trembled. She quiet-sobbed, feeling every bit of her loneliness.

Shelby reached for the phone, her movements a little jerky, since the handle was heavier than her plastic spoon. That jarred her. And it took some effort to press the digits, but the nurse came in back in, holding up her cell phone.

"Look what I found," she singsonged.

All this cheerfulness grated on Shelby's nerves. But she gritted her teeth and thanked the woman. She inspected the phone. It was severely damaged, and the glass was shattered, but it was working. She didn't remember purchasing this, but her code worked. Thank goodness. She had been using the four-digit code since her first debit card. Shelby called her bestie.

After a couple rings, she heard Jewel's voice.

And suddenly, shockingly, she was too overcome to utter a word. She gasped. Tears dripped down her face, the words stuck in her throat. Shelby cut the call and cried. Her friend was alive. She hadn't realized how tense she had been, how crippled with fear, but she knew she would freak Jewel out if she had stayed on the phone feeling like this.

Realizations hit her in waves. She had turned forty. *Forty.* And she didn't remember. She presumed she must have had a party or maybe she and Jewel had gone to Las Vegas to celebrate. Losing her memory was scary and overwhelming. It was like losing herself. Her stomach was as taut as a stretched wire. She shuddered. What if her memory never came back?

Her heart raced, her chest heaved, and she couldn't catch her breath. Drawing deep breaths, Shelby struggled to fill her lungs with enough air. The machine beeped in earnest then, and the nurse returned.

"I can't breathe," Shelby yelled.

The other woman placed a hand on her back. "There now. There now. Deep, long breaths."

Her emotions whirled like a sandstorm. But the nurse's voice penetrated the haze until she calmed. Somewhat. Enough to hear the dull sounds of nothing. The memories stilled for now.

"Did you call your friend?" the nurse asked.

"Not yet."

"Do you want me to call?"

Shelby shook her head. "No. I'll do it." With a nod, the nurse left the room. Shelby reached for the box of tissues on her table and blew her nose. She'd try to reach her friend again as soon as she could speak. Since Jewel hadn't called back, she must have thought it was a butt dial.

A nurse's assistant came in to take her vitals, and then the doctor returned to check on her. It was a few minutes before Shelby had a chance to call Jewel again. And when she did, she got voicemail. Shelby hung up. After some time, she tried again.

This time, Jewel answered.

"J-Jewel?"

"Shelby?"

"Yes, why do you sound so surprised?" she asked. "We talk at least twice a day." She hiccupped. "I guess you must be wondering why you haven't heard from me in six days. Or was it longer than six days? I can't remember." Pain poured through her voice. "Why didn't you call or leave a message?"

Then she chided herself. She shouldn't be fussing with Jewel for not reaching out, especially since Shelby could have died.

"You know why." Jewel huffed. She sounded . . . confused and put-out. "Um . . . what's going on?"

Shelby paused and looked at her phone. Maybe they had an argument? "Hang on, let me call you on FaceTime."

She pressed the app button, and moments later Jewel's face appeared on the screen.

"Jewel! You're . . . you look different." Because of the shattered screen, her face was distorted, but she looked leaner and her wavy hair had been straightened, resting on her shoulders. "What did you do with your hair?"

"What's the matter with you? Why are you calling and . . ." Jewel frowned before leaning into the camera. "Wait. Are you in a hospital?"

"Y-yes." She sniffled. Tears pushing past her eyelids. "I was in a bad car accident and they're saying I'll have to have abdominal surgery tomorrow."

Jewel's eyes widened, her pupils large. "Oh, wow. Wow. Are you okay?"

"N-no. I'm alone." Her lips quivered. "I need you. I—I . . ." She swallowed back the fear rumbling through her insides and said, "I've lost my memory. The doctors said I've lost twelve years because I woke up thinking it was your book release day when it's June 2025."

"Wait. So what does that mean?"

"It means I don't remember anything after the eighth of January 2013 to be exact. The day your book came out. After that, it's all a blank. So I'm all discombobulated, but thank goodness I'll have you to help me figure things out."

There was a distinct pause. One long enough that Shelby wondered what they could have fought about that was so bad that Jewel seemed hesitant to be by her side. But then Jewel whispered, "I'll be there. If you're sure you want me to come, I'll come."

Shelby nodded. "Come," she choked out.

Jewel wiped at the tears on her face. "Despite everything we've been through, I can't not support you. I'll be there."

"What do you mean?" Shelby asked, her stomach muscles tightening.

"Never mind all that. I'll get packed and get on the road early tomorrow morning," she supplied. "See you soon."

"Bring me some black cherry ice cream."

Jewel gave her a piercing look before nodding. The call ended. Shelby searched her phone for text messages with Jewel to see if there were any answers there, but there hadn't been any. She frowned. Not even one. Odd. She rested back on the bed and closed her eyes. She couldn't think straight, and she was confusing her dates and times. She'd ask Jewel what had happened between them whenever she got here. If she had known she was waking up to such confusion, maybe she would have stayed sleeping.

Exhaustion seeped through her being. This was too much to figure out on her own. Jewel would help her, though. Once she got here, Jewel would help her sort it all out. Her eyes fluttered closed, and she welcomed the bliss of sleep and momentary oblivion.

CHAPTER 7

Jewel
June 9, 2025

She hadn't even disconnected the call before Roman was shaking his head. "You can't possibly be thinking of going back to Delaware. There's nothing there but pain, betrayal and the remnants of a toxic friendship that finally met its end. Your words, not mine. And even though you didn't tell me exactly what happened, I know it had to be major to split you two up."

Major wasn't the word. And yes, she had vowed to never cross the state lines again after she and Shelby had had the most explosive argument of their friendship. Not that she had told Roman the whole truth of what had happened. It had been more of a half-truth to appease her conscience and end his questions. To tell him the reality of all that went down would be to lose him.

And when you had a man who loved you the way he did, you knew there was no letting him go.

"She called me on FaceTime. You heard every word. Shelby was in an accident and lost her memory. How could I refuse?" Roman had a leg propped up, showing off his best assets. She diverted her eyes, though the temptation to rejoin him under the sheets almost prevailed. But if she wanted to go to Delaware early the next morning, she needed to get packed. She marched into her closet to pull out two large suitcases.

"How could you not?" Roman popped out of bed, trailing after her. "We don't have money for you to take a vacation, plus I kind of wanted to talk to you about Curtis."

"I hardly call assisting a friend in need a vacation." She purposely ignored his second statement. Jewel wasn't ready to talk about the sixteen-year-old son Roman had fathered before they met. Or his mother, Katrina, who they figured must have been dating Roman and Scott around the same time. A man who Katrina had told Roman was just a friend. Katrina then got hitched and moved out of state to Philly to get away from Roman.

Though Katrina denied Roman's paternity, from the pictures Jewel had seen, Curtis was Roman's imprint. What was sad was the only reason he had even learned that he might be a father was because he had gone to a wedding and an old friend had randomly mentioned that she had run into Katrina and his mini-me at some event. Roman had reached out to Katrina immediately to ask for a DNA test. But all that woman did was hang up and then block him. Word was that Scott, who was now her husband, believed Curtis was his child, and she wasn't about to tip that boat for anyone.

Not even her son.

Roman wanted to hire an attorney to get an injunction for a DNA test, but Jewel wasn't ready to explore that option. She had a lot of drama with her mother and sister, and dealing with this issue would add to the stress.

Jewel huffed, giving the bags a tug. Ever the gentleman, Roman took the suitcases out of her hands and placed them on the bed, unzipping them for her. Whenever he was around, Roman didn't allow her to lift or carry anything with much weight to it. She thanked him for spoiling her, and he responded with the usual *You deserve it.* Jewel dragged open her underwear drawer and picked up a stack of neatly folded undies before dropping them into the smaller luggage.

"Friend?" His brows rose, challenging her. "I don't know if that's how I would classify your and Shelby's relationship."

"We've known each other since kindergarten, and it wasn't all bad. We had drama, yes, but we also had each other's backs when it counted, and we have love for each other and a solid bond," she shot back, her cheeks hot. "That kind of bond doesn't die out that easy. She needs me."

"You haven't spoken to each other in ten years. Ten years, Jewel. Not ten days." He placed his hands on his hips. "And is it Shelby who needs you, or the other way around?"

His words pierced her conscience. "It's both." With a jolt, she realized she spoke the truth. An ache rose picturing Shelby alone and scared. Recalling the genuine confusion in her ex-bestie's voice pulled at her heart. "I'm going."

Roman released a long breath. "As you should. I'm sorry if it seems as if I'm trying to get between you and your friend. Shelby has been nothing short of wonderful to me."

"I'm glad you agree." She couldn't have Shelby lying in a hospital without a familiar face around her. She had seen for herself that Shelby's daughter (it was painful at times to utter her name) was away for the summer.

Roman sighed and rubbed his head. "Believe it or not, I have your best intentions at heart. That's why I'm pushing back."

"I know . . ." She released a long breath and raked a finger through her hair. The urge to talk to him, tell him everything, pressed against her voice box. But Roman hated deception, and he wouldn't understand why she hadn't confided in him, why she hadn't been one hundred percent honest from the start when he had told her all his ugly truths—his short-lived boxing career that ended when he'd broken an opponent's finger; his parents' grandiose lies of affluence; and, of course, Curtis.

Jewel had opened up to Roman about everything except when it came to the collapse of her lifelong friendship with

Shelby. Because that truth wasn't just hers to tell, and voicing a secret that she had kept for almost twenty years was not easy to do. She wasn't sure it was right or humane to do at this point. Especially knowing how Roman yearned to claim the child he thought was his son. He would not understand her and Shelby's actions of long ago. She didn't fully understood why they had done what they did either. Youth? Ignorance? Desperation? All she knew was that at the time it had made sense to them. Shelby had lost everything, and Jewel barely had anything to begin with, and each had been overwhelmed at the thought of caring for a little one.

"Can we even afford a hotel for an extended stay?" Roman asked, boring into her thoughts. "By the time we settle up with the roofers, your family's health care facility, and Mao, we'll have enough to coast for a few months, but a hotel stay is a luxury. Eagle Point Beach is pretty pricey."

"Yes, but I'll be bunking with Shelby."

He pointed at her bags. "From the looks of things, you're thinking of staying awhile." He cocked his head. "How long do you plan on being gone? I'm missing you already."

Aww. She touched his cheek. "You're going to make me miss you more than I already will."

"That's the point." He bent over to kiss her. "I can't sleep when you're not here. It's not the same. I need my baby with me." He wasn't even exaggerating. So many times during her book tours, Jewel would learn he had spent the night on the couch or stayed up for hours.

Her heart squeezed. "I might not even be gone long." She gave a shaky laugh. "For all I know, Shelby's memory could come back before I get there, and I'll be hightailing it back in the middle of the night." Though, she seriously hoped that was not the case. Even with all that still stood between them, she couldn't help but feel that this was the opportunity for her and Shelby to mend their friendship.

"So what happens when she remembers that you two had a falling out?" he asked, his tone gentle. "I watched you cry for weeks on end over the breakup with your best friend, and I just don't want to see you get your heart broken like that again." She lowered her eyes, her tongue heavy to confess that the heartbreak had been mutual. Roman placed a finger under her chin. "I told you I think deep down Shelby is jealous of your success, especially when *That Was Then* hit all those bestseller lists. I don't think she got over the fact that you made it and she didn't."

Jewel had decided to write a book about their experience that summer of 2005, and Shelby had suggested they pen it together instead. It would be therapeutic, a healthy way for each of them to own their mistakes and write that poison out of their friendship. Shelby had even come up with the character names, Sugar and Honey, so that none of the people in the town would be able to tell their true identities.

They were halfway through when Shelby insisted that they include the baby abandonment storyline. Shelby had even written a prologue, but right before she submitted the first hundred pages to agents, Jewel chopped that thread without Shelby's knowledge. Then when Francesca showed interest and wanted to see the full manuscript, Shelby realized what Jewel had done. They'd fought hard, hurling insults at each other, and Shelby pulled out. No amount of beseeching had made her return. Shelby washed her hands of that toxic time of their lives. She just wanted them to move forward.

But Jewel felt to her core that this story was special.

It took a minute, but Shelby allowed Jewel to use her journal entries to round out the story during edits. Many readers bonded with her characters' emotional depth. The truth was Shelby deserved to have her name in print right next to Jewel's, but she wanted no part of that book of half-truths. *If we're going to tell a story, then tell it right* had been her words. She had gone on to write another book, but as far as Jewel knew she hadn't done anything with it.

Jewel shifted and cleared her throat. "I don't think that's it. Shelby was happy for me, and she was my biggest cheerleader when I landed the book deal."

"So what is it with her, then?"

Their actual rift had to do with a twenty-year-old secret, aka the baby between them, that Shelby's actions threatened to implode. Though she typically told Roman everything, Jewel hadn't revealed *that* part of her summer in 2005. Ugh, just thinking about it now made anger burn in her chest. Going back to Eagle Point Beach could ruin her, but how could she not?

"I can't get into that whole fiasco now," she hedged, moving away from his piercing eyes to finish packing. If she kept staring at him, her tongue would loosen and the whole sordid truth would ooze out. "I've got to get on the road early in the morning." Delaware was only a four-hour drive, but with rush hour, it could take as much as five to six. She planned to leave the city long before the commuter crowd. She gathered summer dresses, shorts, shirts, footwear and bathing suits and dropped them into her bags.

"Do you want me to drive you?" he asked. "I can take you there and come back for you."

The way he was willing to spoil her warmed her heart. "No, I'll need my car to get around while I'm down there."

"Okay, that makes sense. Let me know when you're all packed so I can put the suitcases in the car for you. That way all you have to do tomorrow morning is get up, get dressed and get behind the wheel." He dragged on his clothes and picked up his set of her car keys. "In the meantime, I'll go get your car washed and your tank filled and double-check to see if you have your transponder ready to go."

"Thanks, babe." She loved how Roman was helping her, even though he wasn't fully on board with her plans.

She wrapped her arms about her and admitted, "I'm hoping the beauty of the beach will be a muse. That's where I wrote my first book, and my publisher is cutting me a big check, so I have to come through with a product."

"I pray for that for you as well." With that, he left to go see about her car.

Later that night, after they had made love and lay snuggled in each other's arms, Jewel confessed her fears. "I'm trying to provide, to survive. I know what it's like to grow up eating rice for dinner with no meat. I know what it's like to shiver in freezing temps with no heat in the middle of winter. And I can't go back there. If I don't get another novel out there, this could be the end of my career. And our lifestyle." She shook her head against his bare chest.

He pulled her closer into him, and she savored the smell of his sweat mingled with his cologne and his natural scent. "Every time you talk about your childhood it tears me up, and I get why you're so driven." His voice broke. "But I don't need all this. I just need you."

"I love you for that." Jewel sniffled. "But I'm not going back to that state even if it means I have to crawl back to the place I swore I'd never set foot in again."

"Do you think that Shelby would help you with your writing if you told her you were having trouble?"

"There was a time when I would have asked without hesitation. But Shelby and I are at opposite ends of the earth right now, and I don't want her to think I'm using her." She shrugged. "Plus she's lost her memory, so I don't even know what state she'll be in when I get there."

"But her memory loss could be your gain," her husband said.

She lifted her head and frowned. That didn't sound like Roman at all. "Explain your thinking."

"I mean this could be the opening for you to repair your relationship with Shelby."

Jewel pressed her lips to his and placed a hand on his chest. "I was thinking the same thing. You make it so easy to love you." He was so hopeful and genuine that it whipped at her conscience. Roman did have the best of intentions when it came to her well-being, and she wished she was worthy of the faith he had in her. She would be if she fessed up and told him what had really happened back then.

She stared into those earnest eyes and kissed him again instead to keep from blabbering the truth. Though, she knew keeping her secrets was like holding a Pandora's box, and it was only a matter of time before it sprang wide open.

CHAPTER 8

Excerpt from That Was Then *by Jewel Stone*

June 6, 2005

Sugar

There's nothing wrong with a few text messages between friends. Even if said friend is dating your bestie. At least that was how Sugar mollified her guilt for texting Chance without Honey's knowledge.

Stretched out across her lilac bedding in her old bedroom at her parents' summer—now permanent—home, Sugar contemplated her current communication with Chance. Since Honey and Sugar met Chance, the three of them had become as tight as Spanx. *Tres*ties. Honey was so attracted to him that she begged Sugar to tag along most of the time to keep her undies from pooling at her feet too soon. But that meant Sugar was also getting to know Chance, and as a result he felt free to reach out to her.

It started out with a random text about *The Mermaid Chair*.

He'd wanted to say how he agreed with her comment about how passion could be bigger than your common sense.

She'd been flattered that this man—who, unlike the locals she dated, was worldly, having traveled to a few countries including Brazil, Thailand and France (the place she really wanted to go)—had agreed with her point of view. The fact that he was gor-ge-ous, broody and well-read certainly added to his appeal. Chance fascinated her way more than Aaron, the trust-fund guy she had met at a volleyball game on the beach. Honey had lucked out with this one, and she was happy for her bestie, who was glowing.

But now, Sugar and Chance were sharing information: she, her short stories; he, a few snapshots of his paintings. Harmless. Above board. But wasn't that how a spider's web appeared at first? A string woven together with another string until it became a barrier and a weapon.

While she could share the messages with Honey without a problem, it was the low hum of delight when she saw his name pop up on her phone that worried her.

She buried it by going out with Aaron and forced herself respond to Chance hours later or the following day. But she did write out all her angst in her journal, including her current argument with her parents. She had stopped in to have lunch with them at their home a block away from the beach, a weekly requirement so they could *rest eyes on her*, when they broached their favorite topic: her future, and how they wanted it to look. Frustrated, she had stomped upstairs to her old room to clear her head. Her parents had pretty much left her bedroom the same. She and Honey stayed in their other condo during the summer months. They were right at home with the grand European-style furnishings, an antique vanity, walk-in closets and private baths. She grabbed her journal and her pen.

Dear Diary,

Ugh! My parents are still pressuring me, saying that I need to apply to NYU for law school when I'm finished playing with this "hobby." Mind you, they call my passion a hobby when I'm busting through the CFA program and they brag about my writing skills to all our family in Jamaica, calling me the next internationally known Jamaican poet like Ms. Louise Bennett. Even though I don't write poetry.

Mommy and Daddy have been saving for my college fund since the day I was born, and I'm grateful I don't have to take out student loans, but that doesn't mean they get to dictate what I do with my life.!!! From when I was knee-high, they have been drilling law school into me. I was fine to go along with it because I didn't know what I wanted to do. Until Honey. She always knew she wanted to be a writer, and it's because of her I took an elective writing class in high school. Well, I also wanted to share B lunch with her. But to my surprise, the teacher said I was good at writing. Like real, real good at it. That's why I changed my mind.

Though my parents pay my tuition, they call me rebellious. Since when is standing up for yourself rebellious? Writing fits me like a glove. And I am more than happy to wear it.

Ugh, there should be a statute of limitations to parenting. Like once you've crossed sixteen, they need to hang it up.

Sugar gripped her pen, pressing her lips together to keep from screaming. Why were her parents being so impossible? She wished they would behave more like Honey's mom.

Ms. Opal didn't care what Honey did, as long as she got her degree, worked and sent money home. Ms. Opal was just glad that Honey was about to break the cycle and be the first in her family to graduate from college. Sugar doing the same was merely an expectation in her family. Like brushing your teeth twice a day. But if she became a lawyer or a doctor, then "they could pick their head up." Why else had they left their beautiful island to come to this tough country?

When she tried to talk this through with Honey, her bestie praised her parents for being so involved with her schooling. Honey didn't get how constricting parents with good intentions could be. Their ideals were a noose banding her dreams.

She chewed on her pen cap. But Chance did . . . Maybe she could talk to him about it since Honey was at work? His house was literally a few hundred feet from where her parents lived. Nope. Not a good idea.

"Sugar, lunch is ready," her mother called out. "Don't stay in your room and pout. Come on down and full your belly."

If lunch wasn't curry goat with rice and peas and a side salad, she would say she wasn't hungry. But she was upset, not foolish. Sugar wasn't leaving with an empty container. "I'm coming." Tucking her journal into her purse, she made her way downstairs. The smell of curry made her stomach growl, and she sniffed the air with appreciation.

Mommy and Daddy were all smiles, the earlier tiff shelved. Despite her discontent, Sugar couldn't hold back her corresponding smile. Dash it all, she needed to stay mad so they would feel bad. But this was how it was with her parents from when she was a child. Arguments lasted as long as a puff of wind. If they weren't such helicopter parents, she wouldn't have moved into the condo.

"Look at you, you sweet like sugar," her dad said, then pointed to the steaming plate next to him. "Your mother made you a plate, so come on and put some meat on your bones."

Kissing her mother's cheek, Sugar scurried to take her seat. Her mother slipped in the chair across from her father. They joined hands and blessed their meal.

After she took her first bite, Sugar groaned. "You didn't just put your foot in this, Mommy. You put your whole leg in. This is so good. I feel like praise dancing right now."

"Can I get an amen?" her father said jokingly, swaying his arms in the air.

Her mother's shoulders shook with mirth, her cheeks stained pink. "Stop with your nonsense, both of you." But Sugar knew she was pleased.

"Are you coming boating with us?" her father asked. "We're planning to go sometime over the next couple weeks."

"Can I bring Honey and Chance?" she asked, taking a taste of the delicious stew.

"Um, well, we kind of want it to be just the three of us," her mom said, making eyes with her dad.

Sugar looked between them and lowered her fork, ignoring the light clink as it landed on the edge of her plate. "Okay, that's cool . . . What's going on?"

"Now, don't overreact, but we feel you've been spending a lot of time with Honey and Chance when you should be focused on your studies."

"It's summer break. A break is all about hanging with your friends and lounging by the beach."

Her mother squared her shoulders. "Yes, but I heard that your younger cousin has already been accepted for some internship that will give her an edge when it's time for medical school. So we think you need to do the same and start preparing for law school."

And just like that, she felt the heat of their eyes and the weight of their expectations and almost lost her appetite. "I'm not in competition with Antoinette." Her mother's niece was a prodigy. "I'm proud of her accomplishments, but I'm quite comfortable with my career choice. I want to be an author, and you praise Honey for wanting to do the same thing."

"Yes, but Honey is in a different position than you are. The sky is your limit," her mother said.

"And we don't want you to be a starving artist," her father said, reaching over to give her hand a quick squeeze. "We want you to be on top. We want you to be the best you that you can be."

Sugar picked up her fork and resumed eating. As did her parents. For a beat, the only sounds were the scraping of silverware. Her mother put on Bob Marley in the background. She did that whenever there was tension. Nobody could calm a crowd like Bob, her mother would say.

Wiping her mouth, Sugar tried again to make them understand. "I know you mean well and you're coming from a place of love, but I won't be struggling. Grammy left me a fortune that I can access once I turn twenty-five—" Her parents shot each other a look that made Sugar rear her head back. "What? Is something wrong with my money?"

Her father gave an awkward chuckle, pushing his glasses up his face. "No, nothing you need to worry your head about. We have everything under control."

Sugar didn't know what to think. In the pit of her stomach, she felt she should push the issue, but her father looked uncomfortable.

"Continue with what you were saying," her mother said, waving her fork.

"I can't remember what I was going to say. But since we're talking about the trust fund, I wanted to ask if I could use some of my money to go on a trip to Paris. With Honey." Before her parents could object, she rushed on. "You know I've always wanted to go. I've earned all A's, and I think it would be both fun and educational. I believe Paris would inspire me to write my first bestseller."

"W-we will think about it," her father said.

"Please, Mommy. I really want to go. And Honey will be with me, so you wouldn't have to worry about me going to a strange country by myself."

"I'll let you know," her mother whispered.

Sugar bunched her lips and inhaled. She knew what that meant. Her parents hated telling her *no*. But she was going to bring this up every week until they relented. Resentment flooded her chest. She didn't see why she had to beg to use her own funds. It was just so frustrating.

The need to punish them for not allowing her to go pushed her to say, "I don't think I'll be going with you on that boat trip after all."

Sugar hated to see their shoulders droop with disappointment, but withdrawing her company was the only weapon she had to get them to loosen their hold on her life a bit. If she didn't cut those strings, they were going to keep behaving like puppeteers and she was going to be limited by their expectations.

But when she talked about it with Honey and Chance later that night, Honey was quick to say that Sugar shouldn't stay away to spite them, tucking her container of goat meat under her arm. Her mother had packed Honey, whom she called her *bonus daughter*, a generous portion.

Chance, however, seemed to understand her plight.

"I get it," he commiserated. She cocked her ears to listen to what he had to say. Something in his tone said he knew all about feeling closed-in. "Dancing to anyone else's tune but your own will limit your creativity. Trust me, I know all about that. You can't allow anyone to stifle your flow. I'd say to go to the bank, and see what can be done to access your trust fund earlier since they are standing in your way."

His words stoked her ego.

"I disagree," Honey interjected. "Family is everything."

She gave Honey a meaningful glance. "And good friends. Nothing should come between that."

Sugar clamped her jaw. There was no point in arguing with Honey when it came to this stuff, but she was in agreement with Chance on this one. She felt listened to and understood, and that was a balm over her sore disposition.

Thank you for being a friend, she texted Chance later that night.

Friend? he texted back.

Her immediate response was to ask him why the question mark. But she paused on the keyboard. She would leave that one alone, but that one symbol had nicked her heart. A small measure of fear ran through her. She liked that guy. And he knew it. She thought of Honey's words about friends and nothing coming between them. Sugar couldn't allow that to happen. Her only recourse was to stay away from him.

CHAPTER 9

Shelby
June 9, 2025

Knowing that Jewel was on her way calmed Shelby enough that she was able to get to sleep. But now she wasn't sure if she was still dreaming because when she opened her eyes, she found herself staring into eyes the color of gold. Those irises belonged to the man sitting across from her with smooth chocolate skin and perfectly aligned teeth. What a delicious specimen to wake up to. She couldn't hold back the grin spreading her cheeks wide. Talk about hotness personified. A buzz of electricity shot through her when he smiled back at her.

That concussion was messing with more than her head. She berated herself to quit the low-key flirting when she was laid up in a hospital room with no recollection of her current life. But he was looking at her with familiarity.

"How are you?" he asked, gripping the chair to stand, showing off powerful legs in a pair of basketball shorts.

"I've been better," she replied.

He walked over to her, took her hand and gave it a gentle squeeze. "The whole team's praying for you. You don't know how relieved I was this morning when I heard you woke up."

Okay, this was getting a little weird. She had no idea who he or the team was, but she didn't want to admit that to him and have him leave. He had been her first visitor, and she was hungry for company. "Okay, good to hear." She nodded, plucking at the blanket before pulling it higher. The air was cool, and the hospital gown was thin.

"You don't know who I am, do you?" He stepped back.

"Not a clue." She softened the truth with a smile.

"Then why didn't you say so?" Shelby wasn't about to tell him that she had been caught up by his swagger. He smirked then held out a hand. "I'm Kendrick Holmes." He paused and gave her look she would best describe as sultry. A look that made her wonder if there had been something more between them. But then he blinked and cleared his throat before continuing. "Now, this is a small town, as you know, so in addition to being on your cycling team, I'm also going to be your physical therapist. I'm a licensed contractor with the hospital." Maybe it had been wishful thinking on her part and she had imagined that look.

Shelby wrapped the blanket tighter around her. She wasn't sure how she felt about having someone she found attractive working with her while she was in her weakest state.

"No need to feel self-conscious," he said, in a matter-of-fact tone, accurately reading her thoughts. "I'll get you back on your feet in no time, and you'll be challenging me to meet you at the finish line."

"If you say so." All she could do was shake her head and ignore her racing heart. "Hearing you say I'm on a cycling team doesn't even sound like me." She scrunched her nose.

He chuckled. "I have proof." Kendrick pulled out his cell phone, and after a few taps on the screen, showed her pictures of the team posing at different racing events.

"How long have I been doing this?"

"Just the past year, but you were—um, are—good." He scrolled through several photos, and though she definitely recognized herself as the woman in them, she didn't know her. She tapped her head, her heart galloping in her chest. How could this be?

Shelby gulped. "I have a whole life that I don't remember. Not one iota." This was surreal. And overwhelming.

Kendrick compounded that feeling when he held up a photo of her with a young woman. She squinted. There was something vaguely familiar about her companion . . . a resemblance. "Who is this?" she croaked out.

"That's Lacey . . . your daughter. You told the group she was away for the summer, which is why I don't think she's heard about you just yet."

That revelation slammed her chest with force while Kendrick yammered on. She crashed against the pillows and squeezed her eyes shut. Tears trekked down her face, wetting her cheeks and neck. She touched her abdomen, processing Kendrick's words. She was a mother. Somebody's mom. How could she have given birth and not remember? "That can't be. You . . . you must be mistaken . . ."

Kendrick must have seen the panic on her face because he slipped the phone in his pocket. "I'm sorry. I'm hitting you with too much at once. I was hoping it would trigger your memory, somehow."

All she could do was shake her head back and forth. *Daughter. Daughter. Daughter.* That reverberated in her mind.

Suddenly, her emotions were everywhere and all at once, hitting her in waves. It was too much. "I—I . . . I d-don't . . ."

Opening her mouth, she gasped for air, struggling to breathe. The machines sounding off in a fury added fuel to her already frazzled nerves. She tried to grab Kendrick's hand, but her hand refused to listen to her silent command. She could feel herself sinking under as she struggled to breathe. Kendrick called out for help. Then grabbing her hand, he attempted to soothe her, instructing her to take deep breaths, but he sounded far, far away.

More people entered the room. She homed in on the Black woman with short blond hair who introduced herself as Denise. A psychologist. Denise clutched her hand. "You've gone through a traumatic experience, and it's a lot to unpack," the doctor said. "I'm here to help you through that process." She grabbed on to that voice that tried to assure her even as she fought for control, for freedom.

"Take deep breaths," Denise said, as the room emptied. "Focus on something you can see." Heart pounding through her chest, Shelby looked at the clock and nodded. "Good, now focus on something that you hear." Closing her eyes, Shelby zoned in on the beeping of the machine. She felt a pat on her hand and opened her eyes. "You're doing great." Denise smiled. "Now I want you to focus on something you can touch." Shelby reached for her ice cup and gripped it tight. Her breathing calmed. "Wonderful. Now give yourself a safe word. A word that you can repeat that reminds you that are okay."

"Survivor," she whispered. Her insides calmed. *"Survivor."*

"Yes, you are a survivor," the doctor repeated. "You don't have to figure it all out right now. Your brain has the answers, and in time, it will bring it all back to you."

June 10, 2025

Her eyelids felt like they weighed a ton, which was fine with Shelby because she didn't want to open them. The doctor had stayed with her until she had fallen asleep the night before, and she wanted to remain in that peaceful oblivion even as dawn cracked through her window shades. But her mind was awake, despite her sluggish body. She yawned, and even that took effort. Maybe she had imagined the whole memory-loss thing. Maybe she was at home in bed.

Shelby pried her eyes open. Disappointment slumped her shoulders.

She was in the hospital bed, and she was alone. Respite. Because she didn't think she could handle any more surprises about a life she didn't remember. She pressed the buttons on the side of her bed to adjust herself into a more upright position. Trailing her fingers down her right arm, she felt a bit of gauze. They must have given her a sedative, or she might have nicked herself during her panic attack. Her muscles felt sore, and she wouldn't be surprised if she had bruises after her breakdown.

It took some effort, but she put on the television to the local news channel. She needed a window into what the world looked like now. Seeing the face of the local town reporter she recognized put her at ease. At first, the woman was talking about the beachgoers and the summer booklist recommendation, but then Shelby's own face flashed across the screen. A pickup truck driver had lost consciousness and plowed into the pole, sideswiping her in the process.

They showed a picture of her mangled bicycle, and she trembled as goose bumps popped up on her skin. If she had been even a few inches over to the left . . . She couldn't fathom that possibility. Shelby bunched her lips. She had sustained relatively minor injuries considering the remnants of the collision she had seen on the screen.

A thought occurred. What if Lacey—her daughter—heard about her accident and decided to come visit? That would be a natural course of action. Her chest compressed. Shelby really couldn't have that happen. She wasn't ready to meet the daughter she didn't remember.

The door creaked open, and she gasped. Was it Lacey? But in walked her best friend carrying an overnighter on her shoulder. She released a breath. Thank God. She would have to deal with this daughter situation eventually, but for now, she was relieved to see the face of someone she actually knew.

"Well, hello there," Jewel said, strutting into the room at eight a.m., looking perky in her crisp white shirt and blue jeans. "Someone's already awake, I see."

Though her tone was light, to Shelby it sounded forced. Jewel placed the bag on the ledge and lingered there. Waiting. Unsure. Her face was a little rounder and her hips a little wider than Shelby remembered, but they were both twelve years older. Which reminded her—she needed to take a good look in the mirror to see what she looked like now. She must look a fright, but she was alive, and Jewel was here.

"Jewel," Shelby breathed out, her eyes leaking. "How was your ride down from New York?"

"It was fine," she said, her voice soft, cautious. Careful. Almost as if she was talking to a stranger and not her childhood best friend. "I couldn't sleep knowing you were here alone. I left around two a.m., so traffic was a nonissue."

"Well, you must be exhausted." Shelby rubbed her temples, which throbbed.

"My eyes are burning, but I had to come straight here."

Their eyes met, and they shared their first genuine smile. *Ah!* There was her friend.

"Hopefully, you can get caught up on your sleep. You can stay in your old room at the bookstore."

"Ah, thanks." Jewel covered her mouth while she yawned.

"They've got me on some good stuff and I haven't had my surgery yet, so I promise you won't hurt me. But right now I need a hug." Funny, she never had to ask before. Jewel was being . . . standoffish.

After a beat, Jewel dashed over and hugged her. Hugged her tight enough and long enough that it felt like a hug for yesteryears, today and even for the days to come. Shelby patted

Jewel's back. "It's good to have you here. I wouldn't have anyone else but you." Jewel stiffened under her palm before she melted into Shelby. Behind them, she could hear the newscaster talking about summer events for that week.

Rubbing her forehead as Jewel pulled away, Shelby winced then waved at her. "Can you lower the volume, please?" she whispered. "I'm fighting a major headache and a concussion."

With a nod, Jewel took the remote and clicked off the television. "It's probably best you avoid the news channels for now."

"Yeah." She sniffled. "That's probably a good idea."

"Oh, my friend," Jewel soothed, her voice almost a whisper. "I'm sorry I wasn't here. Do you want to talk about it?"

Folding her lips into her mouth, Shelby plopped back on the pillow. "I know I'm supposed to feel grateful for being alive, but all I'm feeling right now is bewildered. My bicycle bore the brunt of the impact, and I don't remember even getting hit." Her eyes felt heavy, but Shelby wasn't about to give in to the need for sleep. If she closed her eyes, she feared she might see the picture of her mangled bike.

"It's a good thing you were wearing your helmet," Jewel said with a shudder before taking her hand.

"I know I'm blessed to be alive." Her eyes filled. "But the driver didn't make it, and all I can wonder is, d-did he have family?" She swallowed to keep the tears from falling.

"Yes, he had a wife and a four-year-old daughter. But don't focus on what you can't control. You have to think of yourself right now."

That was practical. Yet cold. "I don't feel like talking about this anymore at the moment." What she really wanted to do was scream and holler at the injustice of it all. She needed time to absorb the fact that five inches had spared her the same fate as the pickup driver. But letting loose might put her under a psychiatric watch and keep her from seeing Jewel. She gripped the sheets and clenched her teeth.

"That's okay. Sometimes the best thing I can do is listen and say nothing at all." Her voice held a lot of compassion. Jewel gave Shelby's hand a squeeze before going to sit across the room. Having her friend in proximity comforted her in ways she couldn't verbalize, and the good thing was she didn't have to.

After a beat, despite saying she wasn't up for this conversation, she whispered, "I'm so glad you're here." Then after taking a sip of water, she continued. "Besides the fact that there is a little girl without a father, the worst part for me so far is that I have a daughter who is away for the summer. A daughter who could have gotten the same news that other poor little girl did about her dad." Her voice cracked. Jewel came to stand next to her bed. "And the tragedy is that I don't remember having Lacey. She's a stranger to me." She huffed out. "Plus, I'm forty years old. Not twenty-eight." Looking up the ceiling, she said, "This can't be real. I missed two big birthday milestones." She licked her lips. "Or rather, I don't remember them."

Jewel dabbed at the corner of her eyes before giving Shelby some ice chips.

She sucked on one.

"Believe it or not, all these emotions and questions are normal." Jewel cupped Shelby's face. "You're going to feel all sorts of highs and lows, but you're not alone. I'll be here to help you navigate every step of the way."

Shelby cocked her head. "How do you know so much?"

"Research." Jewel quirked her lips. "In my third book, my protagonist was a psychologist, and I spent hours talking to a few."

"Makes sense." Shelby exhaled. "I'm so glad you're here to help me sort things out. It's so good seeing a familiar face and talking to someone who knows me." A realization sank in. "Hang on." She furrowed her brows and grabbed Jewel's hand. "Something isn't adding up. If my daughter is almost twenty, wouldn't I recall giving birth to her?" A fresh wave of uncertainty and panic arose within her. "Something is wrong." She placed a hand over her mouth and started hyperventilating. "Unless I've lost more of my memory than I thought."

Instead of responding, Jewel drew Shelby close to her chest. "The reason you don't remember giving birth is because you adopted Lacey about ten years ago when she was nine years old." Shelby tensed, but Jewel rubbed her back. "We can talk about that later. For now, try to get some rest, and I'll wait here until you fall asleep. You need more sleep before your surgery. I'll come back to see you later today."

"Don't leave me," Shelby said and settled under the covers.

"I'm not going anywhere." Jewel tucked her in.

Shelby tried to sleep. But every time she closed her eyes, she saw her bike twisted beyond recognition or her daughter's smiling face, and she couldn't tell which one made her feel worse.

June 10, 2025

It was close to two o'clock, and she'd had a packed day. Shelby was hungry and parched. Before her surgery, she'd been prepped and not allowed to drink any water or eat. Her stomach was now seriously protesting.

Shelby rang the service bell to ask for water before resting her back against the pillows. The nurse's assistant had been nice enough to give her a couple more pillows and another blanket, but she ached to be home. In her own bed.

Her surgery had gone well, and they had put a great pain management plan in place for her, but she would need physical therapy. Shelby tugged on her hospital gown. She couldn't wait to take an extra-long shower and get into some regular clothes. The doctor had said that since she had Jewel there as a caregiver, she would be able to leave the hospital in a couple days or so as long as her vitals remained stable.

A mysterious benefactor from Eagle Point Beach had heard about her accident and had arranged for Shelby to be moved to a private suite. She wasn't surprised as the Eagle Point Beach community was a tight-knit group of affluent homeowners who took care of each other. Her parents had owned quite a few businesses in town, and when they died the summer of 2005, the community had rallied together to take care of her. She had been too young and grief-stricken to appreciate their generosity then, having leaned into her friendships with Jewel and Declan instead. But she certainly appreciated it now.

Hopefully, Jewel would return soon.

But in the meantime, she could use this time to reach out to Lacey and keep her from coming here. She cleared her throat and wiped her palm on her thigh and then pulled up Lacey's contact information.

"Mom?"

Being called that word punched her in the gut. Right away, Shelby wished she hadn't called. She opened her mouth, but no sound came out, the corresponding greeting stuck in her throat. She chewed on her bottom lip. Should she pretend to have a bad connection and hang up?

"Mom? I've missed you so much. I wanted to call, but I didn't know if you were still low-key mad at me after our argument. Well, it was more of a disagreement, really, but I didn't know what to say." Shelby heard an intake of breath before the young woman broke into a sob. Oh Lord, what had she gotten herself into?

She gripped the phone. *Say something.* But she had no clue how the *mother* Shelby would answer to ease her daughter's distress, especially since she hadn't known that they had been arguing the last time they saw each other. And she had waited too long to disconnect, so she had to respond. But with what?

"Mom?"

Shelby's hand shook, but she made herself respond. "I'm... I'm here," she croaked out, feeling every bit the impostor. "Let's not worry about any argument right now. There's another reason why I'm calling."

"What's going on?"

"I was riding my bicycle and got into an accident."

"What?" Lacey screeched. "Oh my God! Mom, are you okay? Why are you just now calling me?"

"Y-yes. I'll be fine." More crying. Shelby gripped the phone. What should she do to end this meltdown? She had no idea how she would naturally communicate, which made her tongue-tied.

"I'm c-coming to see you. Bea can drive me," Lacey said sniffling.

Shelby pinched her lips to keep from asking who Bea was since she figured that had to be Lacey's friend. She had to say something to ease Lacey's mind. "No, no. Please stay where you are. I'm okay." She eyed the cast on her ankle and touched the bandage around her rib cage. "Or I will be," she said, then coughed. And coughed some more.

"Y-you don't s-sound okay," Lacey said, hiccupping.

"N-n-no. Wait." Shelby held up a hand on pure instinct, even though Lacey couldn't see her. The nurse walked in with a water jug and cup. She thanked him, asking for something to eat. He gave her a thumbs-up and went to check if they had saved her a tray. Shelby took a long sip before adding more water to her cup. "I don't want you to come. Please don't come. At least not yet." Shelby placed a hand on her forehead. She was already overwhelmed with her memory loss and her injuries. Adding a despondent young adult to the mix, one she didn't remember, would tax her strength.

"But, Mom, I don't want you there alone." The sniffling through the line twisted her gut.

"I'm not," she huffed out. *Try to sound "normal,"* she scolded herself. Whatever that was. "Jewel is here with me."

"Who's that?"

"My best friend." Her brow creased. "You don't know her?"

"Um, no. I don't know if you've ever talked about her."

That knowledge frayed the edges of her control, exhausting her mental capacity. "How could you not . . . ? Never mind." She lacked the wherewithal to go down that conversation path. Luckily, the nurse returned with a tray, and she helped herself to some of the apple sauce, just to occupy her mouth while she thought of what to say.

"You don't want me to come . . ." Those words hung between them.

Whoa. She stuffed her mouth with more sauce. Lacey sounded hurt by the brush-off. They must have a good relationship. "Of course I do," she scoffed. "That's not what I meant. I'm thinking of you." Squaring her shoulders, Shelby decided to be honest. "Honey, I really just don't want you to see me like this. I don't want you freaking out. I promise you I feel much better than I look, and I should be getting discharged soon." She hoped. "I'd feel better knowing that you were enjoying your summer. Jewel is taking care of me, and I'll be in good hands."

Lacey gave a small chuckle. "That's so like you, Mom. Thinking about everybody but yourself."

For some reason, the admiration in Lacey's tone made Shelby tear up. Lacey sounded like a sweet girl. She wished she could remember their history. She finished off the dessert and sipped her water. "I'll tell you what you can do. My phone got damaged, and I don't have any pictures. Why don't you email some to me? I'd love that." She was going off the assumption that she still used the same email address and password after all these years.

"I can do that," Lacey said, sounding relieved.

She placed her trash on the tray table. "You and Bea enjoy yourselves. When I was your age, summer was all about fun and relaxation. After a year of hard work, you deserve it. Are you good for money?"

"Whew. Okay. Thanks, Mom. And yes, I'm good for now. I'll be looking for a job too, so I should be fine."

Shelby had done well holding up her end of the conversation, but it was time to get off the line. She didn't want her luck running out. "All right, I've got to rest. I'll text you once I have a new phone."

Jewel poked her head in the room, and Shelby waved her in.

After several exchanges of *I love you* and *Stay safe* with Lacey, she ended the call and released a long breath. That convo was everything she'd feared it would be, but at least Lacey could go on with her summer plans. And Shelby didn't have to continue with the pretense of knowing the correct moves as a mother. She ran a hand through her hair. She was a mother. A *single* mother. That took chutzpah, which she must have had in spades adopting a nine-year-old.

What had that been like?

And why would she knowingly do that to herself, especially considering what she had been like as a teen? Not pleasant. Those were memories she honestly wished she could forget.

She squeezed her head. Ugh, she had so many questions about herself, about Lacey and . . . Jewel. The biggest one being *Why didn't Lacey know Jewel?* How on earth was that possible? Jewel was the only family Shelby had. When her parents died during that fateful summer of 2005, there was no way she could have faced those early days without her friend. A hollow pit formed in her stomach. What if she never remembered the missing pieces of her life? If only her brain would cooperate and return her memories.

Right now everything felt like . . . white noise.

Shelby drew deep breaths and told herself to be patient.

"Um, I wasn't sure if your . . . daughter . . . would be here when I first arrived," Jewel said, interjecting into Shelby's thoughts.

"No, Lacey is hanging with a friend in Rehoboth Beach. She wanted to come, but I convinced her to continue her vacation since you were here," she said, eyeing Jewel carefully. That's why she caught the shoulders dropping. With relief? "What's going on here? Why does it matter if Lacey is here or not?"

Jewel studied her. "You have a lot of questions, but most can't be answered in a day."

"Spit it out," Shelby said with her usual frankness.

"I'm not . . ." Jewel fussed with her dress. "Okay, maybe I am handling you a little, and I'm sorry about that. But you've had life-threatening injuries and are facing what might be a lengthy recovery ahead of you. I just want to spare you any unpleasantries until you're ready."

"*Unpleasantries.* Interesting choice of words." Shelby rapped her fingers on the overbed table and waited to see if her friend would expound on her reasons. Jewel's mouth tightened, and she refused to look Shelby in the eyes. Whatever it was, it had to be big, and by the way Jewel was sidestepping her questions, she knew she wasn't going to like it. A hollow pit formed in her stomach.

"We had a falling out, Shelby."

"A falling out?" She scrunched her nose. "Over what? Yeah, we bickered all the time, but I can't imagine anything breaking our friendship apart." She arched a brow.

"The truth is when you called, I was shocked speechless." Jewel licked her lips. "That's because before that, we hadn't spoken to each other in ten years."

That truth bomb squashed her gut.

"T-ten years," she sputtered. "Say what? What on earth happened to cause such a rift between us?" Shelby cocked her head. "What did you do? Did you tell . . ." Surely, Jewel wouldn't have told anybody about what they had done twenty years ago.

"No. No, it wasn't that." Her tone went sharp. "And what makes you think *I* did something?"

"Because you're hedging like you're guilty . . . So it was me?"

Jewel responded with an edge. "Yes, you ruined our pact."

She lost her breath. "You mean from that summer two decades ago?" She shook her head. "No, I can't see me doing anything to jeopardize our futures."

"Oh, but you did. You very much did."

The doctor walked in. "Are you ready for your postop checkup?" he asked.

Jewel seemed to take that as her cue to escape the room, saying, "I'll go pick up some things for you at your place."

Shelby met Jewel's eyes. "We'll finish this conversation later."

CHAPTER 10

∽

Lacey
June 10, 2025

"I can't believe my mom didn't call me until now to tell me about the accident," Lacey said, dropping the cell phone next to her on the couch in their condo.

Bea squatted on the roomy area rug in the living area, a Kennedy Ryan book on her lap. The very picture of *unbothered*. "I can believe it. I feel like it's very much in line with your mom."

Lacey pulled on the fringes of her shorts, trying to ignore the unease fluttering on her insides.

"I feel like we should still go see her." Her guilt over beginning a search for her bio parents when her mother was in an accident left a bad taste in her mouth. She scuffed the edges of the rug under the coffee table with her shoe.

"Why?"

"Honestly, I think Mom is downplaying everything, and I'm curious about this best friend of hers that she has never mentioned at all before today. It seems . . . suspicious."

"I don't know if I'd call it *suspicious*. *Odd*, maybe, but not suspicious."

"Well, I think it's odd that this friend pops up like a rabbit out of a magician's hat." A friend Lacey had never heard about before today, which was perplexing, considering her and her mother's last conversation before her accident. Mom hadn't corrected her when she said Shelby had no friends.

"I have to agree with you," Bea said. "Did you get her name?"

"Jewel something. I didn't think to ask for her last name. But now this random person is taking care of my mother in my place, and I feel some type of way about it."

"I'm with you, but Ms. Shelby clearly doesn't want you to see her right now. She's been injured, and she's probably freaking out and doesn't want you to do the same."

Lacey folded her arms. "Too late."

"Let's look at the bigger picture here," Bea said. "Your mother was cool with you staying here—in fact, she insisted—so let's explore finding your bio parents, especially since we have limited time before fall classes start. And maybe find us a summer fling or two."

For some reason, Mekhi's face popped before her. "A summer fling might be a good distraction . . ."

"Speaking of flings, I had a good night last night. I met this really cute guy." Bea wagged her brows. "I'm not sure he's into me, but I sure am into him."

"Hmm." Lacey was only half listening since she was used to Bea going on about this dude or that one. Her friend was a wee bit boy crazy, but she was equally as smart. Unlike Bea, Lacey had to study to get good grades.

"This could be *the* one this time," she said. "I'm ready to fall in love for real for real."

"Love doesn't happen upon command, Bea. I think the reason it's called *falling* is that love generally isn't planned."

"Impressive logic." Bea smirked. "But there's something special about Mekhi." The way she breathed out his name made Lacey's jaw clench.

"Mekhi?" Surely they couldn't be into the same guy. But that wasn't a common name. "He wouldn't happen to be tall, polite and have skin as smooth as dark chocolate, would he?"

"Yeah." Bea's eyes went wide. "Wait. Don't tell me you met him too?" She pouted. "Don't tell me he tried to kick it to you?"

"We had a short conversation, but I thought I felt a connection between us." Over the past few nights she had thought about that sultry look they had shared.

"I felt a connection, though," Bea said with a sigh. "He has such dreamy eyes." Bea launched into a recount of how she had bumped into Mekhi while looking for Lacey. He had steadied her, like a knight in shining armor, and then they had locked eyes.

So she must have imagined the strong vibes between them. Mekhi must have been on the hunt for a bed partner, and Bea had been a willing participant. She swallowed the unexpected jealousy swarming in the pit of her tummy. She and Bea had never desired the same man, and Lacey was the pickier of the two. She had never experienced such a sense of awareness and of being seen as she had with Mekhi. To learn that feeling hadn't been special crushed her a little bit. And yes, she felt that way even though they had shared less than a five-minute interaction.

Because she had been struck by a strong magnetism. She was drawn to him. And she wanted to see him again. Lacey peered at her friend. The problem was so did Bea. The bigger problem was she didn't know if that would stop her. What a horrible thought. But the truth was seldom pretty.

Bea scooted close. "Wait. Do you like him?"

She lowered her chin to her chest and shrugged.

"You do. You're blushing," Bea said. Then she lifted her hands in the air in a gesture of surrender. "I'll back off."

"No, no, no. You don't have to," she felt compelled to say. "I thought you liked him?"

Her friend tapped her on the nose. "I like you more. Now, let's get breakfast, head to the beach and find Mekhi so we can get our fill of all that fineness. Then we can stop by the library and begin our investigation."

Lacey gave her a side glance. "What if he likes *you*?" Her heart pounded while she waited for Bea's response.

"Then we let him choose."

She chuckled and gave a jerky nod. "That's a good plan." Lacey departed the condo arm in arm with her friend, her heart in overdrive at the thought of seeing Mekhi again.

THEY HAD ROAMED THE BEACH, BUT THERE HADN'T BEEN a single sighting of Mekhi. Didn't mean he wasn't there, though. The lifeguard stations were portable, and they hadn't walked the entire two-mile length. Just the section along the boardwalk that had the densest group of beachgoers. And they had been distracted by the culinary displays out today. There was an assortment of free goodies to line the stomachs of two hungry teenagers.

Now as they sat at a table in the local library, Lacey admitted to herself that she was both relieved and disappointed that she hadn't seen him. And she was distracted. She and Bea were looking through old microfiche film at news articles from 2006 for Rehoboth Beach, but thoughts of Mekhi filled her mind more than she cared to admit. She kept reliving the moment they were in each other's arms. It was silly, and Bea would laugh her head off if she knew how smitten Lacey was.

With a sigh, she focused on the screen.

Okay, *smitten* was a bit much. She was just really interested in seeing him again, to test if lightning would strike twice. Because being with him had been a shock to her psyche.

Bea sighed, interrupting Lacey's thoughts. "We've been at this for hours, and my eyes are burning. So far I've got nothing." She hunched over and dragged her hands through her hair. "Are you sure you were even born in Rehoboth Beach?"

"That's where my first adoptive parents lived. So I figured it was worth a shot to start here." Shelby had her original birth certificate in her personal safe at home. Ugh. Lacey wished she had thought to ask her mom for her documents. That would help in her search. But she wasn't about to ask now when her mother was in recovery. Lacey didn't want to upset her in any way.

Bea stretched, cracking the muscles in her back. "How about we search Eagle Point Beach instead?"

Lacey scrunched her nose. "But I didn't move there until I was about eight or so. I think."

"How about we just do an internet search and see what pops up?"

"That's just so . . . random." Swallowing her skepticism, Lacey typed in the words *baby, adopted, Eagle Point Beach* and *2006*. The second she hit Send, a news article popped up. When she saw the words *One-Day-Old Baby Abandoned at the Bookstore in Eagle Point Beach*, she gasped. Lacey clicked the link and scanned the words on the page. Goose bumps popped up on her arms. "Bea, you won't believe this, but a day after my birthday, a baby was left at my mom's bookstore. It's dated April 7." Her heart thundered. "What are the odds?"

"Say what?" Bea yelled loud enough to attract the attention of the librarian, who shook her head at them and placed a finger over her lips. The chair scraped across the floor as Bea sped to lean over Lacey's back. Her hair fell over Lacey's face. "What did you find?"

Sputtering, she pulled Bea's strands out of her mouth. "Pin up those locks." Bea apologized and put them in a bun before moving to Lacey's side. She waited for Bea to read the contents on the screen, carefully studying her reactions.

ONE-DAY-OLD BABY ABANDONED AT THE BOOKSTORE IN EAGLE POINT BEACH

"WHEN I HEARD THE KNOCK, A BABY ON MY DOORSTEP WAS THE LAST THING I EXPECTED TO SEE," CARMEN BROWN, EAGLE POINT BOOKSTORE OWNER, SAID.

BROWN REPORTED THAT AT ABOUT 3 A.M., SHE HAD GOTTEN UP TO USE THE RESTROOM WHEN SHE HEARD A RUSTLE BELOW HER WINDOW BEFORE HER DOORBELL RANG.

BROWN WENT TO INVESTIGATE, THINKING THAT IT WAS A GROUP OF TEENS HANGING ON THE PORCH AS USUAL. BUT THIS NIGHT WOULD BE MOST UNUSUAL. "NOTHING COULD PREPARE ME FOR THE NEWBORN SWADDLED IN A PINK BLANKET PEERING UP AT ME," BROWN SAID. SHE SEARCHED INSIDE THE BOX, BUT THERE WAS NO NOTE, JUST A PINK RATTLE.

THE BABY IS NOW IN THE HANDS OF THE DEPARTMENT OF CHILDREN AND FAMILIES. THE EAGLE POINT BEACH POLICE DEPARTMENT IS ASKING THAT ANYONE WITH INFORMATION CONTACT THE HOTLINE.

Bea's mouth dropped. She placed a hand on Lacey's arm and gave it a squeeze. "What if you're that baby?"

"I can't be." Lacey shivered. "I mean, it's highly improbable. There were 12,415 live births in Delaware in 2006. The likelihood of that baby being me is a one in twelve thousand chance."

"How do you know how many *live* births there were?"

"A random internet search result."

Bea shuddered. "Just the use of the word *live* is daunting. I hate to think of those babies who didn't make it past childbirth."

"It's more common than you think," Lacey said with a sad smile. "That's why they call childbirth a miracle." The use of the term *live birth* had jarred her into a tangent exploration into the reasons why babies do not survive childbirth—low birth weight, congenital defects, stillbirths, asphyxiation . . . Lacey had stopped, her heart aching at the morbid picture of tiny little caskets being lowered into the ground. She wouldn't share any of that with Bea, though. Her friend looked shaken enough without that added knowledge. She herself had needed some pizza and ice cream therapy after she had surfaced from that rabbit hole.

"Well, that baby has to be someone," Bea said, returning to her desk. "And you only looked up stats for babies across the state. You need a narrower focus. Like how many babies were born on your actual birthday. Then factor in how many were adopted and how many were females. And that is the correct proportion."

Lacey's mouth dropped. "And that's why, Bea, you are a sheer genius, while I was taking remedial math classes. But the fact that I'm now living at the same bookstore in Eagle Point Beach where that infant was abandoned is the kind of sensationalized story you hear about in the movies. It's probably just a freaky coincidence. It couldn't possibly be the story of my life." Could it? She released a breath and touched her abdomen. "If I were that baby, which I doubt, that would be surreal." Rubbing her forehead, she admitted, "The fact that we're even having a conversation about this is a lot to process." Lacey shifted her body closer to the screen and returned to her original search results. "There are tons of articles here about it too. This baby was famous."

"Whoa." Bea's nails clicked on the mouse as she navigated with her eyes glued to the monitor. "It says here that whoever left her there was never found."

Lacey curled her lips and shook her head. "How can you even live with yourself after doing something like that?"

"Maybe they were desperate," Bea offered, her tone sympathetic. "You never know what you'll do when your back is against the wall."

Lacey looked her way. "You're a bleeding heart."

"I know, but at least they didn't toss her in the garbage or try to flush—" She sucked in a breath and placed a hand over her mouth. "I'm sorry. That sounded insensitive. I didn't mean to put that out there like that. You know I'm a verbal processor and how I blurt out my thoughts at times without thinking."

"What are you apologizing to me for?" Lacey said, ignoring the fresh round of chills on her arms and the fact that her voice was shaky. "There's no way this baby could be me," she blustered. "Like I said, I spent most of my early life in Rehoboth Beach." But still . . . the day after her birthday, though.

"Oh, there very much is, and we can't ignore that possibility."

For some reason she felt like crying, so she cracked a bad joke instead. "Yeah, and if I were that baby there is a zero chance that I'll meet my birth mother." Her weak attempt at humor made Bea's eyes sadden. Lacey's shoulders drooped. "It would be like finding a needle in the sand. I don't think she will ever want to be found." She tilted her head back to keep the tears from leaking. "Maybe Mom was right, and I should leave it alone."

Bea's jaw clenched. Lacey recognized that stubborn look. Her friend wasn't about to let her back out. "No, you have every right to know your heritage. Keep the faith. If she's out there, we will find her." She snapped her fingers. "I got it! You should go live on your socials. I'm pretty sure you would get tons of interest. Maybe someone knows something about that baby."

"Bad idea. I'm not putting my business out there like that." She folded her arms and met Bea stare for stare. "You think I want thousands of people watching my humiliation if nothing pans out? And my mother would freak out. She was just in an accident, and that can't be good for her recovery. There would be no convincing her that I'm not trying to replace her."

"Fine." Bea waved a hand.

Before they left they printed out a few articles about the baby at the bookstore—at Bea's insistence—and Lacey stuck them in her purse.

Bea went to meet up with her mother, and Lacey decided to head back to the beach to put in job applications. With the sun hovering above the horizon, it wasn't as piercing hot as it had been before. But it was still guzzle-loads-of-water hot, so once she was finished applying, she purchased a bottle of water and picked her way across the shore, contemplating the article she had read. If she were that baby, surely she would have known it by now. Surely Shelby would have known about it and told her. Her being that famous baby would be too interesting to withhold.

But even if the baby wasn't her, just the fact that the infant was found where she now resided was too intriguing to let go. Lacey wanted to know more about this newborn. She rubbed her chin.

Pulling one of the articles out of the bag, Lacey walked toward an empty umbrella and sank onto a lounge chair. She held the paper close to her face in the waning sunlight.

Baby Abandoned at the Bookstore on the Beach Finds a Home

Thirty days after Carmen Brown discovered an abandoned baby on the doorstep of her shop, Eagle Point Beach Books, Baby Jane Doe has been placed with a couple who have already begun the adoption process. "She's so precious," Brown said, "and I'm so glad the little one has found a wonderful home."

In her peripheral vision, Lacey saw someone drop into the seat beside her, and a scent she recognized wafted over to her. Her senses went on alert. "Hi, Lacey. We meet again," Mekhi said, giving her a wide grin. "I've been hoping to run into you."

She folded the paper in half and shoved it into her bag. She wasn't about to admit that in the hours prior she had been wishing the same. Donning a blasé attitude that belied her rapidly beating heart, she said, "I've been putting in job applications. Were you working today?"

"No, I came here specifically hoping I'd run into you. You left before we could exchange numbers." She admired how direct he was, and if Bea hadn't told her about her and Mekhi chatting it up the night before, she would have given it to him without question.

"And how many numbers did you get last night?" she asked, her voice calm, light.

"Just one."

Her brow rose. "Oh." She hadn't expected him to be honest about it. Had been fully prepared for his omission. But here he was being forthright, which was both admirable and daunting. Because it made her like him more.

"I didn't ask for it, though." He laughed. "She put her contact information in my phone, took mine and pretty much demanded that I call."

Lacey chuckled. That sounded like Bea. "And do you plan to reach out?" she asked, her stomach tightening.

He drummed his fingers on the table. "The only person I plan to call is you. If you'll give me your number." Her heart smiled, and she quickly provided her digits. He locked it in his phone and then rang her phone so she could record his information.

Her cell buzzed with a notification that one of the places she applied to was asking her to come in for an interview. She texted back that she would be right there.

"Wow. That was fast," Mekhi said when she told him. "Usually, all the job slots are full by now."

She lifted her shoulders. "Maybe someone got ill or something. I don't know, but I'd better get over there."

"I'll walk with you."

Lacey lowered her head so he wouldn't see the blush across

her face. As they walked, their arms grazed, and sparks flew between them. Just as they were close to the boutique store, Mekhi stopped and took her hand. "Do you believe in serendipity?"

She thought of the baby—who might be her—left on the doorstep. She thought of Shelby becoming her parent. "Yes, I do." She tilted her head. "What about you?"

He gave her a piercing look. "I didn't. Not until yesterday."

"Oh." The implications of those words warmed her insides and had her heart beating double time. "What swayed your belief?"

He lifted her chin to look into her eyes. "I met you."

CHAPTER 11

Jewel
June 10, 2025

When Jewel pulled up to the bookstore, there were only a few people out on the boardwalk—the diehard exercise fans, the coffee addicts and an older couple strolling hand in hand. Getting out of the car, she inhaled, lifting her face to the sky, basking in the sounds of the sea gulls and lapping waves, then made her way to the edge of the water to wet her feet. And to release her fears to the sea.

There's nothing like the beaches of Delaware.

Recollections of summers, lazy days hanging at the beach and frolicking in the sand filled her mind. She smiled, splaying her hand. Then she thought of *that* summer. And *him*. And despite the warmth of the water, she chilled.

Jewel shook her head and blinked several times, a futile attempt to return to the nostalgia of past days, before releasing a sigh. It was no use. Rubbing her arms, she walked the short path to the bookstore. This time Shelby occupied her mind. The idea of her friend losing that much time was mind-boggling, yet intriguing.

She drew close to the bookstore and paused. The bookstore. Painted the color of cinnamon with white trimmings, it was remarkably different from the dingy blue it had been when Shelby bought it. She inched closer, her heart pounding as she swayed between the past memories of what the bookstore looked like versus what it was today. The memory of the night she and Shelby had crept up these steps before running, leaving a trail of secrets and of a summer gone wrong behind them. She had vowed not to return.

Yet she had when Shelby purchased the store, determined to make new, joyful memories. Then when she and Shelby fell out, she had made that vow once more. She folded her arms. Yet here she was. Full circle. Again. Twice, this place had made her eat her words, and each time she felt tranquility. She was home.

Jewel picked her way up the dainty steps, appreciating the awning shielding her from the glare of the sun and the birds. Shoot, she had been pooped on more times than she could count going into the store back in the day. So, yes, she approved of that purchase. There were no more creaking boards. Shelby had everything in perfect shape.

The Open sign was lit. The door jangled at her entry, and that sound grounded her. At least something had remained the same.

The smell of apples and books made her tummy grumble and brought a smile to her face. She looked toward the counter and found a young woman scrolling on her phone before looking up to greet Jewel with a cheery hello. A reminder of Jewel's and Shelby's stints here as assistants. The teen wore a pair of cutoff shorts and the bookstore T-shirt, with dark heavy makeup around her eyes, black lips and nails and a lot of piercings. Her blond hair was streaked with different colors, and her name tag read *Abby*. "If you need anything, just holla at your girl," she said, picking her head up to acknowledge Jewel briefly.

There was a small coffee station with apple fritters and cinnamon cookies. Another new, great addition. She would grab some before leaving, but for now, she just wanted to be around the books.

Jewel grabbed a basket and made her way down the aisles, touching the covers. Shelby had a great assortment. She perused a few, deciding to grab a romance by Farrah Rochon and Denny Bryce's historical to add to her never-ending to-be-read pile. Placing her books in the basket, she strolled toward a center display that said *Must-Have Books*. Scanning the colorful covers, she gasped. There were several hardcover copies of *That Was Then*.

Shelby had her book in stock? She so did not expect that. Why would Shelby house her books after all that happened between them? Surely, it wasn't to support her? Jewel flipped open one of the books and read a snippet.

> *A shadow towered over her. Sugar raised her head to see the boy who had filled more of her thoughts than she could ever admit. She licked her lips. "Chance, what are you doing here?"*
>
> *He dropped to his knees and whispered in her ear. "Your friend, Honey, let me in. I had to see you." His deep voice made her shiver, and her heart skipped a beat. No, make that several beats.*

Jewel slammed the book closed. She knew that story, had lived the tale. Picking up the stack, she added them to her pile and walked to the register. Abby was now ringing up another customer. Once the customer departed, Jewel walked up to the counter.

Abby's blue eyes narrowed before her mouth dropped. "You're her," she sputtered. "Oh my gosh, I can't believe this. You're Jewel Stone, the reason I fell in love with books when I was ten years old." Dang. That made Jewel felt a little ancient. Abby gushed on, waving her stiletto-shaped nails. "I've read all your books, but your first is my favorite, though." Jewel stifled a groan. Everywhere she went, at least one reader gushed about that book. She wasn't about to temper Abby's enthusiasm by sharing how she felt like a one-hit wonder.

Instead, she plastered a smile on her face. "I'm humbled by your compliment."

"Is that your real name or is it a pseudonym?" Abby asked, eyes flashing. "You could tell me. I won't tell a soul."

Jewel dipped her head. "It's my real name."

"Gosh, that's so cool." She held up a hand. "I'll be right back. We have some copies in the back that I'd love for you to sign if you're okay with that?"

"I'd love to." Jewel took the copies of her books out of the basket and placed them on the counter. "I'll sign these as well." She reached into her bag and rummaged around for one of her specially designated pens for signing. She never left home without them. Ah! She found one in the small pocket.

Abby returned with the other copies and made space on the counter for Jewel to sign the books. "I can't believe you're here. In Eagle Point Beach and in this bookstore on a random workday. And to think I would have called off if Ms. Shelby—that's my boss—wasn't in that accident." Abby placed a hand over her mouth. "Not that I'm glad that happened. I mean—"

"It's quite okay," Jewel said, patting Abby's hand. "I know what you meant." The door opened, and a family of four entered. Jewel lowered her straw hat. She didn't want to be recognized.

Abby hunched her shoulders. "Um, can you sign one of those to me? The Black Girls Read book club ordered too many of these, so we have a backlog. Shelby is going to be thrilled that we have autographed copies." She tugged open a drawer and took out shiny gold stickers that said *Autographed Copy* and slapped them on the covers as Jewel signed.

Ha! So that explained why her books were here. "Um, sure.

Yes." Jewel autographed the last one, signing just her first name along with her special symbol for a stone. After she allowed Abby a selfie, Jewel added, "I used to hang out here a long time ago."

"Really?"

"Yeah. I know the owner very well."

Abby's mouth dropped. "Wow. Shelby never told me that, and I've been working here two years."

"No . . . We kind of lost touch." Jewel placed a hand on her chest. "But I'm actually here to help her during her recovery. In fact, I'm staying upstairs. I just popped in to get some clothes and other personal items Shelby will need." She held her breath, hoping the younger woman was too much of a fan to question where she'd been all these years or why she had never seen Jewel once.

"Oh, that's great," Abby said. "I have a couple of books that I meant to drop off for her at the front desk. Maybe you can take them?"

"Sure." A thought occurred. Shelby wouldn't know Abby. Pulling out her phone, Jewel decided to snap a picture with the young woman. That way she could show Shelby another picture of her employee since she wasn't sure Shelby wanted Abby to know about her memory loss. Of course, Abby was stoked. "I'll post this on my social media," Jewel said, tucking her phone back into her purse.

"Okay, cool. I'm already following you, so I'll be on the lookout for it." She jutted her chin toward the rear door that would give Jewel access to the upper floor. A steady stream of beachgoers entered the store, snagging Abby's attention.

Jewel searched her bag for the key Shelby had offered her, but she must have left it at the hospital. Mumbling under her breath at her forgetfulness, Jewel went to retrieve the spare. Shelby had a fear of being locked out of her home and hadn't wanted to take any chances.

Sifting through the flowerpot by the staircase, she fished out the spare and ambled up the steps. How many times had Jewel and Shelby dashed up these stairs? Ms. Brown had allowed them to use this space to relax and read, and they would boy-watch through the huge bay windows, the ledge serving as a nook. At the top of the stairs, there was a door. Unlocking it with the key, she entered Shelby's private quarters and got transported in time.

The furnishings, though different, were light and airy and gave her a sense of peace. She stepped inside, traipsing down the small corridor with the linen closet on the left and the half bath on the right. She kept walking to the open-concept living and dining areas with an external door between them, which led to the wooden wraparound porch and steps straight to the beach.

But behind the couch was the nook. Jewel planned to sit there and allow the words to flow. Her fingers tingled to touch a keyboard. She could write here. She knew it.

To the right of the living area were two bedrooms with a Jack and Jill bathroom and an entrance to the porch. Past the kitchen, down another hallway, was the master suite, which had another small bathroom Shelby had built on and sliding doors to the porch. Jewel and Shelby had spent countless hours sitting out there eating ice cream and talking about books. There was another small staircase with a path to the beach so when they were finished, they would run to the waters for a swim.

That was all pre-Lacey-adoption.

Quickly entering the master bedroom, Jewel marched into the walk-in closet, taking a moment to admire its structure and organization before grabbing an overnighter. Filling it with a couple easy over-the-head dresses, socks, toothbrush and paste, hairbrush, loose pants, sweaters and slides, Jewel placed a hand on her chin before snatching up some more hair products, deodorant and lotion and tucking them in the bag. Her next stop would be the farmers market. Jewel knew from her many trips to the hospital with her younger sister that Shelby was going to enjoy the fresh fruit while she recovered.

At the top of the stairs, Jewel paused to look out the window facing the rear of the shop at a small row of neatly trimmed trees. Thirteen years ago—a little over a year after Shelby had repurchased her bookstore, January 1, 2012, to be exact—they had been celebrating both a new year and Shelby and her finishing their books right by those very trees.

Jewel had gone ahead to get her novel published, and Shelby had shelved her book and her dreams for good when she had taken Lacey in. Another thing they had argued about.

With a sigh, she continued down the steps.

After helping herself to the treats by the coffee table, Jewel packed the two books Abby had mentioned in the bag and gave the teen a quick wave. Just as the door closed behind her, a memory hit her. In a flash, she went back inside, rushed up the stairs, reentered Shelby's home and dashed into her closet. Digging around, Jewel huffed. "C'mon. Shelby couldn't have changed that much." Jewel continued her search before she found two brown leather books behind a row of books. "Aha!" Shelby's journals!

She flipped through the pages of the newer one and quickly scanned the pages before giving a grunt. It was as she suspected. Shelby had recorded the good, the bad and the ugly. As usual.

Stuffing the two books in the bag, she took out the books that Abby had given her. Shelby could read those later. Then Jewel sped to the farmers market to get some fresh produce.

Just as she pulled into visitors' parking at the hospital, her cell buzzed with a text message from her agent.

The funds will be in your account within ten days.

Jewel whooped and pumped her fist.

> Thank you, Francesca. I appreciate your coming through for me.

> You're welcome. But that's based on the promise you'll get the first hundred pages off to them soon. How's the writing going?

> Just getting settled by the beach in DE.

> Okay, may your words flow as rich as the waters do.

Jewel hit the Like icon, though she wanted to call out Francesca on her corniness. But that text reignited her apprehension that she was never going to finish this manuscript. Her writing well was dried up, and no amount of best wishes appeared to be changing that.

Her cell dinged again with another notification.

> I need to see something soon.

As you shall, she texted back quickly, though the doubts threatened to consume her. But she reminded herself of the feeling she had experienced at the bookstore. Being home was the cure for her dry spell. And in time, she would write again.

JEWEL RAPPED ON THE DOOR BEFORE STROLLING INTO Shelby's hospital room with the paper bags of fruit and the overnighter. She unzipped the bag to show some of the contents, including the oranges and other fruits that she had purchased before placing them on the ledge.

"I thought you could use some clothes and fruit, so I went by the bookstore and then I made a beeline for the farmers market before coming here."

"Thank you, friend."

"I forgot to ask earlier—how did the surgery go?"

"I'm still here," Shelby teased.

"I'm so glad for that," Jewel said, her tone subdued. "The thought that I could have lost you forever is sobering."

"Aww. I feel the same way about you, which is why I don't get how we could have allowed a decade to pass without contact between us. You said that I did something to jeopardize our futures, and I haven't forgotten that we still have to talk about that."

Jewel pulled out two large leather-bound journals—ones she was sure her friend would recognize since Shelby had been journaling on and off since she was fifteen years old but had begun in earnest since her parents' deaths. "Whatever you need to know will probably be in there," Jewel said, putting the books on the bed. "Your assistant gave me a couple of books for you, but I figured you would prefer to read these."

"Can't we cut to the chase?" Shelby asked. "You accuse me of breaking our pact, and I need to know how."

"I know we have a conversation to finish, but it's hard for me. I'm dreading rehashing the past and messing around in that hornets' nest of past pain. So reading the journals will give you a complete understanding of the full picture."

"I get it, but I feel like until we air the dirty laundry, our interactions will have an awkwardness that I don't know how to resolve because I can't remember what I did."

Jewel whispered, "I agree. But read them first. *Please.*"

Cracking one open, Shelby peered at the first words. "This is dated 2005. I remember that summer well." She opened the other book dated 2013 and held it up. "This is perfect. I'll start reading it today."

Jewel folded her arms. "Good. Going back to the past will explain how we ended up here in the present."

"Thank you for this."

"I met your assistant, Abby," she offered, changing the topic.

Shelby went along with the conversation shift. "Oh, how was she?"

"She's sweet. And a fan of my work." Jewel retrieved the picture of Shelby's employee and gave her a look-see.

There was no hint of recognition. Shelby studied the snapshot for a few seconds before handing back the phone. "Thanks for the photo. It's good to know who's looking after the store while I'm in here."

There was silence for a beat. "Um, I figured you could use a proper shower and something of your own to wear." Jewel bit on her lower lip and looked down at her gold sandals, which she had paired with a burnt orange summer dress.

"The nurse already showered me today, but I'd love to change now if you'll help me."

Jewel took a step forward then stalled, rubbing her arms. After helping herself to some more water, Shelby opened her arms. This time their embrace was brief. Jewel eyed Shelby's cracked glass on her cell phone and made a mental note to order her a new one. Once they had separated, Jewel pulled a sundress out of the bag.

"That's super cute," Shelby said, giving her the thumbs-up sign.

Jewel smirked. "I'm glad you think so, since this came from your closet."

"Oh." Her cheeks warmed. "Let's ignore my obvious embarrassment over not recognizing my own possessions." They shared a chuckle while she helped Shelby out of the drab, itchy hospital gowns, which she had on back to front, and into the soft flexible dress. Then Jewel put a pair of matching socks onto Shelby's feet.

"Thanks, friend."

"My pleasure. I can't have you looking like what you've been through." She searched inside her purse for the hairbrush and a scrunchie. "This will have to do for now. I'll bring some products and get you hooked up next time."

Shelby dabbed at her eyes. "You know exactly what I need to feel like myself again."

"When is your brace coming off?" Jewel asked, starting on Shelby's head.

"In a couple of weeks or so. I'll begin work with my physical therapist tomorrow."

Jewel's mouth dropped. "That soon?"

"When you're in a coma, your muscles can atrophy, so physical therapy will help with all that."

"Oh, that makes sense." Jewel placed a hand over her heart. "It could have been worse," she choked out in a whisper. "Much worse. I'm glad you're here to tell me about it."

"Me too." Shelby cleared her throat and touched Jewel's arm. "I'm sorry our reunion after all this time is in a hospital room."

Jewel looked around. "It doesn't matter where, I'm just glad it's happening and we're together. Ten years is a long time to be without your bestie. This isn't about location. We can have fun anywhere."

Her friend scoffed and splayed her hands. "I'd hardly call this fun."

"No, but your being alive is cause for celebration." Her voice hitched. "I'm glad I get to spend this quality time with you."

"Just having you here makes me feel . . . hopeful. It's like I can face anything ahead, like starting physical therapy tomorrow, knowing you're here. Your presence strengthens me."

Tears flowed down Jewel's face, and she paused the brushing to wipe her face and blow her nose. Washing her hands, she said, "I'm glad to be here for you after all the times growing up you were there for me. Now, let's talk about something else that won't turn me into a blubbering mess."

"How's Roman doing? You've got to tell your husband *thank you* for sharing you."

"Roman is fine," she said, giving her standard response. She wrapped Shelby's hair in a scrunchie, then it struck her. This was her best friend. Jewel could tell her the truth. "Well, he is job-hunting as we speak, and that has been tough. Not to mention he is desperate to have a relationship with his son."

"Son?" Shelby turned her head, her eyes widened with shock.

"Yes. He found out by accident that the woman he was seeing just before he met me actually had a son."

"How old is he?"

"Sixteen. His name is Curtis, and he's Roman's spitting image. Now, all this is hearsay, but the fact that Katrina is so unwilling to talk to Roman makes me believe it's the truth." That knowledge made her smile. She only hoped his child had inherited Roman's integrity along with his good genes. She then went on to explain the entire situation with Katrina, including her avoiding talking about it with Roman. "Roman is gutted over it."

Shelby's brows shot up to her hairline. "Wow. I can't imagine what Roman is going through. Missing all those years of his son's life must be ripping him apart on the inside."

Whoa. That cut deep. All she could manage was a soft "Yes, I can imagine." She could see Shelby's cheeks redden when the implications of her words sank in.

Shelby inhaled sharply. "Actually, yes, we both know." She shook her head. "The first few years without her were tough, tough, tough." Shelby shook her head, and Jewel shifted, desperately needing for Shelby to change the subject. "Have you told Roman?"

"No. It wasn't just my secret to tell." She folded her arms.

"I think the time for that has passed. But I know I have been avoiding talking to him about Curtis because it makes me remember *her*." She dropped the brush in her bag and wandered over to the window, while she thought of something to say to fill the sudden silence and to counteract the resentment rising within.

Jewel returned to the topic of Roman and Curtis. "Roman wants to hire an attorney. The past couple days I've been thinking about going to see Katrina myself to try to persuade her. Woman-to-woman. The last I heard, she was living in Philly."

"That would be a wonderful idea. You should go. Or do you think Roman would be opposed?"

"I don't know if he'd be opposed, but I also don't know if he would think it's a good idea. Truthfully, I'd rather not tell him. He's so eager to see his son that I wouldn't want to get his hopes up. If Katrina changes her mind after meeting with me, then I'd tell Roman. If she doesn't, or Curtis isn't interested, then he isn't any the wiser."

Shelby cocked her head. "If you were Curtis, would you want to know?"

"I think so. But I was so moody as a teenager, and I feel like a younger child might be more forgiving, maybe?" She lifted her shoulders. "Curtis is practically a man, and he might not want us intruding or disrupting his life." She chewed on her bottom lip. "Maybe I should leave well enough alone."

Shelby shook her head before giving Jewel a piercing stare. "Dang, this would make for a great book."

Jewel perked up at those words. She was right, it really would.

But then her bestie shifted gears. "Just a random thought. How do you feel knowing Roman might be a father? Made a whole child with another woman?"

"Are you asking if I'm jealous? Yes. Big-time. Roman would have a permanent connection with this woman. And I don't like sharing. Mind you, I would welcome Curtis into our home and our lives. He's a child and innocent."

"So why not leave well enough alone?"

What a great question. "Because Roman wants to be in his son's life. I want to bring him that happiness, even if it makes me nervous. And if Roman and I don't take charge of the situation, I'd always be on edge, sitting at home wondering if today is the day we get a knock on the door and it's Curtis or Katrina showing up to upend our lives."

Shelby whispered, "Do you have that fear about our child doing the same thing?"

If only she knew . . . "Um, constantly. I grind my teeth at night sometimes because of it."

"Yes, the threat of discovery is like walking around with a hammer over your head. You wonder if today is the day it falls and your world tears apart." She sighed. "I'd like to think if our baby girl showed up, I'd be open to welcoming her."

Oh, she had no idea how truthful those words were. But this wasn't the time. Jewel placed a hand on her hip. "And how would you answer the question? Because what we did has been a secret so long that I kind of want it to remain that way."

"Yes, but what's easier isn't always best." Shelby placed a hand on her chin. "If you do decide to go see Katrina, I'll go with you. We can take a road trip."

Jewel's stomach clenched. "Somehow, I am not surprised that you would suggest that." She did her best to keep her tone light, but the resentment had escalated from a simmer to a low boil.

"This might sound odd or selfish, but maybe helping Roman unite with his son might vindicate us somehow for abandoning another child."

That kind of astuteness punctured her very core. "It doesn't sound odd at all," she whispered, unable to meet Shelby's eyes. Shelby had just pinpointed Jewel's secret motivation.

But Shelby wasn't finished with their conversation. "What I fear most is that if our child ever showed up, I wouldn't be able to answer the question of *why*. You know what I mean?"

"Yes. I also fear going to prison," she snapped. That's why Jewel had stayed away from Eagle Point Beach, the bookstore, Shelby and Lacey. The more she stayed in Eagle Point Beach, the more she increased the probability of that happening. But Shelby had almost lost her life. How could Jewel stay away?

"There are so many moving pieces. Frankly, it hurts my head." Shelby sighed before giving a tentative smile. "You know what I love, though? Being here with you is like old times, like riding a bike. It felt a bit shaky at first, but it's like we never parted. I love that we can still have these discussions."

"Me too. It's nice to talk about this with someone who gets it. But let's change the topic. Please." Because this convo twisted up her insides and made her chest burn. She turned on the television. It was time for them to stop talking before she said too much. Jewel searched the streaming services for one of their favorite movies, *Bring It On*.

"Good choice." Shelby clapped her hands. "Bring it on."

As she and Shelby recited lines from the movie, ate fruit and shared laughs at the antics of the girls in the screen, Jewel felt dueling emotions of happiness and also dread. Shelby was right about this feeling like old times. But that feeling would sour once the truth came out as Shelby read those journals, and she didn't know if she could survive the fallout a second time.

CHAPTER 12

Shelby
June 13, 2025

Sweat poured from her face like crystals, while her eyes were on the finish line. Shelby wore a red cycling suit, along with a helmet and sunglasses that hid most of her expression, but there was a big smile on her face as onlookers around her cheered. The more they cheered, the more she pushed until she got to the finish line.

Wow! That was her. That really was her.

"Will I be able to do that again?" she asked Kendrick. Before their session, he had pulled up an old video of her first race as a cyclist. She had done just under twenty-two miles. Inspiring. "I can't believe that's me."

"You most definitely will. You're in excellent shape, so it shouldn't take long. After studying your X-rays, I'd say you should be able to ride in about six to eight weeks since your injuries are minimal, but under the careful eye of your therapist, of course." He gave her a wide smile.

She nodded. "Can you send that to me?"

"Sure I'll AirDrop it to you now." Seconds later, she accepted the transfer and saved it to her phone.

"Today," Kendrick began when she looked back up at him, "we are going to start out by getting you ambulatory. I'll be right back with a walker. You won't need to use it for long, but

I want you to use it right so you don't cause additional injury to your foot."

"I can't wait," she said with forced cheer.

She hated pressing the call button when Jewel wasn't around to help her with even the most menial of tasks—like going to the bathroom—since the doctor had wanted to make sure she wasn't a fall risk. Having Jewel here with her was such a blessing. Shelby felt fortunate that she had a friend with the kind of career that allowed her to work from anywhere. Earlier today, Jewel had called to say she was in her writing cave, so Shelby had told her to keep working on her book. Jewel assured her she would be by before the day was out.

Taking note of the journals on the table next to her, she picked one up and gripped one in her hand. Her spirit drooped. Today above all days, she needed her friend here. Shelby had no idea how she had faced summers for ten years without Jewel or why. Each time she broached the topic, Jewel seemed reluctant to talk about it, saying she wanted to focus on rebuilding their friendship.

The night before, Shelby had started reading the journal, and among the first entries she had been reflecting a lot on her parents, writing down all the memories she had, and mourning how Jewel wouldn't be there with her on their death anniversary. When Shelby saw the next journal entry was dated June 13, she had bawled her eyes out and had slammed the book closed. She hadn't had the courage to read any more since.

To say she was glad she wouldn't face this date without Jewel today was an understatement. Kendrick returned, and she put the book aside along with her doldrums.

"Let's see how you do," he said. "The doctor said that you should be discharged soon."

"Yes, I could use some good news, especially today," she choked out. Gosh, she needed to hold it together.

Kendrick tilted his head. "Why? What's going on?" He splayed his hands. "Besides the obvious, which is a lot."

"It is." She drew in a deep breath. "Twenty years ago on this exact date, I lost my parents at sea. They went boating, and an unexpected waterspout destroyed their yacht." She gulped. "They were never found."

He rested a hand on her arm. "Oh my goodness. I'm so sorry to hear that. I had no idea. You never said . . ."

"It's not exactly a great conversation starter, and I tend to keep my personal business close to the chest." She cleared her throat. "The thing is, I almost went with them that day. But my best friend had a family emergency, and I got home so late that I backed out of going. I know I sound disjointed now, but that was a tough, dark time in my life." To her utter mortification, she broke into tears. Kendrick stuffed tissues in her hand and waited until she cried it out and regained control.

When she dared to meet his gaze, his eyes held compassion. "How about we do this tomorrow?"

"No, I'd . . . I'd prefer if we didn't." Shelby wiped the corners of her eyes. "I'm motivated to get out of here, and this is how I achieve that."

His lips quirked. "Okay, we'll get to work, but promise you'll talk about all this with your therapist."

She gave a tentative nod. "I will."

Kendrick led her down to the physical therapy room. There were balls of all sizes and various contraptions from the ceiling to assist with mobility. As he passed those and headed to the far corner of the room, Shelby gave thanks that her injuries weren't as bad as they could be. Kendrick walked her through step by step on some strengthening exercises. Through positioning and small hops, she began to walk.

By the time the session was finished, she was sweating and it felt good. Shelby knew a lot of that was due to the exercises Kendrick had put her through, but this man also had her sweating because he was a desirable specimen of manhood. And her body knew that. She felt the first tingling of attraction stir in her gut.

"We'll work on this some more tomorrow." He took her back to her room. "Let's get you back into bed," he said.

"Can I stay in the chair?" she asked. "My friend is coming, and I wondered if we could go out and get some fresh air or something."

"That's fine. Just use a wheelchair. Don't overdo it, and make sure to rest and elevate your left foot." She did a mock salute, which made him laugh.

Their eyes met, and for a split second she detected a personal kind of interest reflected in his eyes, and it scared her. She broke eye contact, looking down at her folded hands. "Tomorrow, then," she said, ignoring the slight tremor in her voice and the unwelcome signs of infatuation.

"Got it," he said, giving her a brief pat on the back and exiting the room.

Shelby wrapped her arms about her, suddenly feeling a draft, feeling the absence of his presence. Luckily, she didn't have long to evaluate that because Jewel entered the room.

"I'm so glad to see you." Shelby held out her hands.

Jewel hugged her and then held up a plastic bag. "I brought black cherry ice cream and a few bags of chocolate candies."

"You remembered."

"Losing your parents was a tough time for all of us. I loved your parents like they were my own. And I'm grateful to bring you some cheer and support you like I did before our estrangement."

Feeling overcome with both an appreciation for her life and mourning her loss, Shelby jutted her chin at the bag. "I take it you brought spoons?"

"Oh yeah." Jewel handed her the bag and left to get a wheelchair. Shelby made a face but she got in it. Together they made their way to the atrium. It felt like being inside a neighborhood. The brick path had names of donors engraved, and there was an assortment of floral arrangements that gave off a pleasant scent.

Shelby splayed her hands, angling her leg so that the bag didn't fall off her lap, and drew in a deep breath. "I love it here, and I love the sun on my face. This is just what I needed."

"Do you want to light the candles first?" Jewel asked.

"No. Right before you came, I had a crying fest with my physical therapist," she supplied. "So right now, I just want to eat ice cream."

"The hunk I met in the hallway? He introduced himself as your physical therapist, but I forgot his name just that fast." Jewel described Kendrick with such accuracy—tall, muscles, broad shoulders, kind eyes—that Shelby knew she had spotted him.

"Yes, that's Kendrick." Why did her voice sound so breathy at his name? "He also happens to be on my cycling team."

"Say what?"

"Yeah. Your girl here was riding marathons and all that. I'll have to send you pictures."

"That's pretty interesting. And, yes, I would love to see them." Jewel wheeled Shelby over to a bench and took a seat. Then she reached for the bag, handing Shelby one of the two pints and a spoon. They were the only people up there, for which Shelby was grateful. The only sound in the space was the rip of the container lid, followed by two appreciative moans.

"This is creamy and delicious and just what my heart needed." She chomped on a sweet piece of dark cherry.

"Well, black cherry ice cream represents so much for us, including a new beginning. A renewal almost." She reached for Shelby's hand. "Our friendship began with black cherry ice cream when we were a couple of five-year-olds in Ms. Hartley's class. I brought it in for Ice Cream and Cake Day. My mom said to get two since it was buy-one-get-one-free at the supermarket, but none of the other kids would eat it, remember? They only knew chocolate and vanilla."

"Yes. Yes, I do. I think I yelled at the other kids and called them stupid dino heads and went to get my spoon." She chuckled. "Ms. Hartley took five minutes off my recess time for that."

Jewel smiled. "But you didn't have to spend it alone. I sat right there with you until she said you could go play."

Shelby gave her hand a squeeze. "And we were inseparable ever since. You were there with me through thick and thin, ups and downs. Not even Declan Welch could split us apart for long." Then she added, "Sleeping with him was one of the biggest regrets of my life."

"Don't be too hard on yourself. We were kids, and when your parents died, you were pretty messed up." She leaned back on the bench and crossed her legs. "You withdrew from me, from Declan. You had a serious case of survivor's guilt, blaming yourself for their deaths, for choosing us."

They finished off their ice cream, and Jewel stuffed their empty containers in the bag. She pulled some wet wipes out of her purse, and they cleaned their mouths and hands.

Shelby curled her fingers around Jewel's wrist. "But to this day I still regret betraying you. No matter how I felt, I shouldn't have deceived you." She lowered her eyes and mumbled, "I don't deserve you as a friend."

"I don't think I deserved you either. Not after what I did with our book. Still don't," she mumbled under her breath.

Shelby frowned. Why did Jewel sound like she was talking about now instead of twenty years ago? Then she shook it off. Maybe she was imagining it. "Hush. We are more than friends." Their heads touched.

Then they chanted together "We're sisters. Sisters of the heart."

CHAPTER 13

Excerpt from That Was Then *by Jewel Stone*

June 10, 2005

Honey

Walking on the beach under the moonlight hand in hand with Chance near the stroke of midnight, Honey knew she was right where she wanted to be. Right where she should be.

Plus she was with the kind of man she could have only hoped for when she was a little girl reading her favorite fairytales and dreaming of happy-ever-afters. Chance was considerate and generous and skillful. Both as an artist and as a potential lover, if his kisses were any indication. Over the past couple weeks, they had engaged in heavy petting, and she was ready to go further.

Oh, so so ready.

And tonight she was going to stop resisting, even though her heart was beating faster than her blowout had fizzled in the heat. If only Sugar hadn't been so scarce of late, maybe she would talk Honey out of what she was about to do. Maybe she would tell her that it was too soon and to slow down.

However, Sugar wasn't here. She had been a little sullen and, Honey suspected, jealous of Honey and Chance's connection. Sugar was definitely crushing on him, but she couldn't fault her bestie because Chance was definitely the *It* guy of the summer.

Honey stole a glance at Chance.

Just being in his presence had her body zing-zanging and twisting in the sheets at night. She was ready to sweat this man out of her system. Or was it into her system? She mopped her brow. Whichever it was, it was going down tonight. She had made up her mind.

They walked to a secluded spot between the rocks and stopped. She dropped her bag to the ground and took out the supersize beach towel to spread it on the ground. She was eager to make love to him with the sounds of the water beside her and the twinkling stars above her head. Nature made for an idyllic, romantic backdrop. But Honey wasn't about to have sand all up in her nether regions, because that wouldn't be cute or comfortable.

Sitting on the towel, she pulled Chance down beside her and scooted close to him. He gave her a peck on the lips before wrapping his arms around his legs and facing the lapping waves.

"Is everything all right?" she asked.

"Yeah . . . I just have a lot on my mind." He twirled a finger in the sand.

Rising up to her knees, she tried to cup his face between her hands, but he held her arm and shook his head. Whatever he was grappling with was bringing down the mood. "What's going on?" She couldn't hide the mild hurt from reflecting in her voice as she sat a few inches away from him. "You're acting like you don't want me."

He gave her his undivided attention then. "Oh, it's the direct opposite. I very much want you." Chance broke eye contact. "That's the problem."

Those words made her scooch closer to him. "Talk to me." She kept her voice gentle but on the inside all sorts of scenarios were going through her head ranging from *Is he ill?* to *Am I coming on too strong?* She knew he adored her full body, so Honey wasn't worried that Chance wasn't attracted to her, but she was worried that maybe she had been too . . . eager. She didn't even play coy when he called. Her enthusiasm was for real. When he hunched his shoulders, the hairs on her arms rose.

Chance touched her face, causing her skin to tingle. She snuggled into his palm.

"Before I met you, I was so unhappy. Lonely. Wondering why I was here in Delaware. I had even stopped painting. But then I met you, and Sugar, and suddenly I spurred to life. I've been painting—small things, nothing meaningful—but considering I hadn't picked up a paintbrush in years, it was huge."

Honey nodded, but she knew a buildup before a letdown when she heard one. So she prodded him on. "Then what's the problem?"

He didn't meet her eyes. "Honey, I've been trying to think of the best way to tell you this, but the woman I live with isn't my aunt." He hunched his shoulders and took her hands in his. "She's my wife."

Whoa. What? Honey snatched her hands away. She rubbed her ears because she must not have heard right. "What did you say? Did you say you were married?" At his slight nod, she jumped to her feet, pulled the towel out from under him and began to stuff it into her bag, calling herself all kinds of fool. "You suckered me real good."

He got to his feet and touched her shoulder. "Please. Wait! Let me explain."

Chest heaving, she wanted to punch him in the face. "My tongue has been in your mouth. A mouth that belongs to someone else. I can't believe I got suckered like this. I am beyond humiliated. I have no idea what you can say that would possibly make things any better." Oh, she wanted to gag. And cry. Honey reached into her shorts for a hair scrunchie and put her hair up. The hair she had spent an hour giving a silk press because she wanted her first time with Chance to be extra special.

Tears threatened to spill, and she absolutely refused to weep over a cheater. She threw her bag on her shoulder and held up two fingers. "I'm out." Stomping through the sand, she was about fifteen feet away when she heard Chance yell from behind her.

"Don't go! I love you."

Honey swung around. "No, you don't get to utter those words," she spat. "You're only saying that to manipulate me."

He raced over to her. "I'm saying it because it's true. Arlena is busy doing her thing. We live separate lives, and she probably won't even come here, so if I didn't tell you the truth, you would never have known."

She did the slow clap. "So I guess this is where I praise you for being the stand-up guy for your confession." She placed a hand on her hip. "Well, I'm sorry, but this has to be it for us. I watched my mother pine for a man who gave her nothing but empty promises and a sick child to care for. I'm not falling into that trap." She lifted her chin. "It was nice knowing you."

He made a move to turn, and dang it but her traitorous heart demanded an explanation. "Why did you tell me?" Honey cleared her throat. "You owe me that much before we part ways."

Chance froze before coming over to her. "Let's go sit by the bookstore so I can see your face."

Avoiding his hand, she trudged behind him. Ms. Brown must have left the outside light on by accident. They sat on the bench in front of the window. Now the sounds of the waves behind her became a lullaby for her aching heart. Dang it.

The tears spilled over her eyelashes and down her cheeks. She tucked her chin to her chest, hating that Chance was seeing her fall apart. Why couldn't she catch a break? Of course the first man she fell for would be someone else's husband. Husband. Not even a boyfriend, which would have been bad enough.

Chance drew her into his arms. "I'm sorry. I'm sorry," he whispered, sounding choked up. "I didn't want to hurt you. You've got to know how much I love you. Seeing you cry is the last thing I'd ever want."

His whispered words were like ointment coating her wounded heart.

Pulling away and wiping her face, she said, "Tell me."

"I got married about a year ago to a woman seven years my senior." Chance raked a hand through his hair. "When I turned eighteen, I left Germany with my paints, my backpack, my passport and the two hundred dollars my mother gave me when I told her I wanted to explore the world. I lived in a small unit near the air force base." He scoffed. "Mami had fallen in love with an American airman, who promised her marriage and a green card until she told him about him about me. Then, surprise, surprise, dude had a whole wife waiting for him in Georgia. A month later, he left her and changed his number." Chance looked away. "All my life, I vowed never to be like him. Now look at me."

She placed a hand over his. He sounded so pitiful that she just had to make contact. "And I said I wouldn't end up like my mother. I didn't realize we had deadbeats for dads in common." Remembering that Chance was a married man, she removed her hand. "Continue."

"After I left home with my pocket stuffed with cash—I thought it was big money then—I grabbed a train to Paris and hitchhiked my way here and there, until I was down to my last dollar." He gave her the side-eye. "And talk about hungry.

I talked my way into a job at a restaurant, and the owner had a back room where I could live. I worked my way up from dishwasher to sous-chef. Scraping all I had, I bought my car and fixed it up. Then I attended art school on a scholarship. That's where I met Arlena. She was beautiful and rich. And I admit, both of those things turned my head."

Honey pursed her lips, hating the jealousy she felt.

He exhaled. "I didn't get to know her true character or her disposition. We got married six months later, and it didn't take a month before the bliss wore off. Being with her was like being inside the eye of a hurricane. It's all calm until it's not. She splurged on me, gave me everything I wanted, but when I didn't do what she said . . . Whew! Arlena exploded. I didn't know what would trigger her temper. Then one month, she ripped my most recent picture my Mami sent me to shreds. That's when I knew I had to get out of there."

"Oh wow. That's horrible." Yet at the same time, she had doubts. How did she know Chance wasn't feeding her a sob story? Or embellishing the details a bit? There were two other sides to consider: Arlena's, and the truth.

"I played nice, though, and told her I needed space to paint." He smirked. "That's the only thing Arlena admired about me. I think she believes I'll make her a fortune one day." Chance looked out at the waters. "I plan to be long gone before then." His voice filled with gravelly determination. "But I won't be broke. I've been dabbling in investments, which has been paying off, so I have a good amount saved up. But nowhere near enough for the lifestyle I envision for myself."

"So that's why you befriended me?" Honey asked, arching a brow. "You thought you were going to snag another rich woman, didn't you?"

He dipped his head. "I admit once I had distance between me and Arlena, it was all about the game. I was partying, going home with different girls. Basically, I was on the hunt, but—"

Honey lifted a hand. "Please don't say that all changed when you met me."

"I was actually going to say I realized right away that Sugar was the one with the deep pockets."

Curious, she cocked her head. "How could you tell?"

"I know designer wear. She pays for most things."

"And you made sure to get her number." She cut her eyes at him. "Then why bother with me?" Now she was pissed off all over again. This man was messing with her emotions. She curled her fists. Right now she felt like slapping him all over again.

"Because."

"That's it?"

"Yup. For the first time in my life, I felt a spark that had nothing to do with finances. Whatever it is, you got it, and I just had to be around you. I like Sugar. She's great, but she doesn't make me feel the way you do. I am head over heels, and I don't know what to do with myself. I wake up, I think of you. I actually started painting you. My muse. I'd love for you to pose for me."

Honey could see she was dealing with a master manipulator. Often, when he didn't know she was looking, she saw him eyeing Sugar. There was an attraction there. She stood and smoothed out her dress. "Well, I've heard you out, and now I'd better get going."

"Are you serious? I just poured my heart to you like I've never done before, and this is what you do." He got to his feet, sounding hurt.

"I told you—I don't mess with married men. So there will be no happy ending for us," Honey said, ignoring her heart twisting like a pretzel and walking toward the condo. Since it was late, she didn't object when he fell in step with her. Instead, she was glad she hadn't been wrong about his decency.

Chance's last words to her were "At least I know I said my piece."

His dejection was almost her undoing. Almost. Oh, so badly she wanted to cave and give in to him, to the pleadings of her heart. But Honey had to hold on to her last shred of dignity and keep her legs closed.

As soon as she was inside the condo, she plodded into Sugar's room and dropped her bag onto the floor. Her bestie was asleep, which was quite all right with her. Slipping under the blanket, Honey quietly cried herself to sleep. Her tears were those of deep regret. A regret that she hadn't given herself even one night with Chance before ending things. She had always prided herself on seeing things in black-and-white. And now she realized how quaint, how naive she had been. But that was all before she had fallen in love.

Because as sure as she knew herself, she knew she loved that man, and in her secret heart of hearts, she didn't know if this fire would die out, and she wasn't sure if she even wanted it to.

CHAPTER 14

Jewel
June 20, 2025

Money was in Jewel's bank account, and all her bills had been brought up-to-date. Her husband had yet another interview lined up. You'd think she would feel like celebrating. But how could she when the typed words on her screen made no sense?

Jewel placed her hand on her head. It was a hot day, and she should be enjoying the view before the sun went down, but instead she had sat for an hour huddled underneath the huge umbrella on the patio behind the bookstore and had yet to come up with an action plan. The past couple days, her routine entailed sitting with Shelby in the hospital and then writing in the evenings. She had completed a hot mess of a first draft of her synopsis and felt like deleting the entire thing as she had done twice before. But Francesca was waiting to send this off to Marina.

A laugh escaped before a sob broke free. She was screwed. Her mother and sister depended on her. Her husband relied on her to keep them afloat until he secured a position. Her publisher was going to demand the money back, and her family was going to be in jeopardy, all because she couldn't spew out a story on demand.

The only time her story had flowed easily was when she had been retelling the true events of a life-changing summer—

and she had done most of it with Shelby as a writing partner. Tears streaked down her face. What kind of writer was she if she couldn't pen the story of her own life?

An impostor.

That's what she was. The only thing missing from this pity party was a tub of black cherry ice cream.

Jewel slammed her hands on the table. Clouds were forming, which matched her current mood. *Okay, Jewel, this isn't who you are. You're not a complainer, and you're certainly not the type who sits around feeling sorry for yourself. Think of something.*

Abby came outside to let her know that she was about to leave for the day. Jewel told the younger woman to head out, then followed her so she could lock up the store. Abby gave her a wave, her eyes glued to her cell phone, before disappearing down the boardwalk.

Jewel then tried to put words on the page but nothing she wrote resonated with her. She closed her laptop and raked a hand through her hair.

A crack of thunder outside came in sync with the idea. The angle. The answer. Beachgoers scampered to gather their belongings, tugging crying children, shoving balls and other items into beach bags, but she remained rooted.

Goose bumps popped on her skin, and she placed a hand to her mouth. She needed to write a Book Two, the *continuation* of her and Shelby's tale.

Right now, Jewel was living a great reunion story involving besties who were no longer besties. She didn't have to tell the truth of what separated them. That was the whole purpose of writing fiction. You got to make things up. All she had to do was age up Sugar and Honey to present day. Her readers would love the themes of friendship, betrayal, secrets, reunion and memory loss.

In a flash, words poured into her mind. Oh my goodness, she needed to write *now*. She needed to unload all this energy from her brain to her hands to the page. Another crack of thunder spurred her into action.

She gathered her things, ran inside Shelby's office and fired up her laptop.

Jumping to her feet, she grabbed paper out of the printer and a pen. She had a new title that she wrote in all caps.

HERE AND AFTER
The story of two friends ripped apart by a secret and reunited twenty years later when one suffers memory loss.

She scrunched her nose. She had to think of a fictitious, juicy secret and that tagline would need some serious work, but oh, was she loving this already. She scribbled furiously, enjoying her burst of inspiration. For now, she would vomit on the page—advice from Victoria Christopher Murray, one of her and Shelby's author faves—and worry about fixing it after.

"I don't think you should return to Eagle Point Beach," Winston said, coming up behind Honey to draw her into him. [note: will need backstory on this new character, Honey's husband]. "From what you told me, your last summer there twenty years ago was a doozy."

Honey snuggled into his chest and inhaled his woodsy perfume. "Yes, but Sugar needs me."

"I need you."

Her chest squeezed. Winston, the man who had slipped in and healed a heart ravaged from the savagery of young love.

Okay, so that last line wasn't exactly true, but this was fiction after all. She could embellish as she pleased. Besides, that meant she could add *second chance* to her tropes. She read the first few lines again. Oh, this was some good stuff.

Jewel cackled. Readers were going to get an authentic tale. It had the makings of a gripping women's fiction read with the potential for lots of drama. She paused and leaned back into the chair. But she would be telling Shelby's story too, and this time without her permission. That would be beyond foul. Guilt slashed across her heart. She would be using her friend.

Maybe she should let Shelby know her intentions.

Yes, that's what she would do. Tomorrow. That would be the first thing she discussed during their visit.

By this time, it was pouring rain. She glanced out the window, welcoming the shower. She knew what it felt like to be under a drought, and boy, did she appreciate the flow.

Before she knew it, Jewel was two chapters in and already at 4,000 words. If she wrote like this every day, she was going to finish this book in weeks instead of months. She was so happy she could cry.

Jewel pumped her fists and fired off a text to Roman.

> Babe, guess what? The water is turned on, and it's a heavy flow.

His answer came fast.

> You're writing?

> Yes. Started tonight. I'm at 4K already.

> Wow. I guess you were right to go back home.

> Yessss.

> Go, baby! Keep at it. I'm rooting for you. You've got this.

Aww. Her man was so supportive. She had lucked out in the marriage market with him. Jewel sent him a few kissing emojis, and then she put her phone on Silent and got to typing. By the time the sun rose, she had written 12,000 words. A good 12,000 words.

The product of a record-breaking writing day and her first all-nighter in years. She texted Roman to tell him about her milestone.

Her eyes burned. Her fingers cramped. Her bladder screamed. But she was back. She was back!

Jewel curled and uncurled her fingers before standing up to stretch her aching back. Tired was too soft a word to describe how she felt, but she was too exhilarated to care. Even now, the words flowed through her, demanding she keep going, but she had used all her reserve energy to get to page seventy and needed rest. If she kept going at this pace, Jewel would hit page one hundred before day's end, and she could send them off to her agent as promised.

Now she just had to tell Shelby about this story arc. Get her blessing. Thinking about that made a knot form in her throat.

Roman texted. **You are flying through! May you have all the words, babe.** She was so tired that all she could do was send him a heart emoji. She would call him later.

Eyeing the numerous coffee cups, take-out containers and the empty ice cream tub, Jewel gathered what she could to toss the refuse in the trash.

What she needed now was a bath. And then she would get a couple hours' sleep before going to visit with Shelby.

Shuffling into the bathroom, exhaustion curving her spine, Jewel started the bath. There was a spa basket that contained bath bombs, salts and bubbles. Shrugging out of her clothes, Jewel tipped her toe to check the temperature and moaned. Perfect. She placed her cell phone within arm's reach then lowered her body into the tub, the water a balm to her muscles.

She breathed in the scent of lavender and jasmine from the bath bombs and smiled, resting her head against the wall and closing her eyes.

Her cell rang.

It was her mother calling. Jewel sat up and looked at her phone. She so desperately wanted to answer, but the problem was she didn't know what mood her mother would be in. Would Beryl be pleasant, which would lead to a thirty-minute conversation of laughter? Or would she accuse Jewel of not being good enough? Of not taking care of her mother and her sister, Hazel, as well as she should? And did Jewel have the patience to bite her tongue and endure the conversation? The fact that she had to use the word *endure* was telling. Before the call went to voicemail, Jewel picked up. "Hi, Mama. How's everything?"

"Hey, baby. It's Hazel."

Immediately, her heart began to pump in her chest. Jewel gripped the phone. "What's wrong with her?" She swung a leg over the top of the tub and got out, water sloshing on the floor. Ignoring the puddle, she put the call on Speaker, then grabbed a towel and wrapped it around her waist.

"She's fine. It's just . . . the doctors want to put her on new meds for her hypertension." Beryl's voice echoed into the space. Her words were like a brick in Jewel's stomach.

Hazel had been born with cerebral palsy and had been recently diagnosed with hypertension due to her high blood pressure. It felt like her younger sister was susceptible to every disease out there, while Jewel had been abnormally healthy. Not an allergy and rarely a cold, while her sister couldn't breathe without having something go wrong.

"They say she needs them to keep up her current quality of life. And there are co-pays . . . The insurance won't cover everything," her mother said, the tremor in her voice breaking into a sob. The pressure of being a single mom with two daughters to care for, particularly one with an illness, had led to diabetes and a heart attack three years prior. That's why Jewel had placed both her mother and her sister in the assisted living facility in Ronkonkoma so they would have round-the-clock care.

"Mom, don't cry," Jewel whispered and wiped her nose. "Please. She'll be okay."

Her mother hiccupped. "My baby. I can't lose her. I'm not ready for her to go just yet. I know she's a lot of work, but I don't mind. I don't mind . . . I don't mind . . ." Her mother's incoherent ramblings whipped at Jewel's conscience. She hadn't visited them in months.

"I don't care what it costs. I'll pay it," she breathed out. "She will be okay." Even as she said the words, doubts weighed her down. "Do you need me to come down there?"

"No, I need you to keep working so you can send the money."

It was always about money when it came her mother. She swallowed down her bitterness and reminded herself that this was about Hazel. What Hazel needed. Not Jewel's feelings. "I'm working on something really good, Mama. I tell you, it's fire."

"I hope so, because you didn't hit the bestseller lists in the top five with your recent books like you did with your first one."

"Hmmm." She bit her lip. This from the woman who hadn't read any of her books. *The New York Times* was still *The New York Times*. Beryl was only invested in where they placed and how that translated into dollars and cents. "I'm doing the best I can, Mama. I hope you know that."

"I do know, sweetheart," her mother said gently. "I don't mean to sound any kind of way, but I'm desperate. I'm afraid for your sister, and I hate depending on you, and I want you to know I'm real proud. I brag about you to everyone who will listen."

The wedge in her chest loosened. See now, that's why she had a wonky relationship with her mother. Only Beryl could make her feel the tiniest of tinies and then pump her up like a blowfish. "I know, Mama. We'll get through this. No matter the cost."

No matter the cost.

Big talk. Jewel had to back that up with some cash.

After a few minutes of affirmations, Jewel ended the call. She rushed into the bathroom to drain the tub. There was no way she was going to be able to relax now. She couldn't. She needed income, and writing books was how she made her money. She was a hamster on a wheel and she had to keep running, keep churning, no matter how her shoulders ached. Jewel banged out the rest of the pages and sent them off to Francesca. Shelby would understand once Jewel explained her situation. And she would tell Shelby everything. In time.

On their video call right before she went to see Shelby, Roman of course said they'd do whatever it took to help her sister. Once again, Jewel felt fortunate to have the man she had met while he was a campus resident assistant finishing his degree.

But when she filled him in on exactly what she'd been writing and her tagline, Roman loved the idea of the secret between them being that it was Sugar and not Honey who wrote the book. He viewed it as a nod to give Shelby her due. But he was adamantly against her decision to wait to tell Shelby. The disappointment in those brown eyes made her shoulders slump. "You went to Delaware to help out your friend who's going through it right now. She's vulnerable, battling amnesia, and you're there to help her navigate all of that. I think you should be straight with her. You should tell her you want to use your reunion story for your book."

That stung. "I'm vulnerable too. I wouldn't do it if I wasn't trying to help my mother and Hazel and . . . and you."

"I know, baby. But this is not the way. To write about her experience without her knowledge is betrayal on a different level, Jewel. She's vulnerable right now, and I don't want you to jeopardize your career or your renewed friendship. Shelby might not be in agreement this time."

"I am going to tell her. I just have to wait for the right time."

"And when will that be? You already sent the pages to your agent. You need to tell her now. Or write something else."

Jewel bit the inside of her cheek. "The words don't come as easy as you think, Roman. For the first time in months, I'm both energized and excited about a story. My fingers hurt like nobody's business, but I'm having fun."

"Oh, you don't know how glad I am to hear that. But your friend could get hurt. And I don't want to see you hurt in the process either. It hasn't been easy seeing you in pain when your friendship ended. You tried to hide it, but I heard your tears. I watched you toss and turn many nights, and I didn't think you would ever recover. I just don't want to see you go through all that again. Guilt is a heavy cross to carry, and it's one I can't help you with, so please think. Think. And do the right thing."

Jewel hadn't realized how much Roman had been paying attention, but she shouldn't have been surprised because that was the kind of man she had married. She sighed. "Telling her is the right thing, but is it the right time?"

"There's never a wrong time for the truth."

Roman's certainty about that gave her pause. "You're right. I'll tell her." Her stomach gurgled with anxiety.

His lips widened into a smile, and her heart lifted at the relief in his voice. He trusted her to be a woman of her word. "That's great, babe. Rip off the Band-Aid. You'll feel better once it's all out in the open. I promise." He tossed a kiss. "I'm going to get ready for my interview. Wish me luck." With a wave and yet another kiss, he went offline.

Jewel touched her abdomen. This phone call would make a

nice scene in her book. It would be good to write it while her emotions were still on a high. Before she knew it, she had her fingers on the keyboard.

> Honey tore her eyes away from Winston's earnest gaze. "You need to tell Sugar that you're writing a book about your reunion. You need to tell her before the truth comes out. Your friendship might not survive a betrayal like this."
> "I will. But I've got to wait for the perfect time." Honey placed a hand on her chest.
> "Honey, I love you, but I know you," Winston said. "Don't shrug this off the way you've done me every time I bring up Janie."

Yes, her husband knew her well, and if he felt she was exploiting him too, he would be crushed. But this added even more conflict and depth to Honey's storyline. She continued writing.

> Ugh. So he had noticed that she didn't want to discuss the woman who had hidden his child from him. A child who was almost a man and who was doing just fine without Winston in his life.

Jewel froze before deleting the last couple sentences. That was a bit too . . . *honest.*

A notification popped up on her screen. It was her agent emailing . . . Already?

> Listen!!! I think you are knocking it out of the park with this one. My eyes are burning. I couldn't stop reading. I need more.

> You have really brought out the emotions in these two women reuniting after years of estrangement. I can't wait to find out what the secret is. When will you have more pages??!!!
>
> ~F

Jewel shimmied. Francesca had used a total of six exclamation points. That meant something. She sent her reply off with a whoosh.

> I am moving as fast as I can. I should have more in a week's time.
>
> Jewel

> I can't wait. Looking forward.
>
> ~F

Squaring her shoulders, Jewel hit the Undo button and put back in the sentences. Roman was a part of her life now, and she did tell him that she was telling her tale. Even if he felt some type of way, her babe would understand. At least that's what she told herself as guilt soured her belly like acid reflux, the only cure being to let it all out on the page.

CHAPTER 15

Shelby
June 20, 2025

Life wasn't the only thing that went on. So did the bills, which were past due. Abby had stopped by the hospital before she went to the bookstore to catch Shelby up on things.

Since Jewel had shown her the picture, Shelby recognized her, which made their conversation more natural. Abby was dressed in black leggings, a crisp white shirt, the tiniest plaid shirt over it, a spiked belt and a pair of clunky black shoes. Her earrings were actual spiked studs. Very interesting and cool.

Shelby was seated in the armchair and the overbed tray served as a small desk for working on a puzzle. She'd had the television on earlier but liked the quiet.

She had a packed day: another consultation with Dr. Downes—er, Denise. She hadn't seen Kendrick since their first session the week before, but the nurses had told her that he would be in later that day. His assistant had been in to take her through some exercises and to get her moving so that she didn't develop bedsores.

The knowledge that she was going to see Kendrick again caused a little flutter in her tummy, but it could be indigestion from the breakfast burrito or residual embarrassment from her breakdown the last time she had been in his presence.

"We only had a handful of paying customers yesterday," Abby said, hovering near the ledge by the huge window. "Lots of browsers. A good number hung out and read, but not that many left with actual purchased books." According to Abby, they had been in the midst of planning some events to boost business before Shelby's accident, but Shelby wasn't prepared to talk to Abby about that as yet. She needed time to process. Abby then assured her that she could hold down the fort at the bookstore until Shelby's release. Shelby knew she had hired well and thanked her loyal employee.

Abby rocked back and forth on her heels and wrung her hands. Shelby sensed the young woman wanted to say something but was nervous. "Well, uh, I was kind of wondering if I'm going to, um, get paid tomorrow." She hunched her shoulders and hurried to say, "I know you have a lot going on, and I don't want to come off as insensitive. It's just . . ."

Shelby slapped her forehead, mortified. "Oh my goodness, Abby. The fact that you even had to ask! I'm sorry. Of course I'll pay you." She paused. "What day do I usually pay you?"

"Every Thursday," Abby said, appearing relieved. Now that she had released what was on her mind, Abby edged closer to the door.

"Oh my. So I'm a day late. I need to get ahold of my laptop so I can pay you right away."

"Uh, I hope it's okay that I brought it." She reached into her bag and took out the laptop, along with a stack of bills and a package, and handed them to Shelby. "I charged the laptop up for you, and I brought your charging cord. I wasn't trying to snoop, but I figured that you might want to take care of the utilities and such. I know you pay those online, if that helps."

Shelby covered her face with her hands. "Okay, I'll figure it out and get you paid." She ripped open the package, grateful to see it housed a new cell phone. She scrunched her nose before searching inside. There was a small note that told her it was from Jewel. Aww. Her friend was so thoughtful.

Right as Abby was going out the door, Jewel was coming in. Shelby lifted her hands. "You've got perfect timing. First, thank you so much for buying me a phone. I hope I didn't put you out, though." Shelby caught sight of the price tag and had to bite her tongue to keep from demanding Jewel return it to the store. Her friend was acting like she had Tyler Perry money. Dang, the prices of cell phones cost as much as a monthly mortgage. The fact that people were willing to pay that, including her, outraged and fascinated her at the same time.

"Don't worry about it. I got a message that it was delivered, but Abby must have picked up the mail before I could."

"I know I have memory loss, but I do know how expensive these can be."

Jewel waved a hand. "It's no problem. Do you need me to help get your new phone set up?"

"Well, thank you again. I really appreciate it. And, yes, I could use some assistance." Shelby slumped. "That would be one less thing for me to navigate."

"I'd be happy to. Do you remember your iCloud log-in information? If you have that, we can get you all set up in a jiffy." Jewel grabbed the armchair and scooted close to her. Shelby lifted the top of her laptop, and it flared to life. Then she plugged in her information. *It worked.*

In a matter of minutes, Jewel had downloaded her apps from the cloud and helped her get her voicemail, notifications and ringtones set up. Fortunately, Shelby learned she had a password-safe app where she had stored all her log-in information. The first thing she did was check her personal accounts. The police had recovered her wallet from the scene of the accident, so at least she didn't need to get new cards or anything. Her personal account balance was decent due to investments and the fact that she didn't have a mortgage, and so was Lacey's. Well, Lacey's was more than decent. Her eyes went wide. It was pretty healthy.

Shelby frowned. Her daughter appeared to be set for life. One of the envelopes included Lacey's tuition bill, which she promptly paid in full.

Where had all this money come from? She rubbed her forehead, not bothering to ask Jewel. Shelby knew what Jewel would say. She needed to start reading those journals. Plain and simple, her fear was holding her back. She was scared to know what had caused her rift with Jewel. Scared that knowing the truth would drive them apart once again.

Jewel left, saying she had to run some errands and then get some writing done.

Shelby decided to text Lacey to let her know she had a new phone. She still hadn't fully come to terms with the fact that she had a grown child.

Her daughter texted her back.

> Cool, Mom. I hope this means I'll get an upgrade too. Check your email. I sent photos like you asked. How are you?

> Thanks. I will. I'm progressing.

As well as could be expected for someone who'd lost twelve years of her memory, but she couldn't say that. She bit her lower lip and instead asked, Are you having fun?

> Yeah . . .

Her eyes narrowed. Now, she was a young woman once and those dots meant something.

> What's wrong?

Um, nothing was the quick response.

Which meant it was something. Should she leave it alone? Or would Mommy Shelby dig deeper? Shelby exhaled and pinched between her eyes before sending another text.

> What's going on?

> I think Bea and I like the same guy, which is weird . . .
> Can I call you? I need to vent a little.

Oh no. She was not equipped for this. Was this what having a daughter was like?

> I'm about to start a therapy session . . .

Great, now she was leaving dots. Lacey sent a crying emoji. Shelby squared her shoulders and typed, I'll call you soon and we can catch up.

> Okay. If I don't answer, it's because I'm at work.
> I got a job at a boutique yesterday.

> You got a job?

Shelby scrunched her nose. Her daughter had considerable wealth. From the sounds of things, she must not have given Lacey access to it. But why? When she was that age, her parents had given her a hefty monthly allowance. Shelby hadn't had to work. Except for the summer when everything changed.

> Yeah. I don't want to burden you.

> It's not a burden. I can up your allowance if you need.
> That way, you can just enjoy your summer.

> Allowance? LOL Excuse me, but who are you and what have you done with my mom?

That text made her drop the phone on the bed. She slapped her forehead. What was she doing playing mother to someone she didn't know? And why wasn't she giving Lacey spending money? Come to think of it, *that* summer when her parents died and she learned how dire their finances were had not been pretty. Maybe that was why she was being frugal with Lacey's funds. Ugh. She had more questions than answers when it came to parenting, and it was beyond frustrating.

Lacey sent her a question mark. Shelby pondered for a beat before deciding she would just laugh it off. Or, as her Jamaican parents would have said, *Smile and nod. Smile and nod.* Gosh, she missed them. Especially now. Picking up her phone, she texted, I'm here. LOL I'll send you a few dollars to tide you over until you get paid.

> Thanks, Mom 😊 Are you sure you don't want me to visit?

> No. I feel good you're having a great summer.
> TTYL XOXO

Her shoulders sagged. Talking with her daughter was the most challenging part of this ordeal so far. She needed a few days to recover after every interaction. But then she groaned. She had promised to talk with Lacey later. Just that knowledge made her stomach knot.

Maybe she should just tell Lacey the truth about her memory. She quickly dismissed that thought. She didn't want to distress her daughter, and she had a feeling Lacey would be here by her side as soon as she knew. Her daughter appeared to be thoughtful and considerate. And they seemed to be close. Like talking–

about-boys-close. But navigating that relationship would be a stressor for Shelby.

Closing her eyes, she prayed, *Please, God, help me remember.*

The door creaked open. "Good morning, Shelby. It's Denise. Are you ready for our session?"

Shelby straightened and released a huge sigh. "Good morning. Yes, I need to unload. I'm feeling a bit overwhelmed. I wish my memory would return already. With each passing day, I'm realizing how much I need to go back to my regular life. But I don't fully know what that is. Yet at the same time, I have a lot going on that I have to deal with so I really need to get out of here."

Denise sat in the chair diagonal to Shelby and placed her notebook on her lap. "You do have a lot that you're dealing with. There is no telling when or if your memory will return, so we will treat your life now as your new normal."

Shelby nodded. "That makes sense."

"Why don't you take a deep breath and tell me what has you feeling overwhelmed the most today?" Denise suggested in a gentle tone.

"My daughter," she said, without hesitation. "Interacting with her feels awkward. I don't remember adopting her. I don't know why I adopted her, why I chose to be a single parent. And I feel like I'm messing up and saying the wrong things." Her chest tightened. "It doesn't help that Lacey's quick on the draw. She keeps catching me with my slip hanging down, as my parents would say. And I promised to call her soon, which has my anxiety skyrocketing because I didn't tell her about my memory loss."

"Why haven't you told her about your memory loss?"

"Because if I did, I'm pretty sure she would come here, and I also don't want to hurt her by telling her that I don't know her. I don't know who she is." Shelby touched her chest. "I do feel the need the protect her."

"That's maternal," Denise noted, with a smile.

"I guess." She chuckled and wiped her brow. "But my reasons are also selfish. I won't have to work as hard if Lacey is off enjoying her summer for now. I can focus on just my healing."

"If that is what works for you, then it is the right thing to do at this time. I do believe in taking small, measurable steps." The doctor tilted her head. "Is there anything you think might work for you right now?"

"Yes," she breathed out. "My best friend brought my old journals." She lifted the journal off the table and waved it in the air. "She suggested that I read them to learn about my life after 2013." She sobered. "But I have a lot of beginning entries about my parents that stirred up a lot of hurt. I lost my parents the summer of 2005, but even though so much time has passed, at times it's like it was yesterday."

"I'm so sorry for your loss. The pain of losing a parent never goes away." She closed her eyes and whispered, "I can relate . . ." then seemed to snap back to attention. "But that does sound like a good game plan." Denise cleared her throat. "There isn't a right or wrong way to deal with your memory loss. But I'll share more strategies on how to relax and keep calm, if you would like."

Shelby nodded. "I would love that."

"My first suggestion is to continue doing what you did today. It's called mindfulness. Being aware of what caused you stress and accepting that stress is normal, then focusing on how to recharge. Writing down your thoughts and feelings is another strategy, as well as physical exercise."

"I'll be getting plenty of that today," Shelby chimed in. "I'm supposed to have another physical therapy session before I leave tomorrow."

"Oh, that's right, you're getting discharged. That's great news."

"I'm scared, actually. But I keep reminding myself that I'm a survivor."

The doctor stood and came over to her then took her hand. "I'm glad you selected that word *survivor* as your safe word. Because that's who you are, and you'll get through this. Do you believe that?"

That question sliced her gut. Tears rolled down Shelby's face. "Yes, I do, for the most part," she choked out, her pulse quickening. "But I do feel quite a bit of survivor's remorse. I keep thinking about that driver who didn't make it, and I wonder how their family is doing." She sobbed. "They lost someone. Meanwhile, I'm here trying to keep my daughter away from me. The guilt eats at me. Especially at night. I haven't been sleeping much."

Denise passed her some tissues from the nightstand. Shelby dabbed at her cheeks. "The guilt is normal. It's healthy. But there are certain things we don't have the answer to, and that's one of them. We don't get to decide who lives and who dies." She rested her hand on Shelby's shoulder. That act grounded her. "But you do get to decide how you handle it. When the guilt presses upon you so hard that your chest is tight, remind yourself that you were given a second chance for a reason." All Shelby could do was nod. "Instead of mourning your survival, begin to celebrate. And make the most of it in whatever way you can. Because when I see you, I see life. Not death."

June 20, 2025

Hello. So I have decided to keep a digital diary this time. That way, I can save it in the cloud. Besides, I type faster than I handwrite. Plus, this is a great way to keep my personal feelings private. But no more using nicknames.

So here goes . . .

For the first time since my accident, I am determined to take back control of my life. I feel a new hope for the future. I am doing well in both my physical and mental health therapy. I still have survivor's guilt, but I am grateful to be alive. I am grateful for Jewel being here and for us rekindling our friendship.

Despite my memory not returning and my fears about motherhood, I do find myself anticipating developing a relationship with my daughter Lacey all over again. I hope to build the courage to interact with her in person. Maybe I will invite her down before school starts. She seems to be a wonderful young woman, and I want her to be proud to call me Mom.

CHAPTER 16

Lacey
June 20, 2025

"Can a concussion cause a personality change?" Lacey asked Bea. She had been mulling on that ever since her phone conversation with her mother who had promised to call but here it was two days later, and Mom had limited their conversations to texts and emails. "Because my mom isn't acting like my mom, and I'm confused. I don't know if I should be worried or elated."

She sat by a bench on the boardwalk with Bea, enjoying the sunshine and slurping on a large chocolate milkshake, her breakfast of choice. Her mother definitely wouldn't approve, but it was worth every delicious sip. And her Instagram followers wholeheartedly agreed. Lacey had abandoned her mukbanging gig once she secured the job at the boutique, but her followers still commented when she posted anything dealing with food. It wasn't like she was good at it, anyway.

"Girl, relax. Be happy your mom is being extra cool right now," Bea said, taking a sip of her strawberry mango smoothie. "Maybe my mom needs a bump to her head because she's trying to get me to sign up for a Summer II course. I had to remind her that summer is supposed to be F-U-N. You know what she said to me?" Bea didn't give Lacey a chance to respond. She snickered. "She said that I was a result of all of her summer fun, so I need to keep my head in my books. And she said my helping you with your search doesn't count." Today Lacey and Bea were headed back over to the library to continue their research before Lacey was due into work that afternoon.

"That's hilarious. Your mom is a trip." She chuckled. "But I'm being serious about my concerns. My mom had a traumatic brain injury, and the repercussions can be lasting." Lacey fretted with her bottom lip.

Bea put her smoothie next to her on the bench and placed a hand over her chest. "I'm sorry for clowning around. You know how much I love your mom. I'd hate to know she suffered any lasting consequences because of her accident."

"I know. You don't have to explain yourself to me, bestie. But yes, I'm really concerned." Her milkshake was rapidly melting under the glare of the sun, so she hurried to get to the bottom of her cup.

"What's making you feel like she's acting different?" Bea asked, drawing close to her. "Because she seems the same to me from what you've been saying."

The birds squawked, flying overhead, and the early morning beachgoers were already setting up their umbrellas. It was going to be a scorcher, and Lacey was grateful that she would be working in the AC. She kept an eye out for Mekhi because he had told her that he was on duty today until noon and had suggested they get together for a late lunch. She had tentatively agreed, depending on when they finished up at the library.

"Yes, for the most part, but something's off," Lacey said, wiping her mouth. "Well, first, she's encouraging me to kick back and hang with you, and I get that she doesn't want me to worry, but just now, when we were texting, Mom talked about sending me an allowance."

"What are you, ten years old?"

Her brows furrowed. "I know, right? An allowance? Once I started working three years ago, that ended. Besides paying my college expenses, she told me that I have to fend for myself."

Lacey made air quotes with her hands and mimicked her mother's words. *"It's all a part of becoming a responsible adult."*

"Oh, yes, I remember that speech. Now, bear in mind that you're talking to someone who lives off a monthly stipend thanks to a very generous mother, so I'm not opposed to your mother doing the same, but this isn't her MO." Bea tilted her head. "Should we go pay her a visit?"

"No, because then she might get upset that I didn't honor her wishes, and I don't want anything throwing off her recovery."

"Hmm . . ." Bea seemed distracted by something in her phone.

Lacey gathered both their cups and tossed them in the trash can nearby. When she returned, Bea was still texting away. "What's going on?"

"Nothing. Just texting Mekhi." She shrugged. Her noncommittal tone didn't fool Lacey.

"Oh, what about?" she asked in a breezy tone, squelching her jealousy and telling herself she had no claim to him. Just because they had hung out a few times—well, almost every day since meeting—and spoke on the phone for hours didn't mean she had a monopoly on how he chose to spend his time.

"Nothing," she said again. Which absolutely meant something. "I asked him if he wanted to meet up after his shift since you'll be at work." Bea dropped that super casual, staring at her unblinking, as if it wasn't a big deal, as if Lacey didn't like Mekhi in a more-than-friend kind of way. The air thickened between them.

"Why him?" Lacey enquired, not caring that her voice held an edge. It was hard to stay cool when jealousy the size of a hydrangea blossomed in her chest. "You have so many other boys gunning for your attention, and you know I like him. That's a major violation of the friend code."

"Because." Bea folded her arms, not the least bit penitent. "And it's more of a minor infraction."

She knew that stance. Lacey lifted a brow. "If there's something more between you two, tell me now."

"There isn't." Bea sighed and lifted her shoulders. "There's just something about him. I like being in his presence. He's a great conversationalist and he's so smart. Smarter than you, even. And he doesn't act his age. He comes off as wiser, worldly."

Lacey blew an errant curl out of her face and lifted her head toward the sun. "I wish I could say I didn't get it, but I do. When I'm talking with him, an hour feels like minutes. I just wish you . . . wouldn't."

"Because you like him."

"I do." Maybe she needed to revisit the allowance conversation with her mom. That would free up her time. Luckily, today she was only on the schedule for four hours, and if they asked her to stay longer, she was going to turn them down.

"But Mekhi says he's not looking for anything serious," Bea said. "He's got to focus on his studies."

"He told you that?"

"Yeah. I asked." Bea's hand crept to join with hers and give it a squeeze. "Better he's hanging with me than with one of those thirsty lionesses on the beach, because they be sniffing around like they're trying to claim their territory. I'm rescuing him. You don't know how many phones be snapping away in his direction aimed at that six-pack."

Lacey giggled. "I do see the logic in your actions in a twisted sort of way."

"We're just hanging. I promise. I'm not after him in that way. Not anymore. What kind of friend would that make me?" Bea made an X against her chest. "I'm just keeping him warm for you."

"Okay, don't ever say that again. What does that even mean?"

"No clue, but I do know I don't want some guy coming between us. That would be juvenile," Bea said. "Honestly, though, Mekhi always circles the conversation back to you. No matter what we're talking about. He brings up your name. So, though I do like him, I'm woman enough to admit that I know where I stand and I'm fine with it. The more I get to know him, the more I realize he's perfect for you."

"Really?" she breathed out before narrowing her eyes. "Are you just saying that so I'll be cool with you hanging with my soon-to-be-man?"

"Nope. It's the honest truth. He's a decent guy. I suspect he's my friend primarily because of you. He tolerates me because he's new in town and doesn't have a lot of friends. He wants to be around you."

During their first phone conversation, Lacey had told him she and Bea were best friends, though the three of them had yet to hang out together. Lacey wanted him all to herself.

"That's interesting . . . I felt like we made a connection when we first met, but he seems to have taken a step back after our kiss. Which has me wondering if he's still into me or if he's friend-zoned me. He hasn't initiated any physical contact besides holding my hand, and even that's sporadic."

"Then make a move," Bea said. "See what happens. It's only been like a week since you met."

"I suppose . . . It feels like I've known him much longer." She shrugged then stood. "Well, we'd better get going. Let me know what you guys decide to get into, and I'll meet up with you after my shift."

"That will work," Bea said, also getting to her feet. They started their walk to the library. "I think we're going to play beach volleyball with another couple."

Couple? She gave Bea the side-eye. "You pushing it, girl."

Bea waved a hand. "You know what I mean. And we're playing against the two guys I hung out with last week."

"That should make for an interesting game," Lacey said, wryly.

"One is to look at and the other is to talk to. I like complicated. What can I say?"

"You are a hot mess."

"But I'm a loyal hot mess. Don't you forget it."

Lacey nodded. She still wasn't too sure she was a hundred percent all right with her bestie hanging out with Mekhi, but she trusted Bea. She hoped she could trust Mekhi, because she didn't do complicated. They arrived at the library just as it opened.

Her cell buzzed. "It's him."

Bea waved her off. "I'll see you inside. Don't take too long."

Lacey nodded as she took the call. "Hey . . ." She tucked her hair behind her ear.

"Hey. So I wanted to let you know that I'm hanging with Bea while you're at work. But I hope you'll come down to the volleyball sand court when you're done."

The fact he was calling to fill her in warmed her heart and spoke a lot about his character. Especially since they weren't in a committed relationship. Yet. "Yeah, Bea already told me. But I like your transparency." She more than liked it. She respected it. Bea was right: he was a decent guy.

"So you're cool with it?"

"I trust my friends, and Bea's good people." The minute she uttered those words, she knew she spoke the truth. She hoped Mekhi picked up on the fact that she had pluralized the word *friend*.

"Great. I'm relieved to hear that. I like Bea, and we've been talking on and off, but I'm not into her like that." His voice dropped. "I'm looking forward to seeing you. The hours aren't moving fast enough." He chuckled. "I have a confession to make. I switched my shift with someone on the off chance you'd agree to see me before your shift."

This didn't sound like someone who wasn't looking for something serious. Maybe those words had been meant for Bea and not her. That thought had her squealing on the inside.

"I'm at the library," she offered.

"Can I meet you over there? Or would that be too much? Because I still want to see you later. I'm out of my depths here. I'm even afraid to hold your hand because when I do, I never want to let you go."

Oh my. These weren't the actions of a shy man. Her cheeks flushed. Lacey exhaled. "Um, sure. Come on over." Her heart pounded. This meant she was going to bring Mekhi into her personal quest. Was she ready for that?

"I'll be right there." He disconnected the call quickly, like he was afraid she would change her mind.

Lacey looked at her phone. Dang, her mother was right. Shelby had told Lacey during one of their boy talks that when a man wanted to see you, you'd know it, you wouldn't have to wonder. And that if she felt anything less than that, move on. There was no mistaking Mekhi's intentions because he had her pulse racing. He was so open and direct that it had her hormones in overdrive. Her insides were hotter than the temps outside, which was scary yet exhilarating at the same time.

She fired her mother a quick text.

> **Mom, just reaching out to let you know that you were so so right. I'll fill you in when we talk later Xoxo**

CHAPTER 17

Shelby
June 21, 2025

Apparently, having a daughter meant you had to be prepared to devote an hour—at least—when they said they needed to talk. Because Lacey was a magpie—with a friend. And you had to be prepared to have that conversation at any time, even if your eyes were burning with dark circles and you looked a horrid fright on a video call.

Before going to bed at about one in the morning, Shelby had reread Lacey's text message saying how right she was about something and reacted by applying a heart to it, not daring to ask about what since she had no clue. She hadn't expected Lacey would text her a half hour later with **Are you up?**

The ding on her phone had actually awakened her, but Shelby wasn't about to tell Lacey that. Her concern had outweighed her sleep, so she responded. **Yeah . . . What's up?**

Cue the video call with two giggling young adults.

Honestly, she didn't mind. They were infectious, and she was getting to know her daughter again right along with Bea.

"So you both like Mekhi?" she asked, zeroing in on the two smiling faces. She kept her tone light to cover the tiny frisson of concern about how similar this was to her and Jewel.

"Well, yeah, but Lacey *likes* likes him," Bea said, jabbing Lacey in the ribs. "I've got my eye on someone else."

Whew. So it wasn't quite the same.

"That's because Mekhi isn't interested. He's hot, Mom. Think Miles Truitt," Lacey breathed out.

Shelby made a mental note to look up the name. In the meantime, she smiled and nodded like she knew who it was. That small-sized fear was now the size of a cotton ball. How was she supposed to navigate this conversation when she needed help with navigating herself?

Bea crooked her finger. "She's got it bad."

"I think the feeling is mutual." Lacey leaned closer to the screen, her eyes shining. "He's got me all bothered in ways I never imagined."

Good Lord. Her armpits were sweating now. It was evident that she had great rapport with her child about any and all topics. Even about sex and attraction. She would be patting herself on the back if she wasn't so scared.

"So, yeah, you were right, Mom. Remember when you said that if a man is interested in me, I wouldn't have to wonder?"

"Uh-huh." Okay, yeah, now the fear had the weight and size of a tennis ball.

"Well, I am certain about Mekhi. Emphasis on the word *certain*."

Shelby wiped her brow. "Just be careful," she croaked out.

"Don't worry, we have protection. We're safe," Bea piped up, bobbing her head as if that information was supposed to put her mind at ease.

Wait. Did Lacey call him a *man*? "How old is this Mekhi person?"

"Relax, Mom. He looks like he's about our age."

"Um, you need to see his license. Some dudes have baby faces."

"Ms. Shelby, you are so funny," Bea said, cracking up. "He's in school like us."

"I'll ask," Lacey said.

"Good. Get proof. Trust, but verify."

Lacey snickered. "If I had a dollar for every single time you've said that, I'd be rich."

Good. She was glad she was sounding like herself in this conversation. Maybe she could pull this off. "So what else are you doing when you're not working or hanging with Mekhi?"

"Um . . ." Lacey gave Bea a pleading look.

There was now a boulder in her gut. What was her daughter up to? Shelby bit the inside of her cheek to keep from asking.

"We've been hanging out on the beach mostly. Playing volleyball and all that," Bea said. The friends exchanged a look. Shelby knew there was more that they weren't saying, but did she really want to know? Lacey couldn't meet her eyes.

She scrutinized them. "As long as you're looking out for each other and being careful."

"Yes. You don't have to worry, Ms. Shelby," Bea spoke up again. "We're good. I promise."

Shelby decided to take them at their word.

"So you sure you're okay, Mom?" Lacey asked.

Shelby wiped the frown off her face. "Yes, I'm getting better every day."

"I'm glad to hear that," Lacey said. "I wasn't sure if you had any lasting side effects from the concussion. You didn't sound like yourself, and I was low-key worried you would never be the same."

Shelby met her eyes. "I am on the mend. No need to worry."

Lacey's shoulders slumped. "Okay . . . Do you need anything? We can come visit you, if you'd like. Or do you need me to work the bookstore?"

She relaxed her brows and reassured her child, "Aww, that's sweet. But I am well taken care of. I have Jewel here and my books. Plus, Abby has things covered at the bookstore." There was no way she was going to tell Lacey about her financial woes. "I'm good. I'll tell you what you can do. Go visit the aquarium, the zoo and the fair for me. I'll need you to tell me all about it and take lots of pictures."

Lacey smiled. "We can do that." Then she fretted on her bottom lip. "Mom, do you miss me?"

Shelby's mouth dropped open. "Of course I do. What kind of a question is that?"

Her daughter shrugged. "You used to text me hugs and *I love you*s, and I know that I'm older and used to roll my eyes, but I like it. Don't stop, okay? I like knowing you're thinking of me."

Her heart became like putty. "I will. I'm sorry I haven't kept up with that like I should." The knowledge that her daughter hadn't received such a text in days made Shelby's heart squeeze.

"Me too, please," Bea chimed in.

"Got it."

Lacey blew her a kiss. "I love you lots."

"I love you lots more," Shelby naturally countered. Judging by Lacey's grin, she had answered right. When the call ended, relief flooded her insides. Even though she hadn't been comfortable talking sex with her child, they'd had a great conversation.

She told Jewel as much later that morning when her friend was brushing Shelby's hair to redo it, for which Shelby was grateful. Jewel stiffened for a moment but then continued brushing and said, "I'm glad to hear that."

Sitting on the edge of the bed, with her back turned to Jewel, Shelby shook her head. "Mother–daughter talks sure are different than when we were growing up. My mother pretty much stopped talking with me once I started dating. All we did was fight after that . . ." Sorrow tightened her chest. *If only she was here to yell at me now. I'd give anything to hear her voice again.*

"Yeah, I remember that," Jewel said from behind her, greasing her hair. "My mother–daughter talks consisted of my mother telling me to get a job to help out with the bills. Remember how I had to hand over most of my paycheck every two weeks?"

"How could I forget? I remember leaving campus to drive to your mother's apartment, then helping you cook dinner because they hadn't eaten all day."

"You never told a soul about the roach infestation. I was so mortified when we spotted one crawling on the wall, but you used your shoe and whacked it so hard a paint chip fell off the wall."

Shelby chuckled. "I was so scared, girl. It was either the roach or me."

"You don't know the terror that racked my body at the thought of you telling the other girls in school about my rickety old place. College was my escape and rescue."

Shelby reared her head back so she could look Jewel in the face. "You were my bestie. And, though my parents were wealthy, they never let me forget their humble beginnings. My father used to walk to school in Jamaica with a piece of wood strapped under each foot because he couldn't afford shoes. My mother had to get a whole row of teeth replaced because her family couldn't afford to send her to the dentist. As soon as they could, they bought land in their hometown of Westmoreland and built a home."

"Still, I didn't think you would eat any of the food after your battle with the roach."

"Listen, I was hungry. I was going to eat no matter what, and I wasn't going to share my meal with any of those critters." They cracked up. "But look at you now. How far you've come. You're an international bestselling author, and you're living your best life in the Hamptons."

"I don't know about the best life, but yes, I've come a long way."

"We both have." Their eyes filled. "Okay, we need to stop before we get into a crying fest." Shelby fanned her face and turned back around. "I need you to finish my hair."

Jewel tilted her head. "Say, did you ever visit Jamaica? I know you wanted to go see about their property and all that."

"I don't think I did . . . I don't remember." She hadn't read about it in her journal so she would say she hadn't. But it could also be that she had been all about having fun and not recording it.

She patted Shelby on the back. "You will." After a beat, she said, "I've missed you, Shelby."

"There's no replacing a good friend. You're worth more than gold."

"I want the friend and the gold, but I do agree with your sentiment." Jewel's words sent them into another fit of laughter.

Shelby picked up the remote, turned on the television and logged into her Hulu account so she could put on *The Kardashians*.

Jewel groaned. "I don't want to watch this. If you were going to forget anything, why couldn't it be how much you are fascinated with these women?"

"They're my guilty pleasure," she cackled. "I've been catching up on them and Taylor Swift's music."

"Okay, but you're limited to two episodes, and then we're going to watch something else. And we're going to play Rihanna."

June 22, 2025

Like a caged bird set free, Shelby wanted to sing to celebrate her release from the hospital. But since she couldn't carry a tune, she settled for lifting her hands in the air and shouting, "I'm going home." When the nurse wheeled her out to Jewel's car, Shelby lifted her face and drew in a deep breath, basking in the warmth of the sun.

"I can't wait to look out to the beach and take in the sounds of the water," she said once she was inside in Jewel's SUV.

"That sounds like a plan. But before we head home, how about we go get some black cherry ice cream?" Jewel singsonged.

Shelby pumped her fists. "Bring it on."

"Great. People have been raving about this place in the Eagle Point Eats Facebook group."

"Well, I'm always down to sample another great ice cream spot."

Jewel's Mercedes couldn't be more than a year or two old, and Shelby was stoked at her friend's success. She shifted into the leather seat, ready to relax and enjoy the smooth ride. "This car feels like butter."

"Whipped." Jewel grinned, giving her a quick glance, before gliding onto the freeway. "You want to get behind the wheel?"

"No, no. I'm good with enjoying it from this side." Though she couldn't deny the kick of adrenaline. She ran her hand on the leather. "Remember when I backed my Acura into a tree?" As soon as she asked that question, Shelby could have kicked herself.

"Oh snap. I remember that." Jewel laughed before she tensed. "I remember what happened after that as well," she said, her voice brittle. The comradery between them fizzled.

Shelby cleared her throat. "I know it was over twenty years ago and I've apologized a gazillion times, but I really am sorry about sleeping with Declan."

Jewel shrugged. "I fancied myself in love with him, but technically, we had split up." She changed lanes and veered to the right of the highway.

"I know you said it wasn't really love, but it doesn't excuse my horrible actions. I was in mourning, and my head wasn't in the right place."

"Are you seriously still trying to apologize for something that happened twenty years ago? I forgave you."

"Eventually." She didn't think the guilt would ever ease. Shelby hated that she had allowed her hormones to override her common sense.

"Well, yeah. You did betray my trust. That took a minute to get over." She pulled up to a creamery and parked. "It did help, though, that you said the sex wasn't that great." There was a lineup that stretched down the street. Both Jewel and Shelby took off their seat belts, in silent agreement that they would wait for the crowd to thin.

"It was a four at best. Truth is, I don't think he was into me. I think he went along because he was sorry for me. That man lay there and let me do all the work." She slapped her head. "That was mortifying."

"Oh, it was off the charts for me." Jewel fanned her cheeks. "I married the only man who has ever topped him in bed."

Shelby gave her a playful shove. "Dang, you don't have to rub it in." Secretly, though, she was glad they could joke about a dark time in their friendship. Because after she had slept with Declan, she had raced all the way to the apartment and confessed everything to Jewel. The fallout had not been pleasant.

Her bestie must have been thinking along the same lines because she grew serious. "No matter what, all paths led us back to each other."

They held hands.

"At least you got a bestseller out of it," Shelby joked.

Jewel cocked her head, sizing her up. "Are you salty about that? Because if it was reversed, I would feel some kind of way about it."

"No. I'm not. And the only thing I feel is happiness for you."

Except there was a small part of her that was disappointed in herself for not pursuing her own writing dreams.

"Your name should have been on that book right along with mine. I begged you to change your mind."

Shelby waved a hand. "I didn't want that."

"Of course you did."

All she could do was purse her lips during the stare-down that ensued.

Jewel broke eye contact first and placed a hand on the door handle. "Let me go get our ice cream. I'll be right back."

AT THE ENTRANCE OF THE BOOKSTORE, SHELBY'S EYES narrowed. "I just thought of a dilemma I didn't consider before we came here." She lifted her chin toward the back of the store. "There are stairs, and I don't my ankle is ready to tackle steps."

Jewel nodded. "It's handled. We set up your office space as a temporary bedroom for tonight and tomorrow. Once I heard about your discharge, we moved a few of your personal items down here. I can fetch as you need. That's why I'm here."

"Did I tell you that you're wonderful? I get to recover with books all around me. How lovely." She furrowed her brows and tapped her chin. "That doesn't solve the problem of a shower, though."

"Kendrick will be coming by to help you upstairs until we get the stairlift installed."

"Stairlift?"

"Yes. Kendrick was able to borrow one from the hospital until you've recovered. It should be here in a day or two."

"Oh my. A stairlift seems like an extreme option for an ankle injury, but I'm grateful for the gesture. It looks like you've thought of everything." She cocked her head. "When did you arrange all this?"

Jewel smiled. "I have my ways. Can't share all my secrets."

Once Shelby was in her office, she logged into her business account to review her finances. She wished she had the funds to hire an accountant instead of handling things herself.

Shelby bunched her fists, her pulse quickening. Ugh. She needed her memory back. "Survivor," she voiced aloud, then exhaled. "Survivor."

"What's wrong?" Jewel probed again. She lowered her accounting program page and gave Shelby her full attention.

Shelby looked up at the ceiling. She patted her hair, grateful that Jewel had hooked her up with two slick cornrows the day before. "I just need a moment to process."

"Okay, I won't push. I'm here."

"My bookstore is in danger," she blurted out. "It isn't turning a profit, and I have no idea if I had a plan in place to try to save it."

Jewel stood. "Um, you have me. I'm still a big draw. I can do a few signings to lure a crowd." She pointed to her chest. "Plus, I can do a poster reveal for the upcoming TV series for *That Was Then*."

"Wow. Those are great ideas." She tapped the top of her laptop. "I'm willing to try anything."

"Have you thought about setting up online sales instead of just in-store purchases?"

"I don't know. I figure that direct to customer would be my bread and butter."

"Well, maybe you can offer special sales and gift certificates and raffle off some giveaways."

"Okay, thanks for those suggestions." Although they sounded like they required more staff, which she didn't have and couldn't afford. "In the meantime, I'll schedule the first signing soon."

"Do it quickly. A pop-up signing. I'll announce on my social media pages. Then we can announce the date for the other two."

"That's a great idea." Shelby beamed. "I wonder why I never reached out to you for help before."

"Because of our rift." Jewel folded her arms.

Silence hung between them. Suddenly the thought of wading through the journal entries overwhelmed her. She needed answers. Now. "I don't understand. What would make besties like us not besties anymore? You said that I broke our pact, but how?" A thought occurred. "If I hadn't had this accident, would we have ever reconciled?"

"I don't know. I'm here now." Jewel's shoulders curved. She released a long plume of air. "It was the child."

Shelby's brows furrowed. "What child?"

"*That* child."

It took a moment for her words to sink in. Shelby straightened and gripped the handles of the desk chair. "Wh-what? How?" Shelby gasped and placed a hand over her mouth. "Where is she?"

Jewel's voice grew bitter. "Right under your nose. You adopted her."

JOURNAL ENTRY

June 8, 2014

Dear Diary,
Serendipity!! I didn't believe such a thing existed until today. It was an unbelievable day. A few months ago, (yeah, it's been a minute. Sorry!) I had my own Casablanca moment because, of all the bookstores that she could have walked in, she walked into mine. At first, I didn't know it was HER. But the moment I saw her, I was drawn in by those large dark brown eyes on that round face. She was stunning in a red-and-black polka-dot dress and black wings. A ladybug. The first thing she did was head for the books, her eyes bright and shining at all the pretty covers.

Her parents—foster parents—hung out by the counter to tell me they had no idea how to feed her voracious appetite for books. The little bug loved to read. But there was something familiar about her. I took that to mean we had a shared love, a shared passion for reading. Those little legs pumping back and forth while her eyes remained glued in a book tripped my heart.

I started to babysit her on and off. Give the foster parents a little quiet time.

But it wasn't until today that Benedict and Carla let it slip that this was the baby abandoned at the bookstore.

The baby Honey and I left at the bookstore. Yes, that one. There, I've written it out in black and white. My confession, as Usher would say, even if this is for my eyes only. That knowledge was my cue to back off. And I tried. I really did. But how was I supposed to withstand those large, sorrowful eyes and downturned lips, which struck me with a force akin to a Category 5 hurricane? I couldn't keep saying no.

Lacey Phillips. Beautiful, brilliant Lacey was the baby from the beach. But she'd been adopted—how did she end up here? It took some doing, but I pried the truth out of Carla. Lacey's adoptive parents had gotten into legal trouble. Trouble big enough that they lost custody. Well, as the saying goes, their loss is my gain.

For me to learn this information on the anniversary of my parents' deaths, it was like they had sent me this gift. And although every part of my brain protested—screaming, Danger, danger!—my heart sang a cappella, that this was my chance. My chance to right a wrong and be there for a little girl who needed love, who needed me.

Now, the question is do I tell Honey?

Of course. I must. I cannot violate the friendship code.

June 11, 2014

Dear Diary,
So Honey didn't respond the way I expected. To my surprise—and it shouldn't have been—she took the news of my crossing paths (okay, babysitting) Lacey Phillips way worse than I anticipated. Our fallout was volatile. Lots of tears and snot, but I held my ground. I knew her reaction was attributed to fear. Fear of discovery. Fear of the domino disaster effect of the fallout for the both of us and our careers.

Come see for yourself, I told her. Come see.

If you looked at her, you'd understand.

If you looked at her, you'd know why I can't turn her away. Why my heart is bursting. But Honey dismisses my pleas. She is protecting us. Me and her. Can't I see that? Or so she says. This contention is a vine, ever-growing, creating a yawn between us. A divide that I don't know will ever be stitched together again. Not even with mutual love.

But Lacey is my joy. She's filled my heart.

I cannot turn her away.

CHAPTER 18

Jewel
June 23, 2025

"Losing our friendship wasn't easy for me either, you know," Jewel whispered, closing the diary and facing Shelby as the tears welled. When they went out to eat at the nearby diner, Shelby had given her the journal with a napkin bookmarking the pages she wanted Jewel to read, and she had obliged.

Now Jewel cupped the brown book close to her chest.

However, Shelby's reddened eyes hadn't prepared Jewel for the contents within. She knew after her revelation the day before that Shelby would skip to those pages, wanting to know more of what she might have been thinking when she'd adopted Lacey and put both their livelihoods at risk. But Jewel hadn't known that she would have to read the heartache poured out on the page.

"No, I don't really know that," Shelby choked out, her voice tender. "All I have is the diary, and though I know it's a one-sided account, you come across as . . . selfish. A word I would never have used to describe you. Before." She sniffled. "You are many things, but not that . . ." Clearing her throat, she challenged her. "Enlighten me."

"For one thing, I sent you an invitation to my thirtieth-birthday party. I begged you to come. Begged," Jewel said. "I needed you there with me to celebrate a major milestone in my life. You refused to come unless I invited Lacey too.

You wouldn't budge. Not even when I told you that Roman would be curious and would ask questions . . . I cried in his arms all night that night."

"I'm sorry. So Roman doesn't know about . . . ?" Shelby gave her a look of sympathy. "For some reason, I imagined you would have confided in him, as close as you two are. You're like peas in a pod."

"No. No, I never told him. That's our secret. And it's one I plan to take with me to the grave . . ." Her lips quivered. "But the day after my birthday party, you and I had a nasty standoff, and we both dropped an ultimatum about our friendship. You said it was Lacey and you, or no relationship at all. I said it was either Lacey or me." Her chest heaved. "You now know the result of that ultimatum."

"Ten years . . . Man, I feel really sad hearing that." She touched her chest. "My heart literally hurts."

Jewel wiped her face. "Keeping my distance from you nearly broke me. If it wasn't for Roman, I don't know how I would have survived. You're thinking of her, but I'm thinking of you. Of me."

Shelby arched a brow and gestured for her to explain.

"This might sound odd, but you're my one connection to her. Only you understand the sorrow I have in my heart," Jewel said. "You wanted to replace that feeling by having a child, but it's the opposite for me. What we did that night is seared into my heart and brain. I can't experience that heartache ever again."

"But you can have a relationship with her if you choose."

The temptation was so strong, it overwhelmed her. Jewel shook her head. "And what if she learns the truth? That would cause more harm than good. Are you prepared to answer the hard questions? Like, why did we abandon her?"

"I don't plan on her ever finding out." Shelby couldn't meet her eyes.

"She knows she's adopted. You don't think she's going to get curious to know her history? Because I'm scared. Our past is like a Pandora's box filled with secrets I don't want ever discovered. But if Lacey is anything like either of us personality-wise, she's going to want to know."

"The girl I'm getting to know is all about having fun. I think that's the last thing on her mind."

Jewel placed her hands on her hips, annoyance making her snappy. "I believe you are one hundred percent wrong. Everybody wants to know their heritage. And when she goes looking, the truth is going to crush her like a boulder." She huffed. "I wish you had left her alone like I said."

"I love her. That's why I adopted her." Her tone came across as slightly accusatory.

Jewel gasped. "You think I don't love her? It's because I do that I know I need to stay away." She couldn't keep the edge out of her voice.

Shelby's eyes narrowed. "So you've never seen her? Aren't you curious?"

Yes, of course she was. "No. Not in person." She flailed her arms. "I've seen her online. But I didn't go seeking her out on purpose." She couldn't quite meet Shelby's eyes.

"Liar."

"Okay, fine. I stalk her pages. You gave me her handles, and you'd send pictures. It was hard not to get attached in some way." She crossed her arms. "But I have my fill, and then I delete them. I'm satisfied with a brief mental image." She pointed an index finger toward Shelby. "You moved her into your space."

Shelby shrugged. "Well, I don't remember all the finer details, but I'm sure I have no regrets about my decision."

"Thus, why we are—er, were—estranged." Jewel covered her face with her hands. "I will say this. I love Lacey with everything within me. But we were both accomplices in her abandonment, and I'd rather she never gets to know me than comes to hate me."

Tension crackled between them. Jewel wasn't surprised. The cause of the chasm in their friendship was very much around and could pop up at any minute. She thought about that all the time.

"I think that logic is flawed. Even though I didn't know who she was at first, and I'm scared to talk to her because I don't want her finding out I have memory loss, I was drawn to her the moment I knew about her. I have a natural maternal instinct to protect her. Now that I know who she is, that feeling has been magnified. I can't wait to have my memory back or fall in love with her all over again, once I'm better."

"Why am I not surprised?" Jewel released a frustrated sigh and massaged her temples. "Can we stop this? We can't get into a spat before the book signing. We will never agree, so how about we declare a truce?"

Shelby lowered her lashes. "I do have a question first."

The waitress came with their check, halting their conversation. But as soon as Jewel got Shelby settled into the vehicle, Shelby said, "So can I ask my question?"

"I really don't want to keep arguing with you." Jewel sighed.

"I know, but I need you to be patient with me. I've got questions."

"I'm sorry. It's difficult arguing with you about the same thing all over again." She drove out of the diner's parking lot.

Shelby touched Jewel's arm. "Have you talked to Roman about his son yet?"

Jewel groaned. "Not yet. We've been having—" She didn't want Shelby knowing about the extent of her financial struggles. Even though she knew Roman wasn't working, Shelby might think they had a healthy nest egg to sustain them. If she knew that wasn't the case, that might lead to a discussion about her problems with book writing, and she didn't have the bandwidth to cope with the possible repercussions for her actions. Shelby would be livid with Jewel for writing another story about them, which is why she had returned to her decision not to tell her just yet. She had promised Roman to come clean, but it might be better to wait until the book was completed and ask for forgiveness instead of seeking permission.

"Having . . . ?" Shelby prompted, raising her voice slightly.

Jewel had to think of something else fast. "Um, having such good news about the series. Did I tell you that I have quite a few sponsors interested in purchasing limited commercial space for *That Was Then*?" She slapped the wheel. "I can't wait until I can announce more about this on social media." She tensed, awaiting Shelby's reaction. After all, this had been the book she had essentially stolen from Shelby. Jewel would completely understand if she had a lukewarm reaction. But that wasn't her friend.

"Oh my goodness! That is wonderful." Shelby clapped her hands, unaware of the relief pulsing through Jewel's body at her conversation shift. "Congratulations. I'm beyond happy for you."

That her friend had the capacity to be genuinely happy for her made Jewel feel grimy. Again the push to come clean, to tell Shelby about the new book she was writing, was strong. Again she ignored it. "Thank you," she breathed out. "You know you'll get your cut once the money clears." Even as she said that, she thought about the promise she had made to her mother. How was she going to manage all those expenses plus help save the bookstore? The weight of delivering the sequel soon pressed on her shoulders. As soon as she got Shelby settled for the evening, she needed to get to writing. Time was literally money, and she needed it.

"You don't have to do that," Shelby said.

"But you could use it." And it would assuage her guilt.

Sweeten the pot for when she finally had the nerve to share the details about her new book with Shelby. Gosh. Jewel didn't like the woman she had become.

"Friend, you are generous to a fault, but I can't take your money like that. I know I said the store was in danger, but it's my problem to work out."

"Nonsense. You would do the same for me." She forced a smile onto her face. The fact that Roman wouldn't react well to this added responsibility made her stomach bubble, but she wouldn't dwell on that now. Jewel didn't want Shelby picking up on the worry on her face.

"I know, but it's different when you're the recipient and not the giver."

Jewel chuckled, even as the churning in her stomach grew. She pulled up to the bookstore and assisted Shelby out of the vehicle. They made their way inside. The air was muggy, but Shelby breathed in the ocean air and smiled.

"Does Lacey need anything? Tuition money?" Goodness, she needed to cut her tongue out. She kept offering money like she was related to the Kardashians. Jewel was a fan of the show, but that didn't mean she needed to adopt their extravagant lifestyle.

"Oh no. Lacey is set for life."

"Is she?"

"Yeah. She has a trust fund, and the bank has made some wise investments on her behalf. At least, that's what they told me when I called them to inquire about it. I already sent off her payment for the upcoming semester. She's all good. I'm pretty sure she doesn't know of her affluence yet, but she definitely will when she turns twenty-five and can access the funds."

Surprising tears welled in Jewel's eyes. "We deserted her. But God looked out for her in ways I didn't even know." She unlocked the entrance to the store. The cool blast of air welcomed them.

"He sure did, and then some." Shelby used her walker and made her way to one of the couches by the front of the shop.

Jewel's shoulders shook. This time the tears fell of their own volition, and she let them. "I loved her. It's important that you know I love her now. It's hard for me to let her go. It's hard, but I care." She hiccupped, tears pooling in her eyes. "I care."

"Hush, I know. I know." A few minutes later, Shelby drew back and wiped Jewel's hair out of her face. "We don't want your eyes red and your cheeks puffy at the signing later."

Nodding, Jewel drew in a deep breath. "I've gotten a lot of traction on my pages. My readers are excited that I'm back where it all began. So I think we'll get a good turnout tonight and even at the other two signings."

"Yes, we've gotten quite a few calls for preorders. I've had to order five cartons of your books. And as you see, the traffic into the store has increased, with fans knowing that you're lurking about."

Jewel smiled. "I'm glad to be of some help. I haven't done more than a signing or two each year after my debut release, so I'm excited as well. Readers have an energy that fuels your writing. They are great for your ego, and you need it because the editing stage can kick your butt like nobody's business. It's like getting your work bleached, sanitized and stripped apart and put back together in one day."

"It sounds daunting but amazing." Shelby smiled, her eyes dreamy. "No wonder people call books their babies."

"Yes, girl. It's labor." She puffed her chest. "But I love it." Then tapping Shelby's shoulder she whispered, "I wish this for you one day."

Jewel half expected Shelby to come back with her usual banter, but instead her friend gave a small smile, which gave her hope. Maybe the sleeping writing bug had finally awakened, and if so, Jewel couldn't wait to cheer her on.

SINCE SHELBY HAD SET UP A *SIGNING UNDER THE STARS* banner at the front of the bookstore, Jewel took a moment to hide out on the private balcony on the second level. Jewel sipped some of the coffee Abby planned to sell, loving the feel of the sun on her skin. *Roman would love it out here.*

From her vantage point, she had a breathtaking view of the beach and the horizon and the crowd below. With her oversize shades, large hat and white maxi dress, she'd stand out if she wasn't so high up. It was just after six o'clock, and thankfully the heat would be bearable for all the people waiting just to meet her.

Unfathomable.

The line was wrapped around the building. Jewel would be sitting at a desk under the awning by the entrance, and Abby had gotten her little brothers to hand out close to two hundred flyers. Plus they had promoted on social media, and the bookstore's and Jewel's websites. There were boxes and boxes of her books stacked inside. Shelby had commenced sales about thirty minutes ago so that once her appointed time began, Jewel would have a nonstop queue. She had autographed about fifty books in advance for those who didn't want to wait to meet her.

Honestly, when she'd suggested the signing, Jewel hadn't anticipated this level of enthusiasm. Was it because she had only done a handful of signings in her career? Did that give her that je ne sais quoi? Or was it because her book was about to be a major television series?

Shelby thought it had a lot to do with her accident and the fact that Jewel was one of the community. Eagle Point Beach supported their own.

Either way, she was touched.

The only thing that would make the evening better was if Roman was here. As much as she had enjoyed reconnecting with and helping Shelby, she missed her husband. Big-time.

It hadn't taken but six hours for her heart to be like, *Where's my babe at?* She missed resting her head on his shoulder, inhaling his scent and making him laugh. Roman said she gave him a reason to laugh or smile every day. Meanwhile he was the reason she felt loved every day. Consistently, completely, he cherished her, every single day. She got her morning texts and nightly emoji kisses.

Glancing at her watch, Jewel snapped a picture of the beach, sent it to him and then gave him a call. As she held the phone near her eyeline, Roman's beaming face lifted her heart. He had gotten a fresh haircut and a tight lineup. Gosh, her honey was looking so handsome. Guaranteed, he had turned a few heads while at his interview today.

"I was just about to call you," he said. "How are you?"

"Nervous. I wish you were here to hold my hand."

"Aww, babe. You don't need me. You're a powerhouse."

"I know. But it's an act. I have to be on, cheery, smiling, even if my fingers are cramped. When I'm with you, I get to chill out and I don't have to be anything."

"Yes, but I would also be a distraction, and you have a deadline. How's your word count?"

"It's good." She pouted. Secretly, she'd hoped Roman would offer to come down to Eagle Point Beach for a few days. They could rent an Airbnb.

"Oh, sweetheart, I don't like seeing your sad face. You know if I didn't have these interviews, I'd be right there by your side."

"I know." Sheesh, his thoughtfulness was irritating at times. Just be selfish and come see me, she wanted to say, but she knew Roman wouldn't budge if he believed he was doing the right thing. "I'd better get going," she mumbled. "I have to freshen up and use the restroom because I think I'll be signing for a good two hours nonstop."

Roman's brows shot up. "You're kidding!"

"See for yourself." Jewel walked close to the ledge, turned

the screen and panned the crowd. Someone looked up and called out, and others joined in. They did an impromptu wave that made her wave back with a giggle.

"It looks you're going to be too busy to miss me," her hubby said once she was finished.

"Never."

Roman blew her a kiss. "Go do your thing. We'll talk later."

Grabbing the kiss, Jewel placed it on her cheek. She blew one to him, and Roman mimed putting it in his pocket, then they ended the call.

"You two are so corny," Shelby said, coming up to her. She was wearing the bookstore T-shirt. "I came to tell you that we're almost ready for you and saw you two exchanging air kisses. It's downright corny, and it warms my heart."

Jewel smiled, slipping her phone in her dress pocket. "Everybody needs a Roman in their life."

Shelby cracked up. "I could say that about a bestie as well."

"Don't forget about books. Books and a bestie are a great combination." Jewel slipped her arm through Shelby's.

"Books, beaches and besties are our bond. Indestructible," Shelby added, splaying her hand toward the water. Arm in arm, they marched in sync, mindful of Shelby's cast. Hips and elbows bumped, but they didn't break stride until they got to the top of the staircase. Shelby settled into the stairlift and they went downstairs.

It wasn't until she was seated at the table that Jewel thought of Lacey. The exception. Fighting over what was best for both the two of them and Lacey had severed Jewel and Shelby's friendship for ten years. And even though they were basking in their reunion, the source of their contention was very much present and could turn up at any minute. Their friendship was as shaky as Humpty-Dumpty balancing on the wall, and if they fell this time there would be no putting them back together again.

JOURNAL ENTRY

December 10, 2014

Oy! Diary!
I have a dilemma. A conundrum.

Lacey's foster parents are moving to Seattle. Since they own their home here, they plan to make it a vacation home or even use it as an Airbnb. Feels like it's the other end of the world. Lacey doesn't want to go. She has finally made friends. The ladybug has grown into her wings (I know I'm being dramatic here). My heart pounds at the thought of never seeing that face again.

I tried to keep it to myself, but I had to tell my bestie. She cried with me. Then she told me to let her go. Letting Lacey leave will keep our secret safe. But the state didn't approve the foster parents' request to move her out of state.

Serendipity.
Again.

I knew what I had to do. Yes, it was risky, but I told Honey I was doing it. I was going to foster and then adopt Lacey. The child we abandoned had returned home. Honey begged me not to, even though I could see she was torn. Self-preservation won. The day I signed the papers and stood smiling in court was the day I lost my best friend. My true friend.

But I gained a daughter, and I can't look back even though there is a gaping hole in my heart. All I have to do is look into Lacey's face and I know I would do it again. And again.

Honey will come around. All she needs is time.

April 6, 2015

Dear Diary ☹
Lacey turned nine today. We had a big celebration and there were dozens of little feet running around the bookstore. All day I hoped that Honey would call. I get that she wouldn't have accepted the invite, but I expected a gift, an acknowledgment. Something. Anything. This was our child.

But there was only silence.

I understand why, but that doesn't stop my heart from breaking. For me. And for my little girl. How could I reject her a second time? That's what I asked Honey. Crickets. Then after days of nothingness, all she says is "You made your choice, I'm making mine. It's what's best for the BOTH of us."

Even if it is best, it isn't right. I remind myself of this often, even as my tears wet my pillow at night.

May 17, 2015

My Diary, my friend (pitiful),
Today I turned 30. Today was the day that Honey and I should've been on our dream vacation. We were going to shop in Italy and skip over to Paris and then Spain. Our plan was to eat our way through Europe. We had been talking about it ever since we read Eat, Pray, Love. *But, did I do that?*

No.

Lacey and I baked a cake, the kind with the 3 and the 0. She ate the 3 and I ate the 0. I felt like the most blessed person in the world, and I have the pictures to prove it.

But Honey wasn't far from my mind. It hurt my heart that she wasn't with me. That she wouldn't agree for Lacey to travel with us. But my answer was easy. I didn't need to travel the world to find what I already had. Lacey.

After Lacey went to bed, I dashed into my closet and cried. I cried until my chest hurt and my eyes were puffy and red.

I don't know what I'll do when Honey turns thirty later this year. I'm pretty sure she won't want Lacey tagging along.

I did sneak on her socials to see the giant picture of a house key. Her dream home in the Hamptons. She is having a fabulous life. The highlight of my day is that I had to write a $3,500 check for Lacey's braces. And, I wonder, which of the two of us is richer?

Motherhood . . .

CHAPTER 19

Excerpt from That Was Then *by Jewel Stone*

June 11, 2005

Sugar

Chance Hudson was the perfect blend of moody and dark, which gave Sugar a secret thrill, and staying away from him hadn't dimmed the yearning. This fascination refused to die and was like a storm that had picked up speed and was now a full-fledged hurricane.

Sugar needed an outlet.

Some days she wrote, and some days she felt like hurling. Especially when she woke up to find her best friend with her eyes red and puffy from hours of crying. Yet Honey wouldn't say what was wrong as Sugar held her while she rocked back and forth, sobbing out variations of *It's over* and *I'm done with him* and *He's not who I thought he was.*

It had taken serious prodding, but Sugar convinced Honey to come with her to lunch at her parents' house. Her mother had made chicken noodle soup, festival and salad—Honey's favorites—at Sugar's request. And her father had purchased two pints of black cherry ice cream.

She toyed with the idea of inviting Chance. Despite her crush, she did believe he and Honey belonged together. Although Honey might get upset at her interference.

Or she might thank her.

Pulling out her phone, she sent Chance a text.

>						Hungry?

I could eat.

>						Meet me at my parents'.

She gave him the address, rattled off the menu, then ended with **Honey will be here.** There seemed to be some hesitation as the three dots moved across her screen before she received an **Okay.**

Whew.

Selfishly, Sugar wanted her friends there not only because she enjoyed them but because they would be buffers against her usual argument with her parents on her career choice. Sugar stepped over the threshold near noon, optimistic that at the end of lunch, bellies would be full and relationships would be restored or mended.

She had dressed in a long flowing dress and a pair of wedges, and Honey had chosen a royal blue jumpsuit with a pair of black sandals. Despite her heartache, her friend looked cute. Eyeing herself in the mirror, Sugar loved how her curls popped and her skin shone. Mommy would be pleased that Sugar had used the skin products she had purchased.

Within ten minutes of everyone gathering around the dining table, Sugar realized her confidence had been misguided. The tension was heavier than a foggy Delaware morning, and after introductions and a few attempts at conversation, there was nothing but awkward silence.

Mommy smoothed her beige blouse and ran her fingers down her black pants as she cut her eyes at Chance's tattoo of an anchor on full display on his right leg. After a disapproving glare, Sugar's ears were already ringing in preparation. Sugar had assumed he would know to show up in a pair of slacks and a collared shirt, but he was wearing shorts, a torn tank and sandals, which was surprising since he was usually so well put together. He sat across from Honey, and Sugar could see him trying to make eye contact.

But Honey was shooting Sugar daggers with her eyes and had sent texts Sugar knew better than to read. Meanwhile, her father was busy eating his soup, unbothered by anyone and anything around him.

Sugar almost didn't want to bring up Paris. But she had to if she wanted to be able to book her vacation. There was a tour due to leave in a week, and she wanted to be on that airplane. With or without Honey. She needed time away.

"Daddy, have you made a decision about Paris yet?"

Her mother frowned. "You're still on that? Do you not listen to the news? People have gotten arrested in foreign countries for minor infractions. I don't think it's a good idea. If you want an adventure, then come fishing with us day after tomorrow. Your father is excited to go deep-sea fishing. We're leaving at about four in the morning."

"Mrs. Bean, traveling abroad is quite safe, actually," Chance piped up. "I've—"

"I don't think you need to insert yourself in this discussion," Honey spoke up, glaring at him.

Chance stood, excused himself and headed to the door. After a quick hesitation, Honey said her goodbyes and rushed after him. The minute the door closed behind them, Sugar heard them yelling at each other. Wow. What was going on with those two? She would have to find out later.

But right now, she needed her dad to quit ignoring her and answer her question. Daddy was so passive-aggressive at times, but she wasn't going to back down. Sugar kept her eyes pinned on her father, who was steady eating his meal. "Daddy, I don't mean any disrespect, but you need to cut the apron strings. I'm about to be twenty years old, and you're treating me like a toddler. Lots of people my age have gone solo backpacking, and they were just fine. I studied French in high school and college, so it's not like I won't be able to communicate."

Daddy bit into a festival, and she gritted her teeth while he chewed and nodded. Chewed and nodded. Her mother gathered Chance's and Honey's bowls, fussing. "Woeful waste make woeful want," she said, shaking her head.

"Mommy, just box it up," Sugar said, striving for patience. "I'll take it to them."

Her mother pursed her lips and retreated into the kitchen.

Finally, her father wiped his mouth and dropped his napkin. Then, facing her, he exhaled. "If you insist on going, despite my wishes, then I'll buy your ticket."

She slumped before his words kicked in. "Whoa. You're letting me go."

"Yes, but your mother and I would plan to come with you."

"Ugh, I don't need chaperones." Sugar jumped to her feet. "I need you to trust me."

"I do trust you," Daddy said. "It's the world I don't trust. The world doesn't empower strong Black women the way it should."

Sugar could scream. "Yes, there's bad, but there's also plenty good."

"It's your choice."

"Why would I want to go anywhere with you and Mommy?

I wish you both would get a life of your own and let me live mine!" Furious, she stormed out of the house, not even bothering to take her leftovers. Her phone buzzed showing her mother's cell phone number several times, but Sugar sent it to voicemail. However, by the time she had pulled up to her condo, her anger had diffused considerably and she regretted disrespecting them. Her parents watched the news for hours at a time and all they saw were dangers. They meant well. And they wanted to spend time with her. Was that so bad?

She released a long hiss of air. In two days, when they returned from boating, Sugar would mend things. No, she was going to go boating with them, and while they fished they would have a discussion like rational adults. Sugar slipped under the covers and put on a Netflix movie. She couldn't wait tell her father to book the flight, and all three of them would have a grand time in Paris.

CHAPTER 20

Excerpt from That Was Then *by Jewel Stone*

June 12, 2005

Honey

She could officially be labeled a home-wrecker, but she was hard-pressed to feel bad about it. After Honey and Chance had left the Bean residence, she had unleashed her fury at him, at her impossible situation, at the fact that they couldn't be together.

And the more she yelled, the more he told her how much he loved her.

Then, before she could question her common sense, they had gone back to his place to make love—in a spare bedroom—leaving a trail of clothing in their path. For the first time ever, Honey had turned off her cell phone. She didn't want anyone or anything interrupting her time with Chance. Even as she kissed him and he heated her body from head to toe, Honey said emphatically, "This will be the only time."

And it had been the only time three more times before she had fallen asleep in his arms.

Now as the sun awakened them, her body and her heart thanked her, and she shimmied with delight. Her gyrations made Chance pop an eye open. Honey loved how his eyes warmed when he spotted her looking at him.

"Last night was impressive," she said, pinching his chin.

His lips spread into a smile. "I can say the same for you. Do you want to catch a movie or something?"

Reaching up, she ran her hand through his tendrils. "I can't. I have laundry and chores to do since I'm off today."

Chance sighed. "I guess I'll see if I can get some painting done since you're determined to leave me all to myself. There's a project I've been tinkering with that I should finish."

Honey cocked her head. "Oh, what are you working on?"

"I've always wanted to do a nude painting. But I have yet to find the perfect muse." Hmm . . . the perfect muse. It sounded like a guise he used as a legitimate reason to get girls out of their clothes. But she wasn't an artist, so what did she know?

Her brows rose. "I could help with that," she offered, even as her heart hammered at the prospect.

Studying her under hooded lashes, Chance quirked his lips. "Nah. You don't seem like you'd be adventurous enough to do it."

See now, Honey wasn't one to back down from a challenge of any kind. But Chance was a hard read. She gave him the side-eye. "What would I have to do?"

He studied her.

"You have all these curves and clean lines. You have an interesting side profile. I think it would translate well onto canvas," he said, his voice a low rumble. "I have a rough sketch already. I really just need you to sit for an hour or two to fine-tune some details. I'd take a picture if you gave me permission, and then I could work off that still to finish it."

"Okay, I could do that," she said, shyly looking up at him from under her lashes.

"Great. When do you want to do this?"

Honey lifted her shoulders. "No time like the present."

Chance flipped out of bed. Taking her hand, he led her into the huge walk-in shower, and they enjoyed another session of frolicking and lovemaking. When Chance exited to give her privacy to use the restroom, she rummaged through the cabinet for toiletries and whooped when she found spare toothbrushes and linens. Grabbing some, Honey told herself they didn't mean anything. Rich people entertained all the time. Made sense for them to stack up on supplies.

Honey swallowed the bile of mortification and headed out the bathroom.

"All right, let's do this," Chance said with a grin, drying his hair. He had a pair of shorts on but remained barefoot and bare-chested.

To her surprise, once they entered his studio, Chance was the ultimate professional. The studio was actually a converted sunroom that boasted its own entrance. Since they had been all about getting under sheets the prior day, she hadn't seen the rest of his place. Curious, she asked for a tour, and Chance promised to give her one after their session.

The huge windows provided great natural lighting and an impressive view of the ocean. Because of the angle, there was a small measure of privacy. So she felt comfortable posing with an artfully placed blanket. His detached, warm tone of voice put her at ease as she sat on edge of a chaise lounge. He adjusted her and tilted her just so before he was satisfied. Standing behind the easel, he worked for an hour before getting out his camera. He took so many pictures, but he was charming and funny, and soon Honey found herself having fun. She forgot she wasn't wearing a stitch of clothing. Though Chance was hidden behind a lens, she felt seen.

Desirable.

It was a heady sensation. And it made her feel closer to Chance. He had a great eye. Honey dropped her guard and her misgivings. At the end, she could honestly say that she'd had a good time.

While Chance cleaned up his tools, she shimmied into her jumpsuit, hating how wrinkled it had gotten—it had a distinct day-after look—then turned on her phone.

Notification alerts buzzed four times. There were two texts and a phone call from her mother, as well as a text from Sugar. Honey pulled up her mother's first and gasped before listening to the voicemail. She had to play it twice to decipher her mother's frantically spoken words.

"What's wrong?" Chance asked.

"It's my mom." She covered her mouth with her hand. "My sister had a nasty fall, and now Mom's being investigated for abuse and neglect." She tapped her feet before pacing as she tried to return her mother's call. "C'mon, pick up. Pick up."

Chance came up behind her to rest a hand on her shoulder, but she shooed him off. Honey didn't need his comfort right now; she needed her mother to answer her call. 'Cause if she didn't, that meant . . . A visual of her mother getting a mug shot caused tremors on her insides. No, she couldn't make assumptions.

"I'm going to have to call a cab and get up to Wilmington. Ma said they were trying to put Topaz into foster care. We can't have that." She tugged through her curls tangled by sweat. Her bank account had exactly $23.13. That wasn't enough. Her heart rate was in overdrive at this point, and she had to draw deep breaths.

"I'll drive you up there," Chance said.

"No. No. You don't have to."

He placed his hands on his hips. "I want to. You're my

girlfriend. You really think I would let you go through this on your own?"

Girlfriend? Despite her worry, his words warmed her heart and also made her cringe. Chance was married. Even if his wife was a shrew, he had still put that ring on her finger. So that made Honey the side piece. That knowledge didn't sit well with her. Her ma would be ashamed at her actions, and now she felt icky. She rubbed her arms. Remorse lashed her conscience. If she hadn't been with Chance, she would have gotten the messages much earlier.

She called again, but it rang and rang. Honey hung up when the voicemail came on. Her chest tightened at the sound of her mother's voice.

"I'm sorry but this is a mistake," she choked out. "I have to get out of here." She moved toward the exit, her legs wobbly and her hands trembling. *Please, God. Let my family be all right.*

"Wait, what? Are you saying *we* are a mistake?" Chance was on her heels. "Honey, you're giving me whiplash here. I love you. I get that you're in a panic, but don't do anything hasty."

"Whatever. I don't have time for this."

Ignoring his pleading look, she tried her ma once more. Voicemail again.

Honey snatched open the door and stepped out then stopped cold. Life was going on right outside the door. The beachgoers were out, and someone had decided to feed the birds, thus the squawking. Shielding her eyes, she peered out at the horizon. The skies looked calm and bright, which seemed odd when her mind and heart were in turmoil. Honey sniffled and wrapped her arms around herself. She needed to get to her mom, and she needed her bestie.

"At least let me take you to Wilmington. A cab that far might be too expensive. Regardless of anything else, I consider you a friend. Let me help."

"Can you stop talking, please?" Honey snapped. "I can't think." She tried her mom again with no success. "Why isn't she responding?" she screamed.

A pair of hands held her shoulders. "Take deep breaths."

Following his directive, Honey calmed. Then she called Sugar, who told her to accept Chance's offer and demanded that Chance swing by to get her. Fighting back tears, Honey acquiesced, getting into the passenger seat. It felt good having her friend take charge because she was too anxious to think past trying to get her mother on the phone.

Five minutes later, Sugar was jumping into the rear seat holding her purse and a bag. Sugar rattled off her mother's address to Chance since Honey had drawn a blank.

"Get in the back," she told Honey. "I brought you a change of clothes and a brush."

"Oh my goodness, I love you." Honey wrangled her way to the back while Chance drove. Sugar gave her a hug, and Honey broke into a sob.

"Shhh, it's okay." Sugar rocked her, swaying back and forth. "No matter what, you've got me. And Chance."

After a few minutes, Honey pulled away and wiped her eyes. She changed her clothes and dragged the brush through her hair. Once she was ready, she climbed back to the front seat. Leaning her head against the headrest, Honey closed her eyes and prayed she wasn't too late to aid her mother and sister.

THOUGH THE ONE-BEDROOM APARTMENT WAS PRISTINE, it was hard to ignore the squeaky wood, faded paint, worn carpeting and the huge hospital bed in the middle of the living room. Her mother fussed around to get Topaz settled with Honey's assistance. Though she was ambulatory, she still required a lot of physical assistance, so Honey and her mother had put their money together to purchase the bed since Medicaid said Topaz wasn't eligible yet.

On the drive from Eagle Point Beach, Honey had finally received a phone call from a social worker who filled her in on her mother's and sister's whereabouts. Her mother had been taken to the police station for questioning, and her sister was at the hospital.

Chance had taken Honey to the county general hospital just as her mother arrived in the back of the police car. Their tearful reunion had been quick and brief before they dashed inside to Topaz's room. In between their tears, Ma had shared that there would be no charges against her. The doctors and social worker concurred that there was no evidence of ill-intent or neglect. However, it had taken hours before they were released to go home.

Now Chance and Sugar sat squished together on the worn leather couch, looking out of place, and for the most part Honey avoided eye contact. It was close to two in the morning, and her eyes burned, but she knew her mother couldn't have handled getting Topaz back inside the apartment on her own. Chance had hoisted her sister in his arms and carried her up the stairs to the second floor, for which they were all grateful. But that meant both of Honey's friends were inside instead of waiting in the car.

In their younger years, Honey hadn't cared when Sugar came to visit. She hadn't known there was a difference in their places of abode. But as they got older and her awareness grew, Honey had elected to visit Sugar's place instead.

Having Chance and Sugar in her home highlighted the disparity of wealth between her family and theirs. Her mother's entire apartment had to be the same size as Chance's and Sugar's bedrooms. Okay, maybe that was a slight exaggeration, but her embarrassment at her living situation was very real.

"Thank you so much for the ride home, Chance," Ma said. "You were a godsend. If you weren't there, I would have had to get a cab at this hour."

Honey clenched her cheeks as her face warmed. Of course her mother would slight her. She would have a vehicle if she wasn't giving her mother almost all of her paycheck.

"You're quite welcome, Ms. Opal. I'm glad I got to see where Honey got her good looks from."

"Go on, now. Quit that." Her ma tittered. Actually tittered. It seemed like Chance's appeal spanned all ages.

"Yes, and I'm sure that you're grateful for Honey as well," Sugar said, piping up to defend her.

"Uh, let me go check on the kettle on the stove." Ma gave Honey a pat on the arm and then walked the few feet into their tiny kitchen.

"Nice try, bestie," Honey mumbled. "But I'm used to my ma's ways. I'm just glad everybody is fine, and now we can head out."

Sugar yawned. "Oh boy, I don't think I'm going to go fishing with my folks. I'm way too exhausted." Sugar had told Honey of her intentions to go with her parents on their boat and had even invited her to come with them to Paris. Honey had been sad to decline because she didn't have a passport.

Chance jumped up and went to hold the door open. "We'll be there in time for you to ship out."

Sugar waved a hand. "Nah. It's okay. Just take me home. It's all good."

They were asleep within minutes of getting home.

Honey was in such a heavy slumber that it took a moment to register the bloodcurdling screams were coming from inside the condo. Bolting out of bed, she darted into Sugar's room.

"What's going on?" Honey yelled.

Her friend sat with the covers around her, her phone in one hand, bellowing, "No. No. Please, God, no. It can't be true!" She was too frenzied to register Honey's words.

Shaking her, Honey asked, "Sugar, tell me. Tell me what's wrong."

"It's my parents. They're gone. They're gone, and they're not coming back."

"What do you mean?" Honey got into the bed and snatched Sugar into her chest.

Sugar tossed the phone toward her. "The coast guards called. A waterspout came out of nowhere and capsized my parents' boat. They can't find the bodies."

"No, no, it can't be true."

Chest heaving, Sugar shoved out of her arms. "It is. It is. Their vessel is missing. And I should have been with them. I should have been there."

CHAPTER 21

∽

Shelby

June 27, 2025

So Kendrick and I have been texting back and forth, which is nice. Random inspirational sayings and jokes. Keeping things light, which works for me. At times when Jewel doesn't see me watching, she seems . . . sad.

She sits with her arms wrapped her, staring into space. I think it's because she misses her husband. She hasn't seen him in weeks. I think I have borrowed Roman's wife for long enough, and it is probably almost time for her to go back home. She has been steadily writing, and I think she might be waiting until after the signings and her book is finished to leave.

Which is fine with me.

The first signing was a success. Jewel really is a pro at what she does. My heart swelled with pride watching her in her element. And Abby sold coffee and hot chocolate, even though it was hot as ever, all because we ordered reusable cups with Jewel's book title and autograph on them.

Meanwhile, I got the old flash drive out of my nightstand, printed out my old manuscript and sent Abby to Staples to have it bound, all 336 pages double-spaced. I can't wait dig in. I will as soon as the knot in my stomach loosens.

CHAPTER 22

Lacey
July 1, 2025

From her chair by the computers in the local library, Lacey glanced over at her friend and her potential bae and wondered how she had lucked out with so many people around her who cared. They had been faithfully helping her in her search, spending hours over the past couple weeks cooped up inside the library or on their devices reading through countless articles about the baby at the bookstore.

Then Bea suggested they review other news clippings in the archives to see if there was any interesting information that would give a clue about the happenings in Rehoboth Beach or Eagle Point Beach at that time.

They had spent the morning at the beach before venturing to the library. But the librarian hadn't cared that they were in bikini tops and shorts, leaving sand in their wake. She had waved them in with a pleasant smile, especially once Mekhi offered to vacuum before they left.

Since her mother had sent her a generous sum, Lacey had decreased her hours at the boutique, so she had more time to spend on this task, as well as with Bea and Mekhi. Opening up to him about her suspicion that she was the baby on the beach had been difficult since she'd feared he would laugh at her, but from the first day that he met up with them at the library, Mekhi had jumped into their investigation with gusto.

The more she hung around him, the more she knew she was falling for him.

Falling in love for the first time.

Poor Bea. Lacey had filled her ears with talk of Mekhi. Mekhi this. Mekhi that. She didn't think she would ever tire of talking about him. Or scribbling his name on her pay stub or on her napkin like she was back in high school. Even she was sickened with her antics, but she was too into him to stop. Her only saving grace was that he was just as infatuated as she was, and though he was a talker, chatting it up with everyone, Mekhi only shared personal things with her. Like his odd relationship with his parents.

He was an only child like she was, but his relationship with them was . . . detached. He had everything he needed: the newest Jeep, his own place and a spending allowance that was bonkers. His father was a retired NFL player who had invested in a lot of businesses, and his mother used to be an airline attendant. That's how they had met. Mekhi could hang out with celebrities, yet he chose to be with her. And Bea.

He was . . . a beautiful monarch butterfly. Mekhi had balked at that analogy, but the more he opened up to her, the more she saw the beauty within and his vulnerability. He had a wicked sense of humor too.

After she had called him a butterfly, he had called her a belt, saying she held him up. She was a thermometer because she could heat him up or cool him down. He would send her those kinds of texts at all odd hours of the day. Once, she had busted out laughing while helping a customer.

Yep, she was a goner. And they had only kissed once. Not because she didn't want to again, but she was afraid to. The energy between them crackled, it was combustible, and she didn't want to light that cherry bomb until she was ready to deal with the fireworks.

"I think I've found something," Mekhi said, hunched over

and staring at the computer screen in the library. "I'm not sure it's relevant. It's a gossip mag, but . . . it's dated in August. Around the time you would have been conceived."

"Anything that stands out could mean something," Lacey said. "We have to explore all possibilities even if we end up with nothing but loose threads."

Bea sidled next to him on the left and Lacey sat on his right. She held back a chuckle when Mekhi shifted his seat closer to her. He didn't even seem aware that he had done that, which made him even more appealing. Tingles shot through her body at his proximity.

She directed her attention to the screen as Bea read aloud. *"Where is Declan Welch? That's the question on the lips of everyone in Eagle Point Beach. Local and upcoming artist and self-proclaimed ladies' man Declan Welch is the talk of the town. Allegedly, his much older wife kicked him to the curb with just the clothes on his back, but Augustina refused to comment. Declan, if you're alive, hit us up. We suspect he's skipped town."*

Lacey read it again. "I'm leaning on the side of it's probably nothing, but let's put in his name and *artist* to see if anything pops up." Bea jumped on the computer and started tapping away.

"I'll look up *Augustina Welch*," Mekhi offered. She eyed his long fingers gliding across the keyboard and wondered what they would be like on her skin. This man was such a distraction.

Snap out of it. Lacey blinked a few times and typed the words *baby, beach, bookstore, Declan Welch* and *artist* in the search bar. A gaggle of random articles popped up. A quick scan of the results included something about Florida schools. Ugh. She was going in circles. Lacey rubbed her forehead. "I'm not getting anything of substance. Maybe we need to call it a day. I could use an ice cream break."

The ice cream truck music had been playing in the background, teasing her taste buds.

"Hang on," Mekhi said, reaching over to squeeze her thigh. Her traitorous pulse accelerated. "Augustina Welch lives on the beach."

"Which beach?" Bea yelled.

"Shush," the librarian called out.

"Sorry," Lacey loud-whispered.

"Is she here in Rehoboth?" Bea whispered.

Mekhi nodded. "Yes, and if the internet photo I'm looking at is accurate, her house is about a half-mile down on the beach. I think I've seen it." The excitement in his voice was palpable.

Bea grabbed her bag off the back of the chair. "Let's go down there now and see if she's willing to talk to us."

Ever a man of his word, Mekhi went to retrieve the vacuum.

Lacey froze. "Wait. We're not suitably dressed."

"We look like we've been on the beach," Bea insisted.

"I feel like we're grasping at straws. Like we're three broke-down Sherlock Holmeses. Like we're fabricating a tale about my existence by stringing clues together." Lacey wet her lips with her tongue, suddenly feeling parched. "We have no actual proof that I'm the baby that was left at the bookstore." She sure wished she had the funds to hire a private investigator instead of playing amateur sleuth.

Bea touched her abdomen. "We're moving on gut instinct here, and even if nothing pans out on your behalf, we aren't hurting anyone by into digging into the bookstore-baby mystery."

"There's no written connection between Augustina Welch and the baby." Lacey shook her head. "Going to talk to this woman based on a hunch just doesn't make sense." They could hear the low hum of a motor getting louder as Mekhi approached.

"But it might make her day."

"How so?"

"Every old person I know loves to start conversations because they're lonely. They hang out in the checkout lines or toddle out to the beach in droves, just waiting for one of us to make eye contact or share a smile. And then it's on."

Lacey couldn't argue with that point. "I have regular chatters at the boutique. And they never buy anything." She relaxed her shoulders. "Okay, I feel better knowing that we might be doing a good deed keeping her company for a bit."

"Yeah, I think so too."

Mekhi zigzagged this way and that, handling the vacuum like it was an attack weapon. They scuttled out of his way.

"He's enjoying that way too much," Bea said, wryly. "The sand doesn't stand a chance."

Lacey giggled. "I agree."

"I'm all for a proper shower and change before going to see Mrs. Welch." Bea raked her fingers through her hair. "I need to give my hair a good wash."

"Great. That's what we'll do. I'll let Mekhi know, and then we can be on our way."

WELP. THEY WERE WRONG ON TWO COUNTS. FIRST, Augustina Welch wasn't ancient. She was stunning and appeared to be fifty, a retired supermodel.

Second, though she was friendly—letting them inside her stately home and offering them a slice of pineapple upside-down cake and Pellegrino—she didn't appear to be lonely or in need of conversation.

But she was bitter.

The minute Mekhi mentioned Declan Welch's name, her face contorted, and her tongue wagged. Twenty years hadn't softened her stringent feelings about her ex. It was like she was waiting to denounce him to anybody willing to listen, and

Lacey's and her friends' ears were open. "I don't care to know where that usurper is. Imagine coming home to find your husband and his lover asleep in your bed."

Enthralled, Bea gasped. Stunned, Lacey placed a hand over her mouth. Unconcerned, Mekhi stuffed his mouth with cake. He had his head buried in his phone. Smart man.

"Yeah, I filed for divorce faster than he could vacate my house. Unfortunately for him, I had a tight prenup. He left Eagle Point Beach with only the clothes on his back and that fancy car he drove around with like he was a Rockefeller."

"Good for you," Bea said, bobbing her head.

"Yep. I donated his clothes, his jewelry and his sneaker collection to charity."

Mekhi stopped munching. "Whoa, not his sneaker— " A cutting glare from Augustina made him shove another piece of cake in his mouth.

Another dead end. Maybe Lacey should just give up.

She had an overwhelming urge to cry, but she reminded herself that she did have a mother who loved her. No matter what, she had Shelby.

As she shuffled out of Augustina's home, Mekhi said, "I did find a small ad saying that a Declan Welch is going to be having an art show in New York."

Bea slipped an arm around Lacey's waist. "That could be promising."

"Humph. I don't want to get my hopes up."

"We can make a day of it and go see his art show," Mekhi said. "The best that could happen is that he is the Declan Welch that we are seeking, and if he's not, we can check out a Broadway show."

"Or go shopping," Bea said.

She shrugged. "It wouldn't hurt, I guess."

"I'll get us tickets to the art show," Mekhi said.

"And I'm happy to drive," Bea offered.

Lacey wiped at her tears. "You two are the best friends in the world."

LATER THAT NIGHT, LACEY AND MEKHI LAY ON THEIR backs, their faces to the sky, holding hands. Bea had driven to Ocean View to have dinner with her mother, and she would probably spend the night there, so it was just Lacey and Mekhi hanging out. Lacey would have curled within herself if Mekhi hadn't stuck by her side, setting up dinner picnic-style on his lawn and watching her with hawk eyes as she forced a slice of pizza down her throat. He had drawn her out with conversation around the summer's latest blockbusters.

Now they rested side by side, admiring the stars. There wasn't any other place that Lacey would rather be. She curved her body into his. "I don't want this evening to end."

He twisted to face her and played with a tendril of her hair, before framing it across her face. "It doesn't have to. You could stay with me tonight."

"What about your parents?" she asked.

His jaw jutted. "They are away. And even if they were home, they don't care what I do. I have the guesthouse all to myself." Underneath his gruff tone, she could hear the hurt and the loneliness. Her heart moved. Sometimes the people who seemed to have it all had very little. She thought again how she was grateful for her mother. Even though they were at odds about her searching for her bio family, she knew she was loved. Wanted.

Lacey reached out to cup his beautiful face. "I'd love to stay with you."

He smiled. "Awesome, and this is a no-pressure visit. I'm just glad for your company."

Sitting up, she brushed pizza dough crumbs off her skirt. "Have you thought about telling your parents how you feel?"

"I don't know if that would be a productive discussion."

"Because if it was me, I wouldn't hesitate to have a heart-to-heart with my mom."

Mekhi sat up as well and squared his shoulders. "They were attentive until I turned eighteen. Then it was like their job was done. They are now focused on each other. I don't mind, but even though I'm grown, I still value their opinions. I want a meaningful relationship with them. They act more like my managers than parents. I think it's because their own parents had control issues, and they don't want to do the same to me. So they check in to make sure I have all I need, and that's it."

"It sounds like every young man's dream."

He chuckled. "The reality is . . . lonely. Now, I'm not gonna lie. At first, I was living it up. Girls. Parties. Drinking. But it got tired fast, and I realized that I need something with . . ." he gave her a meaningful look ". . . substance."

Her face warmed. She moved her hand lower on his chest. His heart rate was a steady pump underneath her palm. "You sound like an old soul. Are you a vampire who has been twenty-one for a hundred years and you didn't tell me?"

His lips quirked. "I'm very much an old soul. And I'm very much human. My father taught me well. He's the antitype of what you think a football player's like. He treats my mother with so much respect and spoils her. They are best friends, and they like each other even after all these years together." There was a flash of lightning. Mekhi jumped to his feet and assisted her to stand. "One day I want what they have."

"So this is getting a little too deep for me." She looked down at her feet. "I'd like that too, but I'm not in a rush."

He took her hand in his and smiled. "Neither am I."

Her shoulders sagged in relief. "I'm glad we're on the same

page." They put their heads together, content to stay in that position and just be. At a crack of thunder, they jumped apart. Together, they gathered the blanket and the empty pizza box and arm in arm went into Mekhi's place.

Lacey and Mekhi camped out in his living room watching movies. He sat with his back against the couch. She settled between his legs with her head resting against his chest. Their conversations centered around which movies had the best on-screen kiss and coming up with new flavors for potato chips. Soon, her eyes began to flutter closed, and he lifted her in his arms and took her into his bedroom. They fell asleep wrapped in each other's arms.

When he'd said *no pressure*, he meant it. As the sun rose, she opened her eyes to see him looking at her. Covering her mouth, aware of morning breath, she asked, "How long have you been awake?"

"I've been up about five minutes. I already hit the bathroom and everything." He kissed her forehead, his breath minty and sweet. "Did you know you do this cute little snort when you're sleeping?"

She placed a hand on his bare chest. "There's nothing cute about snorting." He cracked up. She got out of bed, tossing a pillow at him.

She went into the bathroom to take care of her morning rituals, happy to see he had spare toothbrushes, loofahs, et cetera. Images of other girls who had spent the night gave her pause, but she shook it off. Whoever was before her was before her. She wouldn't be bothered by the past. Lacey had slept in one of Mekhi's T-shirts, which hung just above her knees. When she had brushed her teeth and combed her hair, Lacey went to stand beside him. He was now out of bed and looking out the huge sliding doors, which led to the swimming pool. There was a light breeze rustling the leaves, but all else was quiet. Peaceful.

Even though the sun was out, there were heavy dark clouds. "It looks like it's going to pour. I'd better get home."

"Stay?" he said, drawing her close.

Since she wasn't on schedule to work today, she nodded. "I swear this is the most grown-up relationship I have ever had."

Mekhi turned her around, his brows lifted high. "We're in a relationship?" He hugged her, and she folded her body into his.

"Well, what would you call this thing between us?"

"No arguments here. I'm all for a permanent Netflix-and-chill partner." He lowered his head and pressed his lips to hers. The kiss was as special as she thought it would be, and Lacey knew she never wanted it to end. Bea would not believe her when she told her that thunder had cracked on cue.

CHAPTER 23

Excerpt from That Was Then *by Jewel Stone*

~

June 30, 2005

Sugar

This pain was intense, like being gutted in the same part of your body a hundred times. It was as if she had fallen into an abyss and just kept falling and falling with no end in sight. Grief engulfed her, and survivor's guilt overwhelmed her.

Sugar couldn't look herself in the mirror of the tiny parlor room of the Eagle Point Funeral Home and Cremation Services. She shouldn't have chosen her friends over family. If she hadn't, she would have died with her parents. Then her world would be right. Because she had loved them. How she had loved them!

Yet for all the money in her bank account, she couldn't remember the last time she had told them that she loved them. All throughout the search and rescue, that was the question that plagued her mind. She had stood by the ocean and yelled, "Mommy, Daddy, Come back. Come back to me!" until her voice was hoarse, but the water remained calm, lapping at her feet.

The ocean refused to give up its dead, and eventually, without looking her in the eyes, the coast guards had mumbled, "I'm sorry for your loss," before their hasty retreat. Her parents' faces had been plastered across the screen, and then the entire nation sat riveted for news while they searched for any souls to rescue. Submarines, divers, hours . . . all for naught.

Now she was expected to be composed and memorialize them today. Down the hall, in the gathering space labeled *Room A*, were close to life-size portraits of her parents and a significant amount of the townspeople from Eagle Point Beach waiting for her to make an appearance.

Why were they even doing this? Holding a service? Her parents weren't here. Their bodies had been lost at sea. An unexpected waterspout had seen to that, tearing their yacht apart, making a mockery of its name, *Indomitable*, her mother's favorite word. That their bodies weren't located was the worst part. If only she could touch them and tell them how sorry she was for being spoiled and selfish, then maybe she could heal one day.

She had a meeting with her parents' estate attorney, Jeff Lundgren, right after the service. He'd said it was best to meet quickly since he was leaving the next day for his vacation. An acute reminder that even in the darkest hours, life kicked you in the face and then went on.

There was a rap on the door. It was probably Honey and Chance coming to check on her. Again. She released an exasperated breath. She wanted to yell at them to leave her alone, but she knew they meant well. Still, the words were a dam on the tip of her tongue and with the right push . . . She bunched her fists.

Behave yourself, Sugar, her father's voice whispered in her ear. *You better not show your shirttail at our funeral.*

But it wasn't a funeral. She smoothed her hands down her simple black dress, her only adornments a pearl necklace and pearl studs that had been her mother's and a watch that had been her father's.

The knock again. "Sugar? Are you in there?" Honey asked. Where else would she be? There was no hiding in this place. Nowhere to mourn in secret. "I'm worried about you. Please answer. The service is about to start, and everyone's asking for you." Honey's concern made anger flicker in her chest.

"Leave me alone, will you? I don't want to see anyone."

"Well . . . okay, I guess . . . I'm here if you need me." Sugar hardened her heart against the pain in Honey's voice. Her own pain was ten times that. And keeping away from her friend was better than telling her the truth. Sugar blamed Honey and Chance. If she hadn't been so caught up with them this summer, she would have spent more time with her parents.

Quit being surly, girl, and put a smile on that face.

But, Daddy, I'm tired of seeing the pity on their faces.

Smile and nod, dear daughter, smile and nod.

A harder rap this time, followed by a confident "Sugar? It's me. Let me in." Chance.

She rolled her eyes. "I want to be left alone." She leaned onto the marble sink. "I'm sorry. I don't mean to be nasty. I'm just—"

"It's okay, I know you're going through a lot. We understand. Honey and I. We love you. Come on out. We plan to each sit by your side."

Now the tears came. She was a horrible daughter and now a terrible friend. Here they were trying to be supportive, and she was being distant and churlish. She washed her face and went to unlock the door.

Two pairs of concerned eyes stared back at her, though Honey stood a few feet away from the door. "I don't know why you guys put up with me. My behavior is abominable."

"Because we love you," Honey said, coming to put an arm around her. Chance and Honey flanked her sides. She drew from their strength and somehow made it through the service, the fiery eulogy, the well wishes and the repast. The best part was hearing how much her parents had helped people, how much they had been respected and loved.

As her father would say, *Live how you would want to be written about on your tombstone.* She had wept so hard and blew her nose so much both her eyes and nose were brick-red.

A FEW HOURS LATER, SHE WAS ON HER OWN WHEN IT WAS time to meet with Jeff. He had reserved a meeting space at the law offices nearby. Honey and Chance would be waiting by the beach, and they would go out for black cherry ice cream when she was done. Well, Chance would have cookies and cream.

She walked into the small room five minutes earlier than her appointment time, squelching the resentment balled in her chest. She knew Jeff was only doing his job, but arranging their meeting right after such an emotional service bordered on heartless. So once he arrived and greeted her, she took a seat and let out a gritty, "Let's get on with it."

Jeff didn't mince words. "I'm sorry to be the bearer of bad news, but your parents mismanaged their funds—against my advice. I have an accounting degree and dabbled in investment banking." He made sure to point that out. Mr. High Achiever. It's not like her parents were here to counter what he was saying. "They took investment risks, which, had they paid off, would have made them very wealthy. But that didn't happen. So they were in grave financial straits."

"What does this mean?" she asked. "In everyday terms?"

"Their deaths don't erase their debts, unfortunately. So to clear up all that they owe, I recommend you downsize. Sell their assets. I've worked out a plan where you'll still end up with a healthy bank account to fund your college expenses." He leaned back in his chair. "After that, well, you'll be in a good position to get a job."

The reality of her new situation sank in. She gripped the chair to steady herself. She had heard the phrase *Life can change in an instant*, but in this case it wasn't for the better. It was earth-shattering. "Are you saying I'll have to sell my parents' home?" That idea was preposterous. She took short, choppy breaths. "I grew up there. It's the first house my father purchased when he came to this country."

"Yes. But I can connect you with a great realtor who will get you a fair price." That punctured her gut.

But this did explain why her parents had sold the bookstore to Ms. Brown last year, despite Sugar's protesting.

"What about our condo? It's paid in full. Can I keep that? I need somewhere to live when I'm not in school."

"Yes, but it is better off being used as collateral."

She gritted her teeth. His sympathetic tone did nothing to ease the fury raging insider her. She wanted to hurl and scream and yell at God, but this was not the time or place. So she bottled it up. "I need to see all the papers. I need to see everything in black and white."

"I'll do that. I'll need your signature, as their next of kin, before I can begin liquidating their assets."

"I'll sign once I've had a chance to review."

With their business concluded, Sugar left the office, drained and in need of another good cry. She sent Honey and Chance a quick text.

Sorry. Got caught up in something. Talk to you later.

Then she turned off her phone and drove to her parents' place.

Over the next few weeks, she stayed in her parents' home, sending variations of that text message and refusing to answer the door. Instead, all her efforts went into resolving her parents' financial woes and into her writing.

Her newest motivation, at the encouragement of her therapist, was to write her parents' love story. But even as she wrote page after page, nothing could cure the hole in her heart left by their absence. And the chasm widened with each passing day.

CHAPTER 24

Jewel
July 16, 2025

Honey watched as Sugar went up and down the stairs to her three-bedroom apartment above the bookstore with ease. "I can't believe the progress you've made in such a short time. I think Theo is a great motivator," she teased, waggling her brows.

"Stop. He's my physical therapist. Nothing more." Yet her cheeks were looking rosy.

"If you think so . . ." She put a hand to her chin. "I wonder what other kinds of therapy services he provides?"

"Quit it." Sugar giggled. "I'm glad to have migrated from the walker to the cane so quickly. Having *you* here has been good for my mental and physical health. There's nothing like a true friend to help you through life's toughest challenges."

Honey rested a hand on her heart. "Aww. I know if the situation was reversed, I could count on you above everyone else. That's the true meaning of friendship."

> Sugar smiled. "There's nothing we can't face together."
>
> Except the truth. The truth would definitely divide them.
>
> Speaking of truth, Honey had no idea how she was going to tell Winston that she had located his son's mother and planned to have a heart-to-heart with Janie, woman-to-woman.

Sitting behind a small desk by the window of Shelby's spare bedroom, Jewel reread the last paragraph several times. Something didn't sit well with her. She didn't know what, though, and she had spent the last twenty minutes trying to figure it out.

But she was in writing mode, so this was the time for getting her words down, finishing her draft. She would fix whatever was bugging her in her rewrite. Jewel inserted a comment to remind herself to revisit it later.

When she heard a voice behind her, she jumped, grabbing on to the edge of the desk to keep from falling out of her chair. Jewel slammed the laptop screen shut hard enough to crack it. She whispered a silent prayer that that was not the case.

"Oh, I'm sorry," Shelby said, coming farther into the room with her cane. Shelby had purchased a few in what she called her staple colors—purple, yellow and pink—with studs for bling. Today, she was dressed in a pair of yellow slacks and a colorful blouse, so she carried the yellow cane to match. She looked lovely and confident. "I was calling you to say that it was time to go, but you must have been really into your book." She eyed Jewel's laptop with curiosity.

They were going to try out to be movie extras in one of the scenes an hour away in Dover. Jewel had been excited when Francesca called to ask if she would be up for a cameo.

After letting out a scream to wake the roosters, she had asked if Shelby could be on as well.

However, they officially had to be approved by casting. And there was a good chance their scene could get cut, but they were too excited to care.

"Yeah, I've got a deadline, and I'm about to hit 250 pages. I'm in a zone," Jewel said, laughing to cover her jitteriness.

Jewel was dressed in all-white with rose pink accessories and shoes, so she would stand out even if she was in the background. That was for sure. She had been practicing her smile all morning. It was hard to act natural when there was a camera about, but she would try. Not that she hadn't been in front of a camera before—but that had been for her book tour. This was a movie. Two different things.

"I can't wait to see what you've written," Shelby said.

She tucked her laptop in her shoulder bag. Even though she was pretty sure she would be too busy to write, Jewel had to have it with her. Just in case.

"Don't you miss it?" she asked Shelby once they were on their way. She wished she could put the sunroof down, but she couldn't risk messing up their hair.

"Miss what?"

"Writing."

"Funny you should ask, because I was thinking about it other day." Shelby glanced out the window briefly. "Seeing you tapping away at the keyboard is inspiring me." She smiled at Jewel. "You are inspiring."

Jewel shifted in her seat. She didn't deserve that compliment, and this was a good time for her to divulge the truth about what she was writing. But she found herself hesitating. She would hate to see Shelby's admiration turn to disgust. Why jeopardize their friendship when it was already so fragile?

Because Shelby would read this novel. And it would look

weird if Jewel kept hiding it from her. Shelby, however, dropped a piece of news that blew her topic into the wind.

"Do you remember that novel I wrote all those years ago?"

"Um . . . I think so."

"You probably forgot," Shelby said, tucking an errant curl behind her ear.

She braved a quick glance Shelby's way. "What about it?"

"I printed it off and got it spiral-bound, but I haven't done anything else—yet. It's in my nightstand right along with my flash drive." She cleared her throat. "What do you think about me dusting off that old manuscript?" Shelby gave a self-conscious laugh. "Ridiculous, right?"

"No. No. You have a gift. You know that." Jewel poked a finger toward her chest. "You know better than anybody else that I truly know that."

"Yes, but it's been a while. Writing is a muscle. What if I've lost it?"

"Are you serious? That's an incorrect analogy. Writing is like riding a bike. You just have to get back on and pedal. Or in this case, put your butt in the chair and get to writing. Er, revising, since you already have a draft."

Shelby squeezed her arm. "You are such a cheerleader. I'll think about it."

"What's there to think about? That book was good. Unlike me, writing came easy for you. Shoot, if you don't want it, I'll take it." Jewel gave a little laugh.

"Nah, once was enough, don't you think?" Shelby said. Her voice was light, but Jewel knew there was an undertone of seriousness. Shelby wasn't going to have Jewel take credit for her work twice.

"Ha ha. You know I'm messing with you." Now she knew for sure, Shelby wouldn't agree with Jewel writing about their reunion story. And just like that, she knew what had been bugging her earlier about the last paragraph she had written. Roman wouldn't be happy about her dumping their personal business in her novel. And he read her books. He would be so hurt to discover she had used his situation with his son as a storyline. Her stomach cramped, and her heartbeat thundered in her ears. What was she going to do? Both Francesca and her editor loved the pages. Jewel wiped her brow. Her upper lip was now sweating. She bumped up the AC, though that did nothing to soothe the guilt boiling in her veins.

But she couldn't back out now.

There was the matter of her sister's hospital bills, plus Roman still hadn't secured employment. Jewel's account was fat again, and her savings had a healthy balance, but if anything happened to Hazel, that would deplete her stash in no time. She had to keep churning out the books.

As soon as she finished this one, she would have to start another. And there was one sitting all pretty and ready to send in Shelby's nightstand. The temptation to have a look-see at it was strong. But it was one she would resist.

"If you need me to refer your book to my agent, I'd be happy to do that," she said, softly. "It's not like Francesca hasn't read your work before." Those words hung between them.

But Shelby only fussed with her hair. "I'll give it some thought."

She pressed her point home. "People are pursuing their dreams and getting published in their sixties and seventies. Do you need examples?"

"No. Point taken. I'll start tinkering with my book."

"I like that plan."

"New topic." The sun's rays were blocking her view. She adjusted her visor. "Now that you are doing better, does that leave you free to explore a possible relationship with Kendrick?"

"Let me out of here." Shelby made a show of trying to get out of the car before she said, "I don't think that's a good idea.

I'm pretty sure that's an ethical violation for him. And he's a good physical therapist. If things went sour, it would make for awkward sessions."

"But it won't matter once he's finished."

"You just want to see me settled so we can take those trips we always wanted without me being a third wheel."

"Correction. Roman would be the third wheel. Kendrick would make a good travel partner while we're shopping or at the spa."

"You're a mess." Shelby chuckled. "I can't with you. But the answer is *no*. Kendrick is a nice guy, and nice guys tend to be nice to everyone. I decided not to interpret anything he says or does as more."

"For the record, I think you are wrong. That man is interested, and you are keeping him at a distance."

"How would you know that? Have you been listening in on our PT sessions?"

"Yes. And he's flirting, but you're cool as a cucumber, as your father used to say."

Shelby cracked up. "That was one of Daddy's favorite phrases."

"I'm just saying, let the man take you out somewhere other than the perimeter of the bookstore. You might surprise yourself and have fun."

"If you've been listening, then you know he hasn't officially asked me out."

"Poor excuse." She slapped the wheel. "You go ahead and ask him out. And make sure you tell me all about it."

Her conscience taunted her. *So you can put it in your book?*

CURLED ON HER SIDE IN BED THAT NIGHT, JEWEL SCROLLED through her social media pages to check out fan reactions to her posts about being on set this afternoon. They were eating it up. It had been a fun day, but acting was exhausting—even though she was just in the background. Once they'd returned to Shelby's place, she had trudged up the stairs, eager to shower and sleep.

Now dressed in a plush robe, she was sure sleep would come easily tonight.

Tomorrow night would be her second signing for Shelby. She planned to do a book talk and host a few giveaways open to all who purchased a copy of her book from Shelby's bookstore. She just had to decide on what to give.

She tapped her chin then snapped her fingers. Maybe a few gift cards and a certificate for a spa day. That should be perfect. She made her purchases then rested a hand under her head and continued perusing the fan comments.

One particular name stood out that made her sit up in bed. Katrina Morrison. *Oh my goodness!* Roman's baby mama had liked one of her posts. Katrina was a fan? Hmm . . . highly unlikely. More like Katrina was low-key stalking her pages. Not that Jewel had anything to say about that when she had done the same. It appeared as if they had mutual curiosity about each other. She shook her head. What were the odds that she would even have spotted Katrina's name among the other admirers?

Nothing but God.

Jewel pulled up Katrina's profile. She was stunning with her olive skin tone and curly tresses, and her husband was well-groomed. There were a couple pictures of them with Curtis, but they weren't recent. She zoomed in on Curtis's features. There was definitely a resemblance to Roman, but they would need a DNA test to confirm his paternity.

On a whim, Jewel decided to DM Katrina.

> Hey. I'd love to have a conversation woman-to-woman if you're up to it.

Her fingers felt clammy, and her heart raced while she waited to see if Katrina would accept her message request and reply. Almost immediately she saw **That can be arranged. Just you?**

Good. Jewel was glad to see Katrina wasn't being coy about why she had reached out. Still, Jewel hadn't expected it to be so easy, especially since Katrina had moved to a whole other state to get away from Roman. She hadn't even responded to Roman's attempts at communication. But Jewel wasn't going to think too much about that. She would go with the flow and see where it took her.

Roman won't be there but maybe I'll bring a friend.

Hmm . . . When and where?

How about Maggiano's in Philly for lunch?

It took some back-and-forth but they settled on a date in the middle of the week.

I'm not making any promises. But I'll be there.

Fair enough.

See you then.

A few seconds later, Katrina wrote, **I really am a fan of your work. That's why I liked your page.**

Jewel bit the inside of her cheek. Now, how was she supposed to answer to that? She didn't want to offer signed copies of her books and have Katrina think she was trying to bribe her . . . So instead, she just typed, **Thanks LOL**

Dropping her phone on the bed, Jewel debated whether

or not to tell Roman. Just as quickly, she decided not to. She didn't want him to interpret this as Katrina being ready for him to be a part of Curtis's life. And she also didn't want him nagging her about it because she could see him pressing her for details during the lunch meeting. Plus, for all Jewel knew, Katrina could really be a fan and just interested in meeting her.

Either way, the door had opened a crack, and she had to slip through it. Hopefully, Jewel was prepared for whatever was on the other side. But at the very least, meeting Katrina would give her insight on creating a new angle to Honey's storyline and a chance to introduce tension between Honey and Winston. Because those two were so sweet they were corny. Unlike the real world, tension was a necessary tool in fiction if you wanted an unputdownable read. And that was what she wanted, even if it meant playing nice with Roman's ex to achieve it.

CHAPTER 25

Shelby
July 18, 2025

After a great final therapy session with Denise at the hospital earlier that morning—where Shelby had a shorter crying fest, which for her was progress—her cast was removed.

Yippee! Hurray! Because it had begun to itch like nobody's business, which Kendrick had insisted was a good sign. In addition, her ribs had healed nicely, and the doctor had told her she could ditch the medical brace. As they pulled up to the bookstore, Kendrick, who seemed to have been pacing the curb for some time, came over to her passenger door. She was still seated in the car with only her legs hanging outside.

"Now, remember, your ankle is still healing, so you want to be careful with your foot. Don't get all extra with it," Kendrick said, though he was all smiles. And if her heart did a little skip at those beaming amber eyes, she wasn't ready to admit that to anyone, especially not herself.

"I know, but I'm dying to actually walk up those stairs."

"In due time. In due time."

She inspected her foot, moving it gently this way and that. "My leg is a little swollen." Jewel got out the driver's side to get Shelby's walker. She plopped it next to Kendrick before waggling her eyebrows at them. Shelby gave her a pointed look, and with a chuckle, Jewel went inside.

"Yes, that's to be expected." He squatted and took her leg in his hand. His hands were so gentle. "We're going to work together to increase your mobility and activity on your feet because you've definitely lost some muscle."

"Do you still think I'll ride again?" She had played that video on repeat, and it was a definite motivator. Plus, it was her chance to hang with Kendrick as an equal rather than as a client. She had worn a baby doll dress so she could see her calf. It swayed with her movements.

"Most definitely." His confidence boosted hers. "We'll be riding side by side in no time."

Dang. That sounded suggestive, but he was one of those nice guys who you weren't sure if they were being friendly or flirting. It was better to take the cautious route. She shielded her eyes with her hands to peer up at him. "I'm going to hold you to that."

"Go ahead." He helped her stand. And though she felt good, he made her go slow. "You'll regret it later if you don't."

"It kind of feels funny."

He held her waist. "It'll take time. You'll be back to normal before you know it."

"How long?" She gritted her teeth.

"A few weeks."

"Geesh. Remind me never to get into an accident again."

"Ha ha. You gave me—" he coughed "—well, you gave the team quite a scare. I've been providing them with updates on your progress. I hope that's okay."

"Yes, and please let them know I appreciated the plant they sent. I do plan to set it in the backyard once I'm back on my feet. Every time I look at it, I'll remember what I've been through and that I'm here to talk about how I overcame it." Kendrick hummed the tune to "We Shall Overcome," making her giggle. "You are so funny."

"Laughter is therapeutic. I find that having a sense of humor really helps my clients' progress."

Oh . . . So his demeanor wasn't just for her. It was a part of his efforts to help her recover. Noted. She kept her tone light. "Well, it is working." And then some . . . but he needn't be privy to that part. This crush of hers would taper off in time. It was juvenile really for a woman of forty to be nursing a crush on her physical therapist. How cliché was that? At least, that's what she had to tell herself in the hope the flutters caused by his presence would diminish. No success so far, though. Ah well, it would fade in time. Meanwhile, she would be all business.

For the next twenty minutes, Shelby did such a good job at distancing herself mentally that she caught Kendrick giving her questioning looks. But she feigned ignorance. Kendrick didn't leave until he was sure she would be able to maneuver around safely.

"I'll be back tomorrow," he said with a wave.

"That man is putting in some serious overtime," Jewel said, strutting down the stairs. She plopped into the armchair across from where Shelby was situated.

"You think so?" she asked in mock surprise.

"I know so for sure."

"Hmm . . . Maybe it's because he wants me ready to join the cycling team in time for competition."

"Ah. Okay, that's how you're playing it."

Shelby shrugged. She refused to pick up this conversation thread. Kendrick was a loose end who would get snipped when this was all over. Something else she told herself as a matter of self-preservation.

Jewel fanned her face with her hand. "Does it feel hot in here, or is it me?"

"I am feeling warm, but I thought it was because I was

overexerting myself." All of a sudden, a stifling heat hit her face. She struggled to catch her breath. It was so hot she could taste it.

"Do you want me to check the thermostat?" Jewel asked, her brow lined with sweat.

"Would you?" Shelby usually kept the bookstore at about sixty-eight degrees, which was in the range of the ideal temperature for books. *Please don't let it be the HVAC.* They had had three days of intense heat, which could have blown her unit. It was well over twenty years old, and though her records indicated she had kept up with the yearly maintenance, old was old. According to the paperwork she'd been going through, she'd needed to update her appliances last year.

Jewel returned. The look on her face said it all. "The thermostat is set to Cool but all the vents I checked are blowing hot air. I turned it off." She had her phone in hand. "I'm going to see if I can get a HVAC tech to come out today."

Shelby was pretty positive she was going to need a whole new unit. If that was the case, she'd have to do a payment plan. She wasn't worried about securing a loan: she had the credit to do so. The problem was that if the terms were for three to five years, the bookstore could fold before then and she would still be paying for it.

Jewel's second signing the night before had been an even bigger success than the first, so hopefully those events would help with her bottom line. Though, if the AC wasn't fixed by then, they might have to cancel.

It had to be at least ninety-five degrees in here. In the short time they'd been here, the temperature had already risen another several degrees. There was no point in opening the windows, as it was just as hot outside. "I'm going to close the bookstore today." She fretted. That would create a dent in her profits, and the books could get heat-damaged, which would be a major setback to her business.

Shelby called Abby to inform her of the mishap and to assure the young woman that she was still going to get paid. As she wrapped up that call, Jewel bounced into the room and gave her a thumbs-up.

"Someone will be here before the end of the day."

"Thanks."

"Happy to help." She cocked her head. "Do you want to grab brunch in the meantime? They said they would text when they are about fifteen minutes away, so there are plenty of places we could go."

"There's a mom-and-pop diner about a block over I've been meaning to check out."

"Yes, let's do that. I'm definitely ready to eat."

Once she was back in Jewel's car and the AC was on full blast, an idea occurred to her. "Why don't you leave the key under the mat? I can always tell them how to get in." Jewel reared her head back and looked at her as if she had sprouted a unicorn horn. Shelby chuckled. "This is still very much a small town, or are you too bougie now to remember that? It'll be all right."

"Um, this isn't about being bougie," Jewel said. "It's about protecting your assets. It's one thing to hide keys in case you get locked out. It's another to tell a stranger where it is and have them let themselves in."

"It's fine. I do it all the time."

"Okay, if you're cool with it." Jewel dashed out of the car, glancing around furtively before tucking the key under the welcome mat. Then she tiptoed back to the car. She was dressed in a white shirt, black capris and heels, so walking like that would just attract more attention, but Shelby decided not to tease her about it.

As soon as Jewel slammed the door, Shelby patted her arm. "It's so good having you here. I'm loving every moment." Shelby didn't know where that sentimental feeling had come from, but she had faced death. She wasn't going to hold her tongue when she felt the unction to express her feelings.

For a second, Jewel looked . . . guilty? She opened her mouth like she was about to say something, but her phone rang just as she was about to respond. She held up a hand and said, "Hang on. That's my agent," then accepted the call, before turning down the volume in the car.

"Hey, Francesca. I'm in the car right now with a friend, so I can't really talk book right now." She gave Shelby a pensive look before turning away.

Shelby frowned. Now, what was that about? Why would Jewel be uncomfortable talking about the book around her? Come to think of it, Jewel had been real quiet whenever she had asked about it. Besides giving a generic *It's another book about friends and all their shenanigans*, she hadn't been forthcoming with the storyline at all. Maybe she was struggling and didn't want Shelby to know. That could be it. She could offer to help . . .

"Oh, this is not about your work in progress. This is about *That Was Then*. I received word that in addition to your consulting on the series, the network is definitely granting you executive producer rights for the duration of the series."

That news jarred Shelby out of her introspection.

"Ayeee!" Jewel yelled, doing a jig with her hands in the air.

Shelby pumped her fists and shook her shoulders. "Go, Jewel!"

Francesca cracked up. "Enjoy your friend. We'll talk soon."

"Wait! Did they secure a location for the bookstore scenes yet?" Jewel asked.

"Yeah. We were thinking of Books and Bevs in Dover, Delaware. It's Black-owned, and there's been a lot of buzz about it."

Jewel tapped the wheel. "That sounds good. But my friend

owns a bookstore that sits on the beach, and it matches to a T what I imagined for some of the scenes."

"Hmm . . . Okay, we'll work out the logistics. I'll keep you posted."

When the call ended, the friends hugged and rocked. "Your show might put the bookstore on the map!" Shelby squealed.

"Again . . ." Jewel sobered, hunkering down into her seat. "I didn't think of that."

"*That* has nothing to do with this. It's been twenty years."

"It's still an interesting backstory. Interesting enough to make the news. Bring attention to the baby on the beach all over again. People might start wondering what happened to her." She was now tapping the wheel at rapid speed. "I wasn't thinking this through all the way. I was focused on the now and helping you."

"And that's all it will be. One has nothing to do with other," Shelby said, even though it felt like horses were galloping inside her chest. With so many threads intertwined, it would be easy for her past and present to collide. She couldn't risk Lacey learning the truth. A chill ran up her spine, and it wasn't because of the temperature in the car.

"I'll reach out to Francesca and nix the idea."

Disappointment the size of a boulder crushed Shelby's good mood. There went a magnificent opportunity to get her store in the black. Their actions of the past had far-reaching consequences.

Jewel rubbed her yes. "I've got to say I'm getting tired of the pretense." She sound exhausted and burdened with regret. Exactly the way Shelby felt.

"Yes. I am drained. This deception is a never-ending, no-bio-break juggling act." Shelby grasped Jewel's hand. "I just learned about Lacey again, and it's taxing me. How on earth did we keep this secret this long?"

"I admit, it came with a steep price. One that I'm not sure is even worth paying anymore. But we've come too far down these tracks to turn back now. Might as well keep chugging along."

AN HOUR LATER, THEY WERE SIPPING ON SWEET TEA when the AC company called to tell her she would need a new HVAC system. They would replace the entire ductwork system as well, all for the bargain price of twenty-seven thousand dollars. Shelby closed her eyes and told them to go ahead and do the install. Then she went into her bank app to apply for a loan.

Jewel stilled. "I'll help you with the payments." Before Shelby could protest, she lifted her hand. "Don't try to talk me out of it."

"I have no idea how I'll even be able to pay you back."

"I know how you can." She gave a sad smile. "How do you feel about taking a road trip with me?"

"Where are you trying to go?"

"Philly."

The implication of that location made Shelby lock eyes with Jewel. "Have you reached out to Katrina?"

"I did, and I was shocked when she responded. We're supposed to meet up for lunch at Maggiano's near the convention center."

"Their food is delicious. It's been a minute since I've been to Philly. I'll happily be your ride or die. Wherever you're going, you can count me in."

"Road besties." They fist-bumped.

Shelby drummed her fingers on the table. "Your bravery is inspiring. In fact . . ." She held up a finger and then picked up her phone. Ignoring her rapidly beating heart, she pulled up Kendrick's contact information and showed it to Jewel.

"Are you going to ask him out?" Jewel's eyes flashed before she giggled.

"Yes." Gathering her courage, she hit the Call button. The phone rang as loudly as her heart was pumping in her chest.

As soon as he answered, she blurted out, "Would like to go out with me?"

He paused. "On a date?"

"Well, it doesn't have to be if you're uneasy with the idea." She straightened. "We can just be two friends going out to share a meal."

Jewel pursed her lips and rolled her eyes. Shelby lifted her shoulders.

"Yes, I'd love to go on a date or not-date with you. Whatever you're comfortable with," he said. "Now, we should wait until you're much stronger, and I don't want you injuring yourself, but . . ."

Seeing Jewel dancing in her seat, Shelby moved the phone from her ear to join in before returning to her call. Since she was too excited to fully register all his words, she said, "We'll finalize the details and all that the next time you come over." Wow, she sounded breathy. And eager. And she didn't care.

Because she was going out with Kendrick.

"Go, Shelby," Jewel said after she'd hung up the phone, mimicking a roping motion. "Get it, girl."

"Yeehaw!" Placing a hand over her mouth, she said, "I can't believe I just did that."

"I can. Now we'll have to add a third stop on our excursion."

She lifted a brow.

"You've just snagged a cool brother, and it's time to up the cuteness overload. Let's go shopping at the outlets in Rehoboth Beach."

Shelby frowned. "But that's the opposite direction of where we're going. We would be driving from one end of Delaware to the next."

"Good point. We'll pivot and hit up the stores in Philly instead."

Once again Shelby held out her fist. "It's on. Road besties in effect."

"Road besties in effect."

July 18, 2025

Kendrick has been talking about my return to cycling in a month or even sooner, but I don't know if I'll ever get on a bike again. Right now, the only kind of transportation I trust are my own two feet. And I'm not at one hundred percent yet. But I'm getting there.

We decided to go to the Peach Festival. It's held the first Saturday in August, rain or shine. I'm excited about it, but I keep reminding myself that it's a date, not a relationship.

JOURNAL ENTRY

April 7, 2016

Dear Diary,
The gap between entries has been so long, to comment on it would be an embarrassment, so I won't, though I suspect I just did?! Yesterday was Lacey's tenth birthday party, and since she was in a new school, she wanted to invite all the girls in her class for a Cinderella makeover party. I took her to see the movie a year ago, and she has been hooked ever since. So the plan was that we would sponsor up to fifteen girls to get mani-pedis, make jewelry and do a photo shoot at Sweet & Sassy in New Jersey since there wasn't one in Delaware.

Well, that was a success. Nine girls showed up, and a good time was had by all. But on the way back, the driver we hired got a flat tire in the middle of a downpour. Little missy tried to go out in all that rain to help! She is so tenderhearted and kind. Being with her is worth everything and anything I went through to get here.

I have pictures. I have receipts.
Yep, this is my life.
And I am loving it!

September 7, 2016

Dear Diary,
No one tells you how tired you become with motherhood. It's not about you anymore. While the world is celebrating Jewel's success with That Was Then, *I need a round of applause for getting out of bed to*

pick Lacey up from school while fighting a massive allergy and sinus attack.

I've also begun having full-length dreams about Lacey discovering the truth about who she is and her previous connection to me. I've developed real anxiety about this, and I've practiced several scenarios in my mind. Do I tell her now when she is young and unable to grasp the magnitude of my actions? Or do I wait until she is older and confess everything, then throw myself at her feet and beg for understanding?

This all started because she had to do research on all the members of her family, and she made the offhand comment that sometimes she wonders who she resembles. My stomach burned because I know the answer. I know it, but I dare not tell. The fallout is too great a risk, for me, for her. And HER.

Lacey can never know. I have to do all I can to keep her from learning the truth. But I wrote the teacher a scathing note about the lack of sensitivity to children who had traumatic upbringings. Having her fill out this tree was inhumane, I said, and how is this even grade-appropriate? Tagged the principal on it too. Assignment waived. Problem averted . . . for now.

August 8, 2018

Lacey wrote a Dear God letter for her mother today and asked me to proofread it and check her commas. She then asked me for a stamp so she could mail it to the adoption agency. I hid the letter in my closet, the same place where I keep this journal.

My heart broke. I haven't cried like that in years. I have a feeling Lacey isn't going to drop this.

CHAPTER 26

Shelby
July 20, 2025

The early bird catches the worm. How many times had she heard her father say that? And how many times over the years had he been right?

Countless.

That was why, when Jewel flipped their plans to go shopping first at the Fashion District in Philadelphia, Shelby had been quick to agree. They would get there just as it opened, find her an outfit and then walk over to Maggiano's. Parking shouldn't be an issue at that time, and if it was they could always park at the convention center.

Everything was within walking distance, and Shelby was quite all right with walking short distances. She needed continued muscle strengthening and craved the exercise. They entered the Kate Spade store. From the looks of it, there was a huge sale.

Her two favorite words: *sale* and *discount*. They were already making room for fall, so all the summer wear was on clearance. "Ooh, I'm going to rack-up."

"There's nothing like some retail therapy to boost our spirits," Jewel said. "So that no matter what happens at lunch, this trip will have been a success."

"I agree."

Together, they scouted through the stacks and channeled their inner *Pretty Woman* by trying on different outfits. With every *This is cute* and *Check this out*, their must-have pile grew.

An hour later, they walked out of the store, each carrying a large bag. Shelby's foot ached a little, but the total on her receipt made it all worth it. She had saved a bundle, and she had quite a few outfits to choose from for her not-date with Kendrick.

Since they had a few minutes to spare, they decided to drop their purchases in Jewel's trunk before going to the restaurant.

"This was so much fun," Shelby said. "It felt good to splurge on myself today."

"It's good to treat yourself. Sometimes we women can get so caught up in a cycle of paying bills, taking care of our family and working, working, working that we forget to reward ourselves."

"I'm so glad you said that," Shelby said and chuckled, "because though it felt good, I was feeling guilty about it."

"Rebuke that feeling," Jewel advised. "The second signing was a success, and things are looking up at the bookstore. Treating yourself is necessary. It's a form of mindfulness. There's something about slipping into a new outfit when you're going someplace you've never been that boosts your psyche. At least, that's how it is with me."

"I agree." She exhaled then shifted topics. "One thing I can't wait to do is hit the water at the beach. I've been dying to get my feet wet." When she was younger, she used to be in the water for hours.

"That is something we have to fix right away." Jewel nodded. "First thing tomorrow morning, we are hitting the waves."

"Great. I'll set my alarm."

Jewel

Jewel made sure to sit facing the entrance so she could see Katrina arrive.

Shelby sat to her right, and when the door swung open and Katrina entered, Jewel reached for her hand. "I can't remember the last time I was this nervous," she whispered. "Do you think this was a good idea?" She took a sip of her water to calm her nerves.

"Don't you think it's a little too late to ask that?" Shelby gave her hand a squeeze. "It's all good. This isn't an episode of *Real Housewives*. There will be no name-calling or wig-pulling. Just three grown women having a chat." Katrina scanned the room and gave a small wave when she spotted them. The server grabbed a menu before gesturing to Katrina to follow.

"I don't have a wig to pull, and judging by those curls, I'd say Katrina doesn't either." Releasing short staccato breaths, Jewel forced a smile on her face as Katrina followed the server through the crowded restaurant. It was just a few minutes past noon, and the restaurant was packed.

"She's tall," Shelby murmured.

"And beautiful."

"I love what she's wearing." Katrina was in a mustard form-fitting dress accessorized with gold jewelry and a pair of Chucks.

"Me too."

"But Roman leveled up with you."

Jewel cackled. "Thanks for your loyalty, but I'm not threatened. I'm too secure with myself and my husband to be worried about all that. I feel good knowing that Roman has excellent taste, at least when it comes to her physical beauty. Hopefully, she's the same on the inside. That's what I'm counting on."

When Katrina was a few feet away, both Shelby and Jewel stood to greet her. The women settled around the table right around the time the appetizers arrived, and Katrina ordered a seltzer water.

"I ordered truffle garlic bread and zucchini fritte for appetizers," Jewel said. "I hope that's fine."

"Oh yes," Katrina said, clasping her hands together. "The garlic bread here is delicious."

The women then placed their orders for lunch. Each had a salad. Katrina chose the mozzarella alla Caprese, Shelby ordered the Italian tossed salad, and Jewel went with the chopped salad minus the bacon.

Once the server left, Katrina said to Jewel, "Your author pics don't do you justice. You're even more beautiful in person." She spared Shelby a glance. "Both of you." The large diamond studs in her ears twinkled under the lights. Katrina wasn't hurting for cash, that was for sure. In fact, according to Jewel's online searches, her husband Scott was a trauma surgeon, and Katrina worked as a home organizer for major celebrities.

"Thank you," Shelby said, reaching for a piece of garlic bread.

See now, this woman was going to make Jewel like her. Jewel smiled. "I'm glad you agreed to come."

"Right up until an hour ago, I thought about backing out of our plans, but I know in my heart this was the right thing to do."

She wanted to ask why Katrina didn't feel that way about communicating with Roman, but Jewel reminded herself she wasn't here for a confrontation and she should stay focused on the end goal. And she stuffed a zucchini fritte in her mouth to keep her unruly tongue occupied.

"So Jewel tells me you're a fan of her work," Shelby said to Katrina.

"Oh yes, I'm a major fan. I have read all your books. I connected with Sugar and Honey so well. It was like you were reading my mind. I know this might not be a popular opinion, but Chance was just so dreamy. I would have been happy if he had ended up with either of them." She locked eyes with Jewel. "Are your books based on real life?"

Jewel's and Shelby's eyes met. "Some," she hedged. Luckily their salads arrived, sparing Jewel from having to explain. Or lie.

Katrina used her fork to grab a piece of mozzarella. "In reading your book, I feel like you might understand my actions, even if you don't agree." Her voice hitched. "I don't think you would judge me if you heard the truth."

"Trust me, we're the last people who would judge anybody by their mistakes." Shelby stabbed into her bowl a few times to capture a little bit of everything on her fork before stuffing her mouth. "This is good."

"What's going on?" Jewel asked. She had yet to pick up her fork.

Katrina averted her gaze. "I thought I was pretty hot stuff back when I dated Roman. I fancied myself a wannabe groupie. A little after Roman and I got together, I met Scott at a concert. I thought Roman was so boring. His idea of a date was for us to study together, which made my mother love him. Meanwhile, I wanted to party. So when I met Scott, he had that hint of danger that I was looking for. He was edgy and everything my mother would disapprove of, which made him so desirable to me. Before I knew it, I was seeing them both."

"Girl, were you trying to have your cake and eat it too?" Shelby asked.

"I guess." Katrina snorted. "Like I said, I just knew I was all that and then some. But to be on the safe side, I told Roman that Scott was just a friend." She lowered her lashes, having the grace to look ashamed. "He trusted me."

Jewel ate some of her salad to keep from defending her

hubby. Roman's stability was actually what drew her to him. But she supposed that was because her life was so unstable that she needed the kind of security that Roman gave. Still did. He was her rock. Whatever. Katrina's loss was her gain.

"But then I got pregnant." Her shoulders slumped. "And I was in shock. I knew how babies were made, but I never imagined I would get caught out there like that."

"We never think it could happen to us," Shelby said lightly.

"I imagine you had to be scared," Jewel offered.

"Very. But the pregnancy slapped me into adulthood, and I made a tough decision. I chose Scott because regardless of his antics, he was brilliant. Top of his class. But most importantly, my heart somersaulted around him. I just knew he was the one. I told myself that Scott had to be my child's father. I wouldn't allow myself to think otherwise. So I told Scott about the pregnancy. To my surprise and my heart's delight, he was thrilled. Despite how young we were, he asked me to marry him." She lowered her lashes. "We got hitched at the justice of the peace, and I left Delaware. I couldn't chance running into Roman."

"You were desperate," Jewel whispered.

"We understand desperation," Shelby mumbled.

"Yes. I didn't tell either man that I had been with someone else. I didn't want to hurt Roman, and I didn't want Scott to view me as less-than. If he left me, it would have crushed me. But it wasn't until I got pregnant and knew that I would lose him if I told him the truth that I realized how much Scott meant to me." She looked at Jewel. "Not that Roman isn't great . . ."

Jewel held up a hand. "You don't have to tell me that. I live with him. I know it. He just wasn't great for you."

Katrina straightened. "Yeah. That's it. That's it."

"So did you have any regrets?" Shelby asked.

"Plenty. Countless times over the years, I'd have nightmares of Roman finding out and Scott leaving me. I've walked around with this guilt for years. Sometimes I can't even look myself in the mirror. I think that's why I have avoided talking with Roman when he's reached out. I genuinely don't know what to say to him that is going to make up for what I did."

"Secrets can eat away at you," Shelby said, sympathetic. Jewel knew she was thinking of their situation with Lacey, but she couldn't let their guilt over that situation interfere with her purpose for this conversation. This was about Roman and Curtis.

Jewel cocked her head. "What about your son?" she dared to ask.

"What about Curtis?"

"Have you thought about how he would feel if the truth came out?" Jewel could feel the heat of Shelby's eyes on her, but she kept her gaze pinned on Katrina.

"I think he would be hurt and confused. He idolizes his father. I can't have Curtis questioning his identity when he is at the crux of manhood. That would be cruel, I think. I've kept this secret for sixteen years, and I'll keep it for another sixteen years if I have to."

"You're not thinking about Curtis or Scott or Roman," Jewel countered. "You're thinking about you. The damage this revelation would do to you. The impact it would have on your cushy lifestyle as the wife of a trauma surgeon."

"Why do you say that?" Katrina asked, frosty, folding her arms across her chest.

"Because if you were truly thinking of Curtis, you would get the DNA test. You wouldn't want your son to ever even have a hint of doubt about who he is. So though you think this isn't about you, the truth is you're thinking about yourself. You don't want to mess with your status quo." Her words were harsh, but her tone was gentle, and yes, there was no denying that this was a pot-and-kettle situation. But their truth came with the risk of a prison term. Katrina's didn't.

Shelby reached over to take Katrina's hand. "The truth is never easy. But in the end, it's freeing."

Not for us, Jewel wanted to say.

Tears welled in Katrina's eyes. "I don't want my son to hate me. I don't want him to see—"

"That you're human?" Jewel interjected. "You were young and scared. Allow yourself some grace." She leaned forward. "Please say you'll do the DNA test. Roman is gutted about this."

"I—I'm sorry." Katrina shook her head and stood. "I can't. I can't." Then she dashed out of the restaurant before either Jewel or Shelby could say another word.

"Well, that didn't go the way I hoped it would," Jewel said.

"No, but the seed is planted, and it will take root. She'll come around. You'll see."

CHAPTER 27

╮

Lacey
July 20, 2025

DECLAN WELCH. His name was engraved in all caps with gold ink against a black plaque. Standing at the entrance of the exhibit hall in the Chelsea district, Lacey ran a finger over the letters that had been crafted with such detail, such precision, like they had been penned by Picasso himself.

Mekhi and Bea stood to the side, waiting patiently for her to step around the corner. She finally moved, and they traipsed down the narrow corridor single file and stopped in front of a watercolor painting titled *Sea Gull*. The hushed whispers of the other patrons floated over to where they stood.

Bea had been set to drive all the way to the city, but Mekhi suggested they get tickets for the Rockledge Bus and that they spend the night before heading home the next day. So Bea had driven up to Wilmington, and they had caught the 2:15 p.m. bus at Market Street. Before coming to the gallery, they had grabbed something to eat.

"It's beautiful," Bea said.

Mekhi nodded. "He's talented."

By tacit consent, the trio continued through the exhibit, impressed with each of the displays. But it was the last, *The Beach*, 2005, a painting of a nude woman with her face hidden, that evoked a visceral reaction within her. For one thing, Lacey knew that setting—Eagle Point Beach—and this had been painted the summer before her birth. This didn't feel like a coincidence. The hands, round at the palms with long digits, looked like hers. The hair on her arms rose. There could only be one conclusion. She was that baby. The baby left at the bookstore all those years ago.

Bea wandered off to mingle while Mekhi hovered close, though he seemed content to let her mull over her thoughts for a bit. Which she appreciated. She gestured for him to come closer.

"Do you see the year?" she whispered to Mekhi.

He took her hand. "Yes."

"Could this be . . ." She drew in a deep breath. Her eyes welled. "Could this be my mother?" Was she seeing a picture of her actual mother for the first time? If that were the case, then Declan Welch could be her father. That possibility had Lacey's insides quaking. She was beyond grateful that Bea and Mekhi had accompanied her; without them, she would probably run for the door.

A regal woman, who appeared to be in her midforties, approached with bubbly in hand. "Isn't this gripping?" All Lacey could do was nod. She wiped her face with her trembling hands.

The woman placed a hand on her arm. "I'm Vanessa, the gallery owner. Are you a lover of the fine arts?"

Again a nod. She was too choked up to make small talk, and it was surprising and embarrassing to fall apart in front of a stranger. Mekhi pulled a pack of travel tissues out of his pants. He ripped it open and stuffed a couple into her hand. "Thank you," she managed, wiping her nose.

"We would love to meet the artist," Mekhi said, while she composed herself.

"Sadly, he hasn't been here in years. His agent sends his pieces, and I sell them for him."

"How much is this?" Lacey pointed. "I'd love to purchase it." She had to have it. If nothing else came from her search, this would give her solace. The woman in the picture looked peaceful, content with herself. She could look at this for hours.

Bea returned to join them, carrying bottles of sparkling water.

"Unfortunately, this isn't for sale. Declan refuses to part with it, though I have had several six-figure offers for it. He is pretty reclusive."

Her shoulders slumped. "Oh." She twisted the cap of the bottle and took a sip of water.

"I can see why," Bea said. "His photographs are stunning. I had my eye on *Her Wings*, the one where the ladybug is on the leaf in the rain."

"Oh yes, I know the one." Vanessa smiled. "He's what I call a brush-and-lens artist."

"The ladybug looks ready to pounce onto another, and the raindrops on her wings are so distinct. Such talent . . ." Bea said. "I don't even know how he got such a masterful shot."

Vanessa beamed. "Your enthusiasm gives me hope for art in the future. Declan also freelances as a photographer for *Nat Geo* and others." She crooked her head at Bea. "The one you liked is less than two hundred dollars."

Bea's eyes went wide. "Oh. Somehow, I thought it would be way more."

"Declan feels that art should be affordable for everyone," she said, chuckling. "He could get more for that. A lot more."

Lacey pocketed that tidbit of knowledge about her potential father in her heart. Declan's ex-wife had given one perspective—that of a womanizer. But the man Vanessa talked about had a sensitive side—a redeemable quality. A thought occurred. If Declan was her father, then her mother might have been the lover Augustina had caught in her bed. Oh Lord. She couldn't think about that now. She focused on Mekhi's words instead.

"That's incredibly thoughtful," Mekhi said. "We'll take *Her Wings* home. Can we get his contact information to reach out to him?" Mekhi asked. Lacey reached over to squeeze his hand. He had asked the most important question, the one that wouldn't get past her voice box.

Vanessa shook her head. "As far as I know he's off the grid, backpacking in Europe, getting inspiration." She waved a hand and smiled. "Creatives . . ."

Disappointment pierced her chest. Lacey hadn't realized how much she had been hoping until now. She stared at the painting. "Do you think he'll change his mind about selling?"

Vanessa gave her a brief pat on the back. "If he does, I have a long waiting list of interested parties. The exhibit closes in a week, but if you provide your contact information, I'll add your name to the list." Bea gave Vanessa her contact information. "Great. Let me go ring up your order and get your photograph wrapped up. Then I can have it shipped so you don't have to tote it around."

"That's a great idea," Bea said.

They left the gallery and hailed a cab to the Shubert Theatre to catch the 7:30 p.m. show of *Hell's Kitchen*. It was a quiet ride over, and the musical served as a great distraction, but discontent had settled and spread from Lacey's shoulders to her feet.

After the show, they walked a few blocks before popping into a pizza store and ordering a pie. Bea bit into her slice and moaned. "Oh my goodness. There is nothing like a New York slice to set me right."

"I agree," Mekhi said, choosing one of the larger pieces. They had cut the pie haphazardly, but even the smallest piece was generous.

"We need to make this a monthly thing," Bea offered, then tapped Lacey's foot. "Are you going to eat?"

Lacey picked up the smallest piece, the cheese oozing off at the sides. She loved pizza, but her unease rumbled inside her stomach. She made herself take a bite. Chew. Chew. Chew.

Bea finished off her slice and raised the topic on everyone's minds. "This is still a step forward, Lacey—albeit a small one."

Lacey shook her head. "I should have listened to my mother and left well enough alone. Now I can't even talk to her about how I'm feeling. I need to stop. I need to be done with this because it's affecting my psyche."

"See, I don't think you should give up. We're almost at the finish line. I feel it," Bea urged, drinking her fountain soda.

"Whatever you feel is best for you is what we should do," Mekhi said, giving her shoulder a light squeeze.

Lacey sighed. "Thanks. I just need a rest from all this. I didn't know how stressful this would be. And I didn't anticipate that I would be grappling with feelings of dejection. And rejection."

"I understand that very well," Mekhi mumbled. Lacey gave his hand a squeeze. She knew he could relate.

"Oh, honey, you are very much loved and very much wanted. Trust." Bea wagged a finger. "Don't doubt that for a minute."

Lacey nodded. "I know . . . But I keep wondering why *they* didn't want me. Why did they give me away in the first place? Even if I'm not the baby on the beach, I was still adopted." She lifted her shoulders. "Questions that keep you up at night." She looked down at her hands. "Questions that make you feel . . . unworthy."

"But you lucked out. Twice," Bea jumped in. "Adoption isn't a negative. It's God's way of looking out for you."

Lacey gave her friend a smile. "I know you're trying to help, but you have your parents."

"Yeah, and you have a great mom," Bea said. "Shelby is the best. I want you to focus on the positives. Because no matter the outcome of this investigation, you're going to be all right. I know that for sure."

"When you're feeling rejected, it's good to make new connections. It's good to practice self-love," Mekhi chimed in. He gave them both a light jab. "My summer wouldn't be the best I've ever had if it wasn't for you two."

"You're cool people. Although, I think you have a deeper connection with one of us," Bea said, poking Lacey in the chest.

Lacey released a breath. "You're right. Both of you. Thank you. Now, let's drop this and enjoy the city. See what else we can get into before we go home tomorrow."

"I like that plan." Mekhi picked up his phone. "Let me see what's going on."

Just then, Lacey's mother sent her a text to tell her she loved her and was thinking of her. Lacey responded with hearts. The perfect timing of that message gave her warm feels.

"I'm down for anything." Bea picked up another slice. "I'm going to put in double time at the gym tomorrow." She patted her abdomen. "I'm eating only salads for the next three days." Lacey bit back a chuckle, knowing Bea was only saying that so she could eat what she wanted, guilt-free. Not that she required exercise to maintain her waiflike frame.

"We'll go for an extra-long walk on the beach tomorrow when we get home," Lacey said. She took pictures of herself and her friends and posted them to her social media page in case her mother decided to check on her. Her mom had gone back to her first post and had been steadily liking all of her pictures, adding comments to them. Lacey couldn't comprehend that level of patience. Or love.

"Yeah, that's doable," Bea said, cutting into Lacey's thoughts, the relief evident in her voice. She looked at Mekhi. "Do you think we're fat?"

"I think you're both beautiful," he said, stuffing his mouth.

Lacey tapped him on the nose. "You're a smart man."

"I'm only telling the truth." He leaned over to give her a kiss on the lips. Then another. And another.

"Should I have gotten my own room?" Bea asked, looking between them.

"I got a two-bedroom suite," Mekhi offered. "There's room for everyone." Lacey tensed. They hadn't discussed sleeping arrangements. Did he take it for granted she would be staying with him? "I figure you two could take the bigger room, and I'll be in the other."

"Oh, okay. Yeah . . . That works," Lacey said. She bit into her slice, feeling letdown.

Bea touched his forehead, and Mekhi leaned away from her. "What did you do that for?"

"Just checking to see if you are for real," she said, then burped before wiping her mouth. "You are not like other guys our age."

His lips quirked. "So I've been told, but I'm not one to make assumptions. You know what they say when you do that."

They chuckled.

"You're a keeper, Mekhi James. A definite keeper." Bea gave Lacey a pointed look.

Lacey felt her cheeks heat. *I could fall in love with him. He's making it so easy.* To distract herself from that train of thought, she started talking about the show and passersby. Anything but her feelings. Anything but wondering if he felt the same. She knew he was attracted to her, that he felt a connection, but this could be a summer fling for him. She had to be ready to say goodbye when school started, and she had to be okay with it. So yeah, she was sharing a room with Bea tonight.

Because Bea was right: she would be okay with not finding her parents in the long run. And in time, she would find peace with their decision even if she never got answers. But if Mekhi rejected her, this could stay with her for a long time. And she wasn't sure a lifetime would be enough for her to recover.

JOURNAL ENTRY

February 14, 2021

Dear Diary,
My daughter is my Valentine! I don't need to date. She is the best hangout partner ever, and I just want to be there for her in every way I can. It might sound horrible, but when she gets in from the school, it is the highlight of my day. I soak up anything she has to say. Now, Lacey isn't my whole world, but she is definitely a big part of it. What was my life like before her? What did I do with myself all those years prior to her adoption?

It's all a blur.

Plus, I love how close we are becoming. She's now interested in boys, and she loves pointing out who she thinks is hot or cute at the movies, in the checkout line, at the drive-through. I laugh right along with her. But she doesn't know how worried I am.

She is a stunner. And boy, does she look like a perfect blend of her parents. She has his height and eyes. But I know who claims the personality and those curves. I heave a sigh of relief that she loves books more than boys . . . for now. But that doesn't stop her from asking me if I'm going to get married or have children like her friends' parents.

That's so thoughtful. But I'm good. Not that I don't have needs—I have one-offs when the need for physical relief consumes me.

The older she gets, the more my worry increases. Blame it on my social media feed, but there are so many scary things happening out there, and I don't want to be that poster slapping a Have You Seen Her? sign on my timeline. Motherhood comes with all kinds of never-ending anxiety, a low hum in your tummy that only recedes when your child is actually in your presence. The what-ifs niggle when they walk out the door. This is adulting. This is parenthood.

I just want to bubble-wrap her until adulthood . . . Is that legal somewhere?

August 25, 2023

Dear Diary,
I LOVE motherhood. I LOVE my daughter. I wouldn't trade this for anything in the world. My daughter graduated high school, and I have the ridiculously priced senior portraits to prove it. I have never cried so hard in my life as when she walked across that stage. I just left her outside the dorm at UDel, my alma mater.

For the first time in years, I do consider how comforting it would be if I had a husband waiting to hug me and tell me Lacey will be all right, now that I am a semi–empty nester. Or it would be nice to have my bestie nearby to hold my hand.

It wasn't until I dropped her off and I was driving home that the loneliness slapped me in the face.

Maybe it's time to get a hobby. I'll certainly have time for journal writing now for sure. The highlight of my life cannot be waiting for Lacey to come home on break.

CHAPTER 28

Shelby
August 2, 2025

"Thanks for driving," Shelby said to Kendrick as they explored the craft and vendor booths at the Peach Festival. Noon was fast approaching, and she was ready for lunch having only eaten a hard-boiled egg that morning.

She hadn't brought her cane, but with Kendrick's guiding hand she was managing well. He was dressed in a T-shirt, shorts and sneakers, while she had decided on a white tank and linen skirt, plus red cowboy boots with a matching red necklace, from her purchases at the Fashion District.

"No need to thank me. I'm glad to spend more time in your company." His words made a blush rise against her fair skin, but she pretended not to notice. And just like that, she couldn't think of a single thing to say. *Don't talk about the weather. Don't talk about the weather.* People only did that when they needed to fill an awkward silence.

"It sure is hot today." Welp. She had done it. At least there was a huge crowd out with lots of sounds and sights around them.

"Yes, the forecast said it was going to be in the upper nineties . . ." Great. Now he was talking about the weather.

"I'm looking forward to checking out the peach desserts." There. That was better. "I know they usually have a contest."

"Yeah. I wish I had entered," Kendrick said. "I make a mean peach pie, and they are raffling them off for great prizes." That broke the ice, and they began to talk about the different booths, even stopping to sample the peaches. They were delicious, but her tummy still protested. Loudly.

Kendrick cracked up. "How about we get something to eat?"

"Yes. I think we passed a food truck a little way back, and I am eager to try out their tacos."

"I know just the one." He smiled. To the right of them was a vendor with a bicycle up for raffle. Just seeing it made her knees weaken. Every entrant was required to add five dollars to the pot. Shelby would have kept on walking, but Kendrick stopped. "This is a really nice bike. Close to the one you had before."

"You can enter the raffle or buy one at our special price," the owner said.

She lifted her shoulders. "I don't know . . ." She grabbed the handle and twisted the bike in different directions though she didn't know what she was looking at.

"Isn't it great?" Kendrick asked, his face bright. Wow. He was really into bikes. Hmm . . . If she wasn't, would that be a deal-breaker? Because the version of her from a year ago might have been into cycling, but now she was . . . scared and didn't like getting sweaty. Not that she was looking for a relationship or anything. She just didn't want him thinking she lacked courage.

"It looks pretty fancy," she said.

"Yes, and you can't beat the price." Kendrick turned to the owner. "Can we take it out on a test run?"

We? "I don't think he would want us sullying the tires," she hedged, stepping back.

"Nah. I don't mind. Go ahead." He brought a helmet. "If you buy two bikes, I'll add this on for free."

"All right!" Kendrick held the bike and said, "I'll help you on."

Her heart rate kicked up a few notches, but she swung her leg over and settled her butt on the seat. The things she did for men who looked as fine as he did and who were dedicated and kind.

Kendrick had her put her feet on the pedals. "How does that feel?" he asked, his eyes narrowed.

"It feels good, actually."

"Great. I want you to push off, gradually, carefully rotating that ankle."

She did. It was smooth. "I'm good." She heaved a sigh of relief.

Kendrick asked if there was another bike to borrow. Before he could get on, Shelby took off for the paved sidewalk that led to another lot. Since it was the weekend, the empty space made for an ideal area for her to ride. She increased her speed and began to circle the lot. Another biker whizzed by and came to a smart stop a few feet away. She pulled to a stop next to him.

"It rides like butter," she called out to Kendrick. "And I'm loving how fast it goes."

"Why am I not surprised?" He cracked up and gave her a lopsided grin. "I know this area well—and all the back roads. How about we take this on the road? We won't go far."

"Lead and I'll follow." And for the next fifteen minutes, Shelby did just that. She turned her face toward the sun, loving the feel of it and the light breeze in her hair. To think that almost two months ago she had been in a collision with a car, and now here she was back on a bike again. It was simply wonderful. She cheered on the inside. All too soon, their joyride came to an end. Shelby rued getting off the bike.

"Thanks for the test ride," she said, tossing her hair back and taking her credit card out of her fanny pack. "I'll take it."

Kendrick whooped and pumped his fists. "And she's back! She's back!"

The owner took her card. "If you give me your address, I'll drop it off for you later."

"Awesome. I'm at the bookstore on the beach."

"Oh yeah, I know where that is." The owner swiped her card and then rubbed his chin. "I don't know if you lived here then, but a few years back, probably about twenty years, somebody left a baby over there. I'll never forget because my grandmother used to live there."

"Oh snap, I think I remember that," Kendrick said. "I don't think they ever found who did that. I figured it was probably some scared teenage girl."

Shelby's smiled drooped. This time when her heart raced, it was for a different reason. She lowered her head and curved her body away from the men.

"Teenager or not, anything could have happened to the child." The man spoke with contempt. "Probably some spoiled, young rich girl who thought she was above the law."

"At least they made sure the baby was okay. I heard about it from the librarian when I first moved here." Kendrick sounded a little less judgmental.

Wow. Even after all these years, people had strong emotions . . . No wonder Jewel stayed away. Maybe she should have as well. But it was too late now. She had adopted said baby, and Shelby would never let Lacey go.

Her hands shook as she signed the receipt. It felt like the words *I did it* were all across her face as she avoided looking both men in the eye. She had to get out of here.

"I don't feel too well." Those words ended talk of the baby, which was a big relief. The owner went over to talk with a few other people interested in joining the raffle.

"Oh no. Let me get you back home," Kendrick was quick to say. "Or do you need to use the restroom?"

"No, I think I need to get home. But you can stay. I can always Uber there." She backed up, wanting to put as much distance between her and Kendrick as she could.

"My mother raised me better than that," he said, putting a hand on her back.

She forced herself not to stiffen. "Okay, if it isn't too much trouble."

"Not at all. I'm enjoying your company."

The feeling was definitely reciprocated, but Shelby couldn't voice that. She couldn't encourage something for which there was no future. Kendrick was smart, observant. He would figure it out or she would mess up and say something. It was best she let him go once their sessions ceased—and they had about three or four to go.

They meandered through the crowds, retracing their steps back to his car. She hadn't eaten lunch, she told herself. She needed to tell him she had changed her mind and that she needed to eat. Once they were halfway home, her hunger pangs won over her common sense, and she suggested he stop at a fish house. They had some great lunch specials.

While they ate, Kendrick made small talk about his life in the low country—how he loved fishing and hunting, how he had grown up with a next-door neighbor who hung a Confederate flag, yet waved hello to him every day and even had his son shovel their yard when it snowed and mowed their lawn when in the warmer months.

Weird.

But he insisted since he was alive to talk about it that he'd had the best childhood. In her mind, the fact that you had to praise being alive was saying something, but okay. To each his own.

She told him about her parents being Jamaican and how she always wanted to go back there, having last visited at sixteen, but she hadn't wanted to return without them.

He urged her to go, to check it off her bucket list, and asked if she knew how to cook Jamaican dishes. He loved him some jerk chicken. Of course, he was more than hinting, and Shelby found herself agreeing to cook for him later that evening. Jerk chicken with rice and peas coming up. She had to correct him that Jamaicans didn't say *rice and beans*. And yes, she considered herself Jamaican, even though her mother had given birth to her right here in Delaware.

Before they left the fish house, she texted Jewel to see if she wanted takeout, but Jewel told her she wasn't going to be home tonight. Roman had surprised her with a visit. After sending her a raunchy emoji, Shelby realized that meant she had her place to herself. With Kendrick.

They stopped at the Jamaican store where she picked up the jerk seasoning, bay leaves and pimento seed for the chicken as well as coconut milk and a tin of pigeon peas for the rice. Then she stopped at the supermarket to get some quarter legs and a pineapple, having decided she would fire up her grill. Jerk chicken was great in the oven, but it was finger-licking good off the grill. Especially once she added in the barbecue sauce.

Kendrick got a good flame going while she washed, cleaned and seasoned the quarter legs. Her mouth was already watering. She loved the scent of charcoal with the hickory wood in the air. The only thing that would make this night any better was if it was going to end with them between the sheets.

But she had already decided to keep her distance, and she would hold herself to that. No matter how the connection between her and Kendrick intensified. No matter how well they grooved together. They had no future.

He had put on the radio, and love songs from the nineties were setting a tone for a song she wasn't about to sing. She could hum, though. So she closed her eyes and leaned into his hard body, rocking along to the tune while their meal cooked.

His hands moved over her body, and she stopped them from going too far. He kissed her neck, her ear, before she placed a hand over his lips and shook her head. "We can't."

He kissed her fingers and whispered, "Okay."

They ate in silence, eyeing each other, their hunger building for more than food. Then, when she wanted to cave, her eyes fell on the picture of Lacey holding her diploma and smiling over on the mantel, and that cooled her ardor considerably.

A disappointed man walked through her door that night. And she drank the rest of her Sprite to swallow her regret. Then she heard the door jangle, and she raced to it, thinking she was going to give herself just that one night. But before she could answer, it swung open. Stepping back, she gasped and placed a hand over her mouth. "Lacey? What are you doing here?"

Her daughter's face was reddened from crying. "Mom, I can't do this anymore. I have to talk to you. I have to tell you everything."

CHAPTER 29

Excerpt from That Was Then *by Jewel Stone*

July 14, 2005

Honey

"It's not right how Sugar has shut us out of her life," Honey choked out. "The other day, she walked right by me, acting like I didn't exist. We've been friends since kindergarten."

After a month of Sugar freezing them out of her life, even though she had ended things, Honey had reached out to Chance to commiserate. She was lonely, and he filled that void in her heart and in her bed. Now they sat in a diner and, having eaten their burgers and fries, were waiting for their root beer floats. The fact that they had similar tastes wasn't lost on her. "How am I supposed to help her get through this if she keeps rebuffing me?"

Chance rubbed his temples. "I don't have an answer for you because this whole friend thing is new territory for me." Their drinks came. She took a sip, enjoying the creamy vanilla ice cream with the fizz off the soda.

"We have to cut her some slack, though. She was her parents' world, and they were hers. She is drowning in grief. She told me that she blamed herself for their deaths." Honey sighed. "No matter how much I tell her that the waterspout was an act of nature, it doesn't make a difference. At least she's in therapy."

"Yes, I'm glad she's talking with a professional." Chance stirred his root beer and then locked eyes with her.

"I tried to distract her by saying we should go to the beach party in a couple days, but she claimed she had writing to do. Then when I asked if we could get together tonight, she said she wasn't in the mood for company. Do you think we should barge in on her? Just show up with pizza and put on a movie?"

He shook his head. "I think you should give her what she asked for. Space. Maybe reach out again tomorrow."

"I'd better be going." She dug around in her bag for her wallet. "I've got work in the morning." Her tone held finality. She really needed to stay away from him for good this time.

Chance stood as well. "I understand. No pressure. This was fun." He dropped a fifty-dollar bill on the table. "I'll drive you home." He placed a hand on her back, his touch searing into her common sense.

She fretted on her bottom lip. She really should walk home, but Honey was lonely. She had other people she could call to hang out with, but she didn't consider them friends. She missed Sugar, and he was a great fill-in.

Sugar had moved out right after her parents' memorial, and when Honey pushed for more details, she clammed up. Sugar had definitely curled into herself, and all Honey could hope was that she would come out of it in time.

"You know what? We should totally go to that party tonight."

"I'm in." Chance opened the passenger side of his truck for her.

"Thanks," she whispered, wrapping her arms about her.

They were just two friends accompanying each other to a beach party, she told herself as he drove them there. She was dressed in a one piece and a colorful throwover, while Chance wore his usual board shorts with a muscle T-shirt. Those bulging biceps were hard to miss.

They both agreed to dance with other people, so she found herself sandwiched between two ardent suitors. Chance spent most of the time sitting at the table nursing the same glass of bourbon, keeping an eye on her drink. Honey made a point of getting a shot at the end of each song, and Chance ensured her glass remained full. At one point, she caught him frowning at a dance partner who was a bit too touchy-feely for her liking. Then before she knew it, he was hauling the guy off her and dumping him onto the sand.

Embarrassed at his caveman antics, Honey demanded they leave. She fumed all the way back to her place, bidding Chance a hasty goodnight. She had enough drama in her life, and his behavior solidified that she needed to end things for good. Her cell buzzed. It was Chance texting her an apology for his behavior at the party. He added, **I was jealous.**

Her fingers flew across her keyboard. **Save the apology. We're done.**

Sugar
July 28, 2005

Sugar didn't usually drink, but she was pretty sure she was drunk. Or at least a few beats away from sober. She had been packing up her father's library when she came across an unopened bottle of Wray and Nephew Overproof Rum. Mommy used to rub it into her chest when she had a cold, but that afternoon Sugar had decided to take a sip. And then another.

Two sips had been enough to get her giddy, especially since she hadn't eaten all day. She now sat in Daddy's big brown leather armchair, her legs over the fancy armrest. Daddy had forbidden her from sitting like that, but now she was able to do whatever she wanted.

Her heart ached, so she took another sip. Her chest burned. She put the glass on the coffee table without using a coaster. Mommy wasn't here to cluck her tongue at her. Sorrow flooded her being. She slumped against the back of the chair. There was an offer on the house, and the realtor had suggested scheduling the closing right before the next school year started.

All she had to do was sign the papers.

She bounded out of the chair and grabbed her keys off the hook by the front door. Maybe she could get some black cherry ice cream. She slipped into the front seat and put her car into Reverse to back out of the driveway. But in her state, she pressed the gas instead of the break and ended up slamming into a huge tree.

Curling her fingers around the steering wheel, Sugar broke down. She must have cried for over an hour when there was a tap on her window.

Chance.

Shaking her head, she rolled down the window. "What are you doing here?"

"I came to check on you. I texted you, but you didn't respond. So I got worried."

Sugar wiped her face. "You didn't need to do that. I'm perfectly fine."

He splayed his hands. "I can see that."

"Save your sarcasm, and leave me be."

She must have slurred her words, because Chance bent over to look into her eyes. His mouth hung open. "You've been drinking." He opened her door and helped her out of the car.

"I can't leave you alone like this." He started walking toward her door when Sugar froze.

"I don't want to be there."

"Do you want me to drop you by the condo?"

"No." She shook her head. "I'm not ready to see Honey." She spoke her friend's name, bitterness curdling like milk in her heart.

"What's going on with you two?" Chance asked. "The last time I spoke to her, she said you were still avoiding her calls."

"N-nothing." Two weeks? Were they broken-up? Sugar watched Chance from under her lashes. "So are you now a free man?" she asked, moving close to him. What was she doing? Maybe it was the liquor talking.

"Yeah . . ." he said. His eyes dropped to her lips before he stepped back. "What's going on here?"

The air shifted between them. She wasn't going to be the one to admit to anything. Let him do it first.

"You'd better get inside."

She poked his chest. "You feel something? Admit it. Same as I do."

"You're feeling the effects of all that alcohol you consumed. And you're mourning your parents."

She moved into his space. "Take me back to your place."

His brows furrowed. "Sugar, I like you, but I won't take advantage of you. And I care too much about Honey. You're grieving and not thinking right."

"You're a good man, Chance." She placed a palm on his chest: his heart was pumping fast and hard. "I'm not trying to hurt Honey either, but I feel lost," she said and hiccupped, "and confused. And I don't want to be alone."

"Okay, you can come to my place. But I'm putting you in my spare bedroom."

"Give me five minutes."

Sugar took a quick shower, threw on a dress, brushed her teeth and was back in the truck in fifteen. She had the short ride to his home to change her mind, to ask him to take her back home. But she found herself trailing behind him and following him to the spare bedroom.

Three minutes later, she made her way to his bedroom. She climbed into his bed and to her surprise, Chance didn't reject her. Instead, he opened his arms, and she opened her legs. Before she drifted off to sleep, she thought that Chance was a considerate lover but she'd had better.

ONE MINUTE SHE WAS WRAPPED IN CHANCE'S ARMS under the most luxurious covers with blackout curtains and the next she was rudely awakened by a screaming woman who had ripped opened the curtains.

She squinted, the sunlight blinding her. But her ears were working just fine—hearing the profanity spewing from a regal-looking woman. It would be hilarious if the woman weren't so ticked off.

Chance jumped out of bed, his hands over his crotch. "Arlena, what are you doing here?"

Sugar sat up in bed, wrapping the sheets about her. She figured this was his elusive aunt, upset that Chance had a visitor over. He eyed the woman with caution and put on his shorts.

"What am I doing here? This is my house, you highbrow freeloader. Pack your stuff and get out of here before I get my shotgun."

Shotgun? Sugar sprang to her feet. She rummaged around for her dress and slipped it over her head. The woman hadn't deigned to spare her a glance.

"Babe, let me explain. This meant nothing."

"I don't need you to explain what I already saw with my own two eyes." She pumped her fists and looked upward. "I knew it. I knew this ingrate was up to no good, disappearing for hours on end." Arlena paced the room.

"Babe?" Sugar shook her head. "Who calls their aunt *babe*?"

Arlena glared at her. "I'm not his aunt. I'm his wife."

Sugar gasped. *Please, Lord.* She hoped she hadn't heard right. She hoped this other woman was delusional and Chance would set her straight. But Chance didn't answer. He rushed past her, eyes on Arlena. Sugar grabbed his arm and screeched. "You're married?"

Shrugging out of her grip, Chance said, "I've got to get to my studio," then scurried off to save his precious artwork. He didn't even care that Sugar's life could be in danger.

Arlena was on his heels. She had fire in her eyes. "You're not leaving here with anything I purchased. Not even the clothes on your back."

Sugar dashed toward the front door, her heart racing at double tempo. She had slept with a married man. She had slept with a married man who had also slept with her best friend. After hurling herself into a nearby shrub, she dashed toward the beach, to safety, leaving Chance and chaos behind.

CHAPTER 30

Jewel
August 2, 2025

They hadn't made it far past the front door of Roman's Airbnb before making love. The minute he had opened the door, she was snatched in his arms, and they had undressed in a frenzy, all mouths and hands, as need raged between them before the sweet blessed relief.

Roman had then lifted her into his arms and taken her into the bedroom, where they had connected again for a second time, this time their pace languid, though just as intense.

Jewel lay wrapped in her husband's arms, welcoming the air of the ceiling fan above her. She had left her overnighter in the car in her haste to meet up with Roman, who had driven down to Delaware to surprise her and called her with his address.

"It shouldn't have taken you this long to visit." She ran her hands over his hair and face. "I mean, we were creative over video calls, but there is nothing like being together in the flesh."

"I would have loved to have been here, but—" he captured her hand and kissed the inside of her palm "—I was job-hunting, remember?"

"Yes. So what makes this time different?"

"*Was*, as in *not anymore*."

It took a moment before the implications of his words sank in, along with the wide grin across his handsome face.

"You got a job?" she squealed, flopping onto his stomach and plastering kisses across his nose. "I can't believe you didn't tell me."

Roman cracked up. "You don't know how many times I wanted to call during my drive down here, but I needed to tell you in person." He kissed the tip of her nose. "I needed to see your face when I told you that your man is now employed," he choked out. "I'll finally be able to help out and do my part. Take the burden off you."

"Oh, baby, I'm so happy for you." She cupped his head with her hands. "I'm really proud of you, Roman Stone."

His laughter made her bounce on his chest. "You didn't even ask what I'd be doing."

"I don't care if you're behind the counter of a fast-food joint or serving tables. I am proud of you, my man."

"You could have told me that before," he joked, before going on to name one of NYC's top architectural firms. "I'll be overseeing a staff of twenty, and they are willing to incorporate some of my design aesthetics."

"You'll have quite the commute."

"The firm is setting us up with a four-bedroom apartment in the city. So I figure we would stay there during the week and go home on the weekends."

She nodded, not even bothering to question why he hadn't asked if she wanted to move to the city. They were a team, and her honey wasn't going to live anywhere without her there. If she protested, he'd turn down the position and hunt for something closer to home.

"How long will you be here in Delaware?" Already, Jewel was thinking of the jeans and shirt she had packed along with the skimpy nightwear. She would need more clothes if he was staying for more than a day or two. Not that she planned to be dressed at all.

"I have to get back on Wednesday to do orientation and all that. So I'll probably stay the weekend before heading back to New York."

So he would be there for only three days. As much as she loved Shelby, Jewel missed her husband terribly. Nights were the worst, especially if she wasn't writing. She would roll from one side of the bed to the other missing his warmth.

"When will you be coming home?"

"I'll probably be here another two weeks at most," she said. "Shelby has progressed faster than I imagined. She has had a remarkable recovery. But I want to be finished with my book first. I'm actually almost finished with the first draft. I just have to figure out the ending." Unless she improvised and made up the ending, she would like to see what happened for her and Shelby. "For now I'm going through and rewriting. This might sound odd, but I don't want to jinx my rhythm. Since coming here, I have been so inspired."

"Believe me, I understand. Sometimes a change of scene recharges your brain and activates your creativity. Eagle Point Beach is so picturesque and peaceful. I can see why you've felt so inspired." He gave her a pat on the butt. "How about we go get a swim?"

"I'd love to," she said.

Hours had passed, but because she was with him, it felt like minutes. This was going to be a beautiful additional scene in the novel. She could see readers' hearts melting at how much Winston and Honey loved each other.

They got dressed, she in a gold two-piece and he in a pair of blue-striped board shorts, and they raced to the backyard to splash in the pool. Soon hunger drove them out of the water, and she pulled up her DoorDash and ordered them enough Chinese food to feed a family of twelve. Then they dove into their meal. Once they gathered the containers and put the utensils and plates in the dishwasher, they went back to bed to lie side by side playing footsies.

There was a procedural drama playing on the television, but neither was paying attention. She had her laptop on the nightstand, and she intended to finish up the chapter she had started.

Roman turned on his side. "So let me get a look at what you're writing? I'm surprised you haven't asked me to talk through any points with you."

Tension made her shoulders go stiff. It was time she told him the truth. "There's something I need to tell you."

When he turned those brown eyes on her, so full of trust and contentment, she almost chickened out. But Jewel knew that to be the woman she wanted to face in the mirror every day she had to tell him. "I haven't told Shelby as yet about the book." His brows rose high. She held up a finger when he went to speak. "And there are pieces of us in there." Once she said that, whatever he had to say about her not telling Shelby was shelved. For the moment. She was pretty sure he would circle back to it.

"What do you mean, *pieces of us?*" he asked, his tone mild, curious.

"Highlights of our conversations. Things that add realism to the story."

He nodded. "That's to be expected. Why do you think I'd have a problem with that? I don't think this is the first time—" he held up air quotes "—*pieces of us* have made it into one of your books. So what makes this time any different?"

That was the question.

She licked her suddenly dry lips. "Because I might have shared one thing that I haven't discussed with you."

That made him sit up. *"Might have?"*

Jewel ran a hand across the bridge of her nose. "I did. Share one thing."

He reached over to turn on the lamp on the nightstand. "One thing like what? You're being very vague." He was now zoned in on her, his brows knitted closely together.

She sat up, scooted back against the headboard and bunched the sheets about her. He uttered nary a word while he waited for her to speak. But his eyes were on her, piercing her like lasers. She cleared her throat and looked the man she loved in the eyes. "My character based on you has a child he never knew existed, and he wants to have a relationship with him but the mother is selfish."

Just like Katrina.

His jaw clenched as her words sank in. She knew Roman was taking the time to process her words carefully. "So how detailed were you?" He moved close. "I mean, what if Katrina reads your book and realizes this is about her? Or Curtis, if he ever finds out the truth? This could create problems for me. It might make Katrina more adamant about not wanting this DNA test. Isn't there something in the book that says this story isn't based on someone's actual life?"

"Yes, something like that. But this is my life so it should be okay."

"Correction. This is my life. My potential son's life. Can't you write about something else? Isn't that the point of writing fiction? That it's fiction?" he asked, his tone brittle.

Jewel nodded. "Yes, but the best fiction comes from real life. That gives it authenticity. Does that make sense?"

He gave a slight nod. "I think you should change it." His brown eyes held pain. "This feels like . . . exploitation, for want of a better word." Ouch. *Exploitation* cut her deep.

"I see it as exploration, as inspiration."

"Just trying to express how I feel. This situation is too raw for me. I need you by my side as my wife, not as a . . . biographer. Not sure that's the proper term but—"

"I get your drift," she interrupted. "The thing is, everyone at the imprint is excited about this plotline. I haven't seen this level of excitement since *That Was Then*." She touched his arm, a silent plea for him to acquiesce, to understand.

Roman shifted, putting space between them. "Baby, I don't think you're hearing me. I don't want you to write this at all. I feel exposed, and I don't want anything jeopardizing my chances to get to know Curtis if he is my son."

"I'm sorry, I can't change it. I'm too far gone to stop now. Not to mention this is some of my best writing. We need this money."

"This is about maintaining a certain lifestyle, not what we need."

"Yes, but there is nothing wrong with having nice things." She lifted her chin and faced off with him. "And this isn't just about us. I have my mother and sister to think of."

"Both of whom live humbly." He stared at her, displeasure evident in his furrowed brows and folded arms. "So even though I'm asking you not to use that storyline, that doesn't matter? Wow." His words were laced with hurt, which pierced her heart. She had to look away because she couldn't stand knowing he was disappointed with her.

Jewel touched his chest, needing to make physical contact, needing him to understand. "Please don't be upset. Of course you matter. You're taking this too far. No one will know it's you."

He took her hand. "But the key people will. That's what matters to me."

Jewel tipped her head back. "I have a confession to make. I went to see Katrina."

Roman's eyes went wide. "What? When did you do that, and why didn't you tell me about it?"

"I went not too long after the second signing at the bookstore, and I didn't tell you because I didn't want to get your hopes up if Katrina didn't agree to talk to me. I DMed her and asked if I could meet up with her, and to my surprise she agreed."

"And what happened?" She could see the spark in his eyes.

"Shelby went with me and the three of us had a pleasant lunch. Katrina cleared up that she was sleeping with you and Scott at the time. And when she got pregnant, she was young and scared, which is understandable. Weren't we all at some point in our lives? Katrina doesn't want to see her life explode, but this secret is eating away at her." Jewel placed a hand on Roman's chest and whispered, "I think she's going to come around, babe. I really do. But all she needs is time."

The light in his eyes dimmed. "Time is the one commodity I don't have. I missed out on a chance to know my son, if he is mine, and I've missed all the monumental milestones in his life. That's time I can never get back. Katrina cheated me out of that. I didn't get to see Curtis's first smile, his first tooth, his first step. None of that, and by the looks of it I won't get to help usher him into adulthood." He bunched his lips to keep from breaking down. "And I'm going to have to walk around the rest of my life knowing that. Curtis will never know how much I love him, even though I've never even heard his voice."

Jewel hugged her hubby. She didn't relish another argument with Roman, but if she put this conversation in her book, it would immortalize this sentiment. Yet Roman would object, even see it as her trying to justify her going against his wishes.

However, Katrina was a fan. She would read this story. Jewel was certain of this.

She had to use this book as a means to persuade Katrina to consent to the DNA test and bring Roman one step closer to having a relationship with his son. In fact, as soon as the book was ready, Jewel would send Katrina a coveted advance copy.

Roman was upset now, but he would be thanking her in the long run. She was sure of it.

Sure enough to gamble against her marriage. It was rock steady. Roman's objections would be a minor hiccup, and they'd be laughing it out when he was hugging his son.

CHAPTER 31

Shelby
August 3, 2025

Shelby didn't have her memory back, but she had her instincts. And those instincts kicked in when her daughter came home. Unannounced. But wasn't that the point of having a home? That you could do just that. So after her initial shock, she had opened her arms and comforted her child. Amid her sniffles the night before, Shelby had learned that Lacey had taken a rideshare to the bookstore.

"What do you need to tell me?" she'd asked, while rocking Lacey in her arms. But Lacey had been too distraught to put two coherent sentences together. Her daughter had just cried and cried. Shelby's heart had hammered in her chest as all sorts of scenarios hit her mind—pregnancy, abuse, losing her job, fighting with Bea.

Shelby had made two cups of hot cocoa laden with marshmallows before leading Lacey to her bedroom. She made sure to shut the door to the guest room and cleared the connecting bathroom of Jewel's personal items. Then she texted Jewel to stay away, unless she wanted to meet Lacey. She stilled. Twenty years later, and she and Jewel were still trying to keep this secret hidden. That knowledge made her uneasy.

That unease kept her up, but just as she was about to drift off to sleep, there was a light rap on the sliding door that led outside. She sat up with a start, clutched her covers close and cocked her ear. There it was again. Her cell pinged. She reached for it and saw a text from Kendrick.

I'm outside. There was one prior text she must not have heard. **Are you up? I'm coming over.**

Oh my goodness. He is here. There was no need to wonder why. The time and the rap on her door said it all.

Give me one sec, she typed back. Then panic set in. She was wearing granny panties. But it was dark and late, so who cared. She blew her breath into her hands to do a breath check and ran into the bathroom to brush her teeth. Bad breath trumped granny panties. Rinsing her mouth, she skittered over to the door and pushed the curtains aside to let him in. He smelled like man and wood and ocean, and her body zinged into overdrive.

"Sorry to show up like this," he said, hulking over her. "I couldn't sleep. I hope you don't think I'm too forward—"

"Shut up and kiss me," she ordered, tucking her hand behind his head.

With a groan, Kendrick captured her mouth and swooped her into his arms. Her body flicked to life and within seconds, they were under the sheets. Then remembrance hit. She placed a hand on his chest and tore her lips off his. "Wait," she whispered. "I need you to know my daughter is here." Kendrick nodded. She met his gaze. "She can't know that you're here."

"I'll be gone before she wakes up." He got up and locked Shelby's bedroom door, then padded back over to her bed.

Shelby lifted a finger. "One more thing. This is only happening once."

"Understood."

She heaved a sigh of relief before he got to work on giving her the best encounter between the sheets she had had in years. At least, that's what she assumed since her journals hadn't mentioned any past exploits. Or even dating, which was a shame, because—she stifled a moan—dang, she had been missing out.

She had been missing out big-time.

But Kendrick made up for it and then some. He gave her the kind of mind-blowing pleasure that made a woman want to make him breakfast in bed at the crack of dawn. So she did. Then allowing him one more stolen kiss, she kicked him out.

"See you later. And don't expect me to go easy on you in our session," he said, before walking off with the swag of a man who knew he had a very satisfied woman eyeballing him.

Now as the sun rose, she welcomed the morning sounds of the waves as she hurriedly showered and dressed in a pair of shorts and a T-shirt. She didn't know if Lacey was an early riser but she wanted to be up and ready to listen whenever her daughter ventured out of her room.

About a half hour after Kendrick left, Lacey strolled out wearing a tank top and biker shorts. Her hair was a halo, and her eyes were puffy.

"Where's your friend?" she asked, her voice still sounding a little sleepy.

"Oh, she's with her husband at the moment. She'll be back in a day or so."

"Oh, I'm sorry I missed her."

She scuttled over into the kitchen to give Shelby a hug, their bodies resting against the counter. Was this what it was like having a daughter? Because that hug led to another and another and then a round of *I love you*s.

"It's good to be home," Lacey said. "Sometimes you just need your mother's arms." Words that turned her heart into mush. Her daughter gave her a pointed look. "Am I the only one who's benefited from them?"

Shelby shifted. There was no way her daughter had seen Kendrick . . . right? Well, she wasn't about to answer that question. "Hungry?" she asked instead.

Lacey looked like she wanted to say more, but she hid a grin and settled in at the small dining table, then propped her leg onto the next chair.

"What's for breakfast?" She sniffed the air. "It smells really good in here. That's probably what woke me up."

"I made steel cut oatmeal with berries, and I'm about to whip you up some scrambled eggs. I've got turkey sausage in the air fryer."

She got a big smile. "Thanks, Mom."

After finishing cooking and making plates for both of them, Shelby poured them each a glass of orange juice then slipped into the chair across from Lacey and asked, "So what did you want to talk about?" Lacey paused midbite. "Come on, don't tense up on me now."

"There's something I need to tell you, and I'm nervous because I know you'll be mad at me."

She gave Lacey's hand a squeeze. "Sweetheart, please just talk to me, because I've got all kinds of scenarios in my head."

"I've been looking for my birth family," Lacey said. Shelby barely had time to recover before Lacey continued. It all came out in one swoop then, and Shelby sat back and let her say her piece. "So while I'm in vacationing in Rehoboth Beach, Bea and Mekhi have been helping me. We've been going to the library and sifting through old archives. I thought I came across a good lead." Her cheeks reddened, and she ducked her head.

"Go on," Shelby whispered, though on the inside panic raged. She forced herself to take a sip of orange juice.

Her daughter ran her hands through her hair. "This is embarrassing, but I thought for a minute that I might have been that baby on the beach from years ago. The one that had been left by this very bookstore." Lacey outlined in detail how she found that newspaper clipping and her internet search. *The baby on the—? How had she—?* "Have you ever heard about that? You must have . . . I think."

Shelby choked and coughed hard enough to make her chest hurt. "Sorry, wrong . . . pipe."

The chair scraped, and then Lacey patted her back. "Are you okay?" Her daughter's gentle touch made her feel like scum lining the toilet bowl. Lower than that.

She waved a hand and sputtered out, "Yeah. Yes. Continue."

Lacey took her seat again, and Shelby pushed her plate aside as the contents in her stomach soured. Lacey's appetite seemed to have awakened with her confession, because she was steadily eating and talking. Eating and talking. Releasing it all because she trusted Shelby. She believed her mother's ear was a safe space.

"I know it's ridiculous, and I feel foolish even going down that rabbit hole, but there was a baby found right by this bookstore about twenty years ago—one day after I was born—and it made national news. Did you hear about it?" she tossed out to Shelby again but continued before she could respond. "Well, I got it in my head that it might be me—that I might be that abandoned baby—and I started my own investigation. But I kept hitting dead ends. I even went to New York to an art gallery to find out if an artist named Declan Welch could be my father. He is really talented." At his name, Shelby froze in shock. But then Lacey laughed at herself, an undertone of pain in her voice, and Shelby's heart melted. Her poor daughter was trying to make light of what must be a gut-wrenching desire. "I know that was very random—there's no proof he's even tied to the baby on the beach—but with his splashy divorce in the news around the same time, it seemed like a good idea. But this was clearly a case of one plus one equals five . . . Declan had a painting of a woman with hands just like mine, and I stood there thinking I was looking at my mother's hands. Pitiful, right?"

Twenty years of lies unraveled through internet searches by

a couple of amateur sleuths. Truth continually made a mockery of those who dared to keep it hidden.

Fear crashed through all coherent thought. As Lacey blabbed on, Shelby vacillated between wanting to laugh in hysterics and wanting to plead with Lacey that the past was a bone best left buried and to leave it alone.

"I'm sorry, Mom," Lacey said. "I'm sorry I didn't listen when you told me not to go digging in the past." Shelby's breath caught as the words echoed her thoughts. "Because it feels like my heart is breaking all over again. The more I search, the more depressed I get and the more I feel . . . abandoned."

Tears welled in Lacey's eyes, and Shelby reached over to give her a hug. Slumping against Shelby, Lacey fell apart. Her daughter's tears were a whip for Shelby's conscience. There was no pain worse than watching your child suffer and not knowing what to do. But in this case, she had the solution that would ease her daughter's aching soul. Except it wasn't only her secret to tell. There was also Jewel to consider. And they both had a lot to lose.

Finally, Lacey lifted her head and wiped her eyes. "I'm sorry I ever went on that wild-goose chase, but it did lead to one positive." She stuffed oatmeal in her mouth.

"W-what is that?" Shelby asked after she had processed Lacey's words.

"It made me realize how much I value you adopting me. I have the best mother in the world."

Shelby put her tongue between her teeth, but the words *Thank you* remained lodged in her esophagus. She put a hand around her throat and drew deep breaths. Lacey was such a sweet girl. She was trying to find the sunlight through the clouds. But Shelby wasn't being the best mother. She wasn't thinking of what Lacey needed. Instead, she was protecting herself and Jewel.

"Mom? You look . . . pale. Are you sure you're okay? Mom?"

"Yeah." She barely managed a nod as truth tormented her for the liar and hypocrite that she was. Lacey was going to hate her when everything came out, and she could see that there would be no keeping it at bay. It was ready to be loosed, consequences be damned.

She lifted her chin with resolve. Her only absolution might be to help set it free.

CHAPTER 32

Jewel
August 3, 2025

What did you do? What did you do? That question plagued Jewel's mind as she attempted to lock eyes with Shelby. But her friend refused to look her way. Instead, Shelby entertained with Roman, tittering at his conversation about who knew what, munching on brussels sprouts like she hadn't thrown a meteor into Jewel's world.

They had met up for dinner at a steak house that evening. Jewel wanted a neutral spot, since she couldn't be sure Lacey wouldn't make another surprise entrance, despite Shelby's assurance that Lacey had returned to Rehoboth Beach hours prior. Shelby had walked over, since the restaurant was only a few blocks from her place. Said she needed fresh air. But Jewel knew it had to do with the text message she had sent earlier before going quiet.

Jewel read the text message again.

> I'm telling Lacey the truth.

She sent Shelby what had to be her thirtieth response.

> Why?

Thirty-first.

Why ruin things?

Shelby steadily ignored the buzzing, even silencing her phone. Come on, Roman wasn't that funny, so she was being ignored on purpose. Jewel scooted closer to him and took a small helping of his mashed potatoes. No matter what she ordered, the food always looked better on his plate.

She stretched her foot to kick Shelby on the shins. Shelby finally made eye contact. *Answer me*, she mouthed.

Roman must have seen her because he stood. "I'm going to the bathroom to give you ladies a minute to catch up on girl talk." He planted a kiss on her cheek, and she patted his arm. Good, now they were alone.

"What did you do?" she spat out.

"I gave Lacey my journals. Including the one from that summer."

Jewel's mouth dropped. "You did what?"

"She's hurting. Does that not matter to you? You weren't the one hushing her as she cried on your shoulder. Well, I was, and it broke my heart." She blew out air. "And I'm tired of keeping secrets."

Jewel gasped. "I can't believe you would do that without consulting me. I have a right to know because this involves me."

Shelby bit her lower lip. "All summer, she's been secretly looking for her birth parents, questioning whether she was the baby on the beach. She even somehow tied Declan into it all. Her friends went with her to his art show in New York. But she thought she was wrong and was going to give up. She was crying on my shoulder, and I wanted to relieve her."

Jewel placed her hands on the table. "So you give her some ice cream. You don't smash the life we have built to smithereens."

"Don't you mean the life *you've* built?" Shelby shot back. "We relinquished the baby to someone who would get her care. There's no crime in that. Yes, Delaware law says that it should be a hospital, but the main thing was that Lacey was okay. That's what I plan to tell her, and I pray that she will understand."

"We're not done with this conversation," Jewel furiously whispered, spying Roman making his way back to the table.

When he reached them, Roman looked between them. "Everything all right with you two?"

Both women nodded, planted smiles on their faces and carried on with their evening. But on the inside, Jewel fumed. That's why when they left the restaurant she made up the excuse of needing to get her moisturizer from Shelby's place, though she had a spare in her overnighter. Roman drove back to the Airbnb while she and Shelby walked to the bookstore. Or rather, she stomped her way, gripping the handles of her purse.

"You didn't think things through," she began, swerving out of the way of tourists along the path. "You never do. Not then. Not now. She's going to ask who Honey is. That's a given." Worry ate at her. "I'm in the public eye, and this could ruin my life and affect my family's welfare. This isn't just about you."

"You're right. It's about Lacey." Shelby stopped and faced her. "And if she asks who Honey is, I'll tell her that I'm not at liberty to say. That isn't my secret to tell."

There really was no regret in her tone, in her body language. Shelby was okay with her actions. Jewel couldn't fathom that. Her temples throbbed.

There's no point in being angry. Maybe we can contain this somehow. Think, Jewel, think.

"She could hate you . . . and me." Someone almost bumped into them, so they shuffled out of the way and continued their conversation.

"I— I thought about that, but my love for her is stronger than any hate that she has for me."

"What if she decides to run to the press and tell what she knows?"

Shelby stiffened. "The young woman I've gotten to know and love wouldn't do that."

"You don't know for sure." She paced. "And what about our friendship? It was your actions that made us part ways twelve years ago, and now your actions are threatening our lives all over again."

"*My* actions?" She stuffed her hands in her pockets, probably to keep from giving Jewel a shake, though Shelby wasn't prone to physicality. "You have a lot of nerve talking about my actions."

Jewel held up a finger. "I'm talking about your actions now."

Shelby shrugged. "Our friendship will be fine. At least on my end. I can't control what you do." She trudged off without sparing a backward glance. There was a slight limp, but otherwise you couldn't tell she had been in an accident just weeks before.

Really? She just going to walk off like that? Well, Jewel wasn't about to let her have the last word. She caught up to her and cut her off midstride. "I'm not done talking about this."

"It's a waste of breath because I've already given Lacey the journals. She was so close to the truth anyway. Maybe if it comes from me instead of the search she's been doing with her friends, she will come to understand. Maybe she'll forgive me."

Jewel's anger dissipated. She had a point. "I'm mad, but I can't say I blame you. This lie is a burden. It leads to more lies, and I don't think I could resist that face crying all over me."

Shelby smiled. "It is a very cute face."

"Let's head back. My feet are killing me." Jewel bent over and took off her heels. They continued their way to Shelby's place. She loved the feel of the sand under her feet. "Any chance she might decide not to read them?"

"Not a chance. That's like telling a teenager to stay off their cell phone and then going to sleep." They went around the back and trudged up the stairs to Shelby's apartment. Shelby tackled the stairs at a good speed.

"You did good."

"I had a very good teacher." She flipped on the switch and winked. "A *very* good teacher."

"Wait! What does that mean?" Then Jewel held up her index finger. "Hang on a minute." She went into the bathroom to wash her feet and put on her shoes, then returned. "Now, what were you saying?"

"Well, I'm not one who usually kisses and tells, but—" she mimicked blowing a kiss "—that man gave me the best experience of my life last night. At least the best that I remember." Shelby went into the kitchen.

"Say what?" Jewel dropped her bag on the couch. Remembering that her laptop needed charging, she took it out and plugged it into the outlet on the left underneath the end table. Come to think of it, she needed a rough copy of the manuscript to take back with her tonight. There were a few plot points that she wanted to work out, and it helped to have the printed document in her hand.

"Yes. As Michael Jackson would sing," she broke off in tune, "he rocked my world."

"Dang. All right now. I'm not mad at you. The man got you singing and things." Her use of slang made Shelby crack up. Should Jewel include that scene in her book? She had already been hinting at a romance and that would grab that readership. Jewel reached for the laptop and sent her manuscript to Shelby's printer. She would grab it on her way out.

"He is all that and a bag of chips." She came over with their ice cream and spoons, handed a bowl to Jewel and settled in the armchair across from her. Her eyes shone, and her shoulders lifted with confidence. Oh, Jewel was definitely including this in her book.

Jewel took a taste of the ice cream. "I promise you. This is the cure for all things."

Shelby leaned forward and grew serious. "I'm sorry I didn't check with you first. I didn't want you to talk me out of it."

"I get that." She rubbed her chin. "In the grand scheme of things, it does reveal she is the baby from the bookstore, but it doesn't tell my identity. We both decided to use Sugar and Honey, just in case."

Shelby had come up with those names because she felt they had mystery, and if her diary ended up in the wrong hands, she could deny it was hers. It made logical sense at that time. But when one of them became pregnant, the pet names stuck. In fact, Jewel's first words after the revelation were "Sugar, Honey, Iced Tea," the slang used when you don't cuss but really want to. But then inspiration struck. They would call each other Sugar and Honey when it came to talking about anything surrounding the baby. They figured it would be like talking about someone else and help them maintain anonymity.

"Yes, but I wrote in first person. She will probably figure out which one is me."

"But she doesn't know who I am." Now that they had talked it out some more, Jewel could breathe easy. As long as she kept out of Lacey's path, she was good. "I've avoided her all this time, and now that you're doing better, I'll be gone in a matter of days. All will be well."

"I figured you would be," Shelby said. "I'm going to miss you, but I know I have to return you to your hubby."

"We're a short driving distance away, and we'll communicate every day like we're doing now."

"It's a plan. But to use your words, my adopting Lacey broke our pact, which severed our friendship. Lacey is a permanent part of my life. I'm falling in love with the young woman I am coming to know, and I can't see ever letting her down or letting her go. And you're determined to stay out of her life. So I don't see how we can resolve this. As it stands, she's bound to break us apart again."

"Impossible." Jewel splayed her hands. "We're older. Wiser. We've felt the void—well, I remember the void—of our being apart. I can't let that happen ever again. But I can't have Lacey showing up while I'm here."

"I value you. You're the sister of my heart." Shelby straightened. "So we'll do what we did tonight. We'll work together to keep you and Lacey apart. As long as you're not in the picture, she won't figure out that you're Honey."

Jewel had her doubts, but she nodded. She signaled for them to put their heads together. Then they recited their mantra from the past. "All we have to do is keep quiet."

"All we have to do is keep quiet."

They chatted for about another hour before Roman texted. I'm on my way.

"Oh shoot. I didn't realize how much time had passed. I have to get going. Roman and I are supposed to catch up on some of our TV shows before he leaves."

"Aww. You two warm my heart."

"Yes, I don't deserve him. I told him about confronting Katrina."

"How did that go?"

"He seemed hopeful." Jewel filled her in on their conversation, leaving out the part about Roman's objections to her including that storyline in the book. "With how much he wants his son in his life, I can't imagine how he'd react to the truth about Lacey. When I do spend time thinking about it, I picture it happening to Sugar and Honey. Put it this way—I believe the lie I've told. It has become my truth." She picked up her bag and slung it over her shoulder. "I know that sounds cold . . . distant. But it's what I had to do to cope with what we did that summer."

Her cell buzzed.

> I'm here.

The women hugged like they weren't going to see each other for years, and she left with a lighter heart than when she'd arrived.

On the drive back, Roman asked if she and Shelby had enjoyed their girl talk. "It was like old times," Jewel assured him that a bright smile. Worry still gnawed at her, but neither woman was going to let anything destroy their friendship again.

She and Roman snuggled together and hit Start on episode seven of the legal thriller they had been watching weeks ago. Unlike other shows on the streaming networks, they had to wait weekly for this one. But since it had been a while since they'd viewed it, there were a few new episodes. If they weren't watching thrillers, they checked out food shows, with their latest being a barbecue showdown, until Roman drifted off to sleep.

With her eyes burning to close, Jewel joined him under the covers, but she was wide awake. Go figure. Her fingers itched to write. And write she would. Jewel opened the Notes app on her phone and began jotting down her recollection of Shelby and Kendrick's date. She sat back against the headboard and reread what she had written. She had never used this app before, but it could be useful for plot points when she was on the go.

This was some good stuff. Before she closed her eyes, her last thought was: after all Sugar had gone through, a happily-ever-after storyline would be the chef's kiss that made the readers' hearts swoon . . .

It wasn't until early the next morning when Roman lay on his back snoring that Jewel realized she had left her laptop at Shelby's. Her eyes widened. The printout! She had to get over there. If her luck held, she would be back before either Shelby or Roman awakened. Even as she rushed, she acknowledged that she was tired of the subterfuge. Shelby didn't need to stumble over the truth by accident. She didn't deserve that. Maybe it was time for Jewel to come clean. But if she did, it had to be on her terms. She had to control the narrative to ensure she still got the ending she desired.

CHAPTER 33

Lacey
August 3, 2025

Her mom had a man. That juicy tidbit of information temporarily trumped the old leather journals her mother had given her that now rested at the bottom of her bag.

Lacey had gotten up early that morning and had traipsed over to her mother's room, intending to stretch out next to her. She wanted to inhale her mother's soothing scent and soak up all her love. But Shelby's door was locked, which was odd.

When she pressed her ear to the door, Lacey made out the faint sounds of muffled talking before she heard someone leaving her mom's room. The door to her patio had a distinct sound. Lacey had dashed to the window to look at the parking space in the back of the bookstore, but he was too quick for her.

The knowledge that her mother had a love interest, like she did, made her giddy. And relieved. She was so happy she could squeal. That was probably the real reason why her mother had kept her away. It wasn't that she didn't want Lacey around. Shelby probably didn't want her knowing she had a man staying over. Not that Lacey cared, but that made sense.

Lacey decided to get a shower. Before she jumped under the spray, she sent Bea a text.

> Hey, I think my mom has a boo thang.

She cracked up at the chiming that followed. Lacey got a good scrub and washed her hair. Once she was dressed in a pair of shorts and a tank, she checked her phone. Bea had sent a GIF of woman on a saddle. Lacey cracked up.

> A boo thang LOL. Did you meet him?

> Nope. I think I heard him sneaking out this morning. Tried to get a peek but he was too quick for me.

> Go Ms Shelby. She got her groove back.

Lacey felt her cheeks warm at the reference to the old classic, *How Stella Got Her Groove Back*. Funny enough, they had watched that with Shelby, and that title had stuck with Bea. It would be funny if they weren't talking about her mother.

> Eww. I do not want to think about my mother getting it on with anybody.

> Mama's got needs.

Ugh. Another one-liner, from *Baby Boy*. Note to self: no more old movies. Lacey rolled her eyes.

> Stop quoting old movies.

> Sorry. But it fits, I can't acquit.

> Seriously???!!

Well, at least that one had come from Mrs. Bennett, who used her own deviation from that famous line from the O. J.

Simpson trial often, usually when Bea had been trying to get out of some supposedly unjust punishment.

> LOL. See you later?

> Yep. It'll be you, me and Mekhi. Choose a spot.

Bea gave her a thumbs-up. Putting her phone aside, Lacey went to snuggle on the couch with her mother.

That very evening when she arrived at to their meetup spot, Lacey put thoughts of her mother's mystery guy aside. Those two brown leather-bound books were now the central items on her mind. She kept swinging between heavy anticipation and fear of what would be revealed. Her mother hinted that all her questions would be answered after reading.

She planned to show them to Mekhi and Bea. That was the only reason she hadn't given in to the curiosity nagging at her to open the books.

Right as she neared their table, she stopped. Mekhi and Bea were hugging. She told herself not to jump to conclusions.

They had already ended their embrace by the time she arrived at the table.

Mekhi stood to hold out her chair, leaning forward to kiss her. She took a seat and grabbed a napkin to place it in her lap. "Did you order yet?" she asked pleasantly, though jealousy left a sour taste in her mouth.

It wasn't until after they'd eaten that Mekhi cleared his throat. "There's something I need to tell you."

"I'm listening." Bea drew close and moved to take Lacey's hand, but Lacey kept her eyes on Mekhi's. He locked eyes with Bea before glancing back her way then squared his shoulders.

"I've been trying to figure out a way to tell you that I'm leaving," he said.

"What?" She looked at Bea, who nodded. Her eyes held

sympathy. Of all the things she expected him to say, that wasn't it.

"I reached out to my parents, like you said, and to my surprise they responded. We had a long talk yesterday, and they invited me to join them on their escapade to Thailand at the end of this month." His voice held a hint of excitement. "I told them I needed time to think about it. Because I needed to talk to you. But I was so apprehensive, Bea got it out of me."

"Yeah, I told him to rip the Band-Aid off. So what you saw was commiseration. Nothing else."

She lowered her chin to her chest as she processed his news. How could she not be happy for him? Yet she wasn't ready for him to go. They were just getting to the good part of their relationship. This was someone she could fall in love with, if she wasn't halfway there already.

"Bea gave me a good idea," Mekhi said.

Lacey's head popped up. "Oh?"

He scooted close and took Lacey's hands in his. "How about you come with me?" he whispered. "If you say yes, I promise I'll give you the trip of a lifetime."

"What?" she said for the second time that night.

"That's my cue to leave," Bea said. She pulled out her card. "I'll take care of the meal so you two can talk." Then she hugged Lacey who was still shocked at that option. "Thank me later, girl, and remember you're *grown* grown," Bea whispered, kissing the top of Lacey's head.

"I don't know what to say," Lacey voiced, but in her heart she knew. She wanted to say *yes*. Except just as he wanted to be with his parents, she wanted to be with her mom. Or in this case, in the same state just in case something happened and her mother needed her. And Lacey wouldn't agree without talking to her mother first. Regardless of how Bea advised.

Mekhi spoke up. "Your mother is doing better, and she

does have her friend to support her. Do you think she would be all right with you coming with me? All expenses paid? It would just be for a couple of weeks."

It was like he had read her mind. Lacey rubbed her nose. Her mother also did have that mystery man. Maybe she would be all right. "Let me talk to her and let you know."

"Okay. Will you talk to her tonight?"

Lacey eased back into her chair. "I'm not sure . . . but I will soon." He was coming across a little too insistent for her liking. That made her feel pressured. "What happens if I don't go?" she challenged. "Does that mean we're over?"

"Never. Just be prepared to be annoyed with me calling you to show you everything."

She relaxed. "Talk about a first-class answer."

"I mean every word." Sincerity shone in his eyes.

Lacey pinched herself. Mekhi reached over and stilled her hand. "What are you doing?"

"Pinching myself. Because you cannot be real. Boys like you don't exist."

"You're right. But men like me do." Reaching over, he tucked her curl behind her ear and kissed her like they were the only two in the restaurant. Catcalls made them pull apart.

"I'll let you know," Lacey breathed out. Even as she said the words, uncertainty niggled. She didn't relish the thought of her mother here in Delaware while she went off with Mekhi and his parents. Panic whirled in. She hadn't even met his parents. He hadn't met her mother either. Of course, she had to voice that aloud.

"How about we see if your mother is available tomorrow?" he suggested as they left the restaurant. "And I can have you both meet my folks over video call. My parents have a foundation if your mother wants to research them, although I think most people know my father."

"My mom doesn't." She had indeed told her mother that

tidbit to which Shelby had responded, "Who is that?" She smirked. "Not everyone follows football."

Mekhi stopped at the light. "Do you want to come with me?" A throng of tourists filled the pedestrian crossing.

"I do and I don't."

He squared his shoulders and mumbled, "Take all the time you need to think about it." As they reached her place, Mekhi leaned over and gave her a peck—a sad peck—on her lips. "I'll call you tomorrow. Or better yet, I'll wait for you to call."

"All right." Lacey trudged up the stairs. The door closed with a click. She dropped her bag on the floor and plopped on her bed. Her cell buzzed. She almost ignored it. Almost.

> Hi, sweetie. Are you available for a quick chat?

It was her mom. Her entire body exhaled. Her mother had perfect timing as usual. It was like there was some sixth sense she was endowed with when she'd become a mother because Shelby was the only person Lacey would talk to right now.

> Yes.

Her phone rang seconds later.

"I just wanted to hear your voice and check up on you," her mother said, her voice gentle, probing.

"Mekhi is planning to go with his family on their adventure to Thailand at the end of this month, and he asked me to go with him. All expenses paid."

"Okay? I think that's generous."

"I don't want to leave you." The minute she said those words, her mother surprised her with her comeback.

"Might I remind you that I'm the parent here? I'm practically recovered. I'll be fine." She sounded so certain, yet Lacey struggled to believe that all would be well.

"And what if something happens to you and I'm not here? I can't lose you."

"You're not going to lose me," Shelby said. "And I know I can't guarantee that, but you can't hold back because you're afraid of something going wrong. Guess what? If something is going to go wrong, it is. There's nothing you or I can do about it. I want you to go and experience the things I didn't get to do. The young man you've been telling me about sounds trustworthy, and I trust your judgment. I see no reason why you can't go." Whoa. Those words were uttered with such confidence that it lifted her spirits. "Now, before you go anywhere, I'd want to meet him and his family and have your full itinerary."

"I added myself again to your Life App, Mom." Lacey chuckled. "You can track my whereabouts from anywhere in the world."

"Right. Right. But you must promise to check in every day, regardless."

"All right. I'll call Mekhi back," she said. "We would be leaving in about a week. I'll let you know once we've pinned down a departure date."

"Perfect. I'll come over to Rehoboth, and we can have dinner or something. Or pizza. Whatever. I'm not fussy."

This conversation felt so surreal. She thought her mother would object. Instead, it was almost like Shelby was pushing her to go . . . Hmm . . . That's when she remembered the journals.

She ran her sweaty palms over her jeans, bent over to grab to handle of her backpack and dug inside for the brown books. She held them in her hands. They had some weight to them.

"You've suddenly gone quiet," her mother said. Almost as if she could see what Lacey was doing. Unless this was the real reason for her mother's call. To see if Lacey had started the journals.

"I haven't read any of the entries yet," she whispered. "The journals."

"Ah! I've been thinking about that. Maybe you should wait until after your trip. The truth will be there when you get back. In fact, I think that's a good idea. You want to go on your trip without details of the past haunting you."

"Haunting?"

"Heh. Wrong choice of words." Her mother took heavy breaths in her ear. "What I mean is, you want to have a good time and not focus on searching for answers about your birth parents."

Lacey furrowed her brows. Her location wouldn't diminish her desire to know her roots or who she was. Her stomach bubbles multiplied. Oh, her mother was being all stealthy with it, but Shelby definitely didn't want Lacey reading the journals. Maybe she had given them to her on impulse and now regretted her decision. Yes, that's probably what it was, and she was calling to see how far Lacey had gotten and what she had read. Goose bumps broke out on her arms. A hollow feeling whipped her insides. But why would Shelby withhold knowledge of her history from her? She had to know.

She licked her lips. "Sorry, Mom. No backsies allowed. I'll read them and return them before I go."

"Uh, okay, if that's what you want to do." She released a breath. "Okay, then."

Mom sounded flustered. Guilty? Lacey ended the call but not before her mother emphasized how much she loved her and that she was there if Lacey needed to talk. Those reminders increased her anxiety levels. She sent Mekhi a quick text to update him on their change of plans and to request he set up the video call with his parents. Not even his kissing and dancing emojis distracted her from her next task. She was now eyeing the book with laser focus and extremely sweaty palms.

Tossing her phone on the bed, Lacey burrowed under her covers and cracked open the first book labeled *Private* in permanent ink.

CHAPTER 34

⁓

Shelby
August 4, 2025

Worry made for a terrible bedmate. It had kept Shelby from sleeping all through the night so that by the time there was a sliver of light across the sky, she had already been up for hours just like the night before. Except she had begun her day yesterday engaging in some serious tongue action with Kendrick.

This morning, her day commenced with bags under eyes and a headache sawing away at her temples. It was already a muggy eighty degrees and rising. For the hundredth time, she checked her cell phone to see if her daughter had called.

Crickets.

What page was Lacey on? Did she finish the journals? Oh Lord. This waiting in limbo, in uncertainty, was agony. Let's just beef it out already. She needed to know if Lacey would hate her for the rest of her life or if she would understand . . . forgive her, maybe?

She needed a distraction.

Shelby forced herself to get out of bed. She took care of her morning rituals, got dressed and padded into the kitchen. It was now five o'clock. It would be hours before the bookstore opened, and she didn't have a therapy session with Kendrick until later that day. They had exchanged text messages, each keeping it light, neither mentioning their *sex*tracurricular activities. But her brain and body didn't forget, and at odd moments, a flash of what they had done hit her mind. Good Lord, she didn't know how she was going to look that man in the eyes during PT.

After two cups of coffee and an aspirin, and no contact from her daughter, she made her way into her office. Might as well pay some bills and give Abby a magnanimous bonus for all her efforts during Shelby's recovery.

Slipping behind her computer desk, Shelby tapped on her new bookstore point-of-sale software program. Jewel had convinced her to use it, and it was a dream. With a few clicks, she could manage her inventory, track her sales and create purchase orders. She had even been able to set up online purchases, which brought more sales. Abby had fulfilled the first set of orders, but she had twenty new ones for today. Most were for autographed copies of Jewel's books. At this rate, she was going to have to hire someone part-time to handle this side of the business.

Since she now also had a bookkeeping system, she had linked that to her bookstore program so her accounting was a breeze. Again, thanks to Jewel. Jewel had purchased a package that allowed her to get training with an accountant so she was now moderately adept at handling everything.

"No more Excel sheets!" Jewel had said. And there had been a lot. Shelby smiled.

Having her friend back in her life was paying off for her in so many ways. With the signings and the movie, she was going to end the summer with a substantial profit margin. Shelby wished there was a way she could repay Jewel for her kindness.

She printed off the online order requests. When she went to retrieve the paper from the printer, she noticed there was a huge stack in the output tray. Wow. Had she mistakenly printed more than one copy? Odd. She hadn't heard it churning out so much.

She picked up her order sheet and set it aside then glanced at the rest of the pages.

Here and Ever After.

Wait. Shelby fingered the pages. This was Jewel's next book. She was holding it in her hands. She dragged her teeth across her bottom lip. Here she was wondering what she could do to repay Jewel and then this happens. Back in the day Shelby used to help Jewel with her papers, and since she was on deadline now, Shelby could begin to do some content editing for her. That would be a big help when it was time for Jewel to do her rewrite.

Plus, she was dying to read her bestie's next masterpiece.

Shelby had made a point to read all of Jewel's novels in the last few weeks. She wasn't sure if she had ever read them before her memory loss, but they were good. The first was the strongest of the bunch. She could help make this book shine. Who knew? Maybe Jewel had left it here for her to read.

Decision made, Shelby settled behind her desk and flipped to the first page.

It took a moment for the words to register. She gasped and placed a hand over her mouth as she scanned the page. Disbelief set in.

Betrayal.

In black and white.

Her legs felt wooden. Jewel was penning a continuation of their friendship story—though, of course, the characters were called Sugar and Honey. Just like in her diary. Was that the real reason Jewel had returned? To use Shelby's plight as fodder for her next story? Flipping through the pages, Shelby saw that Jewel had been recounting all of their experiences. Tears welled.

This duplicity cut her to the core. She placed a hand across her abdomen. Why not ask Shelby? Why pretend she was here for reconciliation?

She flipped the last pages and saw that Jewel had written a scene with her and Kendrick. Curious, she read that chapter in full. It was a tender, emotional encounter, but it felt like her supposed friend had put her life on blast.

No wonder Jewel hadn't minded helping Shelby. She was helping herself to Shelby's life story once again, but this time without her permission. She scoffed. Now her words about Shelby's old manuscript—*Shoot, if you don't want it, I'll take it*—took on a different meaning. Jewel probably meant that literally.

Hurt burned in her chest. She wanted to lash out, to confront Jewel for her treachery. But what was the point? Jewel would only justify her actions. As usual. Shelby could hear the sob story now, and she didn't have time for it. She had to be ready for when Laccy called. That's where she would center her focus.

A thought occurred, and she searched the pages again. Just like in the first novel, there was no mention of Lacey that she could see. She heaved a sigh of relief. But of course Jewel wouldn't mention Lacey. Jewel was all for telling stories that didn't affect her interests.

Bottling her fury, Shelby tapped the papers against the desk to straighten them and then put them in a manila envelope. She used a Sharpie to write Jewel's name across it with a flourish.

All of a sudden, facts and details came together like puzzle pieces. *Just like that.* Every single detail was crystal clear in her mind! Oh my word, her memory was *back*! Looking around the space, she viewed it with eyes that remembered who she was. She dashed to her desk and picked up a snow globe. She'd bought that in Lancaster, Pennsylvania, in Amish Country three years ago. She and Lacey had spent the night up there. Then she went behind her desk and picked up a few of the autographed copies she had purchased at Nora Roberts's bookstore in Boonsboro, Maryland.

Lifting her hands in the air, she yelled, "I remember! I remember!" Wrapping her arms about her, her jubilation morphed into tears. "I know all of who I am." She felt . . . whole again. Her breath caught. Was this the feeling Lacey sought?

She touched her heart as the tears rolled down her face. Now she understood. There was nothing like knowing who you were. Oh my stars! How many sleepless nights had Lacey spent wondering who she belonged to and what her place in the world was? Shelby wiped her face. With her memory back, suddenly all was right in her world. She snapped her fingers. Just like that.

Would that be how it was for Lacey when her daughter learned the truth? Because truth filled Shelby's entire body. And now with the manila folder tucked under her arm, she strutted back up to her place, touching this and that, and feeling like she belonged here. The thing was, until her memory returned, Shelby hadn't even recognized that she had been walking around in a fog. She had just gone with the flow. Adjusted. Adapted.

Gosh, she wanted Lacey to experience this wholeness. To finally stop having to adjust and adapt and just . . . feel.

Now she knew for sure she had done the right thing giving Lacey her journal. No matter the outcome, she had done the right thing. All she could hope and pray was that Lacey forgave her because Shelby loved her more than anything.

Even Jewel.

She curled her lips. Jewel, on the other hand, even when the right thing was staring her in the face, would deny, deny, deny. Well, she appeared to be all right with cultivating a life of deceit and making a profit from it. It pinched Shelby to know she was also benefiting from Jewel's nefarious deeds, but shoot, that was her story in those pages. Jewel had stolen from her. She wouldn't feel guilty for any help she received. But what she would do was clean house.

She was going to rid her life of Jewel a second time, and this time it would be for good.

Moving with speed, she packed all of Jewel's possessions in the trunk of her car and sped out of her parking spot. Shelby fumed all the way to the Airbnb, proud of herself for doing all that packing without hurting herself. Meticulously, she placed the boxes by the front door and then placed the manuscript on top.

That would say it all.

She had no intentions of seeing Jewel again.

But of course, right as she was about to get back in the vehicle, the door swung open and Jewel rushed outside. She was dressed in a white shirt and black pants, which was surprising, because as a nighttime writer, most days Jewel didn't get up until after nine. Shelby froze, watching as Jewel took in the scene before her. She skirted around her possessions and ran over to where Shelby stood.

"Oh, Shelby. This isn't what it looks like. I can explain."

She shut the door of her car and addressed Jewel. "This isn't what it looks like?" Shelby shot back. "Well, please clarify what this is, because to me it looks like you came back to Delaware to help yourself to my life story. Again. Without my permission. Or are you talking about someone else on those pages?" She flailed her hands. "And if I'm not mistaken, you were probably heading to my place because you forgot to grab your manuscript on your way out."

Jewel held Shelby's arms. "I planned to talk to you about it, Shelby. You've got to believe me. When I realized I left it over there I panicked, and all I could think about was getting it before you saw. But when I was getting dressed this morning, I realized how tired I am of covering up what I was doing. I was going to give it to you to read. I promise."

"How convenient. Well, this is a case of too little, too late." She stormed away and circled back to Jewel. "Ten years ago we parted ways, and I see now that it was for the best. The decision I made then is just as apt now. At your core, you're selfish. Smarmy. Oh, you assuage your guilt by throwing money at people, but there is no buying friendship. We're done." She jumped into her vehicle.

Jewel yelled out, "Please, don't leave like this. Give me a chance to explain."

Shelby rolled down the window. "Keep your explanations and shove them where the sun doesn't shine."

She tore out of the driveway and headed back to the bookstore. Just as she was about to go upstairs, she spotted her bike. It had been a while since she had ridden . . .

She gave Kendrick a quick call. As it turned out, he was about to go riding, and he wasn't far from her. "Come get me," she commanded and then marched into her house to suit up. Kendrick arrived just as she put her helmet on. She straddled the bike and gripped the handlebars. "Let's go. I need to work off some serious tension this morning."

"Anything you want to talk about?" he asked.

"No. I just want to ride."

"Fair enough. But don't overdo it." He pushed off, and she followed his lead before passing him. Looking back, she could see him giving her a nod, so she headed for the trail. Shelby wasn't ready to hit the main roads just yet. She pumped her legs to move faster.

While she rode, she thought about her manuscript in her nightstand. Shelby ducked her head to avoid a branch whacking her in the face. Quite simply, she had been too caught up with her friendship with Jewel and then her new life with Lacey to follow the dream of her heart.

And she was afraid of mediocrity. The entire publishing process from beginning to end—securing an agent, garnering editor interest, getting approval from the acquisitions team then going through rounds of editing—all for readers to potentially slam your book—was hard on the psyche. Shelby didn't want to blend in with the hopefuls, she wanted to stand out.

But she couldn't if her work was hidden in her nightstand. Shelby had to put herself out there, open herself up for criticism, until she got her breakthrough. But ever since her parents' deaths, she had stopped taking risks. She sniffled and blinked to keep the tears at bay. Maybe if she hadn't been all about herself, her parents would still be here. Why was she alive if not to change her ways and help others?

So yes, let Jewel have her book. Let her get all the accolades. She turned the bend. Kendrick caught up to her and tipped his head to the right. She nodded, relieved he had taken the lead.

Yes, she could make the sacrifice to be the mother Lacey needed. The mother she should have been years ago. But Lacey was grown.

And it was okay for her to pick up her dream.

Her parents had been proud of her skill. They had loved her, and they wouldn't want her to carry the blame of their deaths on her shoulders. Maybe she needed to accept the forgiveness they would have given her had they been alive. Maybe the way to honor them was to pursue her literary goals.

Sweat poured from her body. A cleansing of sorts. And she welcomed it.

Shelby smiled and wiped the perspiration off her brow. The heat of the sun now baked her back. She was going to have to take a shower when she got home. Kendrick tilted his body as he went around the curve ahead and she did the same. Then he cut through a path before he led her back home.

Taking off her helmet, she grinned. "That was therapeutic."

"Yes, riding is a good way to clear your head." He jutted his chin toward her. "You did great out there."

"Thanks." She swung her leg over the bike and got off. "I'd like to do that again."

"Sure. Anytime." His eyes held warmth, like those of a lover.

She blushed. "I remember you owe me a date."

"Excuse me?" He shook his head. "We've already been on a date."

"Yes, but I asked that time. A few days before my accident, you sort of asked me out—at least I think you did—and I said *yes*."

"You remember that?" When she nodded, he picked her up in his arms and swung her around. "That's wonderful news! And yes, I'd love to take you out, but we're not going to go cycling. Somewhere fancy, when you're ready. No rush."

Jewel came around the corner and marched toward them. What was she doing here? Shelby kept her focus centered on Kendrick. "I'll hold you to that."

Giving Jewel a wave, Kendrick rode off after telling Shelby he would be in touch. Jewel stopped in front of Shelby. The look on her face said she wasn't leaving until she had said her piece.

Shelby lifted her chin. "I said all I wanted to say to you already. So why are you here?" She steadied her bike on the bike rack and then squatted to put the lock on.

"Because I'm fighting for our friendship."

Those words lightened her heart, but Shelby couldn't allow herself to be swayed. "I can't just roll over and let you use my life as your source of entertainment." She stood and dusted her hands on her biking shorts, kind of like she needed to do with this relationship.

"I came here because you needed me as much as I've always needed you." Jewel placed a hand on Shelby's arm. "And I haven't been forthcoming with my financial situation, but I have been a true friend." She circled the sand with her shoe. "My sister has hypertension and needed new, more expensive medicines. And remember, Roman was out of work for a while, and I had major repairs in my house. It was a lot of stress carrying all that on my shoulders, and I just couldn't write. But then you called . . ."

"And you thought to yourself, *Let me maximize on Shelby's terrifying experience by writing a book about it.*" She pointed to her chest. "Do you know what it's like to lose a part of your life?" She rolled her eyes. "Just save the excuses."

"No. I didn't think about writing that story at first . . ."

Jewel couldn't even meet her eyes. Shaking her head in disgust, Shelby climbed the steps to her bedroom. Jewel was right behind her like a hound chasing a bone. They stopped on the landing.

"I know it looks bad, but I was desperate. If I didn't come up with something, I would have had to return my advance, and the pressure was intense. I couldn't think. I couldn't write." She wrung her hands. "But once I came here, being around you gave me inspiration. I fell in love with us again and all that made our friendship beautiful. And that's when I found the words. They flowed and flowed."

"Yet you didn't tell me." She stretched her hands. "You should have told me the truth. I would have understood, even if I didn't like it. But you were content to use me, and you would have kept it up if I hadn't discovered the manuscript this morning."

"I did plan on telling you, but I was scared to lose you," Jewel pleaded. "I'm sorry. You're my oldest friend, and I love you dearly." Her eyes flooded with tears. "I can't lose you again. I'll do anything. Just please tell me what I can do to make things right."

"Don't publish this story. That's what you can do. Give your publisher something else." She folded her arms.

Jewel stepped back and frowned. "I don't have another story, and I have a deadline. And they are in love with this one. They said it has heart. It has intensity, and it's some of the best writing I've ever done. And I agree. As you can see, I literally can't do this without you." She sounded bitter. "So please, don't ask me to do that. Can't you think of something else? What can I buy for you? For Lacey?"

"Sorry, love is not for sale. Now, hand over my key and leave." Once Jewel placed the key in her hands, she spun around and opened her bedroom door. She didn't want Jewel seeing her tears. She ached at the torment on Jewel's face. Even now, despite learning about Jewel's betrayal, Shelby's heart ached for her situation. She hated to think of Jewel having to return that advance, especially with Hazel and her mother depending on her. Ugh. She was such a softie.

No. She wasn't going to beat up on herself for caring.

"Wait!" Jewel called out, her chest heaving. "I . . ." She seemed to search for words. "I love you. If this is the last time we're going to speak, that's the last thing I want you to remember me saying. I love you, Shelby Andrews. You're my friend and my sister, and I'll love you for life."

Shelby broke. "I can't do this anymore, Jewel. I just can't. I love you, you were my first friend, but I have to love myself first." She walked over to her nightstand and took out her flash drive and tried to place it in Jewel's hand. When Jewel refused to take it, she tucked it in Jewel's shirt pocket. "Use that story instead, if you must."

"No. I can't do that. They want the story I'm telling now."

"Just get out my face, Jewel," she yelled. "I'm done with you. You've dragged my heart over coals, and I don't think I'll ever recover."

"I—" Suddenly Jewel's face paled, her gaze transfixed on something behind Shelby. Shelby spun around to see Lacey standing by the doorjamb looking between them. She held the journals in her hand, but her eyes were pinned on Jewel.

"Lacey," Shelby breathed out, her shock making her mind go blank. She shook her head. This wasn't happening. This wasn't how she'd planned to talk with her daughter this morning. Shelby had known Lacey would want to talk, but she had gotten so angry at Jewel that it had slipped her mind.

"You," Lacey said, hyperventilating, and pointed at Jewel. "I know you. You're the woman from the painting."

"No. No. I—" Jewel shook her head. "What painting?"

"Declan Welch has a painting called *The Beach*, and her face is hidden but you look just like the woman in it. I saw it when I was in New York." Oh yes. *That* painting.

"I was up all night reading the journal." Lacey looked over at Shelby. "Mom, how do you know her?"

"Th-this is m-my friend Jewel. The one I told you about who came to look after me after my accident." She hated how her voice shook. She sounded . . . guilty.

"Yes, but she's the woman from the canvas." Lacey's gaze swung back and forth between Shelby and Jewel. Her brows knitted. "What's going on here?" Then her eyes went wide. "Oh my goodness. *You're* Honey."

"Sweetheart, let me explain."

"No. No." She backed up. "I don't need an explanation. You *are* Sugar and Honey. I can't believe this. All this time I was searching and searching, and you knew. You knew." Lacey cupped her mouth and ran.

"Lacey!" Shelby screamed, grabbing Jewel's hand. "We have to go after her." They took off side by side, calling Lacey's name and racing after her. But her daughter kept running, running toward the ocean.

CHAPTER 35

Lacey
August 4, 2025

A few hours earlier

Thanks for covering for me today.

Lacey texted her coworker at the boutique. From the minute she started reading the journal, she knew she was going to pull an all-nighter. What she hadn't known was how reading Sugar's diary was going to make her feel.

For most of her life, wherever she went, she would study people's faces and if they were about the right age group, she would wonder *Is that my mother? Could he be my father?* Though she had Shelby, her inner heart felt shattered, like broken pieces of glass.

But as Lacey read each entry, it felt like a shard of glass was being reattached, and her identity was being reaffirmed. And as the night moved on, she kept turning the pages, getting a vivid image of the two young women, who had been roughly her age, frolicking one summer with a man who changed their lives.

Above all, she wondered, why did her mother record all this in her journal? She couldn't really be Sugar, right? It was very clearly written in her mother's handwriting.

Propping her head on her elbow and resting on her side, Lacey flipped back to the section of entries that she had earmarked to read again. These entries used a lot of *we* and *us*, so she couldn't tell who the actual birth mother was, but it made her heart soar seeing she was loved.

> April 13, 2006
> The tummy still was flat. No morning sickness, no weight gain.
> A cryptic pregnancy. According to the internet, a cryptic pregnancy until delivery is a 1 in 2,500 probability.
> Our baby was meant to be here. Our miracle.
>
> August 8, 2006
> As the fall semester is about to begin, we vow that we will finish this year of college and never speak of our little one again. Or what we did. It's too painful. But our deed is as a shadow, always in the back of our brains.
> And so we willingly break our word.
> We toss out possibilities of what our sweet girl is doing at the most random times—in the middle of eating a French fry, while walking to class or on our way home from a friend's party. We are always thinking about this tiny tyke, who is four months now.
> I wonder what life would be like for us now if we had kept her. But then I push that thought aside. Keeping her was the one thing we knew we were not ready to do. Raise a child when we were but children ourselves.
> She's better off without us. At least that is what I tell my bleeding heart.
>
> February 14, 2007
> This year, Honey and I decided the baby would be our Valentine. On this day, we allowed ourselves to voice how much we love this child. Because this baby has changed us. It has brought us closer. It has made us

think about someone other than ourselves and each other.

Anyways, Honey and I sat cross-legged in front of each other, each holding a cupcake—one with blue frosting and one with pink. With each bite, we said, "You're loved, little one. You are loved."

Lacey sniffled. She was crying just as much this time as she had the first time that she'd read it. She didn't know if she could put into words the relief, the happiness she felt. Being nineteen, she understood their fear of parenthood. She understood them grappling with what to do.

But as much as she was happy, she was filled with sorrow. And even more questions. Like, if they loved her, why didn't they keep her? But the biggest one was *Which of these two women was her mother?* Because she now believed her mother had to be one of the two girls.

Tossing back the sheets, Lacey decided to get dressed and catch an Uber to the bookstore on Eagle Point Beach. She needed to talk to her mother. Shelby had the answers to all her questions. Lacey only hoped her mother would be willing to give them.

NOW LACEY STOOD KNEE-DEEP IN THE ATLANTIC OCEAN with her arms spread wide and sobbed. Behind her, she could hear her mother and her friend, Jewel, calling.

They were still a distance away. She put aside the worry of her mother hobbling and waded out farther into the water, wishing for the waves to take her away.

Yet even as her body shook and the tears rolled down her face, her heart acknowledged that she had come too far in her quest to run from the truth. Even if it came with the most painful of betrayals.

How could her mother lie to her? And was Shelby actually her mother, who had given her up and then adopted her? All these thoughts raced through her mind while the two women hollered her name behind her.

She folded her arms about her waist and shivered then turned to face them just as they were about to step in. "Don't come after me or I'll keep going." Shelby put a foot in the water. Lacey backed up deeper. Now the water was up to her waist.

"No, no," her mother yelled, stepping back. "Lacey, they have the red flag out. That means there are rip currents and large waves. Please come back." She broke into tears and leaned into Jewel. The women huddled together.

Lacey lifted her chin. "I'm not going anywhere." The waves crashed against her, rocking her body hard. She lost her balance and went under, but she pulled herself upward. Her heart thudded. She was dressed in a tank and shorts, but they were drenched and weighed her down.

"Ask me anything you want. I'll answer," Jewel called out. "Just come out of the water."

"You don't mean that," she shouted.

"I mean it. Anything."

For several seconds, Lacey debated staying where she was in a show of stubbornness and a perverse satisfaction of watching both women shriek with fear. That's what they got for making her feel unwanted for most of her life. But she had too much to live for to continue putting her life at risk to prove a point. She took tentative steps forward.

As soon as she was in reach, both Shelby and Jewel grabbed her into their embrace. They cried and rocked her. "Never do that again, Lacey," Shelby said. "I can't lose my daughter."

"Am I really your daughter?" Lacey mumbled.

Jewel reared her head back, but her lips were bunched tightly together.

Shelby's face reddened. She gave Lacey a pointed look. "We can talk about all that, but let's get you back inside."

"No." Moving out of their embrace, she gave them each a steely glare and then asked, "Which of you is my birth mother?"

Shelby and Jewel looked at each other and joined hands. After a beat, both women stepped forward.

"Are you two serious right now?" Lacey screamed. "I deserve to know the truth. My life isn't a game between two giddy teenagers. I can't believe you guys would pull a stunt like this when I'm asking the most important question of my life."

"I'm your mother, Lacey," Shelby said, with tears in her eyes. "In every way that counts. I have loved you from the moment I saw you."

Jewel locked eyes with Shelby and nodded before facing Lacey. "No, I'm your mother. I held you in my arms, and I've loved you ever since."

They both held out their arms. Lacey looked between them. She didn't know which one to believe. "Even now, after all these years, you're covering for each other, putting yourselves before me." She ran back to the bookstore and dashed inside for the journals her mother had given her.

Lacey plowed her way through the sand back to the beach. The two women stood where she left them, watching her carefully, like she was a rabid animal about to attack.

Grunting, Lacey raced into the water and threw the journals far into the ocean using all her strength.

"No," Shelby cried out. Her knees buckled beneath her, and she sank unto the sand. Jewel stood, a small smile on her lips, giving Lacey the distinct impression that she was relieved.

Within seconds, the water greedily swallowed the journals, taking their secrets to its depths. Jewel folded her legs to sit with Shelby. They joined hands.

"Why would you do that?" Shelby whispered, her voice

raw with grief. "Those meant a lot to me. I have so many memories in them."

"It doesn't make sense," Jewel mumbled, shaking her head. Lacey didn't believe her remorse for a minute.

"I don't quite know why, but I think it's because I knew it would hurt you. As I am hurting. As I have been hurting." Lacey swallowed. A part of her regretted her rash action because the journals held so many hints of her past. But another part of her felt free. She lifted her chin and bit out, "I'm not to be hidden, confined in the pages of a book. I'm not some work of fiction. I'm real. I'm very much alive." She pointed to the waters. "And I'm nobody's secret." Lacey pointed at Shelby and Jewel, hardening her heart. "I'm going to tell the world who I am."

Jewel's eyes went wide and she stood, stretching out her hands. "What does that mean? What are you going to do?" she sputtered. "Please don't tell me you plan to blast this all over the internet? This could ruin us. We could end up in prison. There's no coming back once you've been canceled." She looked at Shelby, desperation in her tone. "Say something. You have to stop her."

The fact that Jewel seemed to only care about her reputation was absolutely distasteful.

Her mother looked up, her eyes ravaged, her voice filled with dejection. "It's her truth. So it's up to her to decide how she copes with it."

Jewel's lips curled as she addressed Shelby. "I told you this would happen. I—" She looked back and forth between them. Stepping back, she almost lost her footing. "It's my word against yours. Maybe everyone will think you're some misguided fan."

"You don't believe that, or you wouldn't be so panicked," Lacey scoffed and started to walk away, before tossing over her shoulder, "But I guess we'll see how this all plays out."

CHAPTER 36

Jewel
August 4, 2025

When she returned to the Airbnb, laptop and manuscript in hand, Jewel found it hard to believe that she had only been gone for ninety minutes. Her body ragged from the battle she had just lost, she opened the door to the house, half expecting Roman to be standing by the entrance waiting for her.

The house was quiet.

Thank goodness. She stripped out of her clothes and headed straight for the shower, her insides shaky.

She needed to wash off the grime of the morning before she talked with her husband. Once Lacey had walked off, Jewel and Shelby parted ways. There was nothing left to say between them. On the drive over, Jewel had calmed herself enough to realize that Lacey could be bluffing. She was hurting and probably needed some time to calm down because her anger was not only understandable, it was justified. Jewel chided herself for goading Lacey. Her reaction had been all about self-preservation.

In retrospect, that was not a good look.

But if Lacey was going to air their business on social media, Jewel had to do damage control. She couldn't chance Roman finding out from anyone but her. She had lost her friend and her daughter all over again, and she couldn't lose her husband. She had to tell him the truth. She had to tell him everything.

Jewel gave her body a vigorous wash before tackling her hair. Just as she turned off the faucet, Roman padded inside. He gave her a sexy, clueless smile.

"Please tell me you brought back coffee." He grinned. "I showered and all that already, but when I didn't see you I decided to get a nap. You wore me out last night, in a good way."

She was too distraught to flirt back with him. "No, I have a heavy dosage of heartache to heap on your shoulders instead."

His head whipped around. "What's wrong?" The concern in his voice shredded her last ounce of control.

Jewel placed both hands on the bathroom counter and lowered her head. "Everything."

Coming over to her, Roman massaged her shoulders. "Tell me."

The dam within her broke then, and her body shook from the force of her sobs. "I messed up, baby. I messed up, and I've lost my friend. I've lost her for good."

Roman allowed her to cry until she was spent. Then he dried her tears, rocked her until she calmed and urged her to get dressed. She put on a light throwover and flip-flops.

Jewel took his hand and led him to the bedroom. She sat on the edge of the bed, and once he was next to her she unloaded. She told him all about Shelby finding the manuscript and their fight afterward. To his credit, Roman never said *I told you so*. But he pointed out that Jewel needed to respect other people's desire for privacy. Including his own.

Jewel hadn't been able to look him in the eyes.

Then he rocked her and reassured that Shelby just needed time and that she would come around. Jewel didn't agree, but she had so much more to share so all she did was nod.

When she got up her nerve, Jewel told him how Shelby's daughter had turned up midfight and how she got upset and took off for the ocean. Her voice box was becoming increasingly tighter with each reveal. Her breath quickened, and her chest tightened. It was time to share her biggest secret of all. So many scenarios about why she shouldn't flashed before her, but she was tired. And the memory of Lacey's pain was seared into her mind.

Gathering her courage, she stood, squared her shoulders, looked him in the eyes and said, "I have a child. A daughter that no one knows about." Her insides quaked, and her legs felt like jelly, but uttering those words freed her. She exhaled.

Roman sprang to his feet to peer down at her. "What did you just say?"

The heavy frown on his face was a tad off-putting, and for a second she wanted to retract her words and go back to their life before. Because there would always be a before and after with her and Roman now. Before she told him. And after she told him. But that twenty-year-old secret had been loosed, and that heavy cloak of secrets had been lifted off her shoulders. And she had zero regrets.

She lifted her chin. "Twenty years ago, I gave birth to a daughter." She marched into the kitchen, suddenly famished. He was right behind her. She picked up the menus and ordered them breakfast. They were going to need sustenance after this conversation.

"Do you remember the baby that was left at the bookstore in Eagle Point Beach almost twenty years ago?"

His eyes narrowed before they lit up with recognition. "Do you mean at Shelby's bookstore?"

"Yes, well, it wasn't hers then, since her parents had sold . . ." She stopped, realizing that she was rambling. "But yes, that one."

"I vaguely recall. But what does that have to do with you?"

Her stomach knotted as she spoke words she had never spoken aloud to anyone other than Shelby. "That was me. Shelby and I were the ones who left the baby there."

His mouth dropped. "Say what?" Then he shook his head. "No. I would have known. You would have told me something like that." She understood this reaction. He was in denial, as she had been for years. He paced the room. "It made national news. You can't be that infamous girl who abandoned her child."

Jewel walked over to him and placed a hand on his arm. "I am." She repeated it several times, claiming her parenthood.

Acceptance gradually came, and his features tightened with anger. And hurt. He stepped back. "You didn't think to tell me you had a child and tossed her away?"

Those words struck her hard. Punctured her to her core. She had read as much in the newspapers back then from irate people, but she hadn't expected her spouse would feel that way.

"I didn't *toss her away*. That would have been cruel. We wrapped her up gently and left her with someone we knew would care for her."

"I apologize for the wording, but no matter how you phrase it, it still comes down to the fact that you abandoned your child." His words held contempt. She was surprised at his reaction. She hadn't expected him to judge her so harshly. His voice broke. "You know how I feel about Curtis and how badly I want a relationship with him, and you did something like that and kept it from me all these years?"

"I—I was a scared teenager, and I wasn't ready to be a mother—"

"So you give the baby up for adoption. You don't run."

She straightened. "I'm ashamed, but I was a baby back then. I have forgiven myself, and I hope in time you will as well."

"Glibly saying this is a case of *all's well that ends well*." He dragged a hand over his head. "I can't believe how you've rationalized this to make it all right. This doesn't even sound like the woman I married. I mean, I know you have a level of self-centeredness, but I always believed you cared about people in your own way. I didn't think you would be so self-serving. Even if you felt you did the right thing long ago because of age, because of resources, you're not in the same position now. Why not step up and claim her during the past twenty years?"

"Whoa. You're being overly critical right now. I did what I thought was best. I couldn't claim her. I could go to prison if all this comes out. Plus, look at how you're judging me, and you know me. Imagine what my readers—"

"Huh. I should have known this was about your readers. What about a little girl longing to know her mother?" His voice cracked. "What if she knows she's adopted but feels like she wasn't wanted? Have you thought about that?" Oh yes, she had married an empathetic man. She loved that about him, but right now his empathy was whipping at her conscience.

"I did keep track of her. I know for a fact that Lacey was—" She gasped. She hadn't meant to say her daughter's name . . . At least not yet.

Roman's eyes widened, and his mouth dropped. He remained that way for a beat. He placed a hand on his hip. "Lacey? Am I hearing right? *Lacey* is the baby from the bookstore? Lacey is your daughter?" He shook his head. "Hang on, because this just got really weird. Are you telling me that Shelby adopted the child you left at the bookstore?"

She wrung her hands. "Y-yes."

"So that's why you and Shelby fell out. The real reason." He flailed his hands. "I can't believe you've been lying to me all these years." He rubbed between his eyes. "I feel like an idiot for trusting you. For opening my mouth and letting you feed me garbage, because now I'm sick to my stomach."

"But that has nothing to do with you and me. Shelby and I promised each other that we wouldn't tell a soul." As soon as she said that, Jewel knew it had been the wrong thing to say.

"I get that. But I'm your husband. I needed to know you had a child. You know how I've been dying on the inside because

I don't have a relationship with my son. That's not my choice. Giving up your child was yours. You didn't trust me or our love enough to tell me the truth. What else haven't you told me?" Roman's body shook with fury. She had never seen him this angry with her.

"That's it." Her lips quivered.

"That's it," he scoffed. Then he marched into the room and grabbed his bag, throwing his belongings inside.

"Wh-where you are going? I've got food coming . . ."

"I'm going home. I don't know who I've married, and I'm questioning everything I thought I knew about you right now. I don't know where to even begin to wrap my mind around this."

Her heart ached and tears welled. "Are you—" her chest heaved "—are you leaving me?"

"I don't know what I'm doing." He zipped the bag closed and stalked toward the front door. "The only thing I know for sure is that I am getting out of here. I can't share the same space with you right now. I can't."

"Roman, please. I . . . I need you. I love you. I've never lied about that, and I have no one else in my corner. I can't lose you too."

"Then you should have been honest. Deceit destroys a marriage."

Those words were a painful pill to swallow. She trembled. "I'm sorry. I'm so sorry."

"What's eating away at me is wondering if you would have told me any of this if your secrets hadn't already exploded in your face."

He sounded so hurt and disillusioned that she wished she could lie to him, but she was done with her dishonesty. She had to stand in her truth and face the consequences. She thought of Shelby's words about her love for Lacey being stronger than any hate that Lacey might feel for her. That's how she felt for Roman and how she believed he felt for her despite his pain.

Her throat constricted, and as her tears poured down her face she admitted, "I—I don't know. I don't know if I would have had the guts to tell you the truth, otherwise."

"That's the first honest thing you've said so far. But at least you can console yourself with the knowledge that you have some more good material for your book. Congrats, you've got another bestseller on your hands." And with that, he sailed through the door.

HOURS LATER, SITTING IN THE DARK ALONE ON THE couch in the living room, Jewel looked at the screen before her where she had finally written *The End* on her manuscript. Her agent had texted her about the final pages, asking when she could expect them.

She wished she could have told Francesca that she wasn't going to turn this book in. But her bills weren't going anywhere. Even though she had lost the respect of her husband and her best friend, she couldn't shirk her responsibilities. So she had allowed herself one big heart-wrenching cry session, and then she had finished her book.

In her version, the besties ended up together, their bond tighter than before. Unbreakable. Honey and Winston's marriage was stronger than ever, and Sugar and Theo had pledged their love for each other. Everything had been wrapped up and tied neatly in a bow. If she didn't have it in real life, she was going to make sure it happened that way in fiction. No one wanted a downer at the conclusion of a good read. They needed to see the hope, which would garner her the four- and five-star reviews: *I love the overall message of hope! I loved reading about the power of friendship! I'm glad it all worked out in the end!*

Nope. Most readers didn't care to see the permanent consequences from the sting of betrayal or the toxicity of a soured friendship. *Geez, bitter much, Jewel?* She sighed and reread her last chapter then smiled. Shoot, she was a reader too and loved the feel-good ending. She sorely wished she could replicate this in her life.

Now all she had to do with hit Send.

Yet, she was hesitant. Because she wanted Shelby's blessing. And she craved Roman's support. He hadn't even texted her once he had arrived home. She'd had to reach out and ask if he had gotten there safely. But at least he had responded with a **Yes**. However, when she said, **I love you**, all she had gotten was a thumbs-up on her text.

A ratty thumbs-up.

Well, all right, she'd leave him alone if that's all he was going to respond. But then five minutes later, she sent **Really???!!!** Because it was better to have any conversation going than none at all. That's when he'd texted, **I need time. Give me time, Jewel,** and her shoulders had slumped. He hadn't called her *honey*, or *babe*, or any other endearment. It was *Jewel*. Roman was mad for real. Her heart sank and she fretted. She'd lost him. Then she had poured all those emotions out on her pages.

And now she had a word count of 99,000.

Exhaling, Jewel composed a cheery email to her agent.

Hey, Francesca,

I'm finished. Can you believe it? When I wrote the last word, I felt like I've written the best book of my life. I hope you feel the same.

Cheers!
Jewel

Sniffling past the tears, she attached her manuscript and hit Send. Jewel helped herself to a bowl of black cherry ice cream, missing Roman. They always celebrated a submission with dinner and a cupcake or something. The tears trekked down her face.

Jewel took a snapshot of her ice cream, her vision a blur, and uploaded it to her socials along with the caption **Hey, Stoners!!** (Her fans had come up that moniker saying they were addicted to her books.) **Guess who just submitted the best work of her life?? XOXO**

The congrats were quick to come, right along with the celebratory emojis. Breaking out in a sob, Jewel shoved her devices away, stuffed a spoonful of ice cream in her mouth and lay on her side. Something hard pressed against her chest. Frowning, she reached into her shirt and pulled out the piece of metal. When she saw it was Jewel's flash drive, she cried even more, before an idea took root . . .

CHAPTER 37

Shelby

August 11, 2025

It's been a week since I've seen or spoken to Lacey. She hasn't answered my texts or calls. I'm pretty sure she's blocked me. Neither Bea nor Mekhi are telling me where she is, but Bea did say Lacey was safe. Well, I'm giving her one more day before I file a missing person report. I have barely eaten or slept, and I have to fight myself not to go knock on every door in Rehoboth Beach and give her the space she needs.

I know my child. I know all she needs is time. But it's tough to give it to her.

Thankfully, I have a lot going on with the bookstore to distract me. I hired a couple of college students to help staff the store and fulfill orders, and I've made Abby assistant manager. Last night was the third and final signing, and I avoided Jewel as much as I could. We faked smiles for the press, and I hid how much I loved seeing her in her element, how proud I was of her, because that would have invited her back into my life. And I'm done. I want to be done. My heart says differently.

She sent me a text that she was leaving tomorrow and then asked for Lacey's number.

I refused.

That's a day late and a dollar short, in my opinion. But I did say I would give Lacey Jewel's contact information if she asked for it.

Was I wrong to do that? She knows Lacey is missing and seemed just as worried as I was. And at the signing she looked . . . alone. It was hard to miss that Roman wasn't here. But that's not my problem. Not anymore. The more I tell myself that, the more my heart will accept that we are done. For good.

On a happier note, I have decided to book my trip to Jamaica. I'll be going in a few weeks, and it will be a solo trip, but I'm looking forward to it. Sometimes, a girl just needs to go home. Return to her roots . . .

Shelby's hands froze on the keyboard. Oh my goodness. She knew where Lacey was. How didn't she think of it before? Worry must have clouded her brain. Whenever Lacey got mad when she was young and claimed she was running away, she always planned to go to the same place.

Gathering her keys, Shelby jumped into her car. Her destination was less than twenty miles away. She arrived in front of the Smiths' home, which was actually a renovated farm. When Lacey's foster family had lived there full-time, they'd kept chickens, goats and pigs. Lacey had great memories there as a child, and Shelby knew she still had a key to their place. There weren't any vehicles outside, but she knew Lacey was inside. She knew it.

After going back and forth about it in her mind, Shelby sent Jewel the address and said, I believe Lacey is here. Then she marched up to the door and rang the bell. A few seconds later, she saw the blinds shift.

"I know you're in there, honey, and I'm not leaving until we talk."

Another few seconds passed before she heard the lock click, and then she was peering into her daughter's beautiful face. They engaged in a face-off before Lacey stepped back. "It took you long enough to find me. Why didn't you use the Life App?"

Shelby chuckled. They were going to be okay. "I forgot all about that. But I figured it out, that's what counts. I've been worried sick about you." She shut the door behind her, making sure to leave it unlocked for when Jewel arrived. They went to sit on the couch to talk. "How are you even eating? There's nothing within walking distance."

Lacey blushed. "I'm not here on my own. Mekhi went to pick us up some pizza."

"Oh, I see." She wouldn't ask her daughter what that meant as far as their relationship, because the implications were obvious. "What about the Smiths? Do they know that you're here?"

"Yes, Mom. Geesh, you're such a mom." Lacey rolled her eyes. "I wouldn't stay here without their knowledge, and they did give me a key."

"Did you tell them . . . ?" She placed a hand across her abdomen. She would hate it if the Smiths changed their views about her if they knew the truth. But it was now Lacey's truth to tell.

"No, I wouldn't do that to you. Give me some credit, Mom. I have no intention of going public about any of this." Lacey's tone softened. "I'm sorry I threw out your journals. I was mad, and I wasn't thinking right."

"It's okay, and I'm not just saying that," Shelby said. She pointed to her head and then her heart. "I have my memories where they need to be. And I'm making more. I'm sorry I wasn't honest with you. But my intentions were pure. When I returned home and bought the bookstore, I didn't know it at the time, but I was looking for you. I was hoping for my second chance to make things right, and then you came through that door. And I couldn't believe my luck." She pointed upward. "God had a hand in bringing us back together. I believe that."

Lacey had tears in her eyes. "I believe that too. You've been the best mother a girl could have. And I've had many." She wiped the corners of her eyes, and they both chuckled. "I'm blessed to have you."

Her heart eased that they were communicating like old times. "Maybe I should record that for the next time you think I'm being unfair about something." After they shared a laugh, mingled with relief, Shelby said, "I'm sorry I discouraged you when you asked about your birth mother. I was scared you would hate me and I would lose you. I know that was incredibly selfish, but I see now I should have been honest from the get-go."

"Actually, I'm glad you were selfish and accepted me into your life. I do wish you had told me, but I also don't know if I would have been mature enough to handle it either. I've been thinking about that a lot this past week. And it helped to talk to Mekhi about it. He said the path to love isn't always black-and-white. We have to allow for a little gray in between. But the end result is what counts, and all paths led me to you. You were meant to be in my life, and that's what matters."

"Dang, how old is he? He talks wise beyond his years."

"Right? That's what I'm saying. He's made this summer one for the books," Lacey breathed out, sounding like she was in love. That made Shelby's heart happy. Especially since Lacey's first love journey wasn't as complicated as Jewel's and Shelby's. *Thank God.* Lacey scooted close and took her hand. "Did you love my father? I know what you said about him in your journal, but was I conceived out of love?"

Shelby could see how important her answer to that question was, and she wanted to give her daughter the fairy tale. "I think I loved him as much as I could when I was about your age, but it was more a love of friendship, and when I lost my parents, he was there for me in every way I needed."

"Oh." Lacey's brows furrowed while she mulled on Shelby's words. "That's fair. I wasn't born out of hate. I'm glad about that."

Aww. Her daughter was so beautiful and optimistic, it hurt her heart. Maybe she could do the same: focus on the good in situations and people. It would make for a more joyful, fulfilling life. "You look a lot like him," she offered.

"Really?" Lacey's eyes held a hunger for knowledge about the man responsible for her being in the world, and Shelby understood that.

She strove to think of more good things to say. "He had his flaws, but he was brilliant and talented and had a zest for life. He was handsome and articulate, and boy, that man could outread me." Lacey was eating it up. "Yes, and he had a great sense of humor. He was an amazing swimmer and had a body that drove all the girls wild. But he only had eyes for Jewel." Her smiled dropped a little.

"Yes, you wrote that she was his muse and that they were in love."

Shelby patted her hand. "If you decide to look for him, we can do it together. He doesn't know he has a daughter, and he should."

Lacey teared up. "Thanks, Mom. I'd like that. Not now. But I will."

"Whenever you're ready." She heard a door slam and then cleared her throat. "Lacey, I believe you've made the assumption that I'm your biological mother, but I'm not."

Lacey gasped. "I thought . . ."

"No, honey. I so wished I had given birth to you. You don't know how much I wish that were the case. But Jewel is your mom. She was the one who spent hours reading to you while you were in the womb, and nineteen hours in labor without medication until you came into this world. That's why I had to invite her here. Whatever happens next with the both of you is all in your court."

The door creaked, and then Jewel stepped inside, followed by Mekhi, holding pizza. The tantalizing smell made her mouth water. They each took a slice of pizza, and Shelby excused herself to give Jewel and Lacey time together while she talked with Mekhi. She wanted to know more about this fascinating young man.

Just as she was about to enter the kitchen, she heard Jewel say, "Hi, Lacey. I'm Jewel, and I'm honored to meet you. I'm your birth mother." Shelby's eyes welled. All was as it should be.

JOURNAL ENTRY

Shelby

September 30, 2025

I broke things off with Kendrick at the end of the summer. It was great while it lasted and that man gave me some toe-curling times, but there is no point in being in a relationship if I could potentially face jail time. What would he think of me if he ever learned the truth? Although, Lacey assured me that she wasn't going to tell and the truth was buried in the bottom of the ocean. I needed time. I needed space.

Besides, I needed to focus on being there for Lacey and on mending our relationship. I had lied to her, and that underlying resentment didn't just disappear because we had hugged it out. Repairing was a day by day, brick by build rebuilding. I encouraged her to do the same with Jewel, even though Jewel and I still aren't talking.

November 11, 2025

In the middle of hurricane season, I decided to take a solo trip to Jamaica for a long weekend. My heart was hurting, and I missed

Kendrick way more than I thought I would. As soon as I landed, I felt like I had come home. I stretched my arms wide. It was like my parents were here and waiting. I felt so close to them. Plus, the food. The food! I stayed at an all-inclusive resort, and you best believe I helped myself to the island cuisine.

I relaxed on the beach and read most of the day, ignoring the catcalls from the Jamaican men, though I admit their off-the-wall comments stroked my ego. I even ventured out of the resort to get a taste of Jamaica's KFC. Daddy used to brag that there is no KFC like back home.

And doggone it, Daddy was right again. I was licking my fingers the entire time while trying not to embarrass myself by moaning after each bite. I had no shame taking a bucket home with me, along with some beef patties.

But the best news of all is that I got a surprise email from Francesca offering me representation. Jewel had sent her my novel about my parents' love story. That her offer came while I visited their home was serendipity!

November 16, 2025

Even though I broke things off, Kendrick has been such a friend. We ride together in the cycling group and he calls and checks on me, making a point to always ask about Lacey. Gosh, he is such a wonderful man. My heart isn't happy with me right now.

But I have my edits to keep me busy! They are kicking my butt. I'm glad I have Jewel to commiserate with. She is my biggest cheerleader. And after a big showdown with Roman, it appears as if they are on the path to reconciliation.

December 1, 2025

So Kendrick and I are now official. Like, follow-each-other-on-Instagram official. Lacey and Bea call us #Kenby. They played matchmaker to bring us together. Lacey sat him down and told him everything, and he showed up on my doorstep with flowers. That man can do no wrong in their eyes. Or maybe they just like his washboard abs because Kendrick is always in the gym. He keeps me active in and out of bed, and for the first time in my life, my heart and hoo-ha are both happy!

December 3, 2025

I am proud to announce that after three decades of only having one best friend, I am in the process of making another. You can never have too many besties!

After all the drama with me and Jewel, I decided to widen my circle of friends. Deena tried to befriend me when I first started riding, and I decided to invite her to lunch. Then to the movies. Now, some of the things she says and does have me giving her the side-eye, but I'm enjoying her friendship. She's a good hangout partner.

Deena is a widow with the clichéd two munchkin cats, Charm and Poppy. She loves them like they are her children. Those two gorgeous felines are better dressed and fed than most children—and much cleaner too.

CHAPTER 38

Jewel
December 22, 2025

Standing by the door where she had paced for the past hour waiting for Roman's arrival, Jewel softly uttered her well-rehearsed words, mindful that her tone welcomed conversation and not dissonance. "We can't continue like this, babe."

For months after she had returned to New York, Jewel and Roman had been at odds, though he had finally agreed to couple's counseling. But even that was a joke if your heart wasn't in it. And his clearly wasn't. At least not at the level it was before. He was still a good provider, he cared for her and, to anyone watching, their marriage appeared unshakable, but Roman was distant. He didn't speak unless he had to, and that's what hurt her the most. She had lost her talk-through partner, and it grieved her.

Especially during the entire editing process, which could be brutal on an author's psyche. If it wasn't for Shelby, there was no way she would have persevered.

They lived more like roommates, and she was tired of it. Not get-out-of-her-marriage tired, but end-this-standoff tired. They were going to come to a resolution tonight, because for the first time in their union, neither one was backing down.

He paused by the doorjamb. "Have you changed your mind?"

Jewel cleared her throat. "We have expenses. I have to follow through."

"We've been through this before. I understand all that. But this isn't about meeting your responsibility. This is about the story that you chose to tell against my wishes."

"I changed it," she shot out. "I worked on a subplot and sent it off to my editor. Since it's so late in the process, I asked if she would push out the pub day. I'm waiting to hear back from her, but she's not happy with me at all."

"So it's not guaranteed?"

"No. But I tried."

He gave her the side-eye. "That's a little too late. Excuse me." Roman brushed past her and walked inside. Disheartened, Jewel closed the door behind him and followed him up the stairs to their bedroom. He was already stripping out of his clothes to get into the shower.

They had been invited to a dinner party for his job, and she wasn't in the mood to go if they were at odds. But she would. She would press down her discontent and smile and make small talk, whatever she had to do to support him. However, the night would be much more enjoyable if she wasn't pretending.

Because the silence . . . The silence was crushing.

Though she had already showered, Jewel undressed and joined him inside their large walk-in shower. They had designed it with durability and luxury in mind. She was going to be all up in his face, and they were going to thrash this out. Roman made room for her and washed her back, and she did the same for him. Like always, except there was no teasing, no touching, no banter. She sniffled. It was just too much.

Her eyes welled. "I hate that we're like this, Roman," she choked out. "It's eating away at me."

"I'm sorry it's like this too, but you're waiting for me to relent on this, and I'm not going to shrug it off and act like I'm good with something when I'm not. You've exposed my private struggle for everyone to see and to blithely comment on," he said as his voice broke. "And you hid the fact that you had a child from me, for the entirety of our relationship. How could you do that?" Turning off the tap, Roman handed her a towel and grabbed another for himself.

And there it was. The crux of the matter.

Her chin wobbled as she cocooned herself in the soft white cotton.

"Please don't hate me. I'm trying to fix this." Her voice cracked.

His face softened. "I don't hate you. I could never hate you." He shook his head. "You don't know how many times these past few months I've wanted to lie to you. I wanted to tell you all that you wanted to hear, but I love you too much to lie to you. And that's how I wanted you to feel about me. That's what hurt so much. That you didn't trust me enough. That you didn't give me the chance to love you despite your past, despite your flaws."

Jewel touched her chest. "I'm sorry for hurting you, but it isn't because your love wasn't enough. Far from it." She took a step toward him.

He took a tentative step forward too.

Then they rushed into each other's arms. Soon, their hands and lips and bodies engaged in a much-needed, much-missed, much-overdue conversation. Later, as they lay replete in each other's arms, Jewel looked at the clock and gasped. "Roman, we've got to get to your event."

He popped up. "I wish I could skip this so bad."

"I know, but it's your first official job function. You have to go."

With a grunt, he got out of bed and then extended his hand to help her stand. They grabbed another quick shower and then put on their fancy garb. They were almost at the venue and stopped at a red light when Roman's cell rang.

It was Katrina.

Roman answered, reaching for her hand.

"I've decided to do the DNA test," she said. From the sound of her voice, she had been crying. "I know the results might shake up my family, but I've got to do this. I'll be in touch soon, I promise. And if Curtis is your son, I won't stand in your way. I truly didn't realize what I was doing to you. Tell Jewel I said thanks for the ARC. I've never cried so hard in my life."

"Thank you, Katrina! Forgive me if I'm not saying much, but I'm in shock. I gave up hope of this happening."

"It's all good. I understand. Talk soon."

Roman ended the call, his mouth ajar. He looked over at Jewel. "You sent her a copy of your book?" A car honked behind them.

"Pay attention to the road. When you've parked, I'll fill you in." It was obvious he was in shock at Katrina's unexpected call. Truth was, so was she. She had taken a big risk, but it seemed to have paid off.

When he arrived, Roman cut the engine and turned to face her. Jewel squared her shoulders. "I sent Katrina an advanced reader copy of the original storyline. When you spoke of your devastation of never having had the chance to be there for Curtis, it broke my heart. I felt every ounce of your pain, and I had to include that scene in the story. I cried when I wrote that, bawled my eyes out. But I needed the reader to feel every drop of emotion. Katrina must have read it, and I think for the first time she understood your side. That's the power of a novel." She lifted her chin. "The power of my books. I needed to give you the happily-ever-after in my book in case you never got it in real life. I have a copy for you as well, but the rest of the world will get the new version."

"The power of the pen." He gave her a look of adoration, his eyes wet. "You are phenomenal. I never thought I would say this, but I'm glad you told the story of your heart, because you've given me a chance with my son." He lifted his hands. "Thank you, Jesus."

Through her blurred vision, she cautioned, "Baby, I think you need to wait for the results before you stake any claim." She wiped her face with the back of her hand.

"He's mine, Jewel. I know it. Katrina knows it too or she wouldn't have fought it this hard." She couldn't argue with his logic. But she needed to see the results on paper before she truly rejoiced.

Roman, however, didn't have any qualms. That man cut it up on the dance floor until Jewel had to leave him to it to rest her aching feet. Roman danced until some of the women dropped money at his feet, and still he kept on dancing. And soon he was the only one left on the makeshift dance floor, and the deejay was egging him on. There was only one thing to do. Kicking off her shoes, she made her way back to the center of the stage.

JOURNAL ENTRY

Shelby

January 28, 2026

Unbelievable. After months of edits and fourteen days on submission, I have an offer. Francesca said that was virtually unheard of. I just see it as my parents looking out for me. Francesca is a shark. She negotiated a six-figure deal for me and is still selling my book in other countries. Not bad for a debut author.

I had to call Jewel personally to thank her and to share my good news. She asked if she could come so we could celebrate together. I didn't have the heart to say no. And I'm glad I didn't. Friendships like ours don't end that easy. The love for each other will always be there.

Knowing Jewel had made that connection for me has contributed to Lacey and Jewel's relationship. Although it's still a sour point between them that Jewel hasn't acknowledged Lacey openly.

April 18, 2026

I have a cover and release date. On October 14, 2026, *Indomitable* will be released!! I pinch myself knowing that my parents' love story will be in the hands of readers worldwide. Plus, the publicity team scored me some great reviews. I have received starred reviews from *Publishers Weekly* and *Booklist*, and *Indomitable* will be on the fall must-read lists.

Lacey is so ecstatic that she had T-shirts made with my reviews! Adopting her was the best decision I ever made.

EPILOGUE

Jamaica, West Indies

October 10, 2026

Shelby

There was no such thing as a birthday do-over, but Jewel was insistent on celebrating her fortieth birthday today, even though she was going to be forty-one tomorrow. And what better way to turn it up than in Jamaica? Her reasoning was that she was still forty today and since she had spent her fortieth birthday alone and scared her marriage and her friendship were over, she needed to celebrate.

Now, in a classic case of lifestyles of the rich and fabulous, Jewel had decided to throw an all-expenses-paid, all-girls exclusive party—even though the men were invited. Go figure. Roman, Curtis, Mekhi and Kendrick were going to be in their man cave.

Right now, Shelby was sipping on rum punch and watching the crew set up all the trappings for Jewel's all-white birthday party. They had already lost about six helium balloons. Shelby had cracked up at their Jamaican bad words. The men had no idea that she could understand them. And she had no intention of making them any wiser. She was having too much fun hearing them cuss out Jewel for her *extraness. Cho!*

Deena from her cycling team came over to where she sat. She looked like she had been partaking of some of the island herbs. Shelby covered her eyes with her hands. "Girl, I told you not to experiment."

"When in Jamaica, do as the Jamaicans do," Deena said at the top of her lungs, bobbing her head and dancing. That would have been fine and good if there was music playing. The men nearby hooted and cheered her on. Deena lifted an arm in the air and wiggled her hips. Shelby didn't have the heart to tell her that the men were laughing at her, not with her. She'd let her know on the plane ride home.

"Where's the birthday girl?" Deena asked, settling on the lounge behind her. "I'm famished. Are you hungry?"

Shelby bit back a chuckle. "No, I just ate. You'll see her later."

Deena wobbled back to her feet. "I'm going to find me something to eat." With a wave, she took off for the dining hall. Shelby cracked up.

Lacey came over and wrinkled her nose. "Who's smoking that stuff? Blat. It smells disgusting."

Shelby tilted her head in Deena's direction. "Smile and nod, baby girl. Smile and nod."

"Whatever. I came to tell you that Mekhi's parents are here. Do you think Jewel would mind if they come to her party?"

"No. Invite them. The more the merrier. Just let them know we all have to be dressed in white, though."

She kissed Shelby on the cheek. "Thanks, Mom. I'll tell them."

"You can ask her yourself, you know," Shelby said gently. "She is your mother."

"Jewel gave birth to me, but you're my mom. So when it comes to me and Jewel—smile and nod, Mom. Smile and nod."

Shelby giggled at Lacey's fake Jamaican accent. Sitting back on her lounge chair, she watched her daughter run over to Mekhi, her grin widening as they embraced.

"They look good together," Jewel said, from behind her.

"Hey!" Shelby said, turning around. "If you were going to rob me, you would have made off like a bandit."

Jewel slipped onto the chair that Deena had vacated, her gaze pinned on Lacey and Mekhi. "Do you think they'll last?"

"I think they have a good shot." She shrugged. "If they do, we'll celebrate. If they don't, we'll be there to pick up the pieces. Because that's what mothers do. No matter what, she'll be all right because she has us."

"You're right. I need to stop being such a worrywart." Jewel and Shelby scooted to the edge of their loungers and put their heads together as they had done many times in the past.

"We're in this together," Jewel said.

Shelby gave Jewel's hand a squeeze. "We're in this together."

★ ★ ★ ★ ★

ACKNOWLEDGMENTS

I am so grateful to God for this opportunity to put my creative talents to use once again. This is a blessing that I don't take for granted and I pray for more opportunities.

Thank you to my agent, Latoya Smith, and my fellow agent-sis, Sobi Burbano, for your support and encouragement.

To my amazingly wonderful editor and talk-through partner, Dina Davis, who helped me reshape *A Summer for the Books* and fulfill my goal of writing a book within a book. After my talk-through with her, I was able to shape Lacey's character, which deeply enriched the storyline.

Thank you so much to the entire team at MIRA and HarperCollins, some of whom I was able to meet in person over this past year: Nicole Brebner, April Osborn, Evan Yeong, Fiona Smallman, Ana Luxton, Ashley MacDonald, Puja Lad, Randy Chan, Pamela Osti, Lindsey Reeder, Brianna Wodabek, Riffat Ali, Ciara Loader, Diane Lavoie, Rachel Haller, Alex McCabe, Ambur Hostyn, Daphne Guima, Jaimie Nackan, Reka Rubin, Christine Tsai, Nora Rawn, Loriana Sacilotto, Amy Jones, Margaret Marbury, Heather Connor, Katie-Lynn Golakovich, Denise Thomson, Bailey Thomas, Melissa Brooks, Tamara Shifman, Gina Macdonald, Vanessa Wells and Jennifer Lopes, as well as Ariel Blake, whose voice served as narrator.

A special, special thank-you for my publicist, Kamille Carreras Pereira, for all the efforts made to help spread the word about this book.

When I saw the cover for this book, I was blown away,

and so thanks to the art team: Erin Craig and Alexandra Niit (special mention).

Thank you to my little Nova, who is a joy and always brings a smile to my face. Thank you to my parents, Pauline and Clive, my sons, Eric and Jordan, my daughter in love, Jasmyn, as well as the children of my heart: Arielle, Erika, Erin, Dezirae, Destinee, Devyn and Siara.

Thank you to my sisters, Zara, Chrissy and Soso, and my brothers-in-law, Sean and Guillermo. Pauline and Clive and weekly prayer fam: Auntie Charmaine (Paula Ann), Andrea and Arlene. Special thanks for my in-laws: (Pop) John and Mom Dorsa. I can sit and talk with you for hours about the goodness of God.

Kisses, hugs and thank-yous to my husband, John, who holds up the household and everything else that falls apart while I strive to meet my book deadlines.

And finally, thank *you*, dear reader, for reading and sharing and talking about my books. You are priceless. Special mention to all the book clubs who have put this on your lists, and to readers such as Ellowyn and Leslie.

Love always,
Michelle